WHERE'S LUCAS?

The helicopter skimmed above the river between forested hills, and Mike scanned the shoreline for any sign of the kids. He and Dana had hardly spoken on the way. The door had been shut between them for years, and when he'd opened it again it was only to square off with her over HARC. They were united only in their goal to find Lucas, their son.

"What's that?" Her voice was strangely flat. Mike focused the binoculars, and dread knifed into him. A red shirt floated from the waist of a half-naked body, face down in the river, trapped by boulders.

"Go down." His heart was a rock in his throat. He pointed to a flat spot, barren except for some ravens on a scatter of rocks. The birds lifted off. It wasn't until Mike and Dana landed and were getting out, crouching under the knifing rotor blades, that he saw: it wasn't rocks that the ravens had been on, but a corpse. He lurched in front of Dana to block her view, but from her face he could tell that she'd already seen.

What in God's name had happened here?

Also by Stephen Kyle

Beyond Recall

AFTER SHOCK

STEPHEN KYLE

WARNER BOOKS

An AOL Time Warner Company

WARNER BOOKS EDITION

Cover design by Diane Luger
Cover art by Stanislaw Fernandez

Warner Books, Inc.
1271 Avenue of the Americas
New York, NY 10020

Visit our Web site at
www.twbookmark.com.

 An AOL Time Warner Company

Printed in the United States of America

First Printing: March 2002

10 9 8 7 6 5 4 3 2 1

Acknowledgments

Special thanks to the following:

Al Zuckerman for invaluable advice and guidance through this book's every stage.

Barry Kent MacKay for detail on Alaskan wildlife.

Penny Wells for medical expertise.

Bill Hunt for tracking down Archimedes.

Jackie Joiner for thoughtful and meticulous editing.

Stephen Best for detail on computers, planes, complexities of character, and twists of plot.

Author's Geographical Note

The Tanana River and the Chena River exist in the vicinity of Fairbanks, Alaska. The Gatana River and the Wahetna River, as well as the villages of Takona and Hanley, however, are fictional; they exist only for the purposes of this story. The suffix "na" means "river" in the Athabascan language.

". . . physicists have known sin; and this is a knowledge which they cannot lose."

—J. Robert Oppenheimer

AFTER SHOCK

GENERAL BENSON CREWE of the U.S. Marines felt a cold sweat as he stood in the Pentagon's National Military Command Center watching his country come under attack, though he knew it was just an exercise. The big board screen showed an enemy missile speeding through space a hundred thirty miles above the Pacific, heading for California. Ben's eyes flicked to the exoatmospheric kill vehicle launched to intercept and destroy. If the EKV missed, the ICBM's nuclear payload would strike Los Angeles in eleven minutes. His heart thudded—the EKV's trajectory was off. It flew past the intercept point, missing by miles, and the missile raced on at fifteen thousand miles an hour, straight for the U.S.A.

"Close, but no cigar," an Air Force major nearby muttered.

Ben let out a tense breath. The ICBM was only a Minuteman with a dummy warhead launched from a U.S. Air Force Base; the EKV had been launched from an atoll in the Pacific. As chief of the Office of Naval Research,

Ben was among a roomful of military, political, and corporate leaders gathered to observe the latest test in the National Missile Defense program, the president's so-called nuclear shield.

But the catastrophe felt almost real. His palms were clammy.

He glanced around. Raytheon and Boeing executives stood critiquing the disappointing results, but looked unfazed. No wonder. The NMD program pumped a hundred billion their way, win or lose. Their calm unnerved Ben. Couldn't they imagine the devastation from a missile strike like the North Koreans' new Taepo-dong 2? Didn't they suffer the nightmares he did, knowing how helpless the country was against such an attack?

And yet, had he expected it to go any differently? This was just the latest in a long series of test failures in the president's overhyped initiative. The success rate was a miserable twenty percent. National Missile Defense was a crock.

He knew what really had him so on edge. Carol's message on his voice mail. "Dad, we have a problem."

Her tone had been businesslike, as always, and she'd left no details, just a time and place to meet for lunch, but he'd heard the undercurrent of fear. *A problem.* His daughter wouldn't use the word lightly. He was seeing her in an hour. Hell, he was feeling too jumpy, but he'd taken too many risks—illegal ones—to stop now.

"What's your call on this, Ben?"

It was Graham Sloan, chairman of the Joint Chiefs. The five-star general was a head shorter than Ben, with a bland face and quiet manner that led some to underestimate his toughness, something Ben had seen him use to his advantage. They'd been friends since the day thirty-two years ago when Ben had carried Sloan's bleeding body off a Vietnamese jungle path under sniper fire and took a bullet in the thigh. In captivity, they'd kept each other sane. Now, as the nation's top soldier, Sloan supported the NMD program. *Can he take the truth?* Ben wondered. *Can't give him anything less.*

"Primitive, inadequate, and impractical," he answered. "Primitive because the EKV intercept principle is like trying to hit a bullet with a bullet. Inadequate because if an enemy launches multiple warheads, your bullet can go after only one, letting others through. Impractical because the program's sensitive to political cancellation—it's already got the Russians crying foul about ABM treaty infractions, barely a year after the president made it top priority. In any event, estimates indicate three years to develop the system plus three more to deploy, so what we get is guaranteed obsolescence—with a hundred billion price tag." He shot a glance at the corporate suits. "This isn't a policy for defense, Graham. It's a policy for defense contractors."

Sloan's smile was wry. "Don't be shy with your opinions."

Ben felt an itch to go the last step, reveal his secret. *HARC overcomes all these obstacles.* But he held back. *Not the time or place. Just a few more months. Then, Sloan will shake my hand and thank me. The country has the capacity to deal with all threats except nuclear missile attack. HARC will truly make our nation safe.*

But the news his daughter brought him that muggy

July day compelled Ben to a change of tactic. If he'd known the horror it would unleash, the lives it would claim, he would never have given his physicist the order he did that night.

▲

Rupert's Grille was Georgetown's "in" restaurant of the moment. Carol always kept up with these things, Ben reflected as he walked into the chrome and terra-cotta atrium. Part of her job: see and be seen. She'd built a hot PR firm in Boston by being on top of trends. At eleven-forty, though, the Washington lunch crowd hadn't yet left their offices, and the string quartet CD was playing to an almost empty room.

He spotted her at a table in the corner, tapping at her Palm Pilot beneath an arty photo of a Parisian street market. Ben thought Carol herself always had a touch of Paris about her. Even in an unadorned blue business suit she looked chic, poised, beautifully turned out, like her mother, with Julia's perfect features, fair complexion, rich blond hair. He felt a raw twinge. Since his wife's death two years ago, he saw her more and more in Carol.

"Not late, am I?" he said as he kissed her cheek.

She smiled. "You're never late."

Ben sat opposite her, dropped his napkin across his knee, and looked around to check that no one could hear. "What's happened?"

Her smile slid away. She folded her arms, elbows on the table, as if it were her desk, and lowered her voice. "Senator Litvak."

As she too glanced around, Ben's fears for HARC rekindled. Litvak was the senior member of the Senate appropriations committee. "I had breakfast this morning with another senator's aide," Carol said. "The word is, Litvak's about to make an announcement. He's fired up about excessive spending on military research and he's going to call for a comprehensive investigation. It'll hit everybody—the Army Research Office, the Air Force's Philips Research Lab, and you at ONR. You know how these things go, Dad. Once teams of accountants start digging, they'll look under every rock."

"Does Litvak suspect anything? Has he got anything?"

"My sense of it is that he's just taking up a cause— 'cutting the waste,' and all that. Good for his reelection. But if this goes ahead—" She stopped, and seemed to shiver. "Dad . . . we could be talking prison."

"Can I take your order, General?"

Startled, Ben looked up at the young waiter at his elbow. He ordered an omelet he didn't want; Carol a crab salad.

"Fresh Malpeque oysters today as an appetizer, Mrs. Ryder. Can I tempt you?"

"Not today, Tony. Thanks."

The waiter filled their water glasses, collected their menus, and left.

Ben's thoughts were already on containment. The appropriations committee chairman was Harley Gustafson, the senior senator from Alaska—and Ben's secret ally. "I'll go see Harley," he said.

"You think he can stop Litvak?"

Ben had never seen her so anxious. Not good. He needed her to stay strong. "Carol, Harley's our best bet. But I'm also going to light a fire under Crosbie to move the schedule ahead. We may have to make this thing fly sooner than planned, before Litvak can get to us."

"And Mike?" she asked. "Do we finally tell him?"

He saw the worry deep in her eyes, and felt at a loss. His son-in-law was HARC's lead scientist, crucial to making Ben's bold strategy work, but Mike Ryder didn't know Ben's full plan as Carol did. HARC was, in fact, Mike's creation: the High-frequency Auroral Research Center, almost operational in Alaska, would focus the world's most powerful beam of high-frequency electromagnetic energy up to the ionosphere, superheating a patch of it into a virtual mirror to reflect back lower frequencies for use in submarine communications. Or so Mike believed. From day one Ben had intended HARC to be a weapon. Still, he thought of Mike as his own son, and he'd found it painful maintaining the deception. It had been necessary, he reminded himself. Still was. "Not yet," he answered. "Not until we have to."

Carol began tidying her place setting, an obsessive habit, moving the fork a fraction, the water glass, the dessert spoon, the yellow rose in its vase. Ben knew she was trying to recover her composure. Hiding the truth from Mike had been tough for him, but worse for her. He felt an impulse to let her know how much her loyalty meant to him. He reached across and covered her hand with his.

"You've shown great courage in this, Carol. I'm proud of you. Proud that I can rely on you. And believe me, once we've demonstrated HARC's capability, Mike will recognize our foresight and be as proud of you as I am. But until then, the course we're on is best—for Mike too. I'll talk to Harley, and I'll get Crosbie moving. It's all going to work out, for Mike, for us—and for our country."

She looked into his eyes. "Oh, Dad. I know."

It was a relief to see her smile again.

▲

A blast of rap music assaulted Ben as he stepped into the college hangout in Tuscaloosa that evening, stale-mouthed from the flight. Why would Crosbie pick this dive? he wondered, heading for the bar. Black walls. Sticky concrete floor. The stink of spilled beer and cigarette butts, and a whiff of backed-up toilets. Raucous talk rose from the clusters of unkempt kids at long tables with beer pitchers, others playing pool.

Meredith Crosbie looked up from her bar stool. "How's life in the nation's capital, General?"

"Hot," he said, taking the stool beside her.

"Hotter here in 'bama—with the added drawback of no intelligent life." She raised her beer glass. "With the exception of yours truly."

Ben looked at her. Mid-forties, no makeup, no flab, the wiry build of a track and field athlete, which she had once been. Her cloud of curly red hair, feathery as a child's, gave an impression of innocence. A wrong impression, Ben had quickly learned in his association with her. Dr. Crosbie was a physicist with a mind like the proverbial steel trap. A professor of physics here at the University of Alabama, she was a fallen star doing time in a backwater, teaching undergraduates, and Ben knew her exile rankled her. He'd made use of that, kept her dependent. Until now. Tonight, he needed her. A speaking engagement in D.C. tomorrow meant he couldn't get out to see Gustafson until the day after. He had to start with Crosbie.

"So, what brings you, General?"

He looked around, wondering if this was a secure place to talk. He'd dressed to look inconspicuous, gray slacks, tan golf shirt, and navy sports jacket, and Crosbie was in a plain black pants suit, but in this crowd they stuck out like teachers at a high school rock concert. On the other hand, their age made them so dull to the kids, they were virtually invisible. And with the blare of rap, plus three bar TVs tuned to the ball game, no one could overhear.

A trio of girls in skimpy summer dresses were laughing at the end of the bar, and Ben noticed Crosbie stealing glances at them. He knew of her taste for nubile undergrads. *That's* why we're here, he realized: it's where she scores. He thought of the official position: Don't ask, don't tell. Crosbie was a civilian, but he figured it still applied. Anyway, he didn't give a shit about her sex life.

"What'll it be?" the bartender asked. Young, laid-back, an Asian face. Ben recoiled inside. Asian features always did it to him. It was reflexive, beyond his control, a bug in his nervous system ever since they'd kept him in that bamboo tiger cage, half-demented under the broiling Vietnamese sun.

"Mineral water," he said.

"Only soda."

"Fine."

The kid scooped ice cubes into a glass, poured soda from the jet, slid the glass toward Ben, and walked away. Ben looked down at it. In the cage, they'd given him water they'd pissed in.

"Maybe you should go crazy for once, order a martini," Crosbie said, amused.

He turned to her. Time to do business. "I need the parabolic capability. How soon can you upload it?"

She looked startled. "Upload? No way. I've just started the beta testing."

"That's not critical. I need you to speed things up."

She shook her head. "I've created a new kernel—that's the core of the software. I think it's clean, but it's inconceivable there won't be bugs. With any new program there are thousands."

"But they're usually insignificant, aren't they? Screen refreshers, details like that?"

"General, you know my work. I don't do sloppy. I've given the software to my lab assistants for beta testing, and I'll await the results. As I said, I think it's fairly clean, but the last bugs have to be worked out."

Ben couldn't let this hold him back. "Could they be worked out on-site?"

Her eyebrows lifted. "At HARC?"

"Yes."

"They could, but . . ." She cocked her head at him, intrigued. "Why the sudden rush?"

He met her gaze. Time she knew. "Doctor, what you've been working on is more important than I've led you to believe. It's not only about improved sub communications. It's a breakthrough in antiballistic weaponry."

Her eyes widened. "The parabolic capability?"

"Yes." Mike had conceived HARC's high-frequency beam to superheat a patch of the ionosphere into a virtual mirror to reflect power back, which was a brilliant development. But it reflected the power in a broad band. Crosbie had taken it one step further: she'd found a way to make the mirror parabolic, to focus HARC's reflected power with precision on whatever its controllers wanted.

She shrugged, her moment of surprise past. "Makes sense. It's the military's job, after all. Weapons 'R' Us." Her eyes narrowed. "There's more to this though, isn't there, General? I've always wondered, Why just me? I could understand you signing me to that secrecy agreement the size of a phone book, but I've never understood why you've had me working alone. Since we're being so candid, let me ask. Is our agreement your *personal* initiative? A little side project, away from the Pentagon's management?"

Ben bristled. "Hardly little. It'll revolutionize our strategic missile defense. At present, we have none. Despite satellites that can show us the moment a missile is launched anywhere on the globe, we still haven't got the means to shoot down an ICBM in flight. We're vulnerable to attack from any of our enemies. And China . . .

they've begun playing hardball, yet we continue to underestimate them, at our peril. In our rush to sell Coke to them, we seem to have forgotten that the Chinese have amassed the largest standing army in the history of the world."

"Really," she said, clearly unmoved. "And HARC's going to change this . . . equation?"

"In HARC we'll have a weapon that can destroy any incoming missile with stunning accuracy. Better, can reach around the world and take out enemy targets without having to fire a shot."

"Great. So why aren't a hundred scientists like me working on it? For that matter, why isn't Mike?"

Ben caught her sourness as she said Mike's name. Mike had been her research partner at MIT until her ambition had led her to publish fraudulent data. They'd both paid professionally for her offense, but Mike went on to build HARC, while Crosbie's reputation had been shattered. Precisely the reason Ben had sought her out.

"Because," he answered, "to openly develop such a weapon would violate our antiballistic treaties. We need HARC, but I couldn't hide such a huge project. So I built it in plain sight, as a research venture."

"Ah. Mike runs the squeaky-clean part, gets it operational, and gets the glory, while I use his data to make HARC your secret weapon, stuck here in the armpit of America. Thanks a million."

Ben allowed her the moment of disgruntlement. No need to tell her that he'd personally risked *everything* to get HARC this far. That for four years he'd illegally held back funding meant for other ONR projects and chan-

neled it into HARC's development. Harley Gustafson
had enabled the money flow, and Carol had managed its
diversion through her PR company. But now this grand-
standing Senator Litvak could rip it all apart. Over my
dead body, he thought. Presenting HARC's capability to
the Joint Chiefs as a fait accompli had always been his
goal: if it impressed them—and he knew it would—they
could black-box the project overnight, make it a classified operation, removing it from congressional oversight. He'd scheduled HARC to be ready by October, but
unveiling it sooner might now be necessary. Unless
Gustafson could intervene with Litvak.

"The point is," he said, "I need the parabolic capability sooner than I'd anticipated, so I need you to upload
the software immediately. Mike's already begun limited
testing, so let's let him work out your last small bugs on-
site. Then, with his results, you can finish the fine-
tuning."

"Only, without him knowing any of this, right?"

"That's essential." Ben was suddenly uneasy. Mike
Ryder wasn't just a brilliant scientist, he was a hands-on
manager. Would he notice Crosbie's changes? "Keeping
him ignorant is doable, isn't it?"

"No problem. The interface stays identical, so he
won't even know the software kernel's been modified.
Anyway, people on his team at a half-dozen university
labs are writing new HARC subroutines constantly—to
optimize calculations, put data in graphic displays, that
sort of thing. Mike *expects* new code. He just doesn't expect me."

She gave Ben a shrewd look. "Seems it *all* comes

down to me, doesn't it, General? Seems now might, in fact, be a good time to renegotiate."

Ben had been expecting this. "What do you want?"

"Out of Tuscaloosa, for starters."

"Once the weapon's operational, I can guarantee you a position at HARC. Not before."

"I could speed things up a lot more efficiently if you gave me Mike's job."

It threw him. She was serious. It wasn't an unreasonable request—she'd done remarkable work, and deserved credit. And he knew she could have been a leader in her field, had it not been for her damaged reputation. But he hated the thought of displacing Mike. He trusted Mike. All he could trust in Crosbie was her ambition. "Let's get where we need to be," he said. "Then, we'll talk."

"I'll hold you to that, General. So I'm with you all the way. Let's upload." Her smile was sardonic. "To Alaska, with love."

Ben looked her in the eye. "Do it tonight."

She raised her beer. "And damn the torpedoes."

Friday, 9:15 A.M.

MIKE RYDER was troubled as he drove his BMW through HARC's gates in the lee of Alaska's White Mountains. He couldn't shake a bad feeling about the image he'd glimpsed last night on the simulation program. An irregular electromagnetic shadow. Across his monitor the normal wave patterns had been undulating in perfect sequence, when the EM shadow suddenly appeared, a phantom image mirroring the waves' crests and troughs, as though someone had penciled a faint band of shading that undulated with the wave. Mike had begun manipulating frequencies so he could examine the phenomenon, but the EM shadow became intermittent, sporadic, the hardest kind of problem to pin down. A ghost in the machine. It had disturbed him all night as he'd drifted in and out of restless sleep. What the hell was it? Maybe just a software bug. But what if it indicated some imminent system failure, like a lightbulb's kick of brightness before it blows?

He had no answer even after his morning workout in

the kayak. His vigorous hour on the Tanana River that skirted Fairbanks was the one time in the day when he could clear his head of problems, and strangely, that very absence of concentration sometimes tricked his subconscious: solutions to the problems often surfaced on their own, like curious seals bobbing up for a peek at you if you sat quietly on the seashore. Not this morning. Nothing had come to him on the ninety-minute drive north from his house in Fairbanks, either. He was worried. HARC's first full-array power test was scheduled for noon. If he had no explanation for the EM shadow by then, maybe he should abort.

Yet, as he drove onto the site in the bright July sunshine, the last thing he wanted was to stand down. It never failed: the vista of the colossal antenna array in the distance always brought a ripple of excitement. Stronger than ever today, with the anticipation of the test. The site layout was rudimentary—a single gravel road, four buildings reminiscent of any industrial park, lawns between them—but straight ahead lay the magnificent heart of the project: a square mile carved out of the bush, studded with thirty-six hundred high-frequency dipole antennas, each seventy feet tall. The array would soon be transmitting the world's most powerful beam of high-frequency electromagnetic energy. Mike had built it to redefine global ionospheric research. Its immediate goal was to improve submarine communications, but he had a dream for HARC: to one day tap into the vast power of the aurora electrojet, that immense natural power line above Alaska, and redirect it to fuel humanity's needs. An inexpensive nonpolluting source of power, there for the taking. What a thrill if he could bring such a gift to the world.

He parked in front of the operations center, and was closing the car door when he spotted an earring on the floor mat. Carol's. One perfect pearl. Good thing he hadn't ground it with his boot. He picked it up, and as he slipped it in his pocket, smiled to himself. Everything about Carol was polished and perfect. And she'd be here tomorrow. Not to put too lustful a point on it, he'd be glad to see his wife. Winters, he was home at his MIT lab in Boston, but the last three summers he'd been here, building HARC. A hell of a commute. He tried to get home every other weekend, but it was never enough. He hated missing the time with his daughter; at nine, she was growing up so fast. But this weekend Carol, at least, was coming here, and he'd reserved a suite at the Chena Hot Springs resort. Hope springs eternal, he thought as he pushed through the ops center doors. Not that he and Carol ever needed anything but each other and a bed. Sometimes not even the bed. It was just that he knew the smart hotel would please her. Alaska wasn't her favorite place. Mike felt differently; he'd grown up here.

He took the open stairs up to the second-floor control room. Carpeted in blue and rimmed with office cubicles, the room was dominated by the console running down the center, with spectrometers and imagers at workstations on each side. A wall of windows overlooked the antenna array that stretched to the Gatana River, the thousands of towers with their crossed dipoles like helicopter rotors, a vast fleet. Walking in, he was surprised to see what looked like his whole research team of four-

teen gathered at the corner coffee nook with several of
the maintenance crew. As HARC's lead scientist, Mike
didn't believe in segregating occupations, and throughout the day hard hats mingled with white coats around
the coffee and donuts. But not usually such a crowd at
once.

"Here he is," Gina DalBello whispered loudly. Her
smile was ear-to-ear as she nudged Roger Donelly, the
senior scientist. Roger turned his tweedy back, struck a
match, then marched toward Mike bearing a plate with a
blueberry muffin sprouting a foot-tall sparkler showering sparks, and declared, in his plumy British style, "In
honor of the day, old chap."

Everyone applauded. Mike felt a pang. All his team
were so eager to run this first big trial. No one more so
than himself. HARC had been his dream for so long, he
was itching to get the project operational. But should he,
with that EM shadow on the simulation still a mystery?

Gina presented him with a small brown paper bag tied
with a red ribbon. She was a Penn State post-doc in astrophysics, and the miniskirt and nose stud and cute face
gave no hint of the mental sharpness that had made her
Mike's protégée. "I was going to get you a hot new
kayak," she quipped, "but it wouldn't fit in the bag."

He opened it. A chintzy brass tie clip that was a slide
rule. He smiled. "Where'd you find this?"

"Flea markets are my life. The damn thing works,
too."

"Great. Next time I'm trying to get off a desert island
I can do the math." Everyone laughed. Mike slipped the
tie clip onto his shirt front.

Wayne Hingerman stepped up next, the maintenance foreman, a burly but fit forty-six. When Mike was twenty, earning his University of Alaska tuition driving a bulldozer on the oil pipeline, Wayne had been the crew manager, his boss, and eighteen years later they were still friends. Wayne shoved at him a butt-ugly statuette of steel rebar welded into a crude Academy Awards Oscar. The inscription read: "For best bullshit invention."

Mike laughed, accepting the statuette. "And me without a speech."

"That'll be the day." Wayne grinned, making way as Lucas James came forward. The sixteen-year-old was half Athabascan Indian, and his shy smile sent a current of love through Mike. Lucas was his son. Mike had always known about the boy, but had met him only three years ago. That first meeting had been tense, and Lucas still called him "Mike," not "Dad," which suited them both. But they'd forged a bond. Mike had given him a summer job this year with Wayne's crew, so he saw him every day, but this new deep affection he felt still had the power to startle him. So did the boy's appearance. It was like looking at a photo of himself at that age. Same lanky build, same permanent hint of a smile, same brown eyes with a shadow of watchfulness, even the same brush cut Mike had sported back then, though his own hair, conservatively longer now, was sandy brown and Lucas's was jet-black. Mike was proud of the kid. He was an A student in Fairbanks, excelling in science and math, and Mike felt he could have a bright future—if he could break free of his mother's influence. She wanted to keep him in Alaska.

"Special test equipment," Lucas said, and held up three shiny plastic balls, orange, yellow, and blue, the size of tennis balls. Mike laughed. He had a habit of juggling while he oversaw the team's work, and Lucas was giving him bird balls—that's what everyone here called them: hundreds were attached to the antenna array ground screen to ward off birds. Lucas tossed the balls to him—one, two, three—with that unhurried grace he'd inherited from his mother. Mike caught them—one, two, three—delighted. Last week, on a kayak trip, he'd taught the boy to juggle.

"You've got to have a dream," Mike had told him that day, juggling riverbank stones as the arctic grayling they'd caught sizzled on the campfire coals. "Mine's HARC. One day, after the sub applications are in place, I'll focus on the goals I've always had for the project. It could do so much good, Lucas. Treat polluting emissions in the atmosphere. Repair holes in the ozone. Eventually, I hope to configure HARC to convey auroral energy to any spot on Earth. Even the poorest areas could access its power for irrigation systems, industry, you name it. I believe HARC can benefit the world in ways I haven't even thought of yet."

He'd brought it up to give a hint of the opportunities for a career, a life, far bigger than Lucas could find in Alaska. He'd even suggested that Lucas apply to college in Boston, where Mike, working next door at MIT, could help him, and he'd been pleased when Lucas said he'd think about it.

"Come on, Mike," Wayne urged, "tell us we're good to go."

He looked at all the expectant faces. How could he let them down? Besides, what did he really expect could go wrong? *Said the captain of the* Titanic . . .

Run it past Ben, he thought. His father-in-law wasn't a scientist, but Mike didn't need that kind of advice; Ben was something better, a cool-headed commander. Mike often turned to him as a sounding board. Telling the team to stand by, he went downstairs to his office and called Arlington, Virginia.

"The general's on another line, Dr. Ryder. Can he call you right back?"

"Please." As he waited, Mike checked his E-mail. Looking at his screen, remembering the elusive shadow on the monitor last night ghosting along with the wave pattern, he felt an unsettling memory surface. Ghosts. It had happened in Boston, in the house he and his family had moved into barely a year before, a lovely old ivy-covered place on a quiet ravine. But they'd got out because of the problems. "Our haunted house" his daughter Lindsay had called it—a nine-year-old's perspective. All three of them had felt distress in that place: headaches, irritability, sapped energy, and once, late at night, Mike thought he'd glimpsed phantom shapes down the hall. He'd investigated possible physiological causes—mold, chemicals in the insulation—but nothing checked out. Determined to find an explanation, he went to his friend Ravi Shakoor, who studied the effects of electromagnetic forces on human perception. Mike made himself an experimental subject in Ravi's lab in an attempt to induce the same "haunted house" effects through electromagnetic stimulation. He felt a shudder now, remembering the sensations the experiment had generated. Coldness in his limbs. Hallucinations. A gut-rush of fear he could put no name to—a sense of an unearthly presence. He'd hated it.

Stupid to be remembering that now, he told himself. Okay, there was a crude connection with the EM shadow he'd seen last night: both concerned phantom images, and both involved electromagnetic irregularities. But really, the only link was plain unease: he'd felt it in that house, and felt it now. It irritated him to be sidetracked by something so irrational.

His phone rang.

"Mike," Ben greeted him, "what can I do for you? I was just about to call Carol."

"You can tell her to be on that plane here tomorrow, no matter what. An obsessed physicist on his own is not a pretty sight."

Ben chuckled. "Well, I don't think she married you for your pretty face."

"Ben, something's come up." He explained the EM shadow and his concern that he didn't know why it was appearing. "About today's test—until I can determine what's causing this anomaly, I'm not sure I want to power up the full array. I'm considering activating just a quadrant at a time, then evaluate the data and see where we stand. It would add another couple weeks."

There was a pause at the other end. "That's a hell of a delay. What's the downside if you go ahead as planned?"

"I don't really know. I'm not even sure what I saw in the simulation, because the shadow was intermittent. Until I can examine it further, all I'm going on is gut feeling." The words were barely out when he realized how lame it sounded. Jesus, a *feeling*?

"Have you told anyone about the shadow? Has anyone else seen it?"

"No, I only noticed it myself late last night. Thought I'd let you know first what I'm considering."

"I appreciate that, Mike. I just wonder if you're being too cautious. As I understand it, you'll be running the test at just ten percent ERP. Right?"

"It's still considerable." HARC's effective radiated power was a hundred billion watts, an unprecedented jolt of power, and ten percent ERP was still a whopping ten billion.

"Look, any new system has anomalies," Ben went on, "and with something as big as HARC, there're bound to be kinks. That's the whole point of testing, isn't it? To find them? Iron them out?"

"Sure. But it's the very scale of HARC that presents the challenge. We're dealing with unknowns."

"Are you telling me size matters?"

"Always. It might be better to go slow."

"Well, I'd be happier keeping the project on schedule. And think about it. Just ten percent ERP, and for just sixty minutes, right? Don't those controlled conditions offer you the best opportunity to monitor this shadow?"

"That's true."

"Mike, I've never known you to make a timid decision. I have total confidence in your judgment. But if possible, go now."

Mike felt a lump in his throat. Gratitude didn't begin to cover what he owed this man. Four years ago, after

Meredith Crosbie's fraudulent research had tainted Mike, stalling his career, Ben alone had had the vision to support him in creating HARC. And Ben's commitment was total: because of him, a project that should have taken ten years had taken four, and was bigger, better, and more generously funded than Mike had dared dream. When he'd planned just a twelve-acre array, Ben had said, "Make it as big as you need to work right," so Mike made it a square mile. When he'd planned for diesel generators to power the transmitters, Ben had said, "I can get you a nuclear reactor from a sub contract we canceled," and Mike gladly accepted. He had nothing but admiration for Ben's military boldness. And never once had Ben pressured him about timetables or procedures.

"Mike, just remember. Big as HARC is, it's only a glorified radio transmitter. Not exactly dangerous."

Mike winced. He *was* being timid. "Ben, you've helped me decide. We'll go as planned." He allowed excitement to course back. Going ahead was what he'd wanted.

He returned to the control room. "All right, folks, let's fire her up."

Just before noon, right on schedule, his team was at the diagnostics console, and Mike walked behind them juggling the bird balls, glancing over people's shoulders at display screens. With a minute to go, as he set down the balls on the console, he felt a thrill, like the moment before shooting a rapids.

He gave the order to activate.

HARC had been running for six minutes when an electronic warning beeped.

"Southeast quadrant, closing at a hundred ten miles an hour," the radar operator said. "Small plane."

Mike regarded the intruder on the display scope. Some bush pilot was about to blunder into HARC's airspace. The plane would fry in the array's powerful EM beam. Of course, before that happened HARC's aircraft alert radar system would automatically shut down transmissions; there was no real danger. But it made the power-up impossible until the airspace was clear. Tense with disappointment, Mike told everyone to stand down.

The plane droned directly overhead. Mike went to the wall of windows. The plane had gone behind the building, but from the engine's change of pitch it sounded like it might be landing. There was a grass airstrip beside HARC's access road. Mike was about to phone down to the gate when his line rang. It was Wayne.

"Mike, you got a visual on that aircraft? It's landing. I'll go check it out while we're shut down."

"Good, and tell—"

"Mike?" He turned. Lucas stood in the doorway. The moment he caught the boy's flustered look, Mike knew what the problem was. He bit back his anger. Telling Wayne to stand by, he hung up and went out into the hall with his son.

"I saw it fly over," Lucas said, looking anxious. "I'm pretty sure it's . . . I mean, I know it's—"

"Your mother." Mike was furious at her.

Lucas looked torn. "Sorry."

It was Mike who was sorry. The kid was caught between warring parents. "Not your fault."

Sending Lucas to rejoin his crew, Mike went downstairs. Outside, he took one of the Jeeps and drove down to the gate. Across the road a DeHaviland Beaver's fuselage shone in the sunlight, and Dana James stood beside it, the center of attention to five people. Mike groaned inside. She'd flown in her own press conference.

She was speaking, composed and authoritative, blue jeans trim on her slim legs, white T-shirt emphasizing her copper skin, aviator sunglasses pushed up in shoulder-length black hair that gleamed like sable. Mike couldn't catch her words, but he could guess: an anti-HARC diatribe. Her Indian village lay three miles downstream, too close to HARC, so a relocation agreement had been negotiated. Dana opposed it. But every village resident had already received a generous cash settlement, and modern homes had been built in the new location for every family, and the move was scheduled in ten days. So what did she hope to accomplish with this stunt? It galled him as he watched her holding forth, the media types hanging on her words like subjects before a queen—three video cameramen crouching, and a woman behind them writing, all of them spellbound. Oh, yes, Dana was impressive. Thirty-four, the owner of an aircraft charter business in Fairbanks, and also a part-time physician, she was known in this remote area as "the flying doc." And undeniably attractive. Mike's eyes went to the man beside her. A tall blond guy in L.L. Bean getup, maybe mid-thirties, he was watching Dana in admiration. And something more. Intimacy—almost smugness, as though she were his prize. It made Mike's skin crawl. He hopped out of the Jeep and started across the road.

He'd almost reached them when the blond guy started talking.

"Ladies and gentlemen, thank you for joining us outside the High-frequency Auroral Research Center for this announcement. My name is Reid D'Alton. I'm an attorney retained to represent Dr. Dana James and the nonprofit Guardians of Alaska in an action they are commencing in the Ninth U.S. Circuit Court of Appeals. In a Statement of Claim filed this morning, we maintain that the agreement by which the Gwich'in Athabascan people of Takona village are to forfeit their lands and be translocated was entered into improperly—that the Takona village council exceeded their authority, and that the agents of the government acting on behalf of HARC used unlawful inducements to secure the agreement.

"Since this case is now before the court, and since the village translocation—should it proceed as scheduled—will cause irreparable harm to the village residents, we have asked the court to grant an injunction to prevent the translocation, and to order all operations at HARC suspended until the court has dealt with this matter. In your press kits you'll find relevant background material. Dr. James and I will now be pleased to answer any questions."

Mike was stunned. An injunction? A final court decision could take months, maybe years . . . with HARC shut down the whole time.

"Ah, here's Dr. Michael Ryder," Dana announced. "The mind behind HARC." The reporters swiveled to him, the cameramen still videotaping.

"Dr. Ryder," the reporter with the notepad said, moving to him—a chunky woman in heavy makeup and an *Anchorage Daily News* baseball cap. "Why are you throwing the people of Takona off their land?"

Mike stiffened. He'd walked into an ambush. He hadn't seen the lawyer's so-called Statement of Claim, had no knowledge of the charges they were making. He felt incensed—and out of his depth. He said, "This is a matter for HARC's project director in Washington . . . an administrative matter . . . not my area." He pulled himself together. "However, if you have questions about the project itself, I'd be glad to answer them."

"Who's paying for it?" a cable man asked, a wiry guy with a gray ponytail.

"Funding comes from grants to a consortium of universities. The grants are administered by the Office of Naval Research."

"The Navy?" a freckled kid asked. His camera logo read KUAC—campus TV. "Is HARC some kind of new weapon?"

Mike had to smile. "No." Impatient as he was to get this over with, he had to correct that misconception. And it was a relief to be on the solid ground of scientific fact. "The Navy's interest in ionospheric research comes from their long-time problem of communicating with deeply submerged submarines. Normal radio signals degrade as they travel through the high electrical conductivity of seawater. To receive conventional transmissions, a sub has to come up to periscope depth, making it susceptible to enemy detection. That's where HARC can help. The lower a frequency, the more deeply a signal can be received underwater. Those in the ELF range—extremely low frequency—can go very deep. HARC will be able to generate those signals far more efficiently than present technology. It will convert ultra-high-frequency energy, in its HF beam reflected off the ionosphere, into ELF waves that can penetrate even to a deeply submerged sub, anywhere on Earth."

"Why build it in Alaska?" the cable man asked.

Mike couldn't help glancing at Dana. Sixteen years ago science had taken him away from here; now science had brought him back. "It's the only state in the auroral latitudes," he answered. "The ionosphere above Alaska carries a current, called the auroral electrojet. During solar magnetic storms the electrojet can induce long terrestrial conductors, much like power lines, potentially very useful back on Earth. Beautiful too—it's what creates the aurora borealis, the 'northern lights.' HARC was built to perform pioneering experiments in these ionospheric phenomena."

He considered mentioning his future goal of harnessing auroral power, but that was beyond the project's present objectives, and these people weren't here for a lecture in theoretical astrophysics. Anyway, he wanted to wrap this up and call Ben. Ben could send in ONR lawyers to tackle Dana's hired-gun lawyer.

"The ionosphere shields Earth from UV radiation," the Anchorage newswoman said. "Won't your beam burn a hole in that shield?"

"Not even measurable. The ionosphere is a plasma—ionized gas—like a vast sea. HARC's effect will be like submerging a household electric heater in the Arctic Ocean. Its impact will be infinitesimal."

"Its impact on my people will be devastating," Dana said.

The cameras swiveled to her.

"Subsistence living is part of a way of life for the people of Takona, hunting and trapping and fishing," she said. "For centuries they've depended on the river, living in harmony with their environment. The new location, two hundred miles west of here, is hemmed in by a timber corporation's land and nowhere near a river. But it is adjacent to a copper mine, and that's where the men of Takona will have to find work, breaking the traditions of millennia. If history is any guide, that rupture will lead to the dissolution of families, alcoholism, drug addiction, and despair. *That's* what HARC's impact will be."

Mike felt all eyes turn to him, hungry to see a confrontation. He wanted to shout at Dana: Subsistence living has left your people in shacks with no running water. But that would only deliver the reporters the sound bite they wanted. He thought of Carol, an expert in managing media. What would she do? First rule of PR: When possible, make friends of enemies.

He lifted his hands in a gesture of conciliation. "I'm just a scientist. So I'd like to let HARC speak for itself. Be my guests on the site, take a look around." He indicated the open gate. "Open house."

Dana looked astonished. The lawyer, D'Alton, did too. "We can look at anything?" he asked, sounding skeptical but intrigued. "Videotape anything?"

"Anything you want." Using his cell phone, Mike called Wayne to bring a van. When Wayne arrived, he drove the whole group onto the site, and Mike followed in the Jeep. They pulled up in front of the ops center and everyone got out. "Mr. Hingerman here will show you the antenna array first," Mike said, ignoring Wayne's frown of dissent. "Look at anything, ask anything. Then come inside and I'll have a senior scientist answer any further questions. But you'll have to excuse me now." He was itching to call Ben.

"Any way I can get an elevated shot?" the cable cameraman asked.

"Sure." Mike turned to Wayne. "Let him go up on the crane."

He watched as Wayne started on foot toward the array, the group following him like overgrown students on a field trip. But Dana, he noticed, stood at the edge of the road by the ops center, alone, discontented. Mike shook his head. She was so determined to resist his world.

He went to her. "Why don't you give up? You can't win this. HARC's not going away."

She turned her steady gaze on him. Her black hair sent off blue sparks in the sunlight. "Neither am I."

A service truck with a crane passed, heading for the array, and Mike saw Lucas at the wheel, the cameraman beside him. It seemed Wayne had called him out to take the cameraman aloft. Lucas liked working the crane, Mike knew, but today? With me and Dana fighting publicly? He felt ashamed to be putting the kid through this.

Dana, too, had her eyes on Lucas as the truck stopped beside the nearest antenna tower a few hundred yards from them. Lucas and the cameraman got out and climbed onto the crane platform, where Lucas, activating the controls, took them up alongside the tower. "This summer job you've given him," Dana said, watching the platform rise. "Did it buy what you wanted? His affection?"

This is pointless, Mike thought. He turned to go, but Dana's voice stopped him.

"Why here, Mike?" There was contempt in her voice. "Why build on the very spot that would force my village away? You really want me out of his life that badly?"

He turned to her. "It's not about that. The magnetosphere is a continuum of earth and space, and I built HARC here because the geomagnetic properties of this area are optimal." The tech talk sounded hollow, even to him. It was all true, but the logic felt meager as he looked into her dark eyes with their depths of angry passion. Her skin smelled faintly of pine smoke. Its effect on him was a jolt of arousal, his body remembering. He squelched it. "Anyway, isn't it a little hypocritical to foist your will on that village? You don't even live there."

"So I should turn my back on its people? That's your style, not mine."

"Their council voted to move, for God's sake. Their council negotiated the deal."

"They negotiated away entitlements they had no right to. They gave away my son's birthright."

"My son too. And his birthright is the freedom to choose his own future—wherever that takes him. Look at *you*, you went to California for your medical degree, you live an urban life, you're a successful entrepreneur.

Why can't you see that Lucas deserves the same opportunities?"

"I went south because there was no med school here, and I came back. I am what I am because of my people. I don't want Lucas to grow up thinking he exists alone, acts alone, *takes* alone."

"You don't want him to grow up, period. He needs to get out on his own, Dana. Test himself against larger standards. Measure up."

"Measure? Life isn't a *lab*, Mike. How do you measure friendship? Or duty? Or grief at losing a way of life?"

"Damn it, Lucas won't be losing anything if he leaves, and when—"

He stopped. Something was wrong. A tremor beneath his feet. And a sound, a creaking behind his back. He turned. The office window they stood beside was shimmying like taut cling wrap.

Dana said, "What's happening?" Mike turned back to her. She was looking at the ground at her feet.

Mike didn't hear thunder, he *felt* it—a rumble in his bones. The core of his brain signaled *earthquake* . . .

The window exploded. Mike lunged for Dana and pushed her to the ground, covering her with his body. If his back hadn't been turned they might have both been blinded—as it was, glass shards barraged his shoulders and back. Dana had cried out as she hit the ground, the breath knocked from her, but she seemed unhurt, and Mike moved to get up off her. Glass splinters scraped under his collar, cutting him, stinging. On his neck he felt the sticky warmth of blood. He got to his feet, glass all around them, and found his legs wobbling like a drunken man's on the trembling ground.

He heard a yell. He whipped around to the tower where he'd seen Lucas. The truck's crane was quivering, and on its platform fifty feet in the air Lucas and the cameraman stood desperately trying to maintain their balance. The camera fell from the man's hands and pitched to the ground. His legs buckled. He tumbled over the edge and fell, screaming. His body struck a guy wire twenty feet down, breaking his fall, then it bounced him off and he hit the ground, still as death.

On the platform, Lucas's legs buckled. The platform pitched like a wave. Mike heard a loud snap from the crane. The platform fell away. Lucas leaped, arms outstretched, for the nearby antenna tower mast. Watching, Mike felt bands of horror clamp his chest—Lucas wasn't going to make it. And he didn't . . . not to the mast. Falling, he grabbed one of the aluminum dipoles attached horizontally to it. He hung on to this protruding tube, swinging beneath it like a gymnast on the high bar. Then his body slumped from the shock and the strain. Clinging to the tube, he dangled fifty feet above the ground.

Mike charged. His boots crunched gravel as he raced for the tower. He heard Dana running behind him. As he passed two stunned crew members, he yelled to them, "Help that cameraman!" Wayne, too, was running. Reaching the base of the tower together, he and Wayne went for the crane truck's cab.

"Lower the platform!" Mike called to Wayne. He grabbed a tool belt from the cab and buckled it on as

Wayne hit the controls. Mike stood ready to jump onto the platform once it was lowered, but the crane's hydraulics were damaged, and the whining machinery seized in the air. A ground tremor made the crane twitch like a broken arm.

"I'll get the other crane!" Wayne called, climbing out, and started on the run.

But Mike knew the other truck was at the maintenance shop, too far away. He'd seen Lucas's white face, and knew he couldn't hang on long. He ran for the utility steps, aluminum rungs like huge staples up the tower's spine, and began to climb. "Lucas!" he called up. "Hold on!" Halfway up, he glanced down. Dana had reached the base of the tower and was crouched over the fallen cameraman—she was the only doctor here—but her stricken gaze shot up to Lucas. Climbing, Mike was dimly aware that blood was soaking the back of his shirt.

He clambered up the rungs, but it felt so slow. Fifty feet . . . *five stories.* Breaths sawed his throat. The tower shuddered from another tremor, like something alive. How long could Lucas hang on?

Mike reached the dipole tube, finally on a level with Lucas. The tube ran at right angles from the mast, and the boy was hanging from it ten feet out. He turned his face to Mike. It was drained of color, and so were his fingers clawed around the tube. Mike called, "Can you move closer, slowly?"

Lucas did his best. Jerking one stiff hand, then the other, he inched along the dipole. But a big balun canister mounted right where the dipole met the mast made an impossible obstacle between him and Mike. Lucas halted, and Mike saw his terror.

Mike pulled wire cutters from the tool belt, sheared one of the antenna's Kevlar guy wires free, and yanked it to him. Cutting a length about ten feet, he tossed it so that it draped over the dipole tube between the balun and Lucas. Reaching out, his feet precarious now on the rung, Mike tied the wire's ends together, making a long loop that hung between him and his son. Then he backed down a few rungs, positioning himself across from the bottom of the loop.

"Lucas," he called, "you've got to grab the wire."

"Too far! I can't!" It was a few feet from him, and must have seemed like a mile.

"Grab it, and it'll swing you down my way." Mike forced a smile. "Like Tarzan on a vine."

"But I'd have to let go first. It won't work!"

"That's right, let go. I'll let go at the same time and catch you." He planned to tighten his leg's grip on the tower and reach out to snatch Lucas's belt. "You've got to, Lucas. If you don't, you won't make it. And if you don't make it, I don't *want* to make it. So let's go together. Either way, together, okay?"

Hope crept into Lucas's eyes. He managed a wobbly smile. "Okay." His look was so trusting, Mike's heart jerked inside his chest. *Please, let me save him.*

"Let's make it as easy as juggling. Ready?" Mike counted slowly. "One . . . two . . . *three.*"

CAROL RYDER paced the mirrored corridor outside the Washington Hilton ballroom's closed doors. Her father was inside giving a speech, and she'd sent in a waiter with a message for Lieutenant Spencer, Dad's aide, saying she needed to see the general. Carol felt miserable, body and soul. She'd suffered the first jab of a migraine on the way, then had left her cashmere wrap in the cab, and now, in the frigid hotel air-conditioning, she was freezing in this sleeveless sheath. She'd been finishing a meeting over drinks at the Marriott when she'd got Mike's call, and it had propelled her here. Bad news does that, she thought grimly as she stopped at the mirrored wall and noted her fading lipstick. Once, as a child, she'd been swarmed by bees, and in terror had run straight for Dad. When she reached him the bees fled, as if they knew—as she did—that her father was invincible. *Now, here I am, bringing a swarm straight to him again.* A burst of applause inside the ballroom startled her. She hugged herself, and shut her eyes, and prayed she would not have to choose between her father and her husband.

An earthquake, Mike had told her on the phone. A minor one, no fatalities, and, of course, the nuclear reactor containment facility was quake-proof; no problem there. But a visiting cameraman had been seriously injured in a fall. "And Lucas got into a little trouble. He's okay now."

Carol had stiffened at the boy's name. At Mike's affection for his illegitimate son. After, she'd called a Fairbanks reporter she knew who'd been on the site when it happened. "A little trouble? Hell of an understatement, Carol. The kid was five stories up a tower, hanging by his fingernails, and Ryder raced up it, snatched him out of the air, and brought him down. Your husband's a true-blue hero."

To Mike she'd said, "Are *you* all right?"

"Fine. I've left a message for Ben, but if you talk to him before I do, tell him it doesn't look like there's any damage to the array or the diagnostic equipment, but we're checking everything. It'll take a couple days. I'm sorry, honey, it means our weekend at the resort is out. You should probably cancel your flight."

"But . . . I want to see you."

"Me too. But I just won't be able to, not this weekend." He paused. "Carol, there's something else. Bad news. Dana was here."

Dana James. And the boy. Carol hated Mike being so close to them. He'd told her about this Indian woman and his son before they were married, told her he sent money to the boy's mother regularly, which she put in a trust fund for him. Back then, Carol had accepted it with equanimity—after all, they were a continent away. But now? She suddenly, badly, wanted Mike home. To stay.

"Bad news?"

"She's filed for a judicial review of the village resettlement and asked for a court injunction. Her lawyer's serving Burdett the papers today." Landon Burdett was HARC's project manager, a D.C. bureaucrat. "Ask Ben to call me about it after he's talked to Burdett, will you? I just . . . about Dana, I wanted you to hear it from me first."

Carol shuddered. First, Litvak's investigation. Now an injunction threat. And Dad hadn't even been able to meet with Gustafson in Alaska yet. He was going right after his speech. Carol herself was booked on a flight tomorrow morning.

"Mike, I'm still coming. I . . . I can help you there with the media."

He paused as if considering it. "Actually, that's not a bad idea. Okay, great. Oh, I got a bottle of the Chablis you like. In the fridge at the house. Sorry I won't get to drink it with you. Gotta go, honey. Love you."

Another jab at her temple. Cringing, she turned from the mirror and rummaged in her purse for some Advil. All out. She looked down the corridor toward the lobby. There had to be a gift shop where she could buy some. Advil, aspirin, anything. Only, what if Dad came out and she missed him? Have to see him before he leaves. Get the painkillers later.

Drugs, she thought—and allowed herself a small rush of pride. Six months ago she'd managed a PR campaign for Rhodale Pharmaceuticals, to counter an FDA proposed requirement for more clinical testing of Rhodale's newest antibiotic. She'd put together a video news release about the drug saving lives, and got it on every major newscast—a coup. The committee had dropped the requirement, and Rhodale's stock rose thirty percent overnight. Sweet success.

If only I could blow Litvak away like that. And Dana James.

She checked her watch. Dad had to finish soon. Pacing again, she noticed a woman at a pay phone. Should call home, she thought, check in with Constanza. A nanny worth her weight in gold. Lindsay's likely gone to the stable after school—the child's in love with her new horse . . .

A chill flew up her spine. All the good things could be taken from her and her family in a stroke. She could even lose Mike.

It wasn't *fair.* She'd kept the truth from him only to protect him, to let him do the work he loved while she managed the real world around him. She'd been so sure of Dad's judgment, and once he'd won, got the Pentagon to black-box HARC, there'd be no need to tell Mike *how* they'd done it. Not ever. But now, if the truth came out, would it turn Mike against her? That fear had got her thinking on the way here: Could she handle Mike better if she told him herself, first?

She felt coldness in the pit of her stomach. Fear about her marriage could be the wrong priority. She should be worried about going to jail.

The ballroom door swung open, and her father strode

out. In full dress uniform, he looked splendid—fit and confident, and still, at fifty-eight, every inch a Marine. Carol felt a glow of comfort, a sense of safety.

He kissed her cheek as the door closed behind him. "Spencer gave me your note."

"Have you talked to Mike? Have you heard?"

"About the simulation anomaly? Yes, he told me this morning. It was probably an effect of Crosbie's software upload. I called her right away, told her to do whatever's necessary to fix it. She's on it."

An anomaly? Carol didn't follow—and dismissed it. "No, Dad, we have a bigger problem."

He frowned. "Walk with me. McRae's bringing the car. I'm on my way to the airport. I'm seeing Harley Gustafson tonight."

Carol felt a clutch of panic. Everything depended on the senator from Alaska. "Make Gustafson understand. If this thing with Litvak happens, it's the end. For us, for HARC." *My marriage.* "Maybe . . . when I see Mike tomorrow . . . maybe I should tell him everything."

"Don't do that, Carol."

She had seen Dad target others with his steely disapproval, seen people shrink back, but never, until this moment, had he turned it on her. It scared her. So did what she was facing. The choice. Her father or Mike.

"Come," he said more gently, "tell me the problem on the way to the airport. Then McRae can drop you at your hotel."

His driver pulled up outside the lobby, and they slipped into the backseat. The glass partition gave them privacy as Carol told him about the earthquake—no apparent damage, she assured him—and then about the injunction threat from Dana James.

"Damn woman," he muttered.

"Amen," she said, feeling overwhelmed.

"What's your sense of it? Of her chance of shutting us down?"

Carol tried to look at it dispassionately. "It's pure harassment, so the court might not grant the injunction. On the other hand, native rights is a hot button. Hard to call."

Maybe her voice betrayed her fear, because he took her hand and gently squeezed her fingers. His hand was large and warm and reassuring.

"Carol, let me deal with these things. Harley Gustafson will know what to do about Litvak. And I've already got Crosbie pushing ahead to solve Mike's anomaly from the upload. As for the James woman, I believe I know of a way to neutralize her. You mustn't worry. I won't allow anything to stop us. Not now, when we're so close."

Relief washed over Carol as she settled back into the leather seat and let Washington glide by. Dad was still invincible.

▲

Because of the time zone difference, Ben stepped off the plane in Anchorage, Alaska, not long past the time of evening he'd left Washington. Saul Rabinsky, Gustafson's aide, met him.

"Good flight, General?"

"No unscheduled encounters with the ground, Saul, and that's my only criterion."

His calm was a front, as it had been with Carol. He seethed at the threat of Litvak's investigation. *All I needed was a few more months.* And now, Dana James was out to stop him too. He heard again Carol's words yesterday: *"We could be talking prison."*

"How's the family, sir?" Saul asked as he drove. "Your daughter surviving the grind?"

"Thriving." His younger daughter Maureen was in her final year at Yale law, and Saul, a Yale graduate, always asked about her. Political instincts, Ben supposed. *Harley's had better be sharp today.* He looked out at the Chugach range in the distance, the snowy peaks a dazzling white under the evening sun, and tried to compose himself. Somewhere, a pneumatic drill was pounding through asphalt. He looked at the opposite lane where traffic was slowed by a wedding party in five white limos. Anchorage always took him by surprise. A quarter-million people—half the population of Alaska—lived here on the state's southern coast, and although the city offered wintertime dog-sled races and mountain scenery and glaciers within driving distance, it also boasted office towers and golf courses, double lattés and world-class chefs, and a New York style energy fueled by oil and by a dynamic population mostly under thirty. Alaskans elsewhere called the place "Los Anchorage."

The specter of failure dragged him back. Court-martial. Prison. Dishonor and shame. He shuddered. Maybe it was a blessing that Julia was no longer alive—wouldn't suffer his disgrace. But his children would.

William, fresh out of the Naval Academy—it would scar his career. Maureen might have to leave Yale. And Carol . . . Carol, too, could go to jail.

"General Crewe?" Saul had stopped. "We're here, sir."

Harley Gustafson had done well and liked to show it, Ben reflected as they walked up to the house. The grounds were artfully landscaped with Sitka spruce and a Japanese rock garden, and the house was an architectural statement of redwood and steel perched on a bluff above Cook Inlet with a spectacular view. Out of my league, Ben thought—or any officer not born with a stock portfolio. Saul brought him out to the deck overlooking the water, where the senior senator from Alaska sat finishing a salmon sandwich at a glass table littered with briefing papers. Saul left them.

Gustafson, stocky, energetic, Ben's own vintage, wore gray sweatpants and a green T-shirt emblazoned "Seelaska Forest Products." A well-worn baseball glove lay on the table beside him. "Game tonight," he said, nodding at the glove as he stood to shake Ben's hand. "Witching hour innings with the North Slope oil men. Care to join us?"

Ben never could get used to Alaskans' mania for packing activity into every moment of the twenty-two hours of summer daylight. Families set out on picnics at ten o'clock. Ballplayers kept on through the brief dusk of midnight. It was like a four-month celebration at surviving another winter. "Not tonight, Harley, thanks. I'm heading up to the site."

"Heard there was a small earthquake in the area. Luckily no loss of life. Was there damage at HARC?"

Ben shook his head. "Minimal, Mike says. He's got it under control."

"Well, I'm going that way myself after the game, to Fort Yukon. If you can wait, I'll fly you to Fairbanks." Gustafson, a former naval aviator, piloted his own plane, a Beech Bonanza. Ben had flown with him and been impressed at the calm, almost a serenity, that overcame the garrulous politician the moment he settled into a cockpit. It was a side of Gustafson that would have surprised his opponents on the Hill, and even his colleagues. In D.C. he was a bulldog. For over twenty years he'd fought for every funding scrap he could snatch for his state, and in the last twelve years, as chairman of the appropriations committee, he had channeled billions toward projects here. Just last month, a nine-million-dollar study of walruses, and triple that for a new center for native crafts, and a seventy-million-dollar refurbishing of Fort Wainwright's airfield. Gustafson's pork was legendary. Alaskans adored him. Ben admired his drive, and considered him a friend.

"Thanks," he said, "but I'm meeting Mike."

"Fair enough." Gustafson indicated the deck chair opposite him. "What can I do for you today, Ben?"

Ben took the seat. "Harley, we've got a problem. Litvak is about to call for an investigation into all military research funding. Army and Air Force labs, and us."

Gustafson looked startled. "Where'd you hear this?"

"Carol got it yesterday."

The senator sat back, frowning. "Shit."

The feeble response sent a shaft of fear through Ben. Couldn't Harley handle this?

Gustafson snorted a laugh. "Ted Litvak's an idiot."

"What?" Harley seemed to be enjoying himself, but Ben saw no humor.

"You can't dump on the military and not get your nose broken. Believe me, he'll pay, big time. Next election, mark my words."

Ben felt his face grow hot. Were votes the only reality for politicians? "*You* may not be around for another election if Litvak goes ahead."

"Don't worry, he won't."

"Damn it, I hear the man's on a mission."

Gustafson looked amused. "Ben, you're an exceptional officer and a great strategist, and your vision for HARC could one day save this country from a missile attack, but you don't know jack shit about politics. Let me explain. Litvak's the senior member on my committee, but on my committee, I'm king. I can pleasantly explain to the jackass that he'd be stringing himself up by putting *any* military appropriation in jeopardy. Or I can offer him a plum. He's been salivating for a proposed new Air Force training camp—it's a toss-up between his state and Colorado—and I could steer that his way, *if* he shows me he's a happy camper. Or, if he still wants to call for this investigation, I simply won't let the son of a bitch's motion see the light of day. It'll end up at the bottom of the agenda . . . over and over. 'Can't be helped, Senator. Pressing matters of national importance. But we'll get to your fine motion one day soon.' That sort of thing."

Ben wanted to hug the guy. Harley—the consummate pol—could defuse this. Glancing out, he noticed killer whales romping in the inlet, and suddenly the clean Alaska air filled his lungs, as if he were taking his first unlabored breath since yesterday.

"But listen, Ben." The senator became serious. "If the jerk truly is a zealot, I can't hold him off forever."

"You won't have to. I just need another month or two. Crosbie will have everything fully tested and deployable by then."

"Glad to hear it. We've been sitting on this too long. It's time, Ben. Maybe this kick in the pants from Litvak is what we needed. It's time."

Ben then outlined the second threat—the injunction.

"That I can't help you with," Gustafson warned. "Can't interfere with the courts."

"I didn't expect you to. Just keeping you in the loop. I think I know how to handle this one."

▲

Crammed in his seat in the twenty-seater prop plane, Ben looked into the eyes of an Indian boy of about five who'd turned around to stare at him. The plane was bucking through turbulence as they descended into Fairbanks. Sprawled in a bowl of tundra between low hills, the city of less than a hundred thousand was the last outpost before what was officially called "the Interior" but Alaskans called "the bush." HARC lay eighty miles northwest.

Ben felt an inner turbulence, too. He faced a foul task.

Lying to Mike again—at least, continuing to obscure the truth. Just as he'd done with Carol, in a way, telling her that Mike would approve what they'd done once the goal was achieved. Ben knew better. He understood Mike. *He'll hate me.* That confrontation was going to be hard to bear, but a necessary price to pay. But first, he had to push Mike ahead with the testing.

The staring Indian eyes unnerved him. Foolish—just a child. It was the Asian effect that did it: black hair, coppery skin, high cheekbones, slanted eyes. The one time Ben had met Dana James, he'd felt the same unease. Equally foolish—she was a beautiful woman. Yet in her face was his Viet Cong torturer outside the bamboo cage.

Seeing her again was his other task here. He could not let her injunction stop him, but neither could he let her village remain. The official reason he'd given for its relocation was that small aircraft—mail planes, supply planes—flew into the village with enough regularity to disrupt HARC's operations. Since that was true, everyone had accepted the resettlement rationale, including Mike. But, in fact, Ben was creating a five-mile cordon sanitaire, a secure perimeter around the installation, ready for when HARC would be black-boxed—made a classified military operation. He'd staked everything on that. He could not let Dana James jeopardize it.

Saturday, 1:00 P.M.

Dana eased the frail little girl up to a sitting position. Seven-year-old Francie Paul coughed, sending a mist of blood over the threadbare blanket and onto Dana's sleeve. The child looked up, eyes big with fear, breathing labored. It wrenched Dana's heart. She had to get Francie to take her TB medicine, but the child was so weak and frightened she could barely suck breaths, let alone swallow pills. Dana had to calm her.

"I've called in a friend, to help you breathe." She dabbed flecks of blood off Francie's lips with a tissue. "It's Juju, my grandmother. She was wise—always made me laugh, too. Except when she died, when I was about your age, and then I cried. See her? She's up there, at your ceiling." Dana pointed at a shadow against the sheet-metal roof, which was bare except for an unlit kerosene lamp. "See? She's perched on one of Thomas's cache poles that keeps his game from bears, and she's going to listen to you and tell you stories of the old days until you're strong again." She followed the child's wondering gaze up to the empty ceiling. "But she says you better hurry, because sitting on a cache pole is hard on her scrawny old ass."

The small mouth twitched in an impish smile. "That's a bad word."

Dana winked. "Juju likes bad words, sweetie. She likes all kinds of words, and all kinds of stories. That's why you're going to like her, because you like stories too. You can tell Juju anything. She'll be a wonderful friend. When I was sad at her funeral she whispered to me, 'What are you crying about? I'm right here, inside you.' She made me strong, Francie. She'll make you strong too." She watched Francie's big eyes fixed on the roof. The child looked eager to commune with her new spirit-friend: her breaths were becoming relaxed.

Dana felt a stab of guilt. *So many like Francie could be helped if I'd said yes to General Crewe.*

"Better?" she asked. "Can you take your pills now?"

Francie nodded, and Dana helped her take them with water: isoniazid, then rifampin, then pyrazinamide. Francie grimaced theatrically with every swallow as though each pill were a rock—the martyr-drama of kids everywhere—and Dana almost laughed. She smoothed the little girl's damp hair back from her warm face, thinking she would have liked more children, would have loved a daughter like Francie. The sun struck a small stained-glass rainbow hung at the window, making colors dance across Francie's face. Like the aurora, Dana thought. The Northern Lights. To her people, the aurora was the spirits of yet-to-be-born children dancing in the night sky.

The smile inside her died. *To Mike, it's just a way to communicate with submarines.*

As Francie lay down again, tired after this small effort, Dana's alarm crept back. Francie was wasting away. The drug regime, if strictly followed, would cure her tuberculosis, but Dana couldn't rely on the child's family to see that she took the pills daily, and noncompliance worsened the disease. Today Francie's father, Archie Paul, was nowhere to be seen, and her sister, Sophy, had gone off fishing with her boyfriend and Lucas; wouldn't be back till tomorrow. This morning Dana had quarreled with Lucas—about Mike, again. Stupid of her. It only alienated Lucas more, pushed him toward Mike. *Can't think about that now.* The urgent problem was that little Francie was alone, as usual. It filled Dana with such angry frustration.

And yet, poor motherless Sophy, she thought, looking around the dingy cabin. Ada Paul had died two years ago after drinking grape juice mixed with wood alcohol from the school's duplicating machine. A sad family. Sophy, just seventeen, did her best looking after Francie, but she needed a break. Such a pretty girl, too. Dana had seen Lucas watching her, longing and dreaming, no doubt.

But TB was a cruel disease, with no respect for Sophy's problems. If noncompliance had allowed Francie's lungs to grow a drug-resistant strain, as Dana feared, then Francie's life was at risk unless she received second-line drugs—ethionamide and cycloserine and PAS. She would need to take them for at least a year, and she should be isolated. She needed to be in a hospital. But when Dana had told Archie that, he'd only shrugged.

"Your medicine's as good as what the hospital's got, ain't it?"

Except, they've got real doctors, Dana thought. It made her very nervous. She should not be treating this child.

Find Archie, she decided. Make him give his consent right now.

"Rest, sweetie." She made Francie as comfortable as she could, then packed her medical bag and let herself out.

The overgrown yard was littered with empty oil drums and abandoned machine parts. In the sunshine, bees were buzzing in a swath of tall pink fireweed. Pinging sounds drifted across the dirt path from the open door of the general store, where Dana glimpsed a couple of boys at the pinball machines. A raven landed on an overhead wire from the village generator and cocked its shaggy head at her, black eyes glittering mischief . . . just like Carla's. Dana missed her sister terribly. The talks, the horsing around, the effortless silent communion. Ever since Carla's death in the spring, Dana had seen her in the raven.

"What do you think?" she asked the bird. "Check out Titus's store for Archie?"

She'd rather not. Leonard Titus spearheaded opposition to her in the village. Dana wasn't a chief in the same way her ancestors had been—she had prestige on the council, but Titus had the power. He owned a commercial fishing trawler in Anchorage, a holiday apartment in Hawaii, the best house in Takona, and its only store. Last year he'd opposed her effort to make Takona dry, but

Dana had fought hard to get the prohibition vote through, and succeeded. On the village relocation issue, though, she'd lost. Titus held sizable shares in the copper mine near the new location; he wanted Takona's men working there. So he'd aggressively negotiated with HARC for cash settlements for every resident. The money was too much for people to resist; council voted for the deal. But later, several in the village came to Dana to ask her to stop it. Knowing she would need help, she went to Reid D'Alton. He'd recently moved to Fairbanks from San Francisco to represent the eco-group Guardians of Alaska, and people said he was the best. Together, they prepared an attack. He was doing the case pro bono, with Guardians of Alaska offering to pay the other costs of the legal challenge. But was it enough? Reid had warned her their chances were slim.

First things first, she told herself: Get Francie to a hospital. Maybe she'd find Archie at the dock.

The trouble is, it's not just Francie, she thought as she started down the path to the river. She was treating three other cases of full-blown TB here, and eleven cases of TB infection. Her patients needed hospital services, but Takona was far from the cities that could provide them. The village of a hundred eighty was isolated, wilderness all around, no roads connecting it to the outside world. Access only by boat or plane. Yet, without proper treatment, over half of those with the disease would die.

Just like Carla.

Was I wrong to refuse General Crewe?

"I have a proposal," he'd said this morning. "Something to satisfy us both." They were in the park beside the Chena River that bisected Fairbanks, and traffic was passing noisily over the bridge. When he'd called from his hotel and asked to meet her, Dana hoped it was to say he was backing down on the village relocation. Far from it, she found out.

"I have access to a discretionary budget at HARC," he said, "and in my discretion, the well-being of HARC's neighbors is a worthy goal. I'd like to give you the means to build a TB center. A facility that could service the whole region."

Dana was stunned. How had he known this was her dream? TB was a huge problem not only in Takona, but in other Native villages too. A regional treatment center could provide lifesaving services: specialists, isolation units, labs with polymerase chain reaction assays and high-performance liquid chromatography . . .

She caught herself. "You'd *give* me the means?"

"I think you know the exchange I require."

Her hope sank. So obvious. "That I drop the injunction."

He was watching her. "How much would you need to build such a center in the new village location? Two million, to start? Five? You'd have complete autonomy to create it exactly as you see fit. I could release the startup funds to you immediately."

His calm determination chilled her. He wore civilian clothes—pressed white shirt, knife crease in his slacks, crisp windbreaker—but General Crewe was a Marine to his core. He was also Mike's father-in-law. How fixated they both were on HARC.

"Your price is too high, General. Reduce it—let me

build a small treatment center in Takona. Let the village stay."

"Sorry, that's impossible. And, I warn you, so is the injunction. You must know that the court will see that you don't speak for the majority in your village. Take what you can get, now."

"A large minority want to stay, and the court will consider that too. I've made my people a promise. I won't let you drive them from the home of their ancestors."

She had refused his money. But now, with speckles of Francie's blood still bright on her sleeve, she wondered if she had any right to do such a thing.

She waved as she passed her cousin Grace, very pregnant, sitting on her doorstep in the sunshine with a can of Sprite. People seemed to have quickly gotten over yesterday's earthquake, but traces of the horror clung in Dana's mind. The cameraman, still in intensive care. Lucas hanging from that tower. If she'd lost Lucas . . . She shut her eyes, silently thanking Mike.

A blush fired her face. She'd been shocked by what had overcome her the moment she'd seen Mike save their son. Deeper than relief—a primal rush that made her heavy with desire, a flash fantasy of Mike taking her then and there. She was ashamed, remembering.

"Hey, Doc, want some nice steaks to take home?"

She turned. Outside Virgil Dell's house a group of men lounged, talking and smoking, preparing to butcher a fresh moose carcass on the grass. His chained dogs whimpered at the smell of the meat.

"Thanks, Virgil," she said. "Can you take them over

to the Pauls?" Francie had lost so much weight, and Sophy always looked hungry.

"Will do."

"Have you seen Archie?" Dana asked.

He pointed with his knife. "Seen him at Pauline's a while back."

Dana turned up the path to Pauline Tansy's, passing a rusting propane tank, half hidden in the grass, and cabins crowded in irregular rows. "Squalid" was the word some city people would use. Indignation stung as she remembered Mike's accusation: hypocritical, he'd called her. *"You don't even live there."* He wasn't wrong: she came once or twice a week to see to council business and make her medical rounds, but her home was in Fairbanks with Lucas. But Mike would not see how much she loved this place. Every path, every stand of trees, every cabin door, held a memory. Over there on the riverbank, where two little kids were poking sticks in the wet sand, was the big table rock where she and Carla, as kids, climbed up to watch for king salmon. It was their job. When they saw the tiny ripples—the salmon "making a mustache"—they'd signal to their uncles in the boat, who'd go after the big kings, dip nets ready, and wrestle them aboard. Carla always tossed a chunk to her favorite sled dog, not letting the grown-ups see.

That swath of pink fireweed was where she'd picked baskets of the spiky flowers for Juju to make jelly. It was part of her grandmother's medicine. Years later, Dana had found that fireweed flower essence was indeed an aid to people recovering from traumatic experiences, and far easier on the patient than Valium. She hoped some of

Juju's wisdom, too, had stuck. *"What causes sickness? Anything that gets in the way of living." "You're sick when you make a habit of shutting out life." "Sickness is what happens when a person falls out of phase with the pulse of the earth."*

The graves of her parents were here too, out in the cottonwoods by Muskrat Creek. Her father and mother had grown up in Takona, then moved to Fairbanks and started a guide business, raising Carla and Dana in town. Both parents died nine years ago when their Cessna crashed in a snow squall.

That old salmon rack on the sand by the aspens was where she and Carla, at twelve and thirteen, hid in the tall grass that day Thomas Fraser came by with his catch. Thomas, eighteen then, and so good-looking. Dana and Carla had grabbed each other, dissolving in giggles, as he passed. He didn't even notice. But five years later, Thomas married Carla.

Dana also loved something indefinable about the village—something in the air. Her ancestors had called this place sacred. She didn't know about that, but she did know her body and spirit always responded to Takona's special "feel." A sense of peace.

Well, I'm not looking for peace now. I'm looking for Archie Paul.

Inside Pauline Tansy's cabin she found the old lady plucking a ptarmigan at the table. The CB prattled softly beside her: "Trapline Chatter." A young woman sat sewing a moose hide. "Seen Archie?" Dana asked.

Pauline shook her head, her hair as white as the bird's feathers. "Maybe over at Thomas's." Dana loved the melodious sound of the old people's voices, a trait of the Gwich'in language that lingered even when they spoke English. But the old language was dying. Dana had never learned enough of it to carry on a lengthy conversation. Lucas knew only a half-dozen words.

People, as usual, strolled in for a visit. One man carrying his saw sat down and started sharpening the blade. Another walked in, settled on the bench, and cleaned his glasses. Dana remembered how, when Reid came here at spring breakup, after they'd been seeing each other for about a month, he'd been intrigued by Takona's ways, especially the casual visiting: no one knocked, people just came in and sat and didn't say much until something needed to be said. "Stay in one cabin long enough," Dana had told him, "and the whole village comes and goes. My grandfather used to say that visiting is what the Gwich'in mainly do." Reid nodded soberly, absorbing it like a lesson, and Dana had to laugh at him.

"Dana?" Pauline asked with a nervous look, her hands full of feathers. "We going or staying?" The others turned to Dana.

"Staying, I'm pretty sure. We'll know in a day or two." It felt like a lie. Reid had warned how slim their chances were. Her reply to General Crewe had been all bravado.

Reid, she thought with a pang. He's committed himself to this fight. And to me.

"Let's make it forever," he'd said that day he was here. He'd stood behind her on the riverbank, his arms folded across her belly, his faintly stubbled chin against her cheek. "Marry me, Dana."

She'd felt a dart of joy. She wanted this. It had taken her so many years to get over Mike. Reid loved her, and he was a decent, dedicated man, and she was happy with him, in bed and out. "Forever?" she said, turning in his arms to smile at him. "I like the sound of that." They planned to be married as soon as the relocation crisis was resolved.

Her brother-in-law Thomas's house was a rough log cabin, one of the oldest in the village. His chained sled dogs, lazing in the sunshine, idly watched her as she passed. In winter, Thomas stacked chum salmon outside, frozen stiff like cordwood, ready to be tossed into the dogs' pot bubbling over a fire in the snow. A few families here used snow machines to travel their trap lines, and Thomas did keep a snowmobile, but he preferred his team. "Dogs don't break down," he said. "Worse comes to worst, you can eat a dog."

Like most houses in Takona, his was essentially one room. Dana went in through the storm vestibule full of dog harnesses, guns, and parkas. In the main room all the furniture, again like every house here, was pushed against the walls, which, for insulation, were covered with cardboard from cartons. The colored brand names—Quaker State oil, Pampers, McCain frozen french fries—lent a kind of cheerfulness. There were two beds, one which Thomas had shared with Carla, one for his son Ron, and their clothes were in boxes underneath. A table and bench, a wood stove, an old fridge that ran on the village generator. Cordwood was stacked waist-high in the corner. A broom hung by the door.

Coming inside in winter, you swept your legs free of snow before it melted.

Thomas wasn't home. His cabin was close to the river, and as Dana stepped outside again she saw him at the water's edge, hauling his aluminum boat up on the sand. She went to help. Not that he needed it. As she struggled with both hands to lift the boat's right gunnel, Thomas lifted the left side higher with just one hand. "Gonna paint her," he said. "Gets on my nerves, everybody moping. Not me. I figure we're staying."

Dana was grateful for the vote of confidence. Thomas wasn't much for words, but she respected him, and he was her most stalwart ally. They shared a grief, too, in their loss of Carla. Out all last winter with Thomas on their trap line, Carla had gone without medication for her tuberculosis. Dana made the drug-resistant diagnosis in May. She still ached to think that she might have saved her sister with earlier treatment.

"Archie?" Thomas replied to her question now. "Gone down to the Grizzly. Took my gas can too, the bastard."

The Grizzly Lodge, ten miles downstream in the white settlement of Hanley. The only bar for seventy miles. Dana was furious. Archie was off drinking, while Francie was suffering alone.

▲

Flying her Aeronca Chief over the muskeg flats toward home, Dana wished she could have just carried the little girl away. But she had a business to run; she had to be up

at four tomorrow to fly some oil executives to Barrow.
She'd come back later and have it out with Archie.

Home, she thought as she flew over the Chena River,
shining in the sun like liquid gold. Her Fairbanks house
felt empty this summer with Lucas boarding on the
HARC site. She'd never forgive Mike for hiring him—a
first inducement, she was sure, in luring him away from
Alaska.

Clouds suddenly veiled the sun, and the river went
dark as oil. Dana felt a shiver. *"HARC's not going
away,"* Mike had told her. Was her battle futile, a waste
of everyone's time? Was her fight to preserve Takona's
way of life already lost?

A call came through on the VHF. It was Thomas.
"Dana, bad news. It's Francie Paul . . . she's dead."

Be objective, be professional, her mind warned. But
pain spread out from her heart like blood poisoning. It
dried up her throat, her eyes. No words . . . no tears.

Just like Carla.

Horror at her guilt rushed over her. She had spurned
General Crewe's offer. How many more would die at her
feet as she looked down from her moral high ground?

▲

She found the lobby of the Princess Hotel in Fairbanks
crowded with a flight-exhausted tour from Germany, the
harried guide instructing his charges in German over a
microphone. Dana pushed past the tourists, went up to
Crewe's suite, and knocked.

No answer. Was he out? Asleep? She raised her fist to

bang again, when he opened the door, reading glasses in his hand and mild surprise on his face.

The sides of Dana's throat felt stuck together. Her eyes were hot and dry. "The TB center." She forced out the words. "How soon could you give me a check?"

▲

Hidden in the woods, Lucas watched them. His cousin Ron was pressing Sophy with his hips against a big spruce, and there was a faint smile on her lips. Ron's hands went up under her thin white sweater and she gave a funny sound, half giggle, half moan. Lucas kept his own breathing quiet, but it was hard. Hard as his cock. He knew Sophy wasn't wearing a bra. As they'd kayaked here he'd tried not to stare at her nipples, clear as blackberries against her sweater in the cool river air. Ron's knee pushed between her thighs, opening her legs. He shoved her sweater up, baring her breasts, and Lucas's breath snagged in his throat. Ron's hand slid down into her jeans. Lucas imagined his own hand there, his fingers touching her . . . spreading her . . . he could feel her wetness. Oh, God, he was gonna come . . .

He backed off. Slinking away through the pines, terrified he might make a noise, he didn't know which hurt worse, his throbbing cock or the shame. Spying like some pathetic freak, and almost creaming his jeans. He walked quickly back to the riverbank.

The two kayaks lay beached on the gravel shore, and beside them was the remains of their meal. At Lucas's arrival three crows flapped away from the fish bones. He felt jittery, and sweaty in the heat, and anxious to push off, get back on the river. At least there, concentrating on paddling, he could get his mind off Sophy. They were on the Wahetna, a tributary of the Gatana, and the salmon were running thick. They'd come for the fishing, and Lucas was planning to take a couple of big Chinook back to the village. He looked downstream and tried to gauge how many miles it was to the place where he and Mike had camped last week. That spot had been so great, he'd told Ron and Sophy about it, and that's where they were heading now. They'd just stopped to cook a meal. Then Ron took Sophy into the woods. Were they doing it? Lucas wondered.

Don't think about it. Might as well start cleaning up. Taking the frying pan to the shore he swished it in the water, rubbing sand on the bottom to scour off the bits of fish. He crammed all the cooking stuff into his pack and shoved it in his kayak. He stowed the fishing tackle too, and the .30-06 Remington that he and Ron always brought in case of bears. Then he turned both kayaks around, ready to push off. He wanted to get going. If only Ron and Sophy would finish.

What was it like? He'd only done it once—with Janice Hodgkins, behind the ShopRite in Fairbanks after school. He'd been too fast, and she'd seemed kind of bored, and it wasn't what Lucas had hoped. Maybe because they didn't particularly like each other. What was it like to do it with somebody you loved? The way he loved Sophy.

She was Ron's girlfriend, and Lucas felt a little disloyal to his cousin—but they said you couldn't help who you fell in love with, right? And Lucas knew he was in love. He'd never known a feeling like this. Not just the hard-on that wouldn't stop. He'd felt that with other girls. But never this kind of . . . tenderness. Sometimes, she was as happy as a kid, and then he could just watch her for hours, her dancing eyes, her beautiful laughing mouth. Other times she'd look so sad, so lost, he wanted to put his arms around her and tell her everything was all right, and take care of her forever. He knew his chances weren't great. Ron was eighteen, two years older, and way more good-looking—people said Ron could be a movie star, with his sleek hair to his shoulder blades, tight jeans that showed his thigh muscles, shiny cowboy boots. Made Lucas feel like a scrub-pine pole in sneakers. But out here, on the river, he had a knack. He always caught more fish than Ron, and he could read the water better for kayaking, too. If he could show Sophy all of that this weekend, maybe it would impress her.

He kicked at stones by the shore and rubbed his sore right shoulder. Usually he could paddle for hours without a twinge, but his arms still ached from hanging on to that tower yesterday in the earthquake. After Mike caught him and they climbed down, people had crowded around, and Lucas felt embarrassed and told his mom it was no big deal, but his mouth went dry just remembering. Hanging there, knowing he was going to die . . . until Mike came. He was amazed by Mike, and so proud he was his father. Made him think of a story an old man in the village once told about a gigantic earthquake way back when—one of those tall tales set back in the mists of time, like Bible stories, where everybody's character gets tested. Lucas wasn't too sure about his own character—he'd been scared green, hanging there—but Mike had saved him, just like an old-time hero.

Afterward, he flew with his mom the three-mile hop to check on people in Takona, and they found the quake had done more damage there than at HARC. Ron and Sophy lived in the village, and he was relieved to see they were all right. But an ugly fissure had opened up all the way from Mildred Dance's cabin to Titus's store, pushing up rocks and earth and small trees, and damming up Muskrat Creek. Nobody had died, but Mildred's cabin wall had collapsed and broken her leg, and Titus had a bad gash on his head from the stove pipe that crashed down off his roof, and lots of people were shaken up. Lucas and his uncle Thomas and Ron and a bunch of other men were patching up people's cabins for most of the night. And his mom was patching up people.

Then, this morning, he'd had a fight with his mom. Lucas walked out on her. His uncle Thomas would have smacked him for such disrespect if he'd known, a thought that made Lucas wince—there wasn't a man in the village he looked up to more than his uncle. But Ron and Sophy had been waiting, and all he'd wanted was to get out on the river with them. Especially Sophy.

What if she went away, to the new village? He could hardly stand to think about that. It was why he was hoping his mom would win her fight to stop the resettlement. Yet he didn't want to see HARC shut down, either, for Mike's sake. HARC meant everything to Mike. Lucas hated that his mom and Mike were fighting. It seemed to him that HARC was spectacular, and Mike was a genius, and such a cool guy. But his mother had to think of Takona, like a good chief, and she was pretty cool herself. So who was right? The most confusing thing was, he loved them both.

Stupid fight. It had started when his mom asked where they were going for the weekend. Lucas said they were heading for the camping spot he and Mike had found, then made the mistake of telling her how he and Mike had discussed his future, maybe a career in engineering, and that maybe he'd apply to college in Boston and go live near Mike.

"Why?" She'd looked so mad. "The University of Alaska's a fine school too, and you have responsibilities here." She was always going on about him becoming a leader in Takona. He'd grown up in Fairbanks, but spent every summer and most weekends in the village. "A leader isn't someone who gets ahead and gets rich," she said. "A leader is someone who helps his people."

Lucas knew what she meant—a bit. He wanted to help Sophy. Her drunken dad wasn't going to. Also, he wondered if Sophy really was okay with Ron. Sometimes she got so sad and quiet, it made Lucas jittery wondering why. He knew his cousin could get mean when he didn't get his way. Ron had moods.

Twigs snapped in the trees. Lucas turned. It was Sophy, coming back. She was clutching her sweater to keep it closed. She gave Lucas a quick smile, looking embarrassed, and went to Ron's kayak. Bending to reach inside it, she let go of the sweater a little and Lucas saw that several buttons were missing. He felt a hot rush of anger. Jeez, what had Ron been doing?

"You okay?" he asked.

Sophy straightened, gripping the sweater closed again. She shrugged. "Gotta change my top." She frowned down at the kayak.

Lucas saw the problem. Her stuff was crammed way behind Ron's gear. "Here," he said, reaching into his own kayak for his backpack. He pulled out a red flannel shirt. "This'll be warmer on the water anyway." He hated himself for the blush heating his face.

She smiled. "Thanks."

As Lucas turned his back to let her change, he saw Ron coming.

"Let's get this show on the road," Ron called out. Reaching his kayak, he fished out a bottle of Canadian Club whiskey and took a long swig.

Lucas felt uneasy. "Where'd you get that?" he asked. Takona was a dry village.

Ron ignored him. Tossing the bottle back in, he pushed the kayak into the water, splashed after it, and jumped in. "Come *on.*"

Sophy hurried to catch up, and Lucas helped her in behind Ron. Then he pushed off his own kayak, hopped in, and paddled after Ron. But he was worried about Sophy. And worried about the booze.

▲

"Working on Saturday, most commendable, Meredith." It was the dean on the phone. "I'm glad I caught you. Mr. Van Cleef asked if you'd give him a personal tour of the physics department. I told him you'd be delighted. Hope that's not a problem. He'll be here at eight Monday morning."

Meredith Crosbie thought: I'd rather stick needles in my eyes.

"Sorry about the inconvenience," the dean went on, "but, as you know, we couldn't have got the new bistatic anechoic chamber without his donation. By the way, he loves talking about his hotel chain, so it wouldn't hurt if you asked him about it. We do want to keep him happy."

What we want is escape from this purgatory, she thought. Tuscaloosa, Alabama. Undergrads with shit for brains, nouveau-riche benefactors who expect a private tour, and a dean who acts like a pimp. She bit back the advice she wanted to give about what he could do with his big donor. Instead, she assured him wearily, "Fine, Henry, I'll be here in the lab," and hung up. The good little hooker.

She looked at her watch—three o'clock—then noticed the apple and packet of pecans by her computer, her only lunch, which she still hadn't got to. She thought: I'm *always* here, working on HARC. It's all that keeps me going. If only Henry knew.

"If . . ." She sat back from her monitor, pulled off her glasses, and rubbed her stinging eyes, then slipped the glasses back on, and stared at her screen. "If . . . endif." Those two words—basic programming syntax—would activate the new routine. She'd been working on it continuously since yesterday when Crewe had called and told her about the EM shadow anomaly that Mike had identified.

"Get rid of it," Crewe had told her. "Fast."

And she had. At least, she'd completed the routine that *would* get rid of it. She'd been going over it for the last few hours, checking. Now she was finally ready to compile it. Just five lines of code to add to the HARC program. So simple. As simple as the command itself: "If . . . endif." It struck her how perfectly the words that bookended a program module fit her situation. If. End if.

If you make one mistake five years ago, how long do you have to suffer in purgatory to pay for it? *Run:* one HARC routine. *End if.*

She picked up the apple and looked at a scab on its skin. Purgatory . . . marking undergrad tests while Mike Ryder runs a world-class project, maybe the biggest undertaking since the Manhattan Project. It'll make his fucking career. After he ruined mine. Sure, sure, he hadn't *intended* her ruin, but the result was the same. Collaborating as research partners at MIT, they'd published a groundbreaking paper, but an enemy of Meredith's in the department accused her of using fraudulent data. Yes, she'd done it, and why not? She'd *known* the experiment's outcome, and collecting the actual data would have slowed up publication for months. At the charges, she and Mike, as co-authors, were called before the department's disciplinary committee. Meredith implored Mike to support her—the data was abstruse, not a clear-cut issue, and his word could have tipped the balance. But no—though he hated to do it, he said, he couldn't lie for her. Meredith had felt the corrosive gnaw of fury that day, like the poisonous effect of mercury. Years later it was still eating at her.

She bit into the apple. HARC was going to be her

ticket out, back to the world of big science. That's where she craved to make her mark. Now that she knew how much Crewe needed her, and where this could take her, it changed everything. If she failed him, she'd have to serve out her sentence here, and she didn't think she could bear even another semester. She was ready to work her ass off to deliver what Crewe wanted. She'd solved this EM shadow problem faster than he could have dreamed, and she would make his weapon work too. Then, she would hold him to his promise of giving her the job she deserved. The *respect* she deserved. Mike's job.

She laid her hands on the keyboard and entered the five lines of code. It struck her: one line for every year of purgatory.

Done. And how perfect, she thought, how delicious, that Mike won't even know why the shadow's gone.

Saturday, 9:50 P.M.

A SECOND ANOMALY. It had appeared on his simulation screen just hours ago . . . a small unaccountable spike. What was going on?

Mike tried to push aside his misgivings about this second irregularity as he stood in the control room, watching the countdown readout and preparing to give the order to power up HARC. He didn't like to push ahead; he was more apprehensive than ever that this full-array test was premature. But Dana's injunction threat was forcing him into action. Damn her. He was ready to give the sequence initiation order, but every scientific instinct was telling him to abort.

This morning, he'd argued about it with Ben.

"I'd rather reschedule, examine the simulation model more closely." They were alone in Mike's office, Ben having flown in the night before, and he'd just explained that in checking the equipment after the earthquake, he'd once again checked the simulation for that elusive EM shadow. The anomalous image had been intermittent before; now, it had simply vanished.

"What's the point?" Ben said with a scowl. "Examine what? You just said it disappeared."

"But *why* has it disappeared? Ben, the fact that it vanished is almost more disturbing than its sudden appearance. It's vital to identify what it was."

"In the best of all possible worlds, I'd agree. But Dana James has made this a whole new ball game. We've got to move forward, and fast. By finishing these tests and establishing HARC's viability, you'll make it much harder for the court to grant the injunction and shut us down. That's the advice of our ONR lawyers. Don't you see? We haven't got the luxury of time."

Mike rubbed the back of his neck, the scabbed cuts still tender from the flying glass during the earthquake. "I hate to push, Ben. It's too much like NASA's 'better, faster, cheaper.' All that the rush for results has brought them is two failed Mars missions."

Ben's tone took on an edge of disdain. "HARC is just radio waves, Mike. It's not as though this power-up could hurt anyone. What do you imagine going wrong?"

"I don't know. I only know something's not right."

"Look, I don't like rushing any more than you do, but given this legal attack, our best defense is a counterattack. I'm not just suggesting, Mike—I'm *asking*. Move ahead."

It galled Mike to be forced into this by Dana. She meant to close HARC and send him packing, and he could see, from this corner she'd backed him into, that Ben was right: the only way they might win was to come

out swinging. Anyway, how could he refuse Ben? He
owed him everything. He stifled his misgivings, and
nodded. "I'll run the test tonight."

But later, he was working again at the simulation
model and noticed the second anomaly. A negative impedance spike. On his screen, amid the smooth hills and
valleys of undulating frequencies, a narrow mountain
peak reared up. Negative impedance indicated more
power returning to the transmitters than was outgoing
from the adjacent antennas. The spike's power disparity
was minuscule, just a difference of a few thousand watts.
Probably insignificant. Could even be an error in the
monitoring systems. Still, Mike wanted to examine it.

But Ben had made it clear. No time.

So here he was in the control room, about to power
up, with Gina and Roger and the rest awaiting his command. Initiation at 22:00 hours. Ten minutes to go.

Wayne walked in and helped himself to coffee. He
gave Mike a thumbs-up, and Mike nodded back, managing a smile. He looked out the wall of windows. A beautiful sunny evening, a few gold-tinted clouds high in the
blue sky. More important, ionospheric conditions were
ideal, very quiet, with no solar flares or coronal mass
ejections.

"Good night for it," he said to Gina, trying to convince himself.

"Great night. So don't look so worried."

He hadn't told her about either of the anomalies. No
point. Anyway, he felt guilty enough about this slapdash
approach. He didn't *want* Gina knowing.

"Here," she said, tossing him the bird balls, "lighten up."

Juggling the balls as he waited through the countdown, Mike thought of Lucas. He was glad the kid had the weekend off, he needed the rest after yesterday's trauma on the tower. It still haunted Mike, how close he'd come to losing his son.

▲

Lucas nervously watched his cousin doing an unsteady dance at the water's edge, the whiskey bottle in one hand, the rifle in the other. Ron was feeling no pain. Lucas had a bad feeling that this night wasn't going to end well.

They were on a gravelly shore at the foot of a bluff. For over an hour on the river Lucas had called to him that they'd already passed the good camping spot, but Ron, in the kayak ahead, kept paddling, Sophy silent behind him. This crummy gravel beach was where Ron finally had decided to stop. There was no reasoning with him after all the liquor he'd drunk. Lucas and Sophy had set up camp. Lucas could see she was nervous too.

"Think we should get the bottle away from him?" he asked her quietly.

"Let me do it. He can get touchy."

Lucas hated to see her kiss Ron, but he had to admit it was a smart way to get Ron's mind off the bottle. Kissing him, she eased it out of his hand. But the bottle slipped and smashed on the gravel. "Shit, look what you did!" He swatted her face.

Lucas sprang at him. Ron turned the rifle on him and Lucas stopped cold. Ron released the safety catch. "I've seen you looking at her."

"Ron, no! Here." Sophy grabbed another bottle from the kayak. "Have a drink."

"You first, dear," he growled.

She took a swig.

"More."

Sophy gulped down more whiskey. Lucas saw tears brimming in her eyes. He wanted to smash Ron in the face.

"Now you," Ron told him.

Sophy passed Lucas the bottle, fear in her eyes, and nodded that he should do as Ron said. Lucas took a mouthful. The liquor hit his stomach like a ball of fire.

Ron smiled. "All friends. Hallelujah." He stuck the rifle barrel in his own mouth.

"No!" Sophy cried.

Ron laughed. He raised the rifle and let off a shot into the air. Crows burst up from the trees on the far bank. "Come on," he cried, grabbing the bottle and shoving it into his pants pocket. "Let's check out the bluff." He took off with drunken, uneven strides.

"Oh, God," Sophy said miserably, and ran after him.

Lucas followed her. He couldn't let Ron hit her again. It was a long way to the top of the bluff, and he clambered up through thorns that snagged him, sweat prickling him all over, the unfamiliar whiskey already making his head ache. He could hear Sophy crying softly as she scrambled after Ron. He could have killed Ron for making her cry. They reached the top, a rocky plateau jutting out from a forested moraine, nothing on it but moss and bracken. Ron staggered forward to the bluff's edge. Sophy hurried after him and grabbed the back of his shirt as if to stop him from going over. Ron turned, a slack disinterest on his face, and walked past her, leaving her at the edge.

Lucas went to Sophy. She was looking out at the view. Lucas, too, even with his mind on her, was aware of the beauty around them. The evening sun gilded the few puffy clouds to gold against the blue sky, and high above the forested far shore an eagle was rising on a thermal, making a living imprint against the white peak of Mount Keetna. At the foot of the bluff, the river was alive with silver salmon.

"You okay?" he asked Sophy.

She turned to him, her eyes glistening with tears, and when he saw the red welt across her cheek his heart tightened in a tangle of anger and love. He acted without thinking. His arms went around her. She stiffened. Lucas held her as gently as he could, and gradually her muscles relaxed—and her warmth, her beating heart, her tears wet on his cheek, her trust, sent him somehow out of himself, spiraling up among the golden clouds and the joyful rising eagle.

He looked back and saw Ron glaring at him.

▲

The clock read 21:55:00. Mike put down the bird balls on the console. "All right, people, this is it."

"Yes!" Gina whispered.

Mike gave the order.

Ten minutes into the test, he was in four places at once. He checked readouts on the HF vertical incidence sounder, monitored the fluxgate magnetometer, kept one eye on the electron content archive, another on the Rayleigh LIDAR. Fifteen minutes into the test, he started to relax. HARC was operating smoothly. Directly above them, ten billion watts were bombarding the ionosphere, superheating a tiny patch of the universe, though the only evidence was on monitors and LED readouts. Calming down, he picked up the bird balls again and juggled.

A faint vibration shuddered up his bones. *Relax*, he told himself. *Adrenaline playing tricks.* Still juggling, he glanced at the clock readout: 22:20:03. He turned to Gina to tell . . .

The motions of his mind halted. A desert of blankness overtook him. A void . . .

He looked down. The three balls were on the floor, spread out yards from his feet, stilled. When had he dropped them? Why hadn't he seen them roll? He glanced at the readout: 22:20:10.

He looked around. People were at work, tapping at keyboards and examining displays, apparently unconcerned. A few, though, were glancing at one another, looking mildly puzzled.

"You feel that?" Gina asked Ibrahim beside her.

"Feel what?"

Mike answered for her. "A vibration."

"That's right," Gina said, "a little rumble."

Ibrahim grinned. "Thought it was my stomach. Haven't eaten since noon."

Steve Wiggins, across the room, piped up, "I felt it, yeah. Kind of like a shudder."

Wayne was mopping spilled coffee from the carpet with paper towels, muttering, "Didn't used to be such a butterfingers."

Mike felt pinpricks of alarm. "Shut everything down," he ordered. *"Right now."* Reaching for the console, he switched off the main controls, then grabbed the phone, called the power building, and ordered the reactor off-line.

His team stared at him. People started talking, some comparing the sensations they'd felt, others saying, "What shudder?" . . . "I didn't feel a thing."

Mike went to Wayne and asked quietly, so no one else could hear, "Did you blank out?"

Still mopping coffee from the carpet, Wayne looked up with a shamefaced smile. "Old-timers' disease. It'll happen to you one day, young fella."

Mike felt sweat sting the cuts on the back of his neck. *So it wasn't just me.*

Gina came over. "Mike, the vibration—think it could be an aftershock?"

Relief flooded him. *Of course.* The earthquake had been just thirty-six hours ago. Aftershocks could go on intermittently for days.

Only, why did I lose seven seconds?

▲

Lucas could see right down the rifle barrel. Ron's aim was steady in spite of the whiskey. Lucas stepped in front of Sophy to shield her, though his heart was banging as Ron's aim followed him. Lucas didn't know what to do next. He didn't want to die . . .

A sudden vibration of the space around them slapped his ears. A heavy fluttering buffeted his head, as if giant eagle wings were beating the air . . .

What's happening?

Darkness swept through him. Inside his head . . . barrenness. Sense of self fled; something alien crawled in. Primal instinct . . . aware of nothing but Ron's rage, Sophy's heat . . .

A moment later, Lucas lost his mind.

Sunday, 7:00 A.M.

BEN GAZED DOWN from the Search and Rescue Jayhawk's rear seat, squinting in the strong morning sun as the Army pilot navigated the helicopter through the White Mountains. Ben was hoping against hope that he'd spot Gustafson's Beech Bonanza parked beside some little lake at the snow line, and Harley himself waving up to show he was fine. Harley was a first-rate pilot—he'd flown A-6s for the Navy. But Ben feared his hope was fantasy. The senator's plane, returning last night from Fort Yukon, had disappeared. There was little indication of why. And in these mountains just east of HARC, little chance of survival.

The one piece of evidence, if it could be called that, was Harley's last radio call. It had dismayed Ben when they'd played the recording for him—foul expletives and incoherent whimpers about enemy "bogeys," utterly unlike Harley. Almost as though he was out of his mind. Had he accidentally gone too high, been disoriented by oxygen deprivation, and blacked out?

The SAR team leader beside the pilot pointed at the chart, indicating the next move on their grid, and the pilot nodded and banked the Jayhawk. Beside Ben, Harley's aide, Saul Rabinsky, bent over a sickness bag, wracked with dry heaves.

Ben caught a flash. Sun on metal? His hope surged. "Captain, three o'clock."

The charred wreck lay on a snowy plateau between peaks, a black smudge on the vast whiteness. Ben's mouth went dry. There was no way Harley could have survived.

▲

Fort Wainwright in Fairbanks was one of the country's largest Army training centers, and though it was Sunday, the airfield was busy with trucks and aircraft and soldiers as the Jayhawk descended. A mob of reporters waited at the edge of the tarmac, the post commander briefing them. At least Louise Gustafson hadn't heard it on the news, Ben thought, still shaken. He'd called her on the way, consoling her as best he could.

"What's this state going to do without him?" Saul said as they touched down and the media pack began to advance. His face was pasty from the flight and from shock. "Harley Gustafson *was* Alaska."

And my friend, Ben thought, grief swelling. He looked across the airfield to the nation's flag snapping in the breeze. Fixing his eyes on it, he said a silent farewell to a comrade-in-arms, a patriot.

Only then did he confront the fear he'd been holding

at bay. What was he going to do? Harley, as appropriations chairman, had been the only politician who could have derailed Litvak and kept the lid on HARC. Now, not only had that safeguard vanished, but Litvak, as the committee's senior member, would take his place. *It couldn't be worse.*

Getting out, he made it around the helicopter just as the reporters arrived shouting questions at Saul and the SAR captain. Ben quickly walked away across the tarmac.

Litvak with free rein to open his investigation. He'll discover the rigged funding and pull the plug on HARC. And on me. A Humvee passed, and he felt the soldiers eyeing him in his civilian clothes. *And our country will remain vulnerable.* The first strike against us could be this very base. These soldiers.

I have nothing to offer Litvak, nothing to bargain. No defense.

Jets screamed overhead. Ben looked up as three FA-18 Hornets in formation blazed across the sky, close enough to read their call numbers. At their magnificence, he was struck by all they represented. Courage and nerve. Power and dominance. An answer sprang into focus, clear and cold, just as it had in the hell of jungle captivity thirty years ago: attack.

But to attack, I need Mike.

He felt a pang. He'd always known this moment with Mike would come . . . but not this way.

He reached the bustling post headquarters where his driver waited outside the JAG office, and from his car he called Mike's house. Carol answered. She'd arrived yesterday, she said, but still hadn't seen Mike; he hadn't left the site. Ben wasn't surprised. Last night Mike had called him at the hotel to say he'd shut down the test after just twenty minutes because of a tremor and was checking everything, though it was obvious to Ben that the tremor was an aftershock. He thought now: Harley must have crashed about the time Mike stopped the test—and I was finalizing the deal with Dana James. He broke the news to Carol about Harley, and she went silent. When she spoke, Ben heard borderline panic. "Dad, without him it's all over . . . we've got to try to cover our tracks, try to—"

"No. Retreat is a *final* option. We're not there yet."

"We are! As soon as Litvak launches his investigation!"

"Exactly, there's still time. I'll finish what I started, Carol. Finish just as we planned. Only sooner."

"Sooner?"

Ben had thought it through. Even if Litvak announced his investigation immediately it would take him weeks to get the bureaucratic wheels rolling. That gave Ben, say, two weeks maximum, to be safe. He told Carol, "Our new objective is a demonstration ten days from tomorrow."

"Ten days! How?"

"I'll accelerate everything. I'm going to tell Mike the truth. It's essential."

She was anxious, flustered. "So sudden."

"So was Harley's death," he said grimly. "Carol, I need your support now as never before. You've got to be prepared to handle Mike, if necessary."

"Yes . . . all right."

"Let's not forget, he's on our side."

But as he told his driver to take him north to HARC, Ben wondered. Mike was no soldier trained to unquestioningly follow orders. What if he refused? Could Crosbie take over? No. It would take her too long to learn the ropes on-site. Only Mike knew HARC well enough to accomplish this in time. Ben could only hope that if Mike did balk, a last-ditch tactic would win him: Carol.

▲

"Too disruptive," Mike said. Standing in the busy control room, he was on the phone with Landon Burdett, HARC's administrative director in D.C., but his mind was on the test data before him. The last thing he needed now was this bureaucrat demanding a new round of drug testing. "And unnecessary," he added. "You got our clean bill of health last month."

"That was before I learned you have a recovering alcoholic running your maintenance crew. Wayne Hingerman."

That did it. Wayne, a friend for twenty years, had been beaten up in a long battle with the bottle, and hit bottom five years ago when his wife walked out and took their two kids, but he'd joined AA, determined to turn his life around, and three years ago Mike had offered him the job at HARC. He hadn't regretted it—Wayne's record had been rock solid. "Look, Landon, I've got some of the best minds in science working here, but put us in a sinking ship, I guarantee the man who'd save us all is

Wayne Hingerman. He stays. And we'll stick to the scheduled testing." He hung up. "Asshole."

Gina shot him a glance. "That's telling him."

Cool it, Mike told himself. Burdett wasn't the problem. He still didn't know what had caused that vibration he'd felt during last night's power-up, and it was frustrating the hell out of him. Maybe it *was* just an aftershock; most people here thought so. Only, what about my mental lapse? Absolutely blank for seven seconds. It seemed too coincidental that both events happened concurrently with the test, yet he couldn't see any possible connection. He'd checked with the reactor technicians, and he'd been examining test data all night, and this morning he and Wayne had inspected all the transmitter shelters—no obvious problems anywhere. When he'd asked Wayne for more detail about *his* lapse, Wayne had shrugged it off. "Hey, Mike, I only dropped a cup of coffee. Don't make an X-Files case of it." But if there was no connection, if it was just coincidence, that only left Mike with more questions. Had he suffered a small stroke? If so, was he fit to continue directing this operation? But he felt fine, never better. Except for his nagging concern about those two anomalies . . . another mystery. It was maddening, all of it—especially having nothing to go on but "feelings."

His eye fell on Lindsay's crayon drawing that he'd taped to the side of the imaging riometer. Quite detailed for a nine-year-old. Titled "Daddy's Dream," it showed a green field of corn bathed in a huge beam of sunlight under a rainbow. Naturally, a horse was grazing. Mike smiled. One spring evening at the Boston stable where he and his daughter were grooming her bay gelding, he'd explained that HARC might one day power irrigation systems for farmers in developing countries, helping to feed millions of poor people. She'd nodded thoughtfully, then said, "And their animals." Mike loved the drawing.

"Mike, can we talk?"

He turned, surprised to see Ben. Usually he called before he came out to the site. Still, Mike was glad to see him. He felt he was going in circles, and could use a little of Ben's military cool. "Sure. What's up?"

"Let's go somewhere private."

Mike indicated the window overlooking the antenna array. "A mile of towers private enough?"

"The good news first," Ben said as they climbed into the Jeep and headed for the array, Mike at the wheel. "Guardians of Alaska is dropping their injunction request. Last night I reached an agreement with Dr. James."

Mike was glad, very glad. Yet he felt the smallest twinge of guilt. He'd never doubted Dana's passion to help her people. It's what had kept her here years ago, though pregnant, and though he'd begged her to come with him. His past with her wasn't something Mike was proud of—and he felt it even more acutely sitting beside Ben, the soul of military honor. The guy couldn't be more different from his own dad, a bitter Vietnam vet. Coming home to Chicago from that war, antigovernment and antisociety, he'd packed up and come to homestead in Alaska, bringing his flower-child wife pregnant with Mike. The crusty old bugger still lived in that wilderness cabin, all alone. Mike always thought his mother might have stuck it out, might not have fled when he was eight, if his old man had given her just one kind word. Ben Crewe, on the other hand, inspired everyone around him. War hero, POW survivor who, despite torture, overcame his captors after three years and helped all his men escape. One of only four Vietnam POWs to receive the nation's highest award, the Medal of Honor. Ben's whole family looked up to him. So did Mike.

"Great," he said about the injunction. "That means we can finally take the time to identify these anomalies. I found another one, a negative impedance spike which—"

"Unfortunately, we can't."

Mike glanced at him. "You said that was the good news. What's the bad?" Ben was looking straight ahead, and Mike could see that something serious was troubling him.

"Senator Harley Gustafson crashed in his plane last night. He's dead."

Mike stopped the Jeep. The antenna array surrounded them. "Ben, I'm so sorry. I know he was your friend. Carol liked him too. What happened?"

"We don't know. The mayday he sent was . . . incoherent. Our only information is that he was en route from Fort Yukon to Anchorage and went down not far from here around 22:30 hours. In any case, he's gone, and that brings us more bad news."

"I don't follow."

Ben looked up at the towers. He seemed deep in thought. "Archimedes," he said, out of the blue. "The greatest scientist of the ancient era. When Roman ships besieged his city-state of Syracuse, he advised King Heiron to have his soldiers burnish their shields and use them to focus the sun's rays on the ships, burning the enemy fleet." He turned to Mike. "A great scientist who used his genius to save his king and his people. That's what you've got to do now, Mike. Something extraordinary, for your country. Let me explain."

▲

Ten minutes later, they stood in front of the Jeep, and Ben's words left Mike so shaken, he felt disoriented. The gravel underfoot seemed unstable. He laid his hands on the hood to steady himself. The steel was hot. His throat felt parched. He looked up. Far above, an eagle soared, though so high it looked more like a cinder against the blue. He and Ben were alone. Not a tree, not a blade of grass, just gravel, and the silent antenna array that stretched as far as he could see. It seemed like another planet . . . some parallel reality. This wasn't Ben Crewe, his father-in-law, his mentor. This was a Ben Crewe who'd just told him that everything Mike had been working toward, everything he'd been living, was a lie. HARC was meant to be the ultimate antiballistic weapon. A secret lab was transforming it for that purpose. Ben had kept it covert because such a weapon broke international law. He'd illegally steered funds to HARC, and Senator Gustafson had been an accomplice, and now another senator, Litvak, was about to launch an investigation that could expose Ben's crimes.

It can't be true. But one look at Ben's grim face knocked all hope of denial out from under Mike.

His first coherent thought was of Carol. *She'll be devastated when she knows what her father's done.*

Then, even that thought was obliterated in a blaze of fury. "Why?" His voice came out hoarse. "Why was I kept in the dark?"

"Would you have built this, knowing you were violating antiballistic treaties? You wouldn't, Mike. And I needed your genius to get it done. HARC sprang from your mind."

The enormity of the betrayal took Mike's breath away. "You lied to me. You've been lying for years!"

"I'm sorry for the deception, believe me. But it was necessary." He reached for Mike's shoulder.

Mike blocked him, fists clenched, as he would a wild-eyed stranger.

Ben winced, and Mike almost regretted it. He'd never made such a gesture of violence to his father-in-law. It shook them both.

Ben quickly recovered. "Put your brain in gear and listen. There's a way out of this. The way I planned from the beginning. I'd always intended to unveil the real HARC in a couple of months, once you'd completed the testing. But Harley's death and this senator's investigation now force me to rush to a deadline. The point is, we can't wait for Litvak's ax to fall—we have to take the offensive. Demonstrate HARC's true capability. And we have to do it ten days from tomorrow."

"What are you talking about? Demonstrate *what*? Who for?" The conversation felt absurd, like reasoning with a schizophrenic.

"An exoatmospheric kill. The target will be an orbiting satellite, the key observer will be the chairman of the Joint Chiefs, and the outcome will be the satisfactory resolution of this crisis. There are two magic words, Mike. 'National security.' The men at the top of our nation's security command have the authority to invoke those words and make HARC a classified operation. When they see what a remarkable defensive weapon HARC is, that's what they'll do. And then"—he snapped his fingers—"HARC disappears from congressional oversight, beyond Litvak's purview. You see? Overnight, we turn an illicit operation into a top-secret strategic defense system."

Mike stared at him. Anger still churned, but he also felt, for the first time, appalled. "Don't the ethics of this mean anything to you? You talk about security, but treaties are the *bedrock* of security."

"Ethics? Maybe you should take a look at your own. You've accepted military money from me for years to build this place, and you never wondered about a possible weapons application? You've been so enthralled by your pure research, blinkers securely in place. You *chose* not to know, Mike. I take full responsibility for what I've done. Can you say the same?"

Mike felt the need to look away, to look at anything other than Ben's face. But there was nothing but the marshaled columns of thousands of antenna towers. The vista had always seemed so clean, orderly, an austere geometry. And all his. Suddenly it seemed foreign, forbidding.

Ben said, as though to seal his argument, "Mike,

there's only one ethic in war. If you lose, you were wrong; if you win, you were right."

"Christ, Ben, we're not at war!"

"We're always at war! Nations have been overrun protesting 'but we're not at war.' The president's exalted National Missile Defense policy, this so-called nuclear shield, cannot protect us. It'll take years to deploy, and probably will never work. And by *openly* violating treaties, it will initiate a deadly new arms race, our enemies stockpiling missiles to overcome it until nuclear attack is all but inevitable. HARC is the answer. Hidden, effective, ready to deploy."

"Ready? No, it's not." Mike had had enough. "Whatever you might *want* HARC to be, it's not possible to reconfigure it in ten days to give you this 'exoatmospheric kill.' It can't be done."

"It can. I told you, others have been at work on this project, thanks to your data. Most of the specifications are complete."

Mike was astounded. "Jesus, who've you got?"

"That's not important. Only you can produce this demonstration in time. Mike, I need you."

It felt like the blade in his gut being twisted. "And if I don't? You'll . . . be charged?" It was impossible to imagine Ben in prison. The shame would kill him.

"I'm prepared to accept the consequences of my actions. No, don't do it for me. Do it for your country, Mike. Do it to save American lives."

Could that be true? He flashed on his antiwar father snarling, *"Don't trust the fuckers."* He shook it off, the whole question of right and wrong—he couldn't deal with that now. "I won't, Ben. I *can't*. I'm not talking about ethics, I mean it might be dangerous. That vibration last night—I don't know what caused it, and I won't power up again until I do. Last night's test was at only ten percent ERP. The demonstration you're talking about would require *full* power. I just don't know what we're facing. But I do know this—the world's most powerful HF beam, plus a nuclear reactor, plus an unidentified vibration, is a mix that tells me to back off."

"The tremor was an aftershock. Everyone, even the state seismologist, accepts that. Everyone except you."

"Maybe." Seismology wasn't his field. "But the anomalies—"

"They're just the result of the off-site lab uploading the weapon capability. The EM shadow you saw, and now this other thing, whatever you called it—they're only bugs in the new software code, nothing more. You can iron them out."

"You . . . uploaded, behind my back?" He was so shocked, he didn't know what to say. What to think or feel. All he was sure of was a deep, burning rage. Not just for these lies about the upload, but because Ben had planned the whole elaborate deception right from the start. Four *years* of lies! And his rage was stoked by the pain of knowing he'd been Ben's dupe. Self-blinkered, just like Ben said, the easiest kind to lead by the nose.

"Mike, I know you're upset. Maybe even mad enough to *want* to see me in jail. But think about this. Without me, the funding for HARC dries up. You need me, and we both need the Pentagon. If I go down, HARC goes down with me."

The lowest blow of all—Ben knew how much HARC meant to him. It only sharpened his fury. "You think you can force me to do something that's not only illegal but pathologically reckless just to keep HARC? The answer's no."

Their eyes locked. Ben said, "It's time you talked to Carol." His voice was calm, almost gentle, but it sounded like a threat. "I've already discussed this with her. Go home, Mike, and talk to your wife."

▲

He pulled into the driveway of his house in Fairbanks and stopped, but didn't take his hands off the wheel. Something made him dread going in. *"I've already discussed this with her."* Why would Ben tell Carol before he told me?

He squinted at the fierce reflection of sunlight off the expanse of windows. The house, overlooking the Chena River, had been built for an oil executive, a lavish West Coast design of California redwood and glass that was an oddity in this frontier town with its heavy military presence and its core of hard-living "sourdoughs." It had been Mike's home away from home for the last four summers, but he'd never felt comfortable in its sprawling rooms. Carol had chosen it, and Ben had arranged the purchase. *Like he's arranged my life*, he thought as he got out of the car. Beneath the bitterness, he felt hollow, felt the rupture with Ben like a loss, as though something valuable had been taken from him.

My illusions, he thought, slamming the car door. *Deal with it.*

He found Carol sitting on the patio, her back to him, drinking Chablis. When he saw the two guests, he wasn't sure whether he felt dismay at being unable to talk to her alone, or relief.

"Mike!" Jacob Porteous, grinning, got up to shake his hand.

Mike forced a sociable smile. Some small talk, he thought, then I'll get rid of them. "How are you, Jacob?" Porteous, a spirited man with a chubby, monkish look, was the director of the University of Alaska's Geophysical Institute, which collaborated with Mike on HARC. His wife was a shy biologist. "Nice to see you, Jeanine."

Carol had turned in her chair, and as Mike came beside her she reached for his hand. Her fingers felt cold. He bent and kissed her. Even her lips were cold. Mike's heart twisted. *Ben's confession is killing her.* Straightening, he squeezed her hand, and she gave him a trembling smile. She quickly composed herself, the courteous hostess, and said, "Betsy's coming for a visit, Mike. Isn't that lovely?"

"Great." Who the hell was Betsy?

"And bringing her new beau from Cal Tech," Jacob said happily. "Looks like it's serious. We came to ask you and Carol to join us all for dinner tomorrow."

His wife blushed. "Awfully short notice, Mike, but we just found out ourselves. But do come. Betsy's so fond of you." The splotches of color on her cheeks brightened.

"Sorry, Jeanine, I'm snowed under this week." Mike

caught Carol's eye, and her anxious look. She turned away.

Jeanine sighed, accepting. "Ah, well, if anyone understands the tyranny of the lab, we do."

Carol went to see them out. Mike heard her voice, faint through the big house: "Give our love to Betsy." He waited for her to come back, thinking how pointless his blast of indignation to Ben had been. Carol adores her father, and HARC is my life's work. If I refuse Ben, I could be sending him to jail, and HARC will die. If I agree, I'll keep his secret safe, and keep HARC alive. Only, how can I ignore that vibration?

Carol came back through to the patio. They were alone. She shot him a glance, then quickly moved past him. "I'd better take in the Brie out of the sun."

She was avoiding him. "Carol—"

"Jeanine has such a crush on you," she said as she gathered up the cheese plate and wine and glasses and set them on a tray, her high heels clicking on the flagstones. "Funny isn't it, at her age?" She finally looked at him. "On second thought, it's not. I'll be crazy about you until the day I die."

Her poise always amazed him. And the look of her. Even in this rugged town, where "dressing up" meant not wearing work boots, she maintained her style, chic as a runway model. A fashionably skimpy dress of silk as blue as her eyes, a cool grace to her movements, as if she'd been born in high heels. And those great legs. She had sought him out at MIT ten years ago on business— she'd wanted to add a physicist's comments to a PR video—but Mike, reared in the Alaska bush, decided the first time she kissed him that she was a princess and her business was to transform him from a frog. He knew he was a lucky man.

"Oh, did I tell you about Lindsay's ribbon?" she asked, licking a dab of Brie from her thumb.

He stared at her. Was she in some kind of denial about Ben's crimes?

"Honey, the horse show," she reminded him. "Lindsay got a *first*. Isn't that wonderful?"

"Oh, boy," he groaned, truly sorry. "I forgot to call to wish her good luck."

"Don't worry, she loved your card."

"Card?"

She cocked her head slyly. "The one I forged."

He felt a ghost of a smile. "Saved again."

"Mike," she said, bustling with the wine bottle and glasses, "her instructor says Lindsay's got real talent, young as she is. We've got to support that. In a few years she could be training for the Olympic equestrian team. Just think."

"Let's not get carried away." It came out more sharply than he'd intended. Why were they talking about this now?

Carol's forehead creased at his rebuke. Tugging off the clip that held back her thick blond mane, she shook loose her hair. It was an unconscious habit; he'd seen her do it whenever something vexed her, from a problem with a client on the phone, to a broken fingernail. Did she know how sexy it was? Probably.

Enough stalling. "Carol, we've got to talk. About Ben. About our options."

Her face paled. "Options? You haven't . . . decided?"

It threw him. She hadn't even mentioned Ben's illegal activity. He knew she loved her father, but didn't she feel even some small fury at what Ben had been up to behind their backs all these years?

"Not yet," he said uneasily. "There are complications."

He began to tell her about the vibration and his mental lapse, when he saw tears glistening in her eyes. Guilt flooded him. He was a bastard for being sharp with her a minute ago; the thought of her father's ruin was tearing her apart. He was about to apologize when she came to him and threw her arms around his neck.

"You're the most precious thing in the world to me," she said, her voice catching. "You and Lindsay. You know that, don't you?"

He held her close, inhaling the perfume of her hair. His fury at Ben flashed again—how could Ben bring this down on all of them? "And you are to me."

She pulled back her head and looked him in the eye. Her tears had vanished. "Mike, you've got to do what Dad says. If you don't, Litvak's investigation will destroy him. Destroy us all. You'll lose HARC."

It startled him, her instant return to self-assurance. "I know, but—"

"Senator Gustafson's death changes everything. You understand that, don't you? Didn't Dad make that clear?"

"Very."

"Then you *do* see." She pressed herself against him,

her arms closing again around his neck. "We can beat this, Mike. I know we can. *You* can."

He stood rigid, unable to return her embrace. "It's not that simple. I'm responsible for the safety of everyone at the site. The vibration is an unknown I can't ignore, and there are also—"

"It was an aftershock."

"And there are two anomalies," he went on firmly. Ben had explained the software upload as the culprit, as though that settled the matter. It didn't. True, the anomalies might mean nothing at all. But they might indicate that this new weapon capability introduced a systemic problem. "I need to collect and examine a lot more data to determine the significance of these things before I power up again."

She let go of him. "But . . . that could take days, weeks. Dad needs you to start preparing the demonstration *now*."

"I'll do the analysis that's necessary, Carol, however long it takes. If Ben has to face the consequences of his actions, so be it. And if I have to lose HARC because of his actions, so be it." His declaration surprised him. He hadn't known his decision until the moment he said it. Part of him, deep down, craved to reverse it.

Color leaped into Carol's face. "You wouldn't even have the *job* if it weren't for him!"

Why did it shock him to hear her say so? It was the truth. He repeated, as calmly as he could, "This is how it is. I'll collect the information I need and analyze it. And then, I'll decide."

"Decide now, Mike. Right now. If you don't, it's me who's going to jail."

It hit him almost like another mental lapse. It wasn't that her words made no sense . . . they made instant, appalling sense: she was Ben's accomplice.

With a glance at the neighbors' yard, Carol said, "Come inside."

Mike stood in the living room watching her slide the patio glass door after them, shutting out the world. The huge house suddenly felt alien. He'd grown up in a cabin, was never comfortable in spacious rooms. Except the sky. Illogical thought, he told himself, his pulse pounding in his ears. When he spoke, his voice sounded false, like an actor playing the jilted lover. But the feeling of near panic almost choking him was real. "How long have you been involved?" he asked. *How long have you been lying to me?*

"From the start. Dad needed two things. Boosted funding to the ONR, and a system by which money meant for other ONR projects could be diverted to HARC. I helped with both, first by bringing Dad and Gustafson together. I knew Gustafson, because I'd done PR for the Poker Flats rocket range up here. He immediately liked Dad's plan of HARC as a weapon. So, he ensured the large appropriations to the ONR, and the three of us worked out the details of its diversion."

Mike was unnerved at her composure. She saw nothing wrong with what she'd done, only with the prospect of being discovered. What had Ben said about ethics in war? *"If you lose, you were wrong; if you win, you were right."* "What are the details?"

"You know Landmark Construction?"

"Contractors at HARC." There had been several, but Landmark did a lot of the heavy lifting—hauling gravel, setting thermopiles, building transmission shelters, erecting fencing, and they still managed site security. "What's the connection?"

"Landmark is a subsidiary of my company. It handles HARC's . . . creative accounting."

"It's a front? To move the ONR money?"

"Yes. Dad isolated monies earmarked in the ONR budget for other projects, and he channeled them to Landmark. Then, I ensured that Landmark delivered that extra funding to HARC. That's how the project got built so fast, and why you've had carte blanche." She said with sudden passion, "Mike, HARC was your vision as well as Dad's, and I saw a way to help turn it into reality. I'm not sorry. It's been the making of you."

He asked the question that had been choking him. "Why didn't you tell me?"

"Oh, darling, it's not what you think. It was never about not trusting you, or *wanting* to hide it. It was just better, safer, for you not to know. That way you could concentrate—we all could, concentrate on what we do best. Dad's gift is for command. He knows better than anyone what kind of strategic defense is really necessary to protect this country, and he's put everything on the line to deliver it. Every one of us will be safer because of what he's done. I knew that the top military people would covet this weapon if there was no political fallout for them, and I saw how I could help him get it. But, Mike, the most wonderful part was that I could help *you*.

Your dream was to build HARC. Mine was to make your dream come true."

She meant it. She wanted what was good for him. He knew it in his bones. For all her poise, Carol had always looked up to him as superior, a "genius." That label never made sense to him—everything he knew, he'd learned from books, and so could anyone. But Carol would forever feel that he deserved special status. Her devotion moved him. But he was terrified of what it was going to do to her. *Jail.*

"This senator's investigation," he said, "are you so sure they'd find the link to you? You said the accounting's been creative. Maybe the investigators would miss it."

She shook her head. For the first time she looked frightened. "A forensic audit . . . they'll find it. And when they do, I'll face charges. And there's more. Because I'm a lobbyist, the charges would include interfering with Congress." She put her hand to her mouth, as if to keep her fear bottled up, but she whispered behind her fingertips, "Prison. I don't think I could bear—"

"Don't." It tore him apart to see that fear in her eyes. He came to her and put his arms around her. "We're not going to let that happen."

She pulled back to look at him, hope lighting up her face.

"You're my wife," he said simply. Maybe it wasn't reason enough for illegal collusion, but it was the only reason that mattered. He would not let his wife go to prison.

"Oh, Mike." Her hands caressed his face, her fingers

cool, smooth. "It's going to be fine. We can get over this, and then it's all going to work out perfectly. Dad's been right about everything, and I know he's right about this." She kissed his mouth, his cheek, his neck, his mouth again. "You're my hero, you know that, don't you?" Her hands slid down his chest and she said throatily, "Oh, God, I wish you'd fuck me right now, right here. Oh, let's." Her hands were on his buttocks and she pressed herself to him. Then, suddenly, anxiously, "No. No, I'd better call Dad. He'll want to talk to you right away."

Mike watched her go upstairs to the bedroom phone, pulling back her hair again into the clip as she went quickly up the steps. He knew she'd manipulated him, knew she had pushed every button perfectly, but that didn't change the fact that only one course of action was open to him. Hers. Ben's. Bizarre, he thought with a pang. He was going to do what he must to save his wife and save the man who'd given him everything, yet he had never felt so distant from them.

▲

Ben came to the house that evening, all military business—a general planning a campaign. He brought a briefcase of specifications and schematics, spreading them out at the kitchen table, and as Mike looked over the papers, the three of them sat there eating cold crab and drinking white wine, pretending as though all that had happened was a family quarrel, patched up now, behind them. But Mike felt sordid, corrupt. As evening sunshine streamed through the kitchen window, he thought darkness would be more fitting, a cover for what he was doing.

As a boy he'd reveled in the long black winter nights. That's when the aurora did its magic. In that silent, windless Alaska cold, with snow settled in ghostly mushroom caps on the tops of posts, he'd stand outside the cabin watching, head back, so mesmerized he forgot to be cold. At twelve, a self-taught astronomer, he'd liked it that the motion of the moon and planets was rationally predictable—but the mad midnight dance of the aurora was not, and that enthralled him even more. Those shimmering curtains of colored electricity—red, yellow, green, purple. They seemed like something alive, both sensual and spiritual. He'd wanted to know the aurora intimately, its heartbeat, its energy, its soul. He'd created HARC to do that. HARC's order and logic pleased him, and its power too, but the aurora itself had remained a mystery, its energy inviolate. Until now. Now, he felt the shame of raping the thing he loved.

Yet the shame went even deeper, down to a reservoir of guilty relief. Because in his most secret self, he rejoiced that he'd still be in control. HARC would still be his.

The specs Ben had brought were first-rate. Scanning them, Mike was impressed at how skillfully his virtual mirror had been rendered parabolic, a refinement that would focus HARC's reflected energy with great precision. The work was exceptional. Who had done this? He looked over a schematic that detailed circularly polarized EM radiation to be transmitted along a field line through the targeted region of plasma, and he felt a chill. He turned to Ben. "Meredith Crosbie?"

Ben's startled expression told him he was right. "No, I'm not clairvoyant," Mike said, "it's this coding style. It's hers."

Ben said, "You'll have to confer with her, you realize, to get this operational in time. Tell me that won't be a problem."

"No more so than all the other problems," Mike said grimly. Meredith Crosbie, his old research partner, forced to leave MIT in disgrace. That debacle had led directly to HARC's creation. In the academic hothouse of guilt by association with Meredith, Mike's research funding had dried up and his career had stalled. Then Ben came to see him. Holding a copy of Mike's published theory, he'd asked, "Can you really build this?" and days later, thrilled at his good fortune, Mike was planning construction of a HARC prototype with all the ONR funding he needed. What a fool, he thought now. And Meredith's reappearance filled him with misgiving.

He reminded himself that feelings had no currency in his business. He was a scientist. He had ten days to prepare a demonstration of HARC's power that would keep Ben and Carol safe. He had to turn HARC into a weapon.

▲

Where's Lucas? The worry followed Dana as she walked up the path to Archie Paul's cabin. Lucas had said he'd be back by this evening, but it was almost ten and there was no sign of him, nor of Ron and Sophy.

Her heart ached at the prospect of seeing Archie about Francie's burial. She could still see the little girl's big eyes looking up at her with such trust. *Trust I abused* . . .

Last night with Reid had been almost worse. She'd gone to see him late, after making the deal with General Crewe. She'd woken him up.

"Dropping the fight?" Reid asked, astonished. He'd pulled on a cotton kimono over his black T-shirt and boxers and they stood in his kitchen, waiting for tea to steep. "I don't get it, Dana. It's not like you to give up. Why?"

She hated herself for holding back on him. "The only stipulation I make," General Crewe had told her as he'd written the check—three million dollars, as she stood watching—"is that you tell no one about the TB center until the village relocation is complete. Media interest would only complicate a smooth operation. It's just a week away, so let's say ten days." He'd handed her the check. Dana had agreed.

"I can't say why, Reid, not yet. Please, just trust me." She longed to tell him that this was the necessary means to a very good end, a regional medical facility that would help so many, like Francie Paul. But she'd given Crewe her word, so she said to Reid only, "In ten days, I promise, I'll explain everything."

"Ten days?" he asked, frowning, puzzled. "The village will be moved by then." He gently took her face in his hands. "I know what Takona means to you. Are you sure about this?"

She was sure of one thing, the goodness of his heart, and it moved her. She smiled and nodded yes. His hands dropped to her hips as his eyes still searched her face. His hands on her were warm. She looked at the golden hairs on the back of his forearm and waited for desire to stir her. But the connection failed. *Because it's not Mike.* Mortified, she said with sudden energy, "Very sure." She wanted the pain behind her . . . death, and HARC, and the past. Wanted a future, with this man who loved her. "Reid," she said, "there's no reason now to wait. Let's get married next week." She wanted it. But she was also thinking, with a certainty that made her ashamed: Now he'll accept my decision, because it means he'll have *me*.

He had smiled, and kissed her, and had led her to his bedroom.

"Saw you coming," Archie Paul growled, opening his door. Greasy hair to his shoulders, eyes bleary, a rip in his checked shirt, he stood unsteady, the habitual tic in his cheek working overtime. Dana smelled the sweet reek of whiskey on his breath. "You said your medicine would make her better." Tears brimmed in his eyes. "You killed my little girl."

He's beside himself with grief, Dana reminded herself. A lost child—what pain could be worse? Was that why, as she stepped into the dark cabin where poor dead Francie lay, the worry inside her whispered again: *Where is Lucas?*

Monday, 6:15 A.M.

Better?" CAROL STOOD BEHIND MIKE, massaging the knots in his shoulders. He was sitting at the kitchen table where he'd spent most of the night going over Meredith's schematics, familiarizing himself with the parabolic capability. Carol's hands felt good, but the way she was hovering made him more tense.

"Coffee's ready," she said, patting his arm. She had come downstairs in her silk dressing gown ten minutes ago and put on a fresh pot. She'd extended her weekend visit, making arrangements with her Boston office and with the nanny so that she could stay here until the demonstration. "Another cup?"

He shook his head. He'd been drinking the stuff since 4:00 A.M. and his mouth was stale.

"Something to eat? Toast? A muffin? I could cook you some eggs." She was fussing with a pile of his notes like a housewife getting a child to school. Mike grabbed her wrist to stop her. "Carol, I'm fine."

She gave him a smile, tentative, insecure. "I just want to help."

He nodded, softening. "I know."

The doorbell rang. They looked at each other. Who'd be calling at this hour of the morning?

"I'll get it." She left in a drift of mauve silk.

Mike sat back, his eyes itchy. Bright sunlight streamed in the windows. He thought wryly, *Another great day for the tourists, and me stuck indoors making a weapon.* He noticed a scatter of mail on the counter, flyers and unopened bills, plus the monthly PR newsletter that Carol put out for HARC. Her office did it up like a community newspaper—articles highlighting how HARC pumped money into the local economy, brought jobs, attracted top scientists, gave the area status. Until yesterday Mike had believed all that, been proud of it. Now . . . what an elaborate whitewash.

He felt grubby. He'd slept in his clothes—a restless nap on the couch around 2:00 A.M.—hadn't shaved, felt stiff all over, and his mind was churning with Meredith's equations. He longed for an hour in the kayak to get out the kinks. Impossible this morning, though, and every morning until the demonstration's done. And then what? Back to normal? How can we? For four years Carol hid the truth. Was she *ever* going to tell me?

And the demonstration itself . . . was it safe? He would confirm today with the state seismologist whether the tremor had been an aftershock, which was probably the case. But what if it wasn't? He asked himself: What exactly do I think might go wrong, and if it did, who'd be endangered, how? He simply didn't know. The sheer magnitude of HARC made this new territory. In physics, scale was fundamental. He was haunted by the image of Robert Oppenheimer a half century ago preparing to detonate the first atomic bomb in the New Mexico desert, apprehensive because the thing was so big that none of the scientists knew exactly what collateral effects might occur. The wind that sucked buildings to rubble. The vaporization of life at ground zero. The staggering radius of lethal fallout. When it happened, it amazed them all. No one knew . . .

He heard Carol's slippers padding back down the hall. He went back to his notes.

"It's Dr. James."

He looked up, astonished. "What, here?"

Carol seemed just as unnerved. "In the living room." There was wariness in her eyes. "She seems upset."

Mike got to his feet. What had possessed Dana to come to his house? Was it about the injunction? Ben said he'd got her to drop it . . . had she changed her mind, decided to continue the battle? He gathered up the schematics and shoved them in his briefcase. Can't let her know what I'm doing. *Can't let her shut us down.*

He found her in the living room. Her face was drawn, as though she'd had as little sleep as he had. "It's Lucas," she said. "He's missing. I came to ask your help."

His thoughts of HARC vanished in a rush of concern. "What do you mean, missing?"

"He went fishing Saturday morning with his cousin and a friend. They were supposed to come back yesterday."

"Went where?"

"I don't know, but he mentioned a camping spot he'd been to with you. That's why I'm here."

Mike thought of his last kayak trip with Lucas, and that sweet spot they'd found on the Wahetna. "If it's the place I'm thinking of, it's a good one. Maybe they just decided to enjoy another night there. Maybe Lucas is on his way now, paddling straight to work."

"No. He promised he'd get back to Takona yesterday evening to help a neighbor fix her trap."

Carol had come to Mike's side, and she slipped her arm through his. "Teenagers," she said lightly to Dana. "Not the most reliable or considerate, are they?"

Dana looked at her. "My son is."

The eyes of the two women locked. It was the first time they'd met, and Mike felt Carol's arm tense around his. But his mind was on Lucas. Dana was right—if the boy hadn't returned when he'd promised, it was for a good reason. Or a bad one.

"I'm on my way to fly over the area, do a search pattern," Dana told him. "Will you come?"

"Give me a minute to change."

"You're going?" Carol looked dismayed. She turned to Dana, "If you're that worried, shouldn't you call the state troopers?" She offered a faint, polite smile, "I mean, why Mike?"

"Believe me, Mrs. Ryder, I wouldn't have come if I didn't need him. And I've notified the trooper post in Coldfoot."

"Carol, I know where to look. Call Wayne and tell him I'll be late, will you? I'll be in as soon as I can." He turned to Dana. "Two minutes."

"I'll wait in my truck," she said.

Carol followed him upstairs where he pulled on a clean denim shirt and grabbed his hiking boots. "One of the kids maybe broke his leg and they can't move him," he told her. "We'll pick them up, and I'll be right back."

"Or this could just be a new tactic," she warned, "to sidetrack you from work. It's what she does, remember? Harassment? And, Mike, you do *need* to get to work."

Tying his boot laces, he looked up at her. For all Dana's aversion to him and HARC, she would never use Lucas as a pawn. No, this was real. And in the wilderness along the Wahetna, only he would be able to find where he and Lucas had camped.

But Carol's anxiety was real too. Her eyes were full of the fear he'd seen in her yesterday. He flashed on a vision of the FBI leading her away, Lindsay crying. It shook him. It was up to him to keep Carol out of jail for what she'd done. *What she did for me.*

"Don't worry," he told her, forcing more conviction into his voice than he felt. "Meredith's specs are very thorough, well prepared. I can do the reconfiguration on time."

▲

The Bell Long Ranger helicopter skimmed above the Gatana River where it cut a V between high, forested hills.

"Whose chopper?" Mike had asked Dana above the rotors' roar as they'd lifted off outside her office at Fairbanks airport. He knew her small charter business was successful, but a Long Ranger, a very expensive aircraft, wasn't part of her fleet.

"A loan from White Fox Mines," she'd answered, flipping switches on the control panel. She'd once stood in for their sick pilot, she said, to pick up a couple of their injured geologists stranded after a storm; the manager had been grateful. "It's equipped for medevacs."

Now, she was keeping as low to the river as possible so that Mike, using binoculars, could scan the shoreline for any sign of the kids. In some spots, dense trees crowded right down to the water; in others, stretches of beach were rubbled with fist-sized gravel. The Gatana was wide, a glacial river, creamy brown from the silt of mountains it had carved for hundreds of miles. "Looks like cappuccino," he remembered Carol saying on her first, and last, flight over this country. Exploring Alaska bored her.

"The camp spot's about six miles up the Wahetna," he told Dana. They had followed Lucas's presumed route, starting at Takona and going thirteen miles down the Gatana, where they'd almost reached the T intersection with the Wahetna, a tributary. "There's a limestone outcropping just before the spot, looks like a marten's head, and there's an eagle's nest in a tilted Sitka spruce."

She said dryly, "You always were more Indian than me."

Mike almost smiled. Dana had grown up in Fairbanks with TV and school buses, in a painted bungalow across from a supermarket; he was raised in the bush by his ornery old man and flower-child mom, and they'd killed or grown virtually all their food. Mike was shooting squirrels and ptarmigan for the family dinner by the time he was seven.

He caught a flash of movement among trees at the river's edge. "Steady," he said as he adjusted the binoculars.

She maneuvered to help him focus. "Is it them?"

He lowered the binoculars. "Just a grizzly catching breakfast." Wouldn't be hard, he thought. The salmon were running thick, a mass of silver arrows pointing upstream.

The bear sharpened his worry about Lucas. He reminded himself that the kid was a good paddler, knew these waters, and always came out here armed, but it was wild country; things could happen.

He looked at Dana. They'd hardly spoken on the way. Mike found it unsettling to be alone with her. She'd changed so little in sixteen years, and because he could still read her so well, he felt the tension in her every muscle. And the antagonism. The door had been shut between them for all those years, and when he'd opened it again it was only to square off with her over HARC—yet now he wished he could tell her how right she'd been to fight Ben's grand plan. She'd lost. *"I reached an agreement with Dr. James,"* Ben had said. What pressure tactic had he used? Mike wondered. It threw him, that after fighting Dana himself he now felt an urge to protect her from Ben. Yet he couldn't even ask her about it. She knew none of this, of course, and he could feel her hostility speaking through the silence, telling him they were united only in their goal to find their son.

"Here's the Wahetna," she said, banking the heli-

copter to the right as the wide river met the narrower
tributary. They flew past sheer bluffs, bone-colored, that
rose above the helicopter on both sides.

An eagle streaked down on a diagonal in front of
Mike, and as he watched it head for the nest, he spotted
the sandy riverbank he remembered: a nook with low
bracken among spruces sheltered by a bluff. "There," he
said, pointing. "The camp spot."

It was deserted. Dana hovered as low and close to the
trees as possible, but Mike could see no trace of camp
debris. No disturbed sand where the kids might have
hauled up kayaks, no trampled bracken where they
might have set up a pup tent.

"I'll land. Maybe they went farther into the trees."

"They weren't here, Dana." He pointed to a bend in
the river ahead. "Let's look upstream."

She scanned the spot one last time, then flew on up
the river.

"What's that?" She was looking down through the
window by her shoulder. Her voice was strangely flat.

Mike craned to look out her window. He caught a
flash of red among boulders in the river, then, as Dana
banked to turn, it dropped out of his field of vision. The
red thing had been floating, like a piece of washing.
Dana sharply circled back, and as Mike focused the
binoculars, dread knifed into him. A red shirt floated
from the waist of a half-naked body, facedown in the
water, trapped by the boulders.

"His shirt," Dana said in a strangled voice.

"Go down." Mike's heart was a rock in his throat.

As Dana swooped down, Mike saw long hair floating

from the body's head like black seaweed. He couldn't help the jolt of joy. *Not Lucas.*

Dana gasped. "It's Sophy."

"Was she with him?"

"Yes." She threw Mike a stricken look.

He grabbed the VHF. "Climb," he said. "I'll make the call." They had to get above these bluffs for radio transmission. "Then look for a place to land." Dana nodded grimly as she took the helicopter up.

Mike raised the Fairbanks airport tower, explained the emergency, read out the GPS coordinates that Dana indicated on the panel, and requested assistance. As he signed off he caught sight of the flat top of a bluff below them to the left, barren except for some ravens crowded on a scatter of rocks at one side. The plateau would be a good place to land, and would also give them a view of the river and surrounding terrain. He pointed to it for Dana. "There."

As she descended, the startled birds lifted off. Dana was concentrating on landing, and Mike was scanning the river for a sign of Lucas, so it wasn't until they'd landed and were getting out, crouching under the knifing rotor blades, that he saw: It wasn't rocks that the ravens had been on, but a corpse. Horror slammed into him. He lurched in front of Dana to block her view, but from her face he could tell that she'd seen: a young man sprawled on his back with half his head blown off, his face unrecognizable in a mess of red-black pulp. Mike had already spotted the unfamiliar cowboy boots, and relief surged again. *It's not him.*

"Ron . . . Carla's boy . . . oh, God." Dana was suddenly unsteady on her feet.

Mike led her to a mossy boulder and eased her down, and as she sat, she flattened her palms against the boulder to steady herself. Mike felt just as shaky. "What the hell happened here?" he said.

Her stricken eyes met his. "And where's Lucas?"

Mike saw the ravens spiraling closer, emboldened to return. As two landed just beyond the corpse, he strode toward them, waving his arms to scare them off. His sharp call "Ya!" echoed across the river canyon. He looked back at Dana. She was watching the birds with clear eyes as they circled again. She said quietly, "It's their nature."

A rifle lay by the boy's body. Mike picked it up. A .30-06 Remington. Dana said, "It's Thomas's. His father's." She got to her feet, still looking rocky. "I'll call again . . . and tell them." She went to the helicopter.

Mike examined the rifle. He ejected the five-shot clip: three rounds left. If the gun had killed this boy, Ron, that accounted for one round. If the clip had been full to start, had the other round killed Sophy? Or . . . Lucas? The morning air was still and hot, but a cold sweat pricked him. He heard Dana on the radio giving information about the second fatality, updating their location, and repeating that there was still a missing boy. She added, her voice breaking, "My son . . . ."

It tore at Mike. Get a grip, he told himself—think this through. If Lucas had been up here too, where could he have gone? The level bluff top was bare, but the bluff itself was the end of a densely wooded moraine. Mike was almost sure that Lucas would not have headed willingly into that wilderness on foot. Besides, the spongy moss here showed no footprints leading that way. He walked to the edge. It was a sheer drop to the river. The only way the kids could have reached the top was by scrambling up the brushy side of the bluff. The only way down, too . . . except over the edge. Downstream, he could just make out the red shirt among the boulders where the girl's body was trapped. Beside his feet, the moss was trampled and gouged. What in God's name had happened up here?

Dana had come back with a canister of flares and distress markers, and from it she'd taken a package of orange dye and was spreading it on the mossy rock surface to designate the area for the search aircraft. Mike said, "Let's fly back downstream and look more closely."

They'd just got airborne when Dana said breathlessly, "Mike, look."

On the riverbank, tucked beneath the very bluff they'd been standing on, were two kayaks on a narrow gravel beach, and a scatter of camp gear. Mike's heart beat faster as he raised the binoculars.

"The yellow kayak . . . it's Lucas's," Dana said. "I'm going down."

But Mike saw no sign of life.

Dana was hovering, unable to land. The strip of beach was too narrow, too close to the bluff. And at both ends, thick bush crowded to the water's edge.

"Go farther downstream," Mike said. "We'll land on the first good spot and beat our way back on foot."

They flew half a mile, a mile, finding no clear spot.

Mike sensed Dana's anguish the farther they went from Lucas's camp, and felt the same himself. Then he spotted something on a barren gravel bar midstream, a mere outline. It clicked in his brain: a perfect rectangle, abnormal in nature. The size of a desk, it was made of large stones. Only human hands could have arranged them that way—a distress signal. He pointed it out to Dana, and her face lit up with hope. As she descended over the gravel bar, Mike focused the binoculars on the shore. A squirrel bolted up a ragged aspen in fright at the helicopter, and a V of geese overhead veered off, but on the riverbank all was still.

He looked to the opposite shore and spotted a row of small rocks on the beach, a line about the length of a man arranged perpendicular to the river. No, not just a line, an arrow. Pointing into the trees. "There!" he told Dana. The moment she landed, Mike swung open his door and jumped into the thigh-high water, its iciness a shock. He splashed across toward the arrow.

He found Lucas lying among the roots of a gnarled hemlock, eyes closed, face scraped and bruised and white as frost, a gash at the hairline. *Dead?* Mike dropped to his knees. He heard Dana splashing behind him. She kneeled at Lucas's other side and lowered her ear to his mouth and placed her fingers on his throat. "Faint breath . . . weak pulse." Her words burst like a searchlight on Mike's stunned mind: *Alive.*

As Dana did a swift examination, ". . . head laceration, left arm broken, dehydration, hypothermia . . ." Mike realized that Lucas had probably been swept down the river all the way from the bluff. Though alive, he was near death.

"We've got to get him to a hospital," Dana said.

Mike started to lift him. "No," she said, "there could be spinal injury. I've got a backboard and splints." She nodded to the helicopter.

Mike splashed back through the water for the equipment. He helped her splint Lucas's broken arm and secure a neck collar, and together they gently lifted him onto the webbed backboard, where Dana taped his head to the frame. Lifting the stretcher, they waded awkwardly to the helicopter and settled Lucas on board. Dana set up an IV, and as she powered up the helicopter, Mike followed her instructions, wrapping a blanket around Lucas, fitting an oxygen mask over his face, and activating the flow. Dana lifted off, and the moment they had altitude Mike radioed Fairbanks Memorial Hospital.

"Talk to him," Dana said as they sailed over the trees.

"Can he hear? Unconscious?"

"Sometimes they can." He heard the ragged edge in her voice, and knew it was fear. "Try it. Please, Mike . . . help him."

He looked down at the battered young face hatched with cuts and mottled with bruises, yet horribly white in near-death, and he ached to beg, *Don't die.* But he forced calmness and began to talk . . . about the river, about rapids, about the kayak trips they would take. All the way to Fairbanks, he talked to his son.

▲

The hospital waiting room had the antiseptic smell of crisis. Orange plastic couches, one with a gashed back. Gaudily green synthetic plants. A pay phone. Not a room, really, Mike thought, just a corridor. He and Dana stood near the swinging doors that led to the ICU. At the other end a frail old man sat squinting at a magazine, and a middle-aged Inuit couple sat looking abandoned and bewildered. A young man in fisherman's boots, his hand wrapped in a grimy bandage, stood answering questions from a stout, tired-looking nurse writing on a clipboard. Mike felt a rising desperation. Why had no one come to tell them how Lucas was? Dana, beside him, was hugging herself, and Mike felt cold, too, his clothes still damp from the river. It made him crazy, the waiting, having no information, imagining Lucas slipping away . . .

"Thomas," Dana whispered in horror, as though to herself, her eyes on the floor. "Got to call him . . . about Ron. And Sophy . . . tell Archie—" She groped for Mike's hand.

Her touch startled him. She wasn't looking at him, but her pain pierced him, having no way to help her. His fingers tightened around her hand.

A young doctor in faded green scrubs pushed through the swinging doors. Wavy red hair, a sunburned nose that was peeling. He came toward Dana, and at his grave look Mike felt the rock again in his throat. Had this doctor come to break it to them?—"Your son is dead."

"Dana," the doctor said, obviously a friend. "We've got him on a cardiac monitor and we're doing the works—X rays, C.B.C., we'll cross and type him, replace electrolytes, and we'll test for renal contusion. I'm

most worried about head injury. I've ordered a C.T. and
a neurological consult. We'll know better once we get
these results." Giving assurances that he and his team
were doing all they could, he left.

Mike watched the door swing shut behind the doctor.
"What's all that mean?" Dana's eyes were on the door
too, and she only gripped Mike's hand tighter. He drew
her closer to his side, the fear in their hearts forging a
bond. "You're a doctor," he said, "what's it *mean*?"

She shook her head, murmuring, "I'm not . . . I'm
not."

He looked at her. "Not what?"

She raised her face, a frantic look in her eyes. "A doctor. Francie . . . now Lucas. I couldn't help . . . can't
help . . ."

Mike didn't know what she meant, but her pain shook
him. "Dana, whatever happened out there, there was no
way you could've done any—"

"I'm not a doctor! I was expelled from med school!
Cheated on an exam . . . I wanted it so badly . . ."

He stared at her, dumbfounded.

She went on in a rush, "I came home . . . didn't tell
anyone. Started to treat people in the bush . . . and the
village. I'm a fake . . . couldn't help him . . ." She
rocked on her feet.

Mike grabbed her arms to support her, to stop her.
He couldn't let her go on like this in front of people. She
groped a fistful of his shirt to steady herself. "Mike,"
she whispered, "if Lucas—"

"Shhh."

"But, if he—"

Dies. "Shhh!" He pulled her to him. Her arms shot around his waist. They held on to each other.

Footsteps sounded down the corridor. Mike turned his head. Reid D'Alton was hurrying toward them. "Dana," he said as he reached them, his face creased with concern. Mike let go of her.

D'Alton took her gently in his arms. "Darling," he murmured into her hair. Mike only had time to catch the glassy look in her eyes over D'Alton's shoulder, and to feel a stab of confusion, before he walked away.

▲

"A demonstration in ten days?" Meredith saw that the excitement in her voice had turned the heads of two students in her outer office in the physics department. She gave her door a kick, slamming it, and continued on the phone, "It's a tall order, General." Ten days didn't give her much time to prepare, yet she was delighted. What a thrill it would be to see her theories in action. A career maker.

"The essential question is, can you do it?" Crewe asked from his Fairbanks hotel. "Can you have everything ready by then?"

She heard an edge in his voice, and wondered again, Why is he in such a rush? She had no answer, but she did know his urgency shifted things in her favor. It kicked her excitement up another level, made her feel bold. "As I told you the other day, General, this acceleration would be no problem if I were running things at HARC."

"That's impossible. There's not enough time for you

to familiarize yourself with the site and with Mike's team. I've explained the new objectives to him. Given this new time frame, it's imperative that he stay at the helm. Surely you can see that."

She paused, weighing the odds. Crewe couldn't manage this deadline without her. And she had a new card up her sleeve. She'd received a job offer from the Beijing Institute of Physics. Finally, a chance to escape Tuscaloosa. It was a generous offer, and moving to a foreign country didn't faze her; life abroad was second nature after her father's many diplomatic postings. But Meredith wasn't interested in challenge in China, and the thought of starting from scratch set her teeth on edge. She wanted recognition at home, and she wanted it now. Crewe could give her that. He knew how good she was: hadn't she got rid of that EM shadow at HARC overnight? And it was clear that something had happened that made him need her more than ever. She thought: *Go for it.* "For the short term," she answered.

"Pardon?"

"I can see that he has to stay for the short term. But after the demonstration, I want my due, General. I want Mike's job. That's my condition. Nonnegotiable."

His voice turned steely. "Let me make this clear, Dr. Crosbie. If we don't achieve success with this demonstration, there'll be no jobs here for anyone. There'll be no HARC. I've already assured you of a position in the future. In the meantime, you'd be advised to refrain from sinking your teeth into the hand that feeds you."

Meredith bit back her frustration. If she'd misread his urgency he might just tell her to get lost; Mike was more than capable of working out her specs alone, given a few weeks. No, she couldn't afford to antagonize Crewe. Making demands was not the way to get what she wanted. Delivering his demonstration was.

"Ten days is tight," she said. "But I can do it."

"Good. How soon can you get to Fairbanks? I'm arranging an office for you at the university's Geophysical Institute, and accommodation. I want you nearby in case Mike needs to consult with you."

Insult to injury, Meredith thought. But it sounded as though Crewe couldn't afford to lose her after all. And she still had the China card, her ace, to play later if necessary.

She smiled into the phone. "I'm packing my mukluks, General, even as we speak."

Tuesday, 8:20 A.M.

AMBIPOLAR DIFFUSION WILL LIFT the plasma to the altitude we need." Mike rapped his marker on the whiteboard diagram. "Here, to the elevation of R squared. It's *obvious*. Come on, guys, keep up!"

At the looks of concern all around, Mike regretted his outburst. His team of fourteen were adjusting to the sudden changes in trial objectives he'd ordered yesterday. Seated around the conference room studying his equations and diagrams, they felt harassed both by the reconfiguration and the deadline. *You're not the only ones*, Mike thought. He had to produce this "kill" demonstration for Ben, but couldn't tell his team why. He gulped down dregs of cold coffee, and his stomach growled. He'd barely eaten, and hardly slept. How could he, with Lucas still unconscious?

He'd gone back to the hospital last night and found that Dana hadn't left the boy's side, though D'Alton was gone. As the two of them sat in silence in Lucas's darkened room, Dana had got up to adjust the IV drip, then shot a glance at Mike, her confession of that morning rearing up like a presence between them. *Practicing medicine without a license.* She looked away, but something seemed to compel her to explain. "It was my final year," she said quietly. "I was alone in Los Angeles with a five-year-old, and falling behind. I wanted so badly to come home with that degree. So I cheated on a test. Got caught. I'm not excusing what I did, Mike, it's just that . . . all my life I've wanted to be a physician."

She looked at him with a plea in her eyes—to keep her secret? "Seems to me you help people who'd never get to see a doctor otherwise," he said in answer. "I don't suppose they care much about a certificate."

He had told her to go home, get some sleep, and he'd sat all night with Lucas. Carol had been upset. "Dad's seeing that he's getting the best care, and what can you do anyway?" she'd said when he called. But he and Dana had agreed, in a communion without words, that someone who loved Lucas had to be there in case he woke up.

He hadn't.

"It won't work," Roger Donelly said now.

Jolted back, Mike said, "It will. Let's go through it again." He turned to the board to erase his diagram, but the eraser had disappeared. He used his sleeve.

"Four A," Gina quipped, the team's in-joke for Mike's pet phrase: "Alternatives are always available." It brought chuckles from the group. Mike almost smiled.

He began to resketch the diagram, but his thoughts dragged back to Lucas. What had happened out there on the Wahetna? Mike had given a statement to the state troopers about the scene he and Dana had come upon,

and the bodies had been retrieved, but no one knew yet
what had happened. Only Lucas could tell them that. *If
he makes it . . .*

He'd frozen in midsketch, and felt them all waiting.
Can't let them see me like this. "Take a break," he said.
"Fifteen minutes."

He went downstairs to check his messages. He'd finally spoken on the phone to the state seismologist, who
had hedged, "We can't say definitively that what you experienced at HARC was an aftershock, but it's likely."
His ambivalence exasperated Mike. He'd called another
seismologist, a guy with Exxon, but he was out, so Mike
had left a message. Now, he checked his phone mail.

"This is Meredith Crosbie." The terse recording startled him. "I'm at the Geophysical Institute. Extension
208. It's time we talked."

She was here, in Fairbanks? Mike was furious. Ben,
with his micro-managing, seemed in his face at every
turn. Sure, he'd expected to confer with Meredith, but
only by phone. He hadn't needed Ben to drag her up
here. He didn't *want* her.

He called Ben's hotel. They said he'd checked out. He
called Carol.

"Oh, honey, you just missed him. He was here for
lunch, but he left about ten minutes ago for the airport."
Her voice became low, vibrant with excitement. "This is
it, Mike. He's got appointments in D.C. with Kaplan and
Montcrief and General Sloan." The national security adviser, the secretary of defense, and the chairman of the
Joint Chiefs. Mike knew why. Ben was going to invite
these men to the demonstration . . . *and their decision,*

either way, will change all our lives. Their approval of Ben's grand scheme would mean that HARC would be classified, and Ben and Carol would be safe. Their rejection would mean the end of HARC, and ruin for Ben and Carol. Mike had to secure that approval. It sobered him about Meredith—made him realize that this was no time to get macho over turf. With only nine days to go, he could use all the help he could get. Even hers.

He was taking the stairs back up to the conference room when Gina caught up.

"Mike, when you get a minute, there's a printout you should check." They continued up the steps together. "It's a glitch from the aborted test the other night. At least, a glitch on the HILAS monitor. I went to square our readout with their log, but it doesn't match." HILAS was a small independent research facility about forty miles away. Their scientists often compared notes with the HARC team, and Mike knew they had followed the Saturday test with their own diagnostic apparatus. "It may not be relevant," Gina added, "considering the ancient equipment they use. But you should have a look."

"What kind of glitch?"

"Their log shows a spike at twenty-two-twenty, though on ours there's nothing. Since we transmitted ten billion watts and they show almost twelve billion returning, it looks like negative impedance."

Mike's heart skipped a beat. Negative impedance— that second anomaly he'd seen on the simulation. The spike.

"As I say, it may be nothing," Gina went on. "Those

guys are stuck with buggy equipment. Our log shows zip."

Mike asked, dreading the answer, "The duration?"

"Seven seconds."

He stopped. They'd reached the conference room and Gina said, suddenly sheepish, "Sorry I didn't mention it before, but I had a little absentminded glitch myself during the test. Spilled water on my notes. I'm blaming the clean air out here—my brain only works right in Philadelphia smog." She shrugged and started back to her seat.

Mike stared after her. Absentminded? *Seven seconds?* "Gina, wait—"

His cell phone rang. It was Dana. "Lucas is awake," she said. A surge of relief collided with his alarm at Gina's news. "Mike," Dana went on, "he's asking for you."

He told his team he had to leave, and hurried back down the stairs. As he pushed out the front door he met Wayne on his way in.

"You okay, buddy? You look like you've seen a ghost."

"Lucas is awake. I'm on my way to the hospital."

"Better let me drive. You don't look so hot."

▲

In the hospital waiting room he found Dana and Reid D'Alton and a young state trooper. Dana told him the doctors were still examining Lucas, then she moved away with D'Alton. Mike watched the lawyer's hand go comfortingly up and down her back.

"Hey, kid," Wayne greeted the young trooper. "Mike, you know my nephew, Eric? Fresh out of the academy at Sitka."

Mike shook hands with the trooper, his thoughts elsewhere, part of him anxious to see Lucas, another part trying to evaluate the implications of Gina's report. Negative impedance, like on the simulation. Seven seconds. And her mental lapse . . . like his own. Yet, she was right that the HILAS apparatus could be unreliable. If there actually had been a negative impedance event, why hadn't the HARC diagnostics registered it?

"Any break on this yet?" Wayne asked his nephew.

"Nope. I hope to question the boy, get his version."

"Hell of a thing," Wayne said with a sympathetic glance at Mike.

"Hell of a night, last Saturday," the trooper said. "Like some super full moon freaked people out. On a patch along the Gatana, anyway, Creemore over to the White Mountains. There's just a handful of folks in that area—a few old prospectors, a couple squatter families, that little campground of Jehovah's Witnesses—but we were checking out action all through there that night. A suicide. And a guy lost control of his boat and smashed a dock. And a bunch of domestic violence."

"Senator Gustafson crashed that night too, didn't he?" Wayne said.

"Jeez, yeah," Eric said, impressed by this extra evidence. "See? Weird night."

Mike tensed. *The night of the test.*

A nurse pushed through the swinging door. "Dr. Ryder?"

"Here." As he spoke, Dana stepped forward too, and so did the trooper. But the nurse held up her hand. "I'm sorry, Lucas wants only Dr. Ryder."

He followed her, and at the sight of Lucas Mike's breath caught in his throat. Pallor, bruises and cuts mottling his face, his arm bound in a cast, and, most terrible, the haunted look in his eyes. Mike pulled a chair to the bedside and sat, laying his hand on Lucas's good arm. He wanted to say something encouraging, but all he could manage was, "Thank God you're back with us."

Lucas ran his tongue slowly over his cracked, swollen lips. It seemed painful for him to speak. "Sophy . . . they told me . . . is it true?"

"I'm sorry, Lucas. Yes. Your cousin too." *What happened?* he wanted to ask, but it was all warring inside Lucas's eyes, and he sensed he'd hear everything if he waited. Yet he realized that Lucas had already told him one thing, just by the misery in those few words. He'd loved Sophy.

Lucas closed his eyes, and Mike could see that he was struggling to not cry. He looked up at Mike with a stricken expression. "Did I . . . kill them?"

Mike was taken aback. That it could even be a possibility . . .

"I can't . . . can't remember," Lucas said. "I'm afraid I've . . . gone crazy. Mike, I'm so—"

Scared, he thought. He could see it all over the boy's face. "There's an explanation, Lucas," he said as calmly as he could. "There always is. Take a breath. Let's go back. Tell me the last thing you *do* remember."

"I remember you. Talking about rapids we should try. I thought, yeah, I'd like to do that. But . . . that's nuts, isn't it?" He looked confused. "You weren't there."

Mike was moved. His words had reached Lucas in the helicopter—maybe even helped him hang on. "What do you remember before that?"

"Freezing water. Lining up distress stones, my arm killing me. Saw a bear. Stood in the water up to my chin to keep my scent from him. When it got dark, shivering . . . so weak."

His ordeal overnight on the shore. "But, before all that."

Lucas seemed to shudder, and tears welled in his eyes. "I lied . . . I do remember. That's why . . . why I could only tell you." The next words sounded ripped from him. "I was . . . going to . . . rape her." His tears spilled.

The story rushed out of him. "Ron hit Sophy. He had the rifle, and I couldn't let him hurt her again. We climbed the bluff. When we got to the top, something . . . happened. In my head. I don't know what. One minute I was looking down the barrel of Ron's gun and the next . . . I went blank. Nothing. And then . . . a terrible mess in my mind, like something exploded there . . . thoughts and feelings like . . . like I wasn't *myself* anymore. And Ron and Sophy, I think they felt it too, because I heard him howl, like a wolf in a trap, and Sophy was crying like she was going to die. I went to her . . . oh, God, she was crying, but I wanted her so bad . . . so bad, I ripped open her shirt and grabbed her, and I was going to—" He couldn't finish. Mike could see the horror and grief in his eyes. "Then I heard the gun go off behind me . . . and Sophy, oh, God, she was going to jump. I held on to her, tried to stop her from jumping, but . . . she pulled. We went over together. And now . . . she's dead. I *killed* her."

Mike sat back, his heart thudding. Lucas, almost raping the girl he loved? It was beyond belief. He locked on two statements. *"Heard the gun go off behind me."* Lucas hadn't killed his cousin, that seemed clear. Nor Sophy—apparently she and Lucas had fallen off the bluff together. But Lucas's other statement filled him with alarm. *"I went blank. Nothing."* Like the rest of us, Mike thought. Me, Wayne, Gina . . .

"That's all I can remember," Lucas said. "It's all a mess in my mind, all dark. If I did it . . . I only wish . . . wish I was dead too."

"You didn't do it, Lucas. Your cousin shot himself, and Sophy jumped. It's not your fault. None of it."

Lucas let out a shuddering sigh of acceptance. But misery and confusion still swam in his eyes. "Mike, what *happened?* What made us . . . go crazy like that?"

"I don't know. Can you remember anything else? Anything at all?"

Lucas shook his head. Puzzlement flitted across his face. "There is something kind of weird. Just when the . . . the craziness happened, I saw the salmon going in all directions. Before, they'd been heading upstream like usual, but they suddenly looked like they were crazy too. Thrashing in the water."

▲

Mike walked back toward the waiting room, his mind churning with questions and misgivings. This tale of disorientation, aberrant behavior, despair. It was a pattern that felt hazily familiar.

He stopped abruptly in the corridor. His haunted house.

It was in Boston, last winter, that's when it had come to a head. Lindsay's listlessness, Carol's irritability, Mike's own edginess, the inexplicable phantom shapes he'd glimpsed late at night, and a low-level, pervasive sense of unease. He'd investigated about chemicals in the insulation, molds, but nothing checked out. Finally, he went to see his friend Ravi Shakoor at his lab. Ravi was the senior psychobiologist at the McLean Hospital where he studied the effects of electromagnetic and geomagnetic forces on the human brain. Mike suggested that if they could duplicate the uncomfortable sensations he'd felt in the house, he might be a step closer to an answer. He made himself Ravi's experimental subject.

"The intensity of the EM fields I will induce is little more than that of a hair dryer," Ravi had explained in his formal Calcutta cadence as he'd settled the wired helmet on Mike's head. "But it is not the intensity that counts, it is the kind of field. The brain operates within a narrow band of predominant frequencies, and my experiments suggest that subtle pulsations magnify emotions, and amplify the brain's own experiences. The brain is slowly aroused to a perturbation point."

"Kind of like great sex," Mike said, thinking he'd feel less nervous about the wired helmet if he could see Ravi smile.

"Quite." No smile. "What we call our *selves* is really no more than an aggregate of neurons firing in a particular EM pattern. Alter the pattern, alter the self."

The experiment wasn't painful, just . . . horrible. Hallucinations. Loss of mental control, helplessness. Then, a cold and nameless fear. Mike loathed it.

After, as they discussed Mike's house, Ravi suggested a connection with tectonic strain theory. Mike was well aware that electromagnetic radiation from tectonic strain could produce measurable effects, even light: orange balls of light had actually been recorded moving along fault lines. So Ravi thought it significant that Mike's house was on a ravine. "Caves and mountaintops emit high levels of electromagnetic fields," he pointed out, and added, on a rather poetic note, "The hiding places of the gods, and perhaps the devil too."

Not exactly hard data, but the experience as Ravi's lab rat had convinced Mike of the source of the "ghosts" at home: a geomagnetic field, very weak, but at just the frequency to subtly affect the brain. Glad to have a rational explanation for his haunted house, he'd moved his family out.

Now, he felt horribly certain there was a connection here. It couldn't be coincidence that the very night he'd activated the world's most powerful beam of electromagnetic energy, Lucas had suffered a mental imbalance, and so had the other kids. Maybe even Senator Gustafson. Ben said he'd crashed not far from HARC, at around 22:30 hours—almost exactly when Mike had had his lapse. Only, how could the power-up cause such results? By what *process*? He felt on the verge of knowing.

In the waiting room he told Dana and the trooper Lucas's story—that Ron had shot himself, Sophy had jumped, and Lucas, trying to stop her, had been dragged over with her. He left out the attempted rape—going into that wouldn't help anyone, and he doubted that Lucas, so traumatized, would speak of it. But he felt like a murderer hiding a bloodied knife behind his back: he knew in his bones there was a connection to HARC. "Let's go," he told Wayne.

"Poor kid," Wayne said as they pulled out of the parking lot. "He'll be out of commission for the rest of the summer. And it'll take a hell of a lot longer to get over losing his friends like that."

Mike only nodded. He was trying to summon some analytical discipline. Reason this out, he told himself. *Think.*

He glanced at the door's rearview mirror . . . and suddenly he *saw.* In the playground across from the hospital, a little girl was pushing a man on a swing. Up, back, and up again, the swing went so high, and scythed back so swiftly, that in its draft a soda can left on the crossbars toppled off.

It hit like voltage to his heart. "Resonance," he said.

Wayne looked at him. "What?"

Resonance . . . and ELF. The full horrifying implication galvanized him. In powering up HARC, he could well have driven those two kids to suicide. Driven Senator Gustafson to crash. Driven his own son literally out of his mind.

One thought burst through the others. *HARC must not be activated.*

"Stop," he told Wayne. "Turn around." He had to reach Ben. Was he too late to stop the flight? "The airport," he said. "Now!"

Tuesday, 2:00 P.M.

Running into the terminal, Mike almost knocked down a frail Japanese man studying a map. At the Alaska Airlines desk, he barged ahead of customers and asked when Ben's flight was scheduled to leave. Ten minutes. He sprinted for the gate. At the security check they stopped him. "I'm Dr. Ryder of the High-frequency Auroral Research Center," he said, catching his breath. "There's a passenger on flight 306 I've got to see. General Benson Crewe. It's urgent."

"I'm sorry, sir," the uniformed woman told him, "that flight's about to depart."

"Then get him off. Call whatever supervisors you have to call, but get General Crewe off that plane. Now!"

An armed security guard was suddenly beside him, and moments later an airline manager arrived, clean-cut as an FBI agent, his expression courteous but wary. "What's the problem, sir?"

"Hold flight 306 and get General Ben Crewe." He showed ID, and as the man studied it Mike added something he never thought he'd hear himself say: "It's a matter of national security."

Magic words. The manager made a radio call as he and the security guard escorted Mike to the gate, and when they reached the vacant waiting area, where a wall of windows overlooked the plane, Ben was already walking toward them. His surprise at seeing Mike was evident.

"Ben, you can't go to Washington. We've got to talk." Mike couldn't go into detail in front of these people, but he had to make the emergency clear. "I'm canceling the demonstration."

Ben's expression betrayed no alarm, but there was an edge in his voice as he asked the manager, "Would you give us a moment?"

"Sir, I can't hold the flight indefinitely."

"I understand. A moment, please." The manager and the security man moved away, but stood waiting. Ben frowned at Mike. "Well?"

Mike hated doing this in public—the area was open to the main corridor where a stream of people were passing—but it was clear that Ben intended to get back on the plane and wouldn't leave the gate. He said as quietly as he could, "The test on Saturday night produced an unexpected result, a *lethal* result. I believe it caused at least two suicides. It might also have killed Senator Gustafson. And if we power up again the death toll could be in the thousands."

Ben looked incredulous. "What?"

Mike had wanted to shock him, make him stay and face the crisis, but he realized that he'd come off sounding crazy. He had to present this scientifically, yet in terms Ben would understand.

"It's called resonance," he explained. "It's a phenomenon in physics, a natural amplification effect, whereby small and steady increments in force can result in overwhelming power. For example, it's what allows a child to propel an adult on a swing higher and higher with well-timed pushes, and even, theoretically, spin the swing over the top. That increase in amplitude is resonance. I believe that HARC's EM beam, reflected off the ionosphere, created an unexpected and autonomous resonance jump. In a process called negative impedance, the power spiked straight back down to HARC, but slightly increased. The transmitters bounced it up again, and the process was repeated, over and over, amplified each time. Up, down, up, like the swing going back and forth, higher with each push. The event lasted only seconds, because the moment I suspected something was wrong I shut everything down. But the damage had been done."

Ben was clearly struggling to take it in. "You say . . . it killed Harley Gustafson? How?"

"With ELF waves." ELF—extremely low frequency—was the range of frequencies Mike had intended HARC to generate for use in submarine communications; it was integral to the system. But he could never have imagined such an extraordinary collateral effect. "Think of the radioactive fallout from a thermonuclear bomb. It's widespread and lethal. In the same way, HARC's resonance jump generated a sidescatter—a fallout—of destructive ELF waves."

"Destructive? How? You think it knocked out Harley's electronics?"

"Definitely. But, even worse—" He was about to explain that it had also incapacitated Gustafson's *mind*, and the minds of Lucas and the other two kids, but he hesitated, overwhelmed, unsure how to begin. On the way here, he'd called Ravi on his cell phone, and Ravi had confirmed that the scenario, at least as it concerned altered brain functions, was indeed possible.

"The uploads." Ben said it in dismay, a sudden realization.

Mike stared at him. Of course—Meredith's modifications. He'd been so engrossed in working out the bizarre chain of cause and effect, he hadn't stopped to realize that the resonance was the direct result of Ben and Meredith's tampering. It snapped something inside him. Heat rushed to his face. "Do you know what you've done? This ELF bandwidth affects neurons in the brain. *Distorts* the brain. Your modifications sent HARC into a resonance jump that induced *insanity*. And my son was a victim!"

"Mike, calm down." Ben's eyes shot to the manager and the security man, who were watching. He took Mike by the elbow and led him farther away, to the wall of windows overlooking the runways. A 747 was landing. A baggage cart train glided along the tarmac. So orderly, Mike thought . . . unlike the chaos inside him. He felt Ben's hand grip his shoulder, a gesture of sympathy, but also of containment and control. "Insanity?" Ben asked in a whisper. "Your son? What are you talking about?"

"Lucas and the two kids with him who died that night.

They each suffered a mental failure that drove them to violence, to suicide. *HARC* did that. And not just to them. Between the Gatana and the White Mountains, I believe the ELF radiation disoriented every living thing."

Mike saw something in Ben's eyes shift, as though his shock had deflated, his sympathy cooled. "Every living thing?" His eyes narrowed in skepticism. "How do you know that? How could you *possibly* know?"

Mike raked his hand through his hair. He *didn't* know, not with any scientific certainty. He'd already used the words "I believe" too many times. He was speaking not from facts, but from conjecture—an untenable position. *Present the evidence*, he told himself. "There were other aberrations. Lucas observed that the Wahetna salmon running upstream suddenly began swimming in all directions. Salmon depend on electromagnetic fields to navigate upstream. It's a function of an element called magnetite in their brains—the human brain has traces of it too. Even a slight distortion of those EM fields would leave the salmon disoriented, confused."

"Lucas's observations? That's your evidence? Mike, the boy was badly hurt in tragic circumstances, apparently some teenage love triangle gone wrong. Of course you're saddened by that, but you can't believe every word of a traumatized adolescent who's just come out of a two-day coma. Let's keep some perspective."

Perspective? Mike remembered Lucas's shame and misery in confessing that he'd felt a lust so violent, he'd been intent on rape. "I know my son. ELF altered those kids' minds. It produced aberrant behavior in Lucas, and it drove the other two to kill themselves."

"Indian kids committing suicide is hardly news. It's regrettable, but true."

A shudder went through Mike. "You don't believe a word I'm saying."

"I believe you're upset about the boy, naturally, and about his friends, and you're groping for answers. But you've got to pull yourself together and carry on. You know how much is at stake."

"Carry on? Christ, Ben, don't you see? We *can't* power up again. The consequences are unthinkable."

"What's unthinkable is the consequences if we don't. Have you forgotten Carol? Forgotten your *real* family?"

Carol. It was up to him to protect her. But . . . there had to be another way. "I haven't forgotten, but . . . Ben, we have no choice. Saturday night was only a *glimpse* of what can happen. I ran that test at just ten percent ERP— the demonstration would be at *full* power. If it causes a resonance event at that level, we're talking a *runaway* event. The whole upper Northern Hemisphere could be bombarded by ELF radiation. Hundreds of thousands of people could be driven out of their minds. It would be like committing mass murder."

Ben frowned, clearly losing patience. "Mike, get a grip."

"Talk to the state troopers, for God's sake. On Saturday night in the Gatana Valley there was a suicide and a rash of domestic violence that—"

"Would you listen to yourself? There must have been a thousand times more violence in Los Angeles alone that night—countless more incidents across the country. Did HARC do all that too? Look, you've often said, 'If it can't be measured, it didn't happen.' Do you have even one shred of measurable evidence for this incredible theory?"

"The HILAS log," Mike said, feeling he was clutching at straws. "It shows a brief spike, a negative impedance event of seven seconds at the time of the test. Also, I personally experienced a seven-second mental lapse at exactly the same time."

Ben scowled. "HILAS is bush league. Did HARC's instruments record this spike?"

"No."

"Exactly. As for your, what did you call it, a lapse? I honestly don't know what you mean by that. These ELF waves obviously didn't make you and your team 'insane.'"

"Because I think the ELF radiation wasn't uniform throughout the affected area. Some places were skip zones. We felt just a brief lapse, and then—"

"We? Who else experienced this lapse?"

He thought of Wayne dropping his coffee, and Gina spilling water on her notes, though they'd both made light of it. "I suspect it affected every one of us at the site, but so briefly, most weren't aware. It hit, we all blanked, then it lifted just before the next spike *would* have hit if I hadn't shut everything down. I suspect it interrupted everything that operates on electricity—brains and machines alike. That's why HARC shows no record of the event, and why people didn't even notice it happened."

Ben gave him a mocking smile. "Sleeping Beauty and all the castle folk frozen in time?"

Mike knew he was sounding crazier and crazier. A girl's laugh reached him from the corridor—a teenager outside one of those self-photo booths. She and her girlfriend were breaking up over pictures. Mike watched the stream of passing people. Blithe tourists. Weary businessmen. A bearded young adventurer under a mountainous backpack. A family—parents and three little kids all wearing T-shirts emblazoned "Yukon Quest Dog Sled Race." If the worst happened, what derangement would these people suffer? It shook him . . . but it also made him think: Is that the way to get through to Ben?

"I know how much you love this country, Ben. I know you did this so that HARC would protect America from its enemies. Do you really want to gamble that I'm wrong? If HARC unleashes a catastrophe, *you* become the enemy . . . and it's innocent Americans you'll be destroying."

He saw he'd hit a nerve. The mockery drained from Ben's face.

"Just give me time to prove it to you," Mike urged. "Let me produce evidence, scientific evidence. Give me that. A few days. Please."

Ben's eyes narrowed, as if calculating odds. "One day, Mike. That's all I *can* give you."

▲

"Resonance?" Meredith Crosbie's face went slack with astonishment.

Ben had never seen her so unprepared. They stood beside the outdoor track on the University of Alaska campus where he'd found her running laps. Leaving the airport, he'd come straight here and told her everything Mike had told him.

"Resonance," she repeated in a hush of wonder. "Holy shit."

"So you agree it happened?" Ben was reeling. He thought of Harley in that disabled plane, his mind unbalanced, plunging to his death. The irony was devastating: HARC, the weapon Ben had risked everything to build, had killed the one politician who could have saved him and HARC. "How *could* it? How could you have missed such a thing? *Both* you and Mike?"

She looked at him. Though obviously unnerved, she appeared to be working to regain her composure. "General, did you know that at the turn of the century there were over two hundred automobile companies in this country? Collectively they held patents on *thousands* of different designs for internal combustion engines. That's how many ways there are to proceed with any new scientific undertaking. The variable designs are countless, every scientist swears his way is best, and every one of us is surprised by glitches. But glitches happen, and bugs. It's endemic. We're all used to it."

Ben stared at her, appalled. "This 'bug' sent HARC out of control and drove at least two people out of their minds. Let's keep things in proportion, shall we?"

"Hey," she shot back, "let's remember who demanded a quick fix, *shall we*? I don't like this any more than you do, but it's not something either of us intended. It was an unexpected result. An accident."

The metallic taste of fear was in Ben's mouth. What was he going to do now? Abort, as Mike was insisting? Impossible. His whole life was riding on HARC. He'd got Mike to promise not to speak about the resonance event until he had evidence . . . but then what? Could Mike fix the problem? Mike . . . so shaken by the event, and by his son's ordeal. Ben sympathized, but he also suspected that he couldn't rely on Mike to find a way out. *Crosbie may be all I have.*

"All right, no one anticipated it, but it happened," he said. "Now, what can be done? Can we prevent it happening again?"

"Don't know yet. Quite a challenge." She was doing runners' stretches, one knee bent, the other leg extended behind, but from her look of concentration Ben could tell that her mind was already on the problem. It gave him hope. Crosbie's love for tackling the seemingly impossible had always impressed him. Before hiring her he'd canvassed some of her colleagues, and although few spoke of her with affection, and some said she'd never redeem her reputation, most of them grudgingly acknowledged her genius.

"I'll check it out," she said. "It might take some time." She started toward the track, then stopped and turned back to him, "There are only three U.S. automobile companies today, General. It just takes skillful refinement—and a little ruthless competition."

Ben watched her as she resumed running laps. Crosbie wanted time; Mike wanted time. But time was the one thing Ben couldn't give either of them. In nine days he had to produce the demonstration.

▲

The next morning Ben parked beside a tour bus at the Alaska Pipeline outdoor viewing station at Fox, just outside Fairbanks. At Mike's bombshell he had postponed his trip to Washington, making excuses when he called to reschedule his meetings. He had to deal with the crisis here first. He walked toward the observation platform that overlooked the pipeline as it crossed the tundra like a giant snake. Crosbie had called back late last night, and this was where they'd agreed to meet. She had been cryptic on the phone, telling him only, "We need to talk," and Ben, after a sleepless night, was trying to control his fear that she'd concluded the challenge at HARC was insurmountable.

He scanned the platform. At one end about two dozen white-haired matrons, from the Midwest by the sound of their nasal chatter, stood listening to a tour guide's spiel about the eight-hundred-mile-long feat of engineering from the seventies that carried crude oil overland right across Alaska, from the Arctic Ocean to Valdez. At the other end of the platform Crosbie stood alone, looking out.

"Well?" he asked as he reached her.

She turned. "Mike was right. Resonance, and in spades. Pretty fucking impressive."

Ben didn't see how she could appear so relaxed at such a moment. She was leaning back, elbows on the platform railing, as though lounging at a bar. She shrugged. "If you let the genie out of the bottle, you take your chances."

"But is there a way to—" He stopped. The tour guide was shepherding his charges into an adjoining open kiosk where an oil promotional video was beginning, and Ben waited as the group shuffled past.

"To put the genie back?" she finished his question. "Sure."

Ben looked at her, hoping . . . but not quite believing. "That's fast work."

She regarded him, condescension in her eyes. "Ever hear of Nikola Tesla? No, not many have. He gave us our electric power system. Everyone thinks Thomas Edison did that, but Edison was just a clever hustler. This was the 1880s, and the system Edison had devised used direct current, which couldn't be transmitted beyond a mile from a power station. Imagine—his DC setup would've needed a power station every *mile*. It was a nightmare, and Edison couldn't see a way around it. Then Tesla invented alternating current, which could transmit over distances—a breakthrough technology. But he needed backing, and the money men in the game were Edison and George Westinghouse. Together, they robbed Tesla blind. Bought his patents for a song, then transformed power delivery using his AC system. Tesla died a pauper, never got recognition. Everybody remembers Edison."

Ben felt his exasperation growing. "Is there a point?"

"Yes, General, there is. Tesla was a genius at lateral thinking, which is what I spent the night doing. Solved your problem. It's just a matter of realigning several antenna banks so their transmissions pulse out of phase. I've already drawn up the preliminary specifications. Then—" She snapped her fingers. "No more resonance."

Ben felt a harsh breath of relief escape him. "Well done." He shook her hand. "Really, outstanding. Let's get the preliminary information over to Mike right away."

She shook her head, eyes fixed on him like a threat. "That's not how this is going to happen, General. Unlike Tesla, I intend to get my due. Mike's job. I've just saved your ass. I think I'm entitled."

Anger surged in him. He'd have any subordinate who spoke to him like that busted on the spot. But he held his tongue. He needed Crosbie's fix. And she knew it. In the silence between them, the tiny music of the oil promotion video sounded from the open kiosk, and Ben glimpsed the tourist group passively watching, like children parked by parents in front of a TV. "That's not possible yet," he told her. "After the demonstration, I assure you, I'll give you what you want."

"The demonstration *is* what I want. That's when the big brass will be watching. That's when I can make my mark."

"Look, we have only eight days. Mike knows the site inside out. His team is used to him, they know him and trust him and—" He'd been about to say "like him." Did anyone like Meredith Crosbie? "You've simply got to wait."

"I don't 'got' to do anything, General Crewe. I've grown weary of campus life, and I've had an offer from the Beijing Institute. A very generous offer, for a very prestigious job. I'd be designing and running a high-frequency auroral research project much like the official face of HARC, for sub communications. Who knows? Given my refinements, the Chinese might take their project to the next level, a weapon . . . maybe someday they'll even use it to outgun you." Her eyes hardened. "I'm not bluffing, General. I want HARC, very much, but I'm quite prepared to get on the next plane for Beijing. The choice is yours." She pulled her Hertz keys from her pocket and bounced them in her hand. "Here's the deal. Give me Mike's job by tomorrow, or fix the problem yourself."

▲

When he returned to his hotel, he was surprised to see Carol in the lobby. "Dad, I called Washington and they said you'd canceled your meetings. What happened?"

Ben felt caught. "Something came up. Mike's working on it. I'm going this evening instead."

She nodded, her mind clearly elsewhere. She looked around the lobby busy with tourists. "We can't talk here."

They went to the coffee shop and took a back booth. "It's happened," she said. "Litvak held a press conference this morning as the new committee chairman. Announced a Senate inquiry into excesses in military research funding. All the networks covered it." She paused as the waitress came. Carol ordered coffee, Ben nothing. Carol went on, "He gave quite a rallying cry,

'There is waste, I can smell it, and I hate waste.' He's got religion, Dad. He wants blood."

Ben felt he was bleeding already, wounds invisible to Carol. She didn't know he was under attack from two other sides as well as from Litvak. The resonance crisis, and Crosbie's ultimatum. The thought of the Chinese getting Crosbie's breakthrough expertise, the Chinese building a HARC-like weapon, made him cold with dread.

Carol let out a tense sigh. "I'll admit, I was pretty shaken up a few days ago when Gustafson died. And it was hard telling Mike the truth. But of course you were right, Dad, Mike *is* on our side. It's made me feel stronger. This morning, when I heard Litvak on the news, I thought: You won't get us, you prick, my dad's got you way outclassed." She managed a smile. "You're going to pull this off. You and Mike. I know it."

He felt a ripple of pride. She'd been his constant ally, had kept their secret from Mike for four years, understanding the greater good. Yet, he also felt a new sting of doubt. Because now, everything had changed. He needed Crosbie's solution: that was prime. To get it, he had to give her HARC, which meant removing Mike. How could he explain that to Carol? Me and Mike . . . she loves us both. *Where does her ultimate allegiance lie?*

He was isolated. Couldn't presuppose Carol's devotion any longer, and could no longer work with Mike. But leadership was his job. He had lives to protect. At stake was the defense of the United States.

First, he had to keep Carol as an ally.

"I'm worried about Mike," he said. "I'm afraid his feelings have warped his judgment. It's about his son."

Carol stiffened.

The waitress brought the coffee and left.

Ben went on, "He's overwrought about this accident the boy suffered with his friends."

"I know," Carol said tightly. She tore open a packet of Sweet'n Low, poured some, and stirred. "He's spending so much time at the hospital. Now, of all times."

"It's worse than that, Carol." Ben kept his voice low. "He came to me yesterday with a theory that's . . . well, it's beyond belief. He's convinced himself that during the Saturday night test HARC went out of control and—" He shook his head. "And produced mind-altering electromagnetic waves. He believes these waves drove the boy and his friends crazy. It's quite incredible."

She stared at him. "He told you that?"

Ben nodded. "I'm partly to blame, asking so much of him, working him 'round the clock. Especially after he just learned about HARC's true purpose and our involvement—a shock for him. Now, his son's accident seems to have been a last straw. Carol, he's become too disturbed by the boy's problems . . . precariously so, in my opinion." He paused to let the weight of this sink in.

Anger flickered in her eyes. "That woman. If only she'd stayed away."

Ben couldn't let this go off on another track. "The point is, I'm going to have to bring in Crosbie, install her in his place. It's the only responsible course, given Mike's . . . behavior. You see that don't you? You know how much is riding on the demonstration."

In her eyes, her trust in him warred with distress for Mike. "Do you have to? It'll hurt him so much. HARC means everything to him."

"Not more than you."

She swallowed. "I hope you're right."

An idea came to Ben. "Come to Washington with me this evening," he said. "I've rescheduled my appointments with Kaplan and Secretary Montcrief. They're each giving me fifteen minutes tomorrow, and I'm having dinner with Graham Sloan. You're so good with those politicians, and Graham would love to see you. Come with me."

She brightened. He remembered that same look when he used to bring her gifts from his overseas postings, silk blouses, silver jewelry. His wife sometimes protested that the gifts were too extravagant for a child, but Carol had preened.

"We *are* going to pull this off," he assured her now. "You and me."

▲

"Mike?" Gina asked. "Got a minute?"

"No." He grabbed the spreadsheet he'd come into the control room for and started for the door. He was hunting for proof. Ben had given him only until the end of today. "We need a full team meeting with you," Gina said, hurrying after him through the busy room. "We're in limbo about these new trial objectives."

"You have the specs. Work through them. You guys don't need me to hold your hand."

Leaving Gina in his wake, Mike felt everyone's eyes on him. He knew they wondered what had come over him. He was hiding too much. He hadn't told a soul about the appalling resonance event—he'd promised Ben he wouldn't until he had evidence. Anyway, who'd believe it until then? In telling Ben, he'd sounded like he was raving. Only irrefutable proof would convince Ben to abort. Yet Mike was all too aware that that would make Carol a potential victim of Litvak's investigation. Aborting was the last thing he wanted . . . but the only right thing to do.

"Mike," Roger Donelly called across the room, holding up a phone, "it's General Crewe, looking for you. He's in your office."

Mike hid his alarm. "On my way."

Proof? he thought as he took the stairs down to his office. He had *nothing*. He'd worked all night, poring over data, eyes buggy at his computer, hadn't even called Carol. He was frantic to find evidence—but in one day? The detailed computer modeling he *needed* to do would take weeks. And even if he did get a compelling result, that still might not convince Ben about the ELF waves' bizarre effects. The victims couldn't speak from the grave, and as for Lucas, what "proof" were the confused feelings of a sixteen-year-old who'd thought he'd gone out of his mind?

"Hey, Mike," Wayne said, stopping him in the corridor, "how's the kid?"

"Better, they tell me. But still in ICU."

"I know this has got you down, buddy, but he's a tough little bugger. Look what he did, arranging those signal stones on the riverbank, broken arm and all. He's got the right stuff. He'll be okay."

"Yeah. Thanks." Mike felt like a liar. His worry came from more profound reasons than Wayne knew.

Lying to everyone, he thought, walking on. Dana was devastated about her nephew and Sophy, and seemed to have accepted their deaths as the latest tragic manifestation of her people's despair. He remembered Ben's words: *"Indian kids committing suicide is hardly news."* That's how the investigating troopers were writing it up: two Native teen suicides, a third one injured but recovering, case closed. But Mike felt the indictment in his heart. *HARC killed those kids . . . and I built HARC. Ben and Meredith's tampering sent it out of control, but I powered it up. I fired the murder weapon.*

And now, I've got to prove my own guilt.

Opening his office door, he found Ben standing at the window . . . and Meredith sitting at his desk. What the hell was going on?

Ben turned. "Mike, let's not beat around the bush. You identified a serious problem—the resonance event. Dr. Crosbie has confirmed it."

Mike's relief was so intense, it was almost painful. *Thank God.*

"Fortunately," Ben went on, "she has devised a solution. And with the demonstration just eight days away, I want to implement her proposal immediately."

Mike was aghast. "You can't be serious. A solution? Jesus, we haven't even identified the conditions that *produced* the resonance!" When Ben's face remained stony,

Mike turned to Meredith. "What possible solution could you come up with overnight?"

"A realignment of selected antenna banks, approximately fifty in each quadrant, programming their transmissions to pulse out of phase. Voilà, no resonance."

"Hell, I could have tried that. It's just more tinkering."

"It's expertise. I've prepared strict specifications."

"There's no way to know if it will *work*, Meredith. And you know why. It's a matter of scale. This is crazy!"

"It appears we differ in our analysis. You may not be sure it will work. *I am*."

"Like you were sure five years ago with your fraudulent data?"

She said, as if biting back fury, "As a matter of fact, yes. I was right about that data. Subsequent experiments at Stanford proved it. I was vindicated, Mike, and you goddamn well know it."

"It's not about being right, Meredith, it's about *knowing*. What you did was an aberration of the scientific method. You winged it."

"I found the solution."

"You *guessed*."

"I guessed *right*!"

"Stop it, both of you." Ben stepped between them. "I don't care what happened five years ago, I want an answer *now*. And there's only one question." He demanded of Meredith, "Will this realignment work?"

"Yes."

His gaze lasered on Mike. "Will it?"

"Christ, Ben, that's *not* the question."

Something shifted in Ben's eyes. He turned to Meredith. "Give us a moment, please."

She shot looks of suspicion at them both, but she left the room.

"Mike, I saw you hesitate," Ben said, coming to him the moment they were alone. "You didn't say it *can't* be done. And I could see you immediately understood the process she's talking about. You could devise these specifications *yourself*." There was an energy in Ben that Mike had never seen before—something on the edge, faintly yearning. "Mike, you're *family*. You're the leader I *want* here at HARC. Litvak announced his investigation this morning, so there's no more time. My life and Carol's depend on this. You can *do* it."

Mike felt wrenched apart. Carol and Ben . . . Lindsay. Their lives in his hands. He had to struggle to speak. "But I won't."

The three words lay between them like felled trees.

"Won't lift a finger to save your wife?"

"We'll get through this, Carol and you and me. We'll survive. Ben, the question isn't whether Meredith's solution will work, it's whether the attempt is too reckless. Powering up HARC again would be immoral, criminal, a potential catastrophe. I can't do it."

"Then I will. I *will* protect my family. And my country."

Mike didn't blink. Ben wasn't the only one with the burden of protecting lives. "And I'll do everything in my power to stop you."

Their eyes locked.

Ben said, "As of this moment, you *have* no power.

I'm relieving you of your position. Dr. Crosbie will assume your duties, effective immediately."

As Ben called Meredith back in, Mike's heart thumped in his chest. Thoughts sprang up of hiring lawyers, suing for wrongful dismissal, demanding an injunction. But what judge would listen when he didn't have a shred of evidence?

"You're in," Ben said to Meredith as she joined them.

She looked at Mike, and victory gleamed in her eyes.

He held up his hands in surrender. "Meredith, you win. HARC's yours. But please, I beg you, look at the resonance equations I've worked out. The data's far from complete, but there's enough to suggest how dangerous this is. Once you see—"

"Been there, done that," she said as she sat at his desk. "Face it, Mike, I've always been able to manipulate the simulations on levels you only dream of. It's all under control."

"Simulation isn't reality, Meredith."

She gave him a withering look. "Well, the reality is, pal, you're out of a job."

"Mike," Ben said, "I warn you not to speak of the resonance event to anyone. I'll deny it. So will Dr. Crosbie."

My word against theirs.

"Go home," Ben said. "Take a rest. Take a holiday."

Mike watched Meredith surfing through his files. He felt unable to move. *It's over . . . I've lost HARC. Lost the chance to prevent a disaster. Eight days . . .*

"Mike," Ben said with a trace of pity, "am I going to have to call security? Go home."

Home. Carol. He felt a spark of hope. I'll tell her everything. The resonance, the mind-altering ELF, the poor kids who died at our hands. She'll make him see. *Ben will listen to Carol.*

Only, will she listen to me?

Wednesday, 4:10 P.M.

MIKE FOUND CAROL in the bedroom, packing. All he could think of was how desperately he needed her help to stop Ben. "No, you can't leave."

She turned, startled. "Oh, darling, I'm not *leaving* leaving. Not leaving *you*." She came and hugged him.

As his arms went around her he thought: How can I ask so much of her? But he was asking more of himself. He couldn't let her be led away to a police cruiser while Lindsay sobbed . . . couldn't do that to them. He'd decided on the way that, if necessary, he'd go to jail in her place. "Carol," he said, holding her, "we've got to talk."

She pulled out of his embrace. "Honey, my flight's in ninety minutes. I'm going to D.C. with Dad." She gave him a reassuring smile. "I'll be back the day after tomorrow, I promise." She ran her finger softly down his cheek. "Mike, we had to cancel our little holiday last weekend, but let's do it once this is all over, shall we? Let's take a week or two. Go to some sinfully luxurious

place in Palm Beach. Forget everything. Okay?" Her
voice was soothing. She stroked his cheek.

Her tone irritated him, as though she were talking to a
child . . . but also because it echoed Ben's voice, *"Take
a holiday."* He grabbed her wrist to stop her caress. She
flinched, and he immediately regretted it. "Sorry. Got a
lot on my mind."

With a hurt look, she turned away. "Don't we all."

He felt like a bastard. Ben said that Litvak had
launched his investigation, and Carol must have heard.
She knew she might be facing jail. He had to settle that
first.

"Carol, listen to me. Everything's . . . changed.
There's a crisis at HARC. I'll explain it, but first, let me
tell you what I've decided. If Litvak's inquiry does lead
to us, I'm going to take the blame for your . . . for the
money laundering. I'm on your board, so they'll accept
that it was me who instigated the diversion of funds."
He'd been a director of Carol's PR company for years,
his name there just to add prestige, though he hadn't
known until four days ago that Landmark Construction
was her subsidiary. Since Landmark had been awarded
the contract at HARC, anyone could see Mike's conflict
of interest. "Given my credentials, maybe the judge will
let me off with a light sentence. You know what they
hand out for these kinds of things, probably just six
months and some community work. And those minimum
security places are like country clubs." Though he hoped
it was true, he really had no idea about such matters, and
it galled him to think of spending even one day in prison.
But he had to convince her. "We'll get the best lawyers

money can buy, and who knows, maybe they'll even get me off. If not, well, it's a white-collar crime—they won't hang me." Unlike murder, he thought; murder was what he *felt* he'd committed. "The point is, we'll survive. I've made this decision because something went wrong with HARC . . . something terrible. On Saturday, the night of the first full-array test, a phenomenon of resonance occurred, against all my expectations, which—"

"Oh, Mike, don't," she said, burying her face in her hands. "I love you so much, I can't stand to hear this from you."

He was taken aback. What had she heard? He gripped her shoulders. "Carol, what's your father told you?"

She lifted her face. Tears glistened in her eyes. "Everything. Oh, Mike, it's my fault. I pushed you to do the demonstration. You were going to do it for *me*, and I love you for that, but your heart wasn't in it, and then, just while you were working so hard, you were forced to go and find . . . the boy. And I know his accident was an awful shock. And you were rushing back and forth to the hospital when you had so much to do at the site. No wonder it's taken a toll. It's been too much. It's pushed you . . . over an edge."

"What are you talking about? Did Ben tell you what happened or *not*? Are you aware that HARC produced an autonomous resonance jump? That it generated—"

"Produced what?"

He told himself to slow down for her. "HARC went out of control, okay? Like a nuclear chain reaction. It generated a kind of fallout radiation, except it was electromagnetic radiation, at exactly the frequency that debilitates neurological processes. It altered the minds of those kids, including my—"

"Yes." She almost snapped the word. "Dad told me. I know what you think happened to them."

"Carol, believe me, it happened. HARC is dangerous, far too dangerous to power up again. This demonstration must not go ahead."

She shook her head and spoke soothingly, as though, again, she were dealing with a child. "No, no, honey, it's all under control. Dad explained it to me. There was a glitch last week but it's been fixed. Dr. Crosbie has it covered. You're just . . . well, you're taking this all too . . . emotionally. It's better for everyone if you're out of it for a while."

Mike stiffened. She *knew* Ben had fired him . . . knew it before he'd walked in here.

She briskly resumed folding blouses and skirts on the bed and packing them. "I'm going to Washington with Dad," she said. "I'm going to help him arrange to bring Ron Kaplan and Secretary Montcrief and General Sloan here for the demonstration. I'm doing it for us, Mike. For our family. You're well out of this. Once it's all over there'll be great opportunities for you again. But right now, you . . ." She broke off, a sob in her voice. "Mike, you need a rest."

So that was it. Fury boiled up in him. Fury at Ben's manipulation . . . at handing over HARC to Meredith . . . at seeing his own wife believe he'd lost his mind. "Damn it, Carol, Ben *lied* to you."

Anger flashed in her eyes. "This is hard for all of us,

Mike. Don't make it worse by saying things that aren't true . . . and that you'll regret."

He couldn't believe this was happening. How had *he* become the liar, and Ben the victim? How was it that he, whose life's dream was HARC, was begging everyone to shut it down, and no one would listen? But, Carol *had* to listen. Only she could convince Ben. *She has to stay on my side.*

"Carol, you've got to believe me. The resonance event happened. There was that vibration. There's HILAS evidence of a negative impedance spike. There are state troopers' reports of violence that night in the Gatana Valley. There's the evidence of my son. If you could have seen him when he told me the hell he went through, he and the other two kids, if you could have heard about his disorientation and horror, seen how Dana and I found him after—"

"Enough!" She covered her ears and shook her head. "Your son, your son . . . Dana, Dana . . . I don't want to hear!"

Mike was shocked by the childish petulance. But when she lowered her hands, her expression hardened, and was anything but childlike.

"I'm sorry for the boy's accident. But it seems to have triggered some kind of breakdown in you. I intend to protect you, and your interests, until you . . . recover. I'm going to help Dad bring the VIPs he needs here, and Dr. Crosbie is going to produce the demonstration for them, and it will all work out, for everyone. And one day, Mike, although you can't see it now, although that woman and her son's problems have . . . unbalanced your judgment, one day you'll thank me."

He saw her pain, saw that he had somehow insulted her about Dana without meaning to, saw that this was entirely personal for her. How could it be otherwise, he realized, when she didn't believe a word he was saying about the danger? Ben had *insured* that she wouldn't. In silence, he and Carol stared at each other across a gulf of mistrust.

The phone rang. Carol tensely went back to packing as Mike grabbed the bedside receiver. "Mike Ryder."

It was Lindsay. "Daddy? You sound funny. You okay?"

He struggled to switch his thoughts from crisis to his little girl. "I'm fine, Lins. Kind of busy, though. What's up?"

"You said to call whenever I need to, and . . . Champagne's got colic, and . . . I'm scared." She sounded like she was fighting back tears. "Daddy, what if he dies?"

Carol asked, with a frown of concern, "Lindsay? Is she all right?"

"Sick horse," he told her, then asked Lindsay, "Has the vet seen him? Has Constanza called the vet?" The nanny was a no-nonsense manager with a soft heart.

"Yes, he came, and he said Champagne'll probably get better, and he's coming back tomorrow. But Champagne looks so terrible in his stall, so sad and sick. I can't stand to see him like this. I just . . . I wish you were here, Daddy. I miss you."

"I miss you too, honey. Now listen. Log onto that equine Web site we found, remember? Check out everything you can about colic. Then write a list of questions to ask the vet when he comes back. And if he tells you you're just a little girl and he'll handle it, you tell him you're responsible for Champagne and you'd like his help in understanding what's wrong and what can be done. Ask him every question on your list. Information, knowledge. That's how you can help Champagne. Got it?"

"Got it."

Hearing the new brightness in her voice, Mike was pleased at guiding her to take control. Bizarre, he thought, when I can't do the same about HARC. "Call me after you talk to the vet, okay?"

"Okay. Thanks, Daddy. 'Bye."

"You want to talk to your mother?"

"No, I wanna get on-line right away. Love you guys. 'Bye."

As Mike hung up he saw Carol smiling at him. "Let me guess," she said, "she can't wait to check out the Web site." She came to him, eyes shining. "Oh, Mike, you're such a wonderful father. We can't do without you, you know. Lindsay can't . . . and neither can I." Tears made her eyes indigo pools gleaming up at him. "I don't want *anyone* to go to prison," she said, her lips trembling. "I want us all to be together. Please, let the demonstration happen, Mike. You don't even have to *do* anything. Just let it be. We'll get through this next week, and then we'll be together always. You, me, Lindsay. Please, Mike. Please." Her mouth was on his, soft, eager. He felt her lips part, felt the warm tip of her tongue. Felt her breasts press against his chest.

All it sparked in him was anger. He pulled away. "You want me to get you in bed? Is that it? You think that's going to make me forget the disaster we're facing?"

Emotions played over her face—surprise, embarrassment, anger to match his own. "What I want is for this to be *over*."

The doorbell rang. Carol groaned. "My cab. This damn hick town—always either early or late." She tossed the last clothes in her suitcase and zipped it up.

The appalling stakes reared up in Mike's mind. Who else could he go to? The police? The governor? *"I'll deny it,"* Ben had warned. "Carol, I'm begging you, hear me out. Ben told you there was a glitch with HARC, but it's far more than that. If they go ahead and run HARC at full power, the ELF radiation could affect thousands of people. Us included. You've got to believe me. You've got to convince Ben to stop."

She looked at him with pity. "Oh, Mike, don't. You know that's out of the question."

He followed her downstairs to the front door, wildly thinking he'd have to physically force her to stay, to listen. She opened the door. Dana stood on the doorstep. Carol stiffened.

Dana looked past her, stone-faced. "Mike, could I have a word?"

Lucas? "What's happened? Is he—"

"He's all right. At least he's . . . the same. That's what I need to talk to you about."

Carol said icily, "I don't believe I'm *invisible*, am I, Dr. James?"

Dana looked at her. "Sorry."

A car horn beeped across the street. "That's my cab," Carol said. She turned to Mike, deadly earnest, "You could drive me, you know."

He saw that she was carving a line in the sand. About Dana . . . about HARC. "I'll do whatever you want," he said, "if you'll hear me out and speak to Ben."

They gauged one another in silence. The cab beeped again.

Dana said, "I'll wait in my truck."

When they were alone, Carol said, with a tremor in her voice, "I love you, darling. Love you enough to see the truth, and look beyond it. I'm afraid anxiety about the boy . . . and his mother . . . has disturbed you out of all proportion. I'm going to do what I can to help get us through this, help you come back to earth. But you've got to help me, too. Me and Lindsay. You've got to re-member that *we* are your family."

▲

"I've only got a minute," Dana said. "And just one ques-tion."

They stood beside her Ford pickup. Mike was watch-ing Carol's cab disappear around the corner. She wouldn't intervene. Nothing would stop Ben now.

He turned to Dana, his mouth dry, knowing she was unaware of the disaster that had happened—and the one that loomed. "Question?"

She looked uncomfortable, looked away to watch a teenager mowing the lawn across the street. "Lucas won't talk to me. I mean, *talk*. He just sticks to the bare facts, that Ron shot himself, Sophy was about to jump, he tried to stop her and fell with her . . . period. He won't open up. Won't tell me what's behind it all." She faced him. "He looks so lost, Mike. As though he's . . . haunted. I came to ask, did he tell you anything? I mean," she said as though steeling herself, "did he tell you that he . . . jumped?"

Mike hated himself, because he saw he could answer honestly and still hide the truth. "Dana, believe me, he didn't try to kill himself."

She let out a pent-up breath. "Thank God."

She opened her truck door, then stopped. She looked down at her keys in her hand, fiddling with them like worry beads. "I didn't mention it before, with all this tragedy, but I'm sure General Crewe has told you. I've agreed to the village relocation. No injunction." She met his gaze. "You've won. I won't be bothering you again about HARC. That chapter is closed. I just want to say, about Lucas . . . thank you."

Mike watched her drive off. Dana had been HARC's only opponent. And Ben had silenced her. Like he's silenced me.

An idea flashed. He remembered Dana flying the media people in last week. She'd used them in her fight against HARC . . . *why can't I?* Bypass the authorities, go *public* about HARC's lethal effects. Then it wouldn't be Ben's word against mine—nothing so rational. People would be terrified. They'd *demand* to have the place shut down.

Then Dana would know it all, though—that he'd

killed her nephew, killed Sophy, and almost killed Lucas. It made him shudder.

My God, he thought, could Carol be right? *Had* his feelings clouded his judgment? Not about the resonance event—that he was sure of. But what if Ben actually did have things under control? What if Meredith's solution really would work? Had he been too shaken about the kids to accept that possibility?

He remembered his own words to his daughter. Get information. Act from a position of knowledge. Meredith had boasted about her simulations on the computer modeling. Check it out, he told himself. Maybe the problem *is* fixed.

He suddenly, desperately, hoped so.

▲

The corridor at the university's Geophysical Institute was busy. Mike passed a lecture room where he'd often briefed the Institute scientists who collaborated on HARC. People were meandering out after a meeting, and he forced himself to smile and nod at greetings as he passed, heading for the lab where computers networked with the HARC system. Meredith would have input her simulations there.

"Mike! Stop!"

He spun around. It was Jacob Porteous, the Institute director, hurrying on his squat legs to catch up. "I'm royally pissed at you. Don't you ever check your voice mail?" His monkish face split into a grin as he reached Mike, showing his anger was an act. "Actually, you can ignore the messages. I'd wanted to touch base about the injunction, but now I've heard that D'Alton and James have withdrawn their lawsuit. Great news, isn't it? A quiet relocation of the Indians, just what we all wanted. HARC's smooth continuation means smooth sailing around here, too." He didn't need to spell it out. Continuing grants for his scientists, enlarged prestige for his Institute.

"Can't talk now, Jacob. Got to check out something in the lab."

Jacob's look turned quizzical. "Has the real thing lost its charm?"

Mike realized how ludicrous it must seem, scrounging information here when he ran HARC itself. *Actually, Jacob, I've been fired.* "Sorry," he muttered lamely, and walked on.

In the lab, four people were at workstations—three students who, thankfully, didn't know him, and a bearded astrophysicist from Cal Tech who collaborated with Gina, and who, engrossed in work, nodded absently as Mike sat down at a computer.

Two hours later, Mike sat back from Meredith's simulations, stunned by what he'd discovered. The array realignment she had conceived seemed, at first glance, an elegant and clever solution, but he had extrapolated from that point, modeling a worst-case scenario. The problem was the parabolic mirror effect she'd designed to make HARC a weapon. Operating under full power, HARC's signals would gather electrons from the Van Allen radiation belts, creating a cascade condition, an avalanche of electrons, amplifying the signals thousands of times in a colossal resonance jump. A magnetic storming. It was a result that defied any physicist's expectations: nonlinear, nonthermodynamic effects that seemed to violate entropy. Mike saw the fatal error in Meredith's logic. When a system is near saturation, you can't predict what will send it over the threshold. In concentrating on the precision and accuracy of HARC's planar array for a solution, she was focusing on the wrong end of the stick. It wasn't the HARC array that was the problem . . . it was the ionosphere itself.

He remembered his warning to Ben at the airport: "The upper Northern Hemisphere bombarded by ELF radiation . . . hundreds of thousands driven out of their minds . . ." He'd flung those words to make a point, not with any real sense of their accuracy, but now he saw how right he just might be.

And the area around HARC—including Fairbanks—would be hardest hit.

That wasn't the worst. This time, the mental instability induced by the resonance event wouldn't last for just a short spell. It would go on and on . . .

He walked out to the courtyard, his legs rubbery, and made his way to an outdoor picnic table in the corner and sat. Students were eating paper-bag lunches, a couple were playing chess, one was napping, head on his arms folded over books. No one looked Mike's way as he unclipped his cell phone from his belt and called his office. Meredith's office. She didn't answer. He left a message saying it was urgent that she get back to him, truly a matter of life and death. But even as he spoke the words he was aware how overdramatic they sounded, and knew she wouldn't call back. Knew, too, that driving out to the site to demand a meeting would be equally futile, because she would refuse to acknowledge his warning. She *wanted* to flirt with that oversaturation; it was how the weapon worked. She would not see that it was also how the weapon would overwhelm her. Like Ben, she was blind to any effect beyond the ones she controlled.

There was one last chance. Landon Burdett, HARC's administrative director—the bureaucrat Mike had brushed off the other day for requesting a new round of drug testing. He called his Washington office.

"Mike, hi, I was going to call," Burdett said the moment he came on the line. "Sorry to hear of your . . . problems. Anything I can do?"

Mike heard the insincerity in the hollow offer that really meant, *This platitude is all you'll get, pal.* "Ben called you?" he asked, knowing the answer, knowing that although Burdett wasn't part of Ben's conspiracy, Ben would have covered himself.

"Yes. He's sorry to lose you. As am I, my friend. But, as I told him, it happens to the best of us. Burnout. You take a rest and, mark my words, you'll be right as rain."

Mike fumed at the condescending tone, so much like Carol's, as if he were a ten-year-old. Still, he gave it his best shot. He outlined the resonance phenomenon, the consequent ELF effects, and warned in the strongest terms of the disaster that another power-up would unleash. Then he gritted his teeth as Burdett replied, just as he'd feared, that Ben had it all under control, that Dr. Crosbie was an exceptional scientist, that there was no need for concern. Burdett thought he'd gone off the deep end and didn't believe a word he'd said. Primed by Ben, just like Carol. Anyway, Mike knew the game. Burdett's very expensive bread was buttered by the Office of Naval Research, and whatever General Benson Crewe wanted for his pet project was fine by Burdett; he would not be sticking his neck out for Mike. Mike felt almost sick, remembering how proud he used to be about Ben's championing of HARC, how cocky that his father-in-law ensured him a free hand running the project, shielding him from Burdett's interference. He'd always treated Burdett as a necessary nuisance. Now, when he needed some of that interference, he was paying for his arrogance. Burdett owed him nothing.

"Good luck, Mike. Give my best to Carol." The line went dead.

Mike looked up at the sky. The glorious summer weather of the last week had changed. The sky was overcast and seemed to be darkening as he watched, and there was a foreboding of rain in the air. He felt the same in his heart, certain now of what he had to do. Go public. It was the only way.

If only he could do it without implicating Carol.

It struck him . . . stay invisible. A leak. No one had to know about Ben's weapon plan, nor about Carol using Landmark as a money-laundering front. *Is it as simple as that?* With rising excitement, he thought it through. If he anonymously leaked just the basic information about the resonance event, including the mind-altering ELF effects, that should be terrifying enough to rouse the public to demand HARC's immediate closure.

Only, what media outlet would accept an anonymous

report of a story so outlandish? He needed a surrogate. Someone who was a credible opponent of HARC.

He needed Dana.

What a hard irony. The person he wanted most to avoid was the only one he could trust to help him.

Or would she? After all, she'd surrendered to Ben. But Mike was almost certain she would. She knew that some dark energy was haunting Lucas, and the moment she learned that HARC was responsible for his suffering, and for Ron's and Sophy's deaths, she would strike back like a she-wolf. Mike was as sure of Dana as of the indictment he felt he deserved for what he'd unleashed, however inadvertently. She would do it . . . and hate him forever.

He started for his car, steeling himself for the confrontation. It felt like he was walking toward prison. Which, he realized with a gut-rush of dismay, he probably was. Dana's going public would shut down HARC, but HARC was the only safeguard between Litvak's investigation and Mike's family. Someone would go to jail for Carol's fraud, and Mike was trapped into hoping it would be him.

▲

"It's . . . too incredible," Dana said.

She sat in the pilot's seat beside Mike, struggling to comprehend what he'd just told her. She couldn't get a grasp on it. That HARC went out of control . . . affected the kids' minds . . . drove them crazy . . .

She stared out the window. The Aeronca Chief float

plane was tethered to the dock, and all around them the airport float pond was bustling with aircraft and boats. When Mike had arrived at Aurora Aviation he'd said he needed to talk to her alone, impossible in her one-room office, where one of her pilots was arranging his schedule and her mechanic was discussing a parts order with the receptionist. So she'd brought him out to the dock. But again there were so many people around, they'd shut themselves in her two-seater Chief for privacy. Now, as he sat next to her in silence, his words reverberated in her head. A water taxi crammed with laughing passengers plowed through the channel in front of them, carving a wake, and the ripples reaching her and Mike rocked them gently. Seeing her plane's yellow wing rise and fall, feeling the gentle bobbing, hearing the laughter from the water taxi, it seemed to Dana as though she were at some fairground midway . . . far away from this horror. *HARC killed Carla's son, and Sophy, and drove Lucas nearly out of his mind.*

Part of her balked at believing him. Mind-altering electromagnetic waves that drove people to despair and suicide? It was so . . . grotesque. If it had been anyone but Mike, she wouldn't have believed a word. But that was the very reason she knew it was true, because it came from him. He'd based his whole life on science and rationality. And he had built HARC.

Disgust overwhelmed her. As the wake jostled her toward Mike, she shrank back. "*You* did this . . . this unspeakable thing." She stared at him, wanting to burn her revulsion into him. "You made the machine."

He said, his face haggard, "I'm . . . so sorry."

Dana saw his devastation, and the vicious urge to blame him drained from her. She remembered him saving Lucas during the earthquake, grappling him out of midair. Remembered him in the helicopter, murmuring into Lucas's unconscious ear during the whole flight to the hospital, urging him to pull through. She had bitterly fought him about Lucas's future, but she had no doubt that Mike loved his son. Now, he'd almost killed him, and she saw that it was tearing him apart.

"There's more." He took a deep breath, as though arming himself to go on. "Ben . . . General Crewe doesn't believe this is a problem. What I mean is, he believes there's a solution. Everything I've just told you, I told him, but he's decided I'm unreliable because I'm . . . too personally involved. He's fired me and brought in a new lead scientist, and she's convinced him she has a plan to prevent another such event. It won't. I've told them it won't, but they won't listen to me. Dana, in eight days they're going to power up HARC for a trial at maximum power. It will hit Fairbanks this time and far, *far* beyond. Hundreds of thousands, maybe millions of people will be affected."

She was aghast. "And I made a deal with this man."

"What?"

The words had escaped her before she'd thought. But what was the point of holding back now? "Money to build a TB clinic, in exchange for dropping the injunction. Crewe said HARC would subsidize the medical facility, and he gave me three million dollars as a start-up fund."

Mike shook his head. "I wondered how he'd got to you."

"We have to stop him somehow."

"I think we can. If we get the facts out to the public. Create a backlash that will force him to cancel the power-up. But I can't do it alone. Will you . . . help me?"

In his eyes, she saw how hard this was for him, and couldn't help feeling pity. "Of course, anything. We'll get the truth out today."

Mike's relief was clear, but he avoided her eyes. "Not we, Dana. You. You've got to take this to the media for me."

"I don't understand. You're the physicist. You're the one who's the authority."

"I can't. I've got to stay anonymous."

"But, you created HARC. No one's word will mean as much as yours." Why wouldn't he do this?

"There are . . . complications. My wife—" He didn't finish.

Dana felt a door close in her heart. "She asked you not to get involved?"

"I have valid reasons, that's all I can say. You're a well-known opponent of HARC, and you have people's respect. They'll listen to you. Will you do it? Will you speak for me?"

Dana squirmed inside. Some primal instinct urged her to trust him, but logic warned her that because he was hiding something it could only mean trouble. But, did that matter? She saw Lucas's haunted face, and Ron, overwhelmed by despair, shoving that rifle barrel in his mouth, and poor Sophy, her mind deranged, leaping off the bluff. And now, countless others stood in the same danger. Whatever was holding Mike back, someone had to come forward. "I'll do it," she said. "But you'll have to tell *one* other person. Reid."

Mike frowned. "D'Alton? Why do we need him?"

"Media relations are part of his work, and he's good at it. Besides, I'm going to marry him." She said it more sharply than she'd intended. Guilty conscience, she thought: after Reid worked so hard for Takona's interests, I made a pact with the enemy. "Mike, don't mention my deal with Crewe to Reid. Now that we're going to put Crewe out of business, the deal's obviously dead."

He seemed to be studying her. "You're going to marry the guy, but you kept that a secret?"

"Guess not," she said, feeling shaken. "I've told *you*."

Their eyes met. Mike asked, "When's the village re-settlement?"

"Five days."

"Dana, I know it's a poor kind of consolation, but you'll be *glad* those people have been moved if the worst happens. Being next door to HARC, Takona would be the hardest hit."

▲

"I worked up a worst-case scenario. Let me tell you what it is." Mike had just explained to D'Alton the resonance event and its apparent effects on Lucas and the others, but the lawyer's stunned silence left him needing to take a breath before going on.

The three of them were in D'Alton's office, one tidy

room above a sporting goods store across from the post office on Fourth Avenue. The furniture was basic, the walls white, the only decoration Alaskan eco-themed posters: Mount McKinley in its mammoth snowy splendor, whales broaching among icebergs, a valley moonscape where timber interests had clear-cut the forest. Weird, Mike thought—days ago I would have called this enemy territory, the headquarters where the environmental lawyer, Dana's lover, was working to kill HARC. Now I'm asking for his help to do exactly that. He thought the two of them could be a poster themselves: D'Alton, boyishly blond, sitting on the edge of his desk in chinos and preppy blazer, Dana standing beside him in black pants and sapphire-blue T-shirt, as beautiful as night. They were holding hands. Getting married. Well, why shouldn't she? Not my business.

He plowed on. Worst-case scenario. "An extreme resonance jump would bounce mind-altering ELF radiation randomly and intermittently over millions of square miles. You know the principle of how HARC works. Its beam superheats a patch of the ionosphere into a virtual mirror to reflect the energy back." He didn't mention Meredith's "improvement" of making the mirror parabolic to focus the energy—that it kick-started the resonance. To explain that would be to expose Ben's weapon, and Mike couldn't let the lawyer see inside that Pandora's box. He had to safeguard his family's secret.

"With the resonance jump," he went on, "the heating and reflecting action will increase in power, and *keep* increasing, and because the ionosphere is a dynamic system, constantly in flux, the mirror will become a chaotic, billion-faceted entity. Imagine one of those dance-floor mirrored balls. Now imagine a giant one spinning in the sky, with every mirror facet bombarding destructive ELF waves back to Earth across the entire upper Northern Hemisphere. Areas farthest from HARC—that is, halfway to the equator—will experience the least frequent barrage. Areas nearest HARC will be hardest hit, meaning all of central Alaska, including Fairbanks. Everything in between—the whole northern half of the United States, Canada, Scandinavia, and Russia—could suffer. It will be like random sniper fire that never quits."

D'Alton found his voice. "But . . . why couldn't they could just turn it off?"

"Because no one on the HARC site will know it's happening." He added grimly, "They won't even know their own names." He explained his lapse during the test, explained that all his team likely experienced the same thing but didn't realize it. "That was just seven seconds, a mere hiccup. The longer the resonance event lasts, the more debilitated the victims everywhere will become. Eventually . . . we're talking permanent brain damage. Meanwhile, HARC's mainframe won't be disabled, because for climate control and earthquake shielding it's in a separate steel-enclosed room. And here's the worst. HARC, as you know, is powered by a nuclear reactor— doesn't need fuel. With everyone at the site incapacitated, the reactor could carry on indefinitely."

There was a long moment of silence. D'Alton finally said, more in shock than reproach, "How could you build such a thing?"

Mike found it hard to hold his tongue. *Ben and*

Meredith did this, not me. But technically it was true—he *had* built it. "The point is," he said, "can we prevent the catastrophe by going public with the facts?"

"Absolutely." D'Alton had got back his balance. "HARC's electromagnetic disturbance killed Alaska's preeminent politician, Senator Gustafson, by disabling both his plane and his mind, and similarly affected at least three others? You'll see HARC's doors padlocked the moment the words are out of your mouth."

"Not me," Mike said. "I stay anonymous. I'm only leaking the background information. Dana's agreed to announce it."

"What?" D'Alton got to his feet, his frown full of suspicion and contempt. "That's absurd. You're the one who has to expose this. It's a moral duty."

"I *am* exposing it. But I can't have my name used. That's a condition."

"Somewhat cowardly, wouldn't you say? Hiding behind Dana?"

Mike controlled the urge to go for his throat. "Look, I know I've always been the bad guy to you. Fine. Just use what I'm giving you against HARC. Let's *do* this."

When D'Alton still resisted, Dana said, "Reid, what's it matter who speaks out? If the three of us don't work together, Crewe will go ahead in eight days. I'm willing. I'm ready."

"It's preposterous."

"It's all we have."

D'Alton regarded her, then Mike. He threw up his hands. "All right. An informed source, we'll say. Let's get started." He went around his desk, opened a drawer, and pulled out a yellow legal pad and pencil. He sat, then looked up, all business. "To prove a crime was committed we need a victim. Is Lucas recovered enough to give a statement?"

Mike exchanged a glance with Dana. He sensed she felt the same way he did. "I don't want him dragged into this," he said. "He's been through too much already."

D'Alton said, "There's an awful lot you don't want."

Mike let it slide. "Why not speak to people in the Gatana Valley? There's only a handful of them in that wilderness, but state troopers were called in over several incidents of domestic abuse. There might be some who went through what Lucas did and would talk about it."

D'Alton thought for a moment, then nodded. "Domestic abuse victims would make sympathetic witnesses, too." He jotted a note, then said to Mike, "Next, I need a written report from you explaining the scientific phenomenon. Detailed, but not technical. I want simple language an ordinary person can understand."

"No problem."

"That's a first," D'Alton said dryly. "Get it to me ASAP. I'll head out to the Gatana Valley and start looking for victims."

"I'll help," Dana said. "I'll fly us."

D'Alton smiled at her. "Thanks." He stood. "Today's Wednesday. If we can get our facts together by tomorrow night, I'll contact Burt Dunlop at the CBS affiliate in Anchorage first thing Friday. I imagine they'll break the story immediately." He turned to Mike. "One question. You said this deadline to activate HARC is for a trial. General Crewe is not a stupid man. What could be so urgent about a mere trial that would make him disregard all the warnings of an expert like yourself?"

Mike stiffened. Smart lawyer.

"I can think of two possible reasons," D'Alton went on. "Either he's got somebody powerful breathing down his neck. Or he's bent on impressing someone."

Both. Mike tried to make his face unreadable. "I can't discuss that."

He caught Dana watching him, anger in her eyes. "Mike," she demanded, "whose side are you on?"

"All I want is to stop this power-up. I can give you enough information to do that. No more."

"While keeping your own nose clean," D'Alton said.

"Look, I don't give a shit what you think about my—"

"That's enough," Dana said, coming between them. "There's too much to do. Mike, go write your report. Reid, let's get started. Now."

▲

"And Crewe's his father-in-law. Imagine," Reid said, shaking his head after Mike had left. Dana watched him pack legal pads and a tape recorder into his briefcase. She didn't want to go into this. She wanted to get airborne.

"Funny," he went on, "I never took Ryder for a traitor."

"The decision was made for him, Reid. It was an accident. It's not like he *wanted* this. Anyway, he's on the right side now." Mike's refusal to come forward unsettled her, but something in her wanted to protect him.

"Dana, you're too generous. Never trust a traitor." He snapped shut his briefcase. "Ryder's a coward. He deserves everything he's going to get."

"What do you mean?"

"You think the media sharks are going to play by his rules?"

"But, we've agreed to keep him out of it."

"Tell that to the sharks. They'll be onto him in a New York minute. He'll be outed before he knows what's hit him."

IT'LL BE ON TODAY'S NEWS. I just wanted you to hear it from me first."

Mike sat beside Lucas's hospital bed, his explanation about HARC hanging between them like toxic fog. He waited, hardly knowing what reaction to expect. Lucas still looked so weak, helpless with the cast on his arm, his face puffy and bruised like a boxer's. Mike thought of him on their last kayak trip, paddling with an easy vigor, alert to the river, at home with the calls of ravens and jays. Now, beaten up by that same river, sluggish with drugs, in a room sharp with the smell of disinfectant.

"HARC . . . made us crazy," Lucas said as though absorbing it, accepting it—and hating it. "HARC . . . killed Sophy and Ron."

Mike could only nod in bleak agreement. Lucas was the first person who'd instantly believed the ELF explanation. Why not? He'd lived through it. Saw his friends die through it.

Mike felt he'd died a little himself in the last two days. So much lying, so much hiding. Yesterday, while Carol and Ben were in Washington, he'd gone out to HARC to try again to convince Meredith—a last attempt before Dana went to the media—and in the halls, passing people who'd asked him in dismay about his abrupt departure and the change in leadership, he'd answered only with a brusque, "I'm taking a sabbatical." He reached Meredith in his office—her office—hoping that away from Ben's influence she might listen to the scenario he'd modeled. Far from it. "Mike, you just can't take it that I found a solution when you couldn't. I'm not even sure you *understand* the solution. And I've had it with your interference. Next time you try to come onto the site, I'll have security throw you out." She'd actually called a security guard to escort him to his car. Backing up in the parking lot, he saw Wayne pulling up in his truck, bewilderment on his face as Mike drove right past him. Since being fired, he hadn't returned Wayne's calls, nor the calls from anyone on his team. He wished he could explain things to Wayne, at least, but knew that would do no good. He had to hang tight until the news story broke. Lying and hiding—he was so sick of it, it was almost a relief to come clean to Lucas. And after he left here he was going to pick up Carol at the airport and tell her that while she'd been away he'd leaked the facts, that Dana was informing the media, that he'd had to do it to put an end to Ben's grand scheme. Who am I kidding? he thought grimly. Compared to telling Carol all that, lying's been a picnic.

Lucas was watching him. The haunted look in his

eyes was gone, and something hard had taken its place. "*You* did it. *You* killed Sophy."

Mike didn't turn away. It was the truth. "Lucas, I'm more sorry than I can say."

Lucas just stared, as though seeing him for the first time. Mike remembered that same look in Dana's eyes. Disillusionment. Disgust. From her, for his refusal to speak out, to take responsibility. It galled him, maintaining this silence to protect Carol. And Lucas's contempt cut even more deeply. *He looked up to me.*

"Mom calls what you do Big Science. She says that kind of science doesn't help people—it's just deals for corporations and the military. HARC hasn't helped anybody, has it? It's *hurt* them. Making people kill themselves . . . you can't hurt much worse than that. Maybe Mom's right about a lot of things. Maybe I don't want any part of your Big Science. Maybe I'll stay put, with people who still look after each other in little places like Takona." He added pointedly, "*My* people."

"People are the same everywhere, Lucas. Good, bad, greedy, kind. You still have to answer for your own life, wherever you are. If you hide away, you might as well bury yourself alive."

"I'm buried alive *now*," he said. "By nightmares . . . about Sophy. And now you tell me she died because of your . . . *machine*." His look was fierce with anger and pain. "The old Indians said there were devils in machines. I don't believe that. But maybe devils *make* the machines."

The insult hurt, but not as much as the sob in his son's

voice. After that, Lucas wouldn't talk anymore. Mike left heavy-hearted.

On his way to pick up Carol at the airport his cell phone rang.

"Mike, have you heard?" It was Wayne. "Did you see Dana James on the news?"

It's started. Mike steeled himself: more lying. "No."

"Christ, she said HARC went out of control last Saturday night and *killed* people. Even killed Senator Gustafson. Said it generated EM waves that messed with people's heads. I mean, what's she been smoking? People here at the site are pretty damned stunned. Me too. Can you believe it?"

"Wayne, I can't talk now. I'm in the car. Gotta go."

"You okay? What's this medical leave they say you're on? And who's this Dr. Crosbie taking over? I mean, is it for good? Mike, are you sick or something?"

"Can't comment. Look, I've got to go."

"Can't *comment*? This is *me*, man." Mike could practically hear the gears suddenly shift in Wayne's mind. "Jesus . . . don't tell me something *did* go wrong with that test. Mike, what the fuck is going on?"

▲

"Don't worry, Dana, you were perfect. Even without Ryder, we're going to blow HARC away."

She looked over at Reid beside her in the cockpit and faked a smile. "Worry" didn't begin to cover it. They were returning from Anchorage where she had made her statement to the Channel 8 people. She'd seen their shock, but that was this morning, and flying back she'd been in limbo, no way to gauge the impact of her news. She knew only that she'd set something in motion that was necessary, but frightening: General Benson Crewe, backed by the might of the U.S. military, against her and Reid. Making her approach to Fairbanks International, she radioed and got clearance, and between glances at her instruments and airspace she looked over at him. He'd gone back to the papers stacked on his briefcase on his lap—yellow legal pages filled with his meticulous handwriting. Dana felt a smile spring from affection and hope. Reid was committed to this fight.

Yet, what good would it do Takona? For months she and Reid had worked on how to kill HARC, but when she realized they couldn't prevent the village relocation, she'd made the deal to get the TB clinic, which at least was something. Now, she *was* killing HARC, but killing that deal too—yet, still, Takona would be moved. The airlift of the residents in three days was all arranged. Then, the village would be razed.

This bleak failure, coming after Ron's and Sophy's horrible deaths, felt like the final nail in the coffin of her people's existence.

She thought of Thomas with a pang. Last Sunday, when she'd wondered why Lucas hadn't come back, she'd visited her brother-in-law's cabin and told him she was giving up the fight, and she'd been stung by the depth of his anger. "Like a good Indian, huh?" he growled. "Same old story—give up, and get out." He grabbed his rifle and stalked off into the woods. The next morning she and Mike had found the kids' bodies, and Dana wondered how Thomas was going to bear it. He'd lost Carla three months ago, now his son.

She still hated the relocation—Takona's people carted away like livestock, and the home of their ancestors burned—yet she saw, bitterly, that it might now be a blessing in disguise. Mike had made it clear that if the disaster did happen, Takona, next door to HARC, would suffer the worst. Should she send Lucas to stay with friends in San Francisco? If the unthinkable did happen, he'd be safe that far away . . .

No, she told herself, it isn't *going* to happen. Her statement this morning would stop it. Which meant carrying on with life. Only, had some rules been rewritten? She'd told Mike that in exposing HARC she was killing her deal with Crewe, but now, as she prepared to descend into Fairbanks, she was rethinking that. Three million dollars was sitting in her bank account. What was she going to do, give it back? Why should she? She'd be dammed if she was going to end up after all this with nothing for Takona. She *would* use Crewe's money to build the clinic in the new location. HARC owed it to her people.

The decision lifted her spirits a little: finally, she could tell Reid.

As she began her final approach, Comm 1 crackled with the air traffic controller's voice. Fred Snyder, it sounded like. Dana acknowledged, and Fred cleared her to the base leg, then added, "And, Dana, a message from your office. There's a media welcoming party."

▲

The moment she and Reid opened the aircraft doors, reporters swarmed them. They seemed to be running from all directions. Dana wished she had a few more minutes to consult with Reid, but it was impossible in the sudden crush of bodies and cameras and lights, and the barrage of questions.

"Dr. James, on what evidence are you basing the accusations you made today about the High-frequency Auroral Research Center?"

She took a deep breath. "I have a reliable source."

"Is your source employed at the HARC facility?"

"I won't divulge my source's identity, but I'll be glad to repeat the facts about the destructive resonance event and its victims. That tragedy is where your focus should be."

"Do you have a background in the field of ionospheric research?"

"No."

"Were you present at the HARC site when the event you allege took place?"

"No."

"Did you personally experience the mind-altering effects that you claim HARC generated?"

"No."

"Dr. James, despite your legal battle against the HARC project, you've been unable to stop the scheduled resettlement of your Indian village. Is your claim about a deadly accident at HARC an act of desperation?"

"There's no—" She was stopped by Reid grabbing her arm. He pulled her with him as he started across the tarmac toward her office. "Don't answer that," he told her under his breath. They walked, and the reporters followed.

"Dr. James," one called, "is this your last-ditch attempt to discredit HARC?"

Furious, Dana turned and faced the pack. "Is this *your* attempt to deflect focus from the tragedy? HARC went out of control. It generated mind-altering electromagnetic fields that drove people to despair, to violence and suicide. That's what happened. HARC must be shut down."

"If you weren't there, and have no expertise in this field, how do you know?"

Dana hesitated, feeling trapped. Reid said in a fierce whisper in her ear, "Tell them."

"No," she whispered back.

"Dana, they'll hang you out to dry. It's not your responsibility to protect him."

"I gave him my word."

"He had no right to ask! And they'll find out *anyway*."

Their hushed exchange ignited the reporters, and the questions became a bombardment:

"How can we corroborate your story?"

"Are you accusing HARC's scientists of mind control?"

"Are you seeking damages?"

"Who's your *source*?"

Outrage and adrenaline priming her, Dana was ready to take a stand on everything she'd claimed, but before she could speak, Reid broke in. "Dr. James has acted bravely in bringing these tragic events to light." His arm went around her shoulder. "Her own son was affected in the calamity, and she is suffering over that. Please, let her alone. Put your questions to the authorities at HARC."

The reporters pounced:

"Her son? What happened?"

"Did he die?"

"*Which* authorities?"

"*Who's the source?*"

Dana felt herself pulled away by Reid toward the building. "They'll be on Ryder's doorstep within the hour," he told her as they left reporters behind. "It was inevitable, Dana. Let him face the fallout."

▲

Mike drove away from the terminal along Airport Way, Carol beside him. He hadn't told her yet. She was talking about Lindsay—Lindsay's horse, Lindsay's horse's vet—and Mike understood that she was rattling on to fill the chasm between them with words. There had been precious few when he'd met her, Ben coming through the arrival doors with her. They had split up immediately, Ben going with the driver who'd come to take him to HARC, Mike and Carol heading home. Mike had no intention of telling Ben what was going on; he'd hear soon enough. It occurred to him uneasily that this was a war tactic—ambush. War was Ben's specialty, only this time it was Ben who would be ambushed.

But Carol was his wife. Carol he must tell.

"She's an overnight expert on equine colic, a real blabbermouth." Carol gave a nervous laugh. "Cham-

pagne's recovered, but Lindsay's infected . . . with the
bug to become a vet."

Her feeble joke died on the air between them.

She launched into a blithe rundown on the stable.

Mike wondered how to begin. He'd planned to wait
until they were home, alone, able to retreat to separate
corners, but he didn't think he could take another minute
of her chattering while the bomb about HARC was tick-
ing between them. Like Lucas, she deserved to know
what he'd done before she heard it on the news.

"Carol, I've gone public. About the resonance jump.
The victims. The danger."

Silence as brittle as spring ice. Keeping his eyes on
the road, Mike felt her staring at him.

"You . . . went to the media?"

"No. Passed on the information anonymously. I didn't
want it to lead anyone to what you and Ben have done. I
only want to stop him."

"So, you leaked it. Who to?"

"Dana James."

Even watching the road, he could sense, in her still-
ness, her chest rising and falling in tight breaths.

"When did the story break?"

"A couple hours ago."

"You're a fool, Mike. Everyone will know it's you."

He was startled by the change in her. Looking at her,
he saw a woman who was not his wife. It wasn't that he
didn't know her; once or twice before, when she was engrossed in a PR campaign, he'd glimpsed this persona:
intensely focused, in control. It struck him that the terrain he had so reluctantly stepped into—public rela-

tions—was a place where Carol became this woman. A place as familiar to her as a combat zone was to Ben. *Or me in the lab.* Now, he was so far from that world he knew.

He turned the corner onto their street. An unusual number of parked cars. One had the mountain-peak logo of Channel 5. And outside their house, a mob of reporters.

Carol said quietly, "You are such a fool."

▲

Dana squeezed her pickup through the vehicles parked on both sides of Mike's street. She'd felt sick when she saw the mob. She'd tried Mike's cell phone on her way but got no answer, but still had hoped to get here in time to warn him. Too late. They were lying in wait for him. Leaving her truck double parked and getting out, she glimpsed him, and her heart crammed up in her throat. He had his arm around his wife and they were hurrying up the walk toward their front door, trying to get past the shouting reporters.

Dana reached the fringe of the crowd and pushed through. Mike opened the door, and as his wife hurried inside, he shot a look back at the shouting mob, and his gaze met Dana's. She opened her mouth, longing to somehow show how sorry she was, but the fury in his eyes made her freeze. He stepped inside and shut the door.

The shouting died down, but none of the reporters moved. It was going to be a siege.

Dana pulled herself together. She should never have come.

Lucas, she thought. *He'll be their next target.* She turned and started back to her truck. She had to get Lucas out of the hospital before they tracked him down.

▲

"Stop," Ben told his driver. From a block away he could see the crowd of reporters on Mike and Carol's front lawn. He couldn't be seen arriving there. "Turn right."

He'd been on the outskirts of Fairbanks on his way to the site when he'd heard the news bulletin on the radio. "Dr. Dana James, a local physician and owner of Aurora Aviation Charters, claimed today that the High-frequency Auroral Research Center was responsible for a deadly accident last Saturday night. HARC officials have declined to comment . . ." Ben had told his driver to turn around, and they'd raced toward the house.

Now, as they reached the entrance to the alley that ran behind it, he said, "Turn here."

▲

"Goddamn vultures!" Mike was closing curtains and blinds, furious at the assault on his home, at being block-aded in his own living room. And at seeing Dana among that mob. Carol was right. How had he ever thought he could stay out of it? As he yanked the strings of vertical blinds on a double-story side window, the strings snagged. *Damn* this house of windows!

"They want you to confirm the story," Carol said. "Mike, you've got to deny it."

He turned to face her, feeling unnerved—by her determination, by the realization that, yes, he must give the reporters an answer, but most of all by the answer she was asking him to give.

"Why can't you see that you've got this all mixed up?" she said. "Dana James isn't on your side. *I am.* I'm trying to save us both. She's got you believing you somehow hurt the boy through HARC. She's manipulating you, because she wants to bring us down. Do you honestly believe my father would go ahead with the demonstration if he wasn't absolutely certain HARC is safe? The technical problem is fixed, Mike. All we have to do is ride out this media storm for another few days. The demonstration will save us. But only if you turn this thing around, here and now. You've got to go out there and deny that any accident happened. You're the expert, you made HARC, they'll believe you. Deny it now, and the story will die."

"Deny that my own son almost lost his life? Deny my responsibility for the deaths of two kids, when I saw their bodies with my own eyes? Let Ben power up HARC again and kill more people?"

"Stop it! You talk like he's some kind of murderer."

"I know he doesn't *intend* harm, but believe me, he will *do* it."

"Do you know how crazy you sound?" The strain seemed to snap something inside her. She began to tremble, and tears welled in her eyes. "Don't you care anything about us? Dad being court-martialed, ruined? Don't you care about *me*? About Lindsay? Don't you care if they send me to prison?"

"Ben has to live with what he's done. As for us, I told you, I'll claim the money diversion was my doing, and we'll get the best lawyers money can buy. My sentence won't be much. Carol, we'll survive this."

"You don't know what you're talking about! You'd have a prison record. How could we live? *Where* could we live?"

"Anywhere. I can get a position at any university in the world that—"

"No, you couldn't," Ben said.

They turned. Ben stood in the kitchen doorway. Came in the back door, Mike realized, his heart hammering.

"I can break you, Mike. I can make it so that no one in the world will hire you in your field. You'll lose your livelihood, lose your family. Do you really think you can survive *that*?"

Mike stared at him. The man who'd given him everything . . . could also take everything away. He tried to hide his fear. "What are you going to do, Ben, have me arrested for telling people the truth? Too late. They already know."

"Don't be an idiot," Carol said. "People don't care about the truth, they only want to know who to *blame*. And if you confirm there was an accident, believe me, they will blame *you*."

"Don't force me to make you a scapegoat," Ben warned. "They'll tear you apart."

Mike was suddenly very tired of his father-in-law's threats. He shook his head. Maybe Ben took it for a weakening, because he said more gently, "Mike, accept it, Crosbie has everything under control. She's very, very good."

Carol said, her voice trembling, "Deny the story, darling. I'm begging you." Her eyes flicked between him and her father. "Please, Mike, don't make me choose."

Choose. He stood to lose so much. And he wasn't even sure anymore if his catastrophe scenario for a full power-up had any validity. It was theory. *Simulation isn't reality*, he'd told Meredith. Was he really prepared to destroy his career, his marriage, lose Carol, maybe never see his daughter again—because of a hunch?

He opened the door. The lounging reporters were instantly alert, jostling closer, readying cameras and microphones. Beyond the crowd, Mike caught a glimpse of Dana's red pickup across the street, pulling out. Seeing her leave, something inside him went cold. He was on his own. He could sense Carol behind him, listening, hoping, praying.

He made his choice.

JACOB, BAD NEWS. It's Mike. He's had a breakdown."

Carol could control the waver in her voice as she spoke on the phone, but not her anguish. She already regretted her vicious words to Mike, wished she hadn't thrown him out. Yet she was relieved at how automatically she could hit her professional stride now, say what had to be said. Jacob Porteous at the university's Geophysical Institute was one of many calls on her list. She only wished she could get her hands to stop trembling.

She glanced across the den at her father. Standing by the desk, he was on the other line, following her instructions, calling the governor's office. Carol felt a pang . . . Mike's desk . . . he liked catching up on work here. He'd left a half hour ago, right after his statement to the journalists.

"As lead scientist with the High-frequency Auroral Research Center until two days ago, I want to confirm the report that an unforeseen result occurred during our tests last Saturday night. It created an electromagnetic

*resonance event of an unprecedented magnitude result-
ing in tragic consequences. Let me explain . . ."*

The moment he'd gone, Carol and her father knew it
was war.

"He didn't mention the weapon agenda. Yet."

"He's trying to protect me."

"He's unbalanced, Carol. And he has all the information. He can ruin us."

"Don't worry. I can take him out."

She'd called her office in Boston, instructing her two
assistants to catch the next flight here, telling them she
was booking a suite at the Princess Hotel, setting up a
war room. "The three of us will be eating and sleeping
this for the next forty-eight hours, minimum," she told
them. "Welcome to your weekend."

"A breakdown?" Jacob Porteous came back to her on
the phone. Carol explained the crisis. Yes, she agreed, it
was an excruciating position for her, but she had a responsibility to everyone who relied on HARC. She
didn't need to spell it out for Jacob: his Institute would
lose millions in grants if HARC was shut down. He was
more than willing to help. Carol told him, "I'll have a
video crew at your office at eight sharp tomorrow morning."

She went back for her address book on the desk,
where her father seemed to be on hold. "When you speak
to Governor Dainard," she told him, "call in every IOU.
Remind him what he owed Gustafson. I need five minutes of him on video, the focus is jobs and a high-tech
future, and tell him I must have it by tomorrow night."

He looked at her. "Carol, are you all right?"

She nodded. A lie. She turned away to hide her face . . . pretended to search for a phone number, but *still* her hands were trembling, and tears clouded her vision. She'd declared open season on opponents before, but never dreamed she'd have to on Mike. *"Take him out."* It left her feeling sick. But that's just it, she told herself—it's *Mike* who's sick. Unbalanced, like Dad says. A breakdown. He needs a rest, that's all. And then . . . he *has* to come back.

A sound startled her. Rain. Fat drops were thumping the glass door to the patio. Yes, she thought, a rest. And once this horrible thing is behind us, we'll get our lives back to normal. Leave this miserable hick state, go home. Mike *has* to come, he adores Lindsay, couldn't bear a separation. I'll make Dad forgive him. Mike will be grateful. His work is everything to him. He'll start on a new project, and we'll settle back into our old life— dinner parties, friends, Lindsay's horse shows. We'll be ourselves again. A family.

"Carol? Are you *sure* you can manage this?"

She turned her back on the rain, the threat of tears subdued, and assured her father, "Absolutely." The thought of going home with Mike gave her new strength. She could make it happen. She had all the skills. She could restore his reputation later. The public forgets— it's why "the news" works: breaking story, or corrected update, people buy whatever's on the nightly broadcast as truth. She could make that work for Mike.

But first, she had to break him.

▲

Mike lay on his back in Wayne's upper berth, hands under his head, listening to rain dripping on the roof of the boat. It was Sunday, suppertime, and Wayne stood in the narrow galley chopping mushrooms and peppers for spaghetti sauce, the aroma of frying onions filling the cramped cabin. The scruffy fifty-foot steel trawler docked on the Chena River at the edge of Fairbanks was a veteran that looked as though it had seen as much hard living as its owner. The boat was Wayne's home.

Mike's, too, for the last two days. A weekend of rain. The skies had opened in a deluge on Friday evening after he'd faced the reporters. Last night, after twenty-four hours of downpour drumming like punishment on the steel decks, he thought he'd go crazy, stuck inside here, waiting for his statement of disaster to sink in with the public, waiting for whatever was going to happen next . . . and unable to get Carol's words out of his head: *"You have no idea what you're in for."* He'd felt tied in knots at what he'd put on the line—his marriage, his career, his whole future. But now the rain was letting up, and he felt as though something inside him had let up too. *Out of my hands . . . nothing to do but wait.* Lying on the bunk, listening to the rain's soft dripping and Wayne's chopping, cocooned by the low-lit coziness of the cabin, it seemed as though the world was holding its breath. That's how Mike felt—holding his breath, hoping that what he'd done was going to work.

He'd confirmed everything to the reporters. Explained the resonance in plain language, and the ELF radiation effects in stark detail, so that no one could be confused about the danger HARC posed, and then he'd answered their questions. He said nothing about Ben's real agenda: HARC as a secret weapon that violated treaties. Whether that came out later in an investigation wasn't up to him. He wasn't doing this to destroy Ben; he only wanted the demonstration stopped. As the reporters ran to their cars and raced off with the story, Mike went back inside. The living room, under such clamorous siege minutes ago, was quiet. Just Ben and Carol, staring at him. Carol was trembling.

"How could you?" she said. "Bastard!" She slapped him.

He grabbed her by the shoulders, wanting to shake sense into her. "I *had* to. *Lives* are at stake. Why won't you believe me?"

Ben's hand clamped Mike's bicep. "Take your hands off my daughter."

Carol pulled out of Mike's grip, coldness in her eyes. "You made the wrong choice, Mike. You have no idea what you're in for."

It was as though she'd slammed a door between them. A complete withdrawal in body and spirit—to Mike, far more painful than her slap. He shrugged off Ben's hand, his eyes still on Carol, wishing he could break through her wall of denial and reach her. But she had shut him out. Decided they were enemies. She told him icily, "I think you'd better leave."

He closed his eyes now, sick at the memory.

Then opened them, fed up. Enough self-pity. And enough of lying here like a bum. He sat up, swung his legs over the bunk. Time to get cleaned up.

"You like hot chili peppers?" Wayne asked.

"What?"

"In the sauce." Without waiting for an answer, he tossed in a fistful of peppers. "If not, open a can of beans."

Mike had to smile. "Sure, peppers—the hotter the better." Wayne had been a good friend, offering him a berth without question or comment. Mike figured he'd endured so much in his lifelong battle with alcohol that a buddy's marriage problems didn't faze him. And the moment he'd heard Mike explain the danger with HARC, Wayne had accepted his judgment. Mike was more grateful for that than anything.

He looked around at the comfortable bachelor squalor. Part boat, part home, part workshop for Wayne's constant tinkering, the place had the snug feel of a kid's fort. Things were far from shipshape. Nothing was stowed for a rough waterway, since Wayne hadn't taken the boat from the dock in years, living on it even when the hull was gripped in ice with knee-high snow on deck, a propane stove heating the cabin. Short paths butted through the piled messes of tools and spare parts, canned food, true-crime paperbacks, small motors in various stages of repair, old *Popular Mechanic*s magazines, and equipment manuals. Despite the dusty clutter, though, Mike knew that every system on board worked flawlessly, from the wind generator that powered the refrigerator, to the solar panels that heated the shower tank. Wayne was a genius mechanic. He could keep an engine running on the fumes from an oily rag.

What Mike didn't see anywhere, and knew he wouldn't however deeply he dug under the junk, was a bottle of liquor. Soda, juice, bottled water, nothing harder. Not even a beer. Five years ago Wayne had hit bottom when his wife walked out of their Fairbanks bungalow, taking their two kids. Mike knew it had been a long haul for him through the years of AA, and he admired Wayne's staying power. Still, he could have used a drink himself right now. He realized that if he was edgy enough to want a shot, it must be far worse for Wayne. He remembered Wayne once telling him, "Hell, I can have a drink anytime I want. See this?" He'd lifted the thick copper AA medallion that always hung around his neck. "When I get the craving, I drop this in a glass and fill 'er up. I can have that drink just as soon as the medallion dissolves." Mike chuckled at the memory.

"What's funny?"

"Not funny, pathetic. Your cooking." He hopped off the bunk. "Don't you know the oregano goes in before the tomato paste?"

"Watch your mouth, if you want any dinner to fork into it. Speaking of your mouth, when's the last time you shaved? You look like shit. Go get cleaned up." Wayne was talking over his shoulder as he opened the fridge and pulled out a bowl of leftover coleslaw. "Go on, the sauce needs to fester awhile anyway."

Mike showered, felt a little more civilized. When he came out, Wayne was ladling sauce over spaghetti mounded in two enamel bowls. "How long do you think it'll take?" Wayne asked. "I mean, before this shuts the place down." He jerked his chin at the TV on a shelf cluttered with screwdrivers and spark plugs. On Channel 5 a local game show host was yammering, the sound on mute. All weekend Mike had been monitoring news reports, but he'd watched his statement replayed so many times he'd got sick of hearing himself and hit the mute button hours ago.

"I don't know," he said, worry gnawing him again. "But it has to be by Thursday." That's when Ben had scheduled the demonstration. Four days.

They sat down to eat.

"Can't stop thinking of what you called it—runaway resonance," Wayne said, shaking a hill of Kraft Parmesan onto his spaghetti. "Puts me in mind of a runaway diesel."

Mike knew of the phenomenon, a result of worn parts or contaminated fuel. "Ever see it happen?" he asked.

"Almost got killed by it. I was working a crab trawler out of Kodiak about ten years ago, a real rust bucket. The skipper treated that engine like shit. Guess a little gasoline got in, and the thing went nuts, three thousand RPM to ten thousand in no time flat, banging and wobbling like it was demented. Then it blew up, just like a bomb. Fired out pistons like shrapnel. One hit the skipper in the chest, killed him right there. Boat sank, we all ended up in the drink. A June night in the Shelikof Strait, cold as a witch's tit. I'd got a mayday out before we abandoned. Japanese freighter picked us up." He shook his head, chewing spaghetti, eyes twinkling at the wonder of surviving. "Fucking runaway diesel, man."

Mike smiled as he ate. Not that the story wasn't chilling—it just felt good, after the hell of the past week, to be with somebody who believed him. Yet he knew Wayne was already paying for it. Yesterday Wayne had told Meredith that given Mike's warning, he couldn't continue at HARC if she planned to power-up again, and she'd given him his notice on the spot. As of tomorrow, he would be on the street.

Makes two of us, Mike thought grimly.

"Thursday," Wayne said, frowning at the deadline. "And Dana's village airlift is tomorrow. Weird, huh? You gotta wonder what's the point, if HARC's shutting down. Gotta feel sorry for Dana."

Mike looked at him. Wayne had met Dana that last summer Mike worked the pipeline to make his tuition. One summer—two months—was all Mike had had with Dana; but he'd fallen hard. She was the one who'd broken things off. Wouldn't leave Alaska.

"Granted, I'm no expert on women," Wayne said, digging his fork into spaghetti, "but let me get this straight. The girl you loved and left is supporting you on this whistle-blowing, and the one you married is busting your balls. Something I'm missing?" He glanced up. "Sorry. Guess I hit a nerve."

"No, just thinking about the village," Mike lied. And the thought did bring a jab of guilt. A hundred eighty people uprooted from their ancestral way of life, because of HARC. My creation. *"Devils make the machines,"* Lucas had said so bitterly, adding that he wanted no part of Mike's world, wanted to stay with "his people." When Mike called the hospital yesterday, Lucas had been discharged into the care of his mother. He felt a hollowness in his chest. Could he ever heal this rift with his son?

"Mike. Look." Wayne was pointing his fork at the mute TV. It was the local six o'clock news, launching with a banner: "Special Report: HARC Scientist Out of Control?" Mike stiffened. The anchor seemed to be finishing some introductory remarks, then they cut to Landon Burdett, HARC's administrative director. An imposing black man, impeccably dressed, Burdett was speaking from his Washington office. Mike grabbed the remote and turned up the volume.

". . . which made this regrettable step necessary," Burdett was saying. "Concern for Mike Ryder's welfare, and for the smooth operation of the HARC research project, led me to place him temporarily on mandatory medical leave."

"Dr. Ryder to you," Mike growled.

"I'd like to stress the word 'temporarily,'" Burdett went on. "We want him back as soon as possible. Mike Ryder's brilliance in both theoretical physics and experimental physics is undisputed. The HARC research project is, after all, his concept. We are doing everything possible to ensure that he receives the best medical treatment, and his team of colleagues, as well as myself, are hoping for a speedy recovery and his quick return to the project."

Liar. Mike's eyes were drawn to the interviewer sitting across the desk from Burdett. Stocky young guy, curly dark hair. Only his profile was visible, but something about him looked familiar. He asked Burdett, "Isn't it true that at issue is Dr. Ryder's psychological health, due to the recent suicide attempt of his illegitimate son?"

Mike felt his jaw drop. *What?*

"I cannot comment on Dr. Ryder's psychological state."

"But he has publicly maintained that irregular radio signals from the HARC research site were responsible for the suicides of two Native Athabascan teens and the suicide attempt of his own son, who's half Native. Aren't these extraordinary claims the reason you had to remove Dr. Ryder? And if so, would you classify him as dangerously disturbed?"

"These personal matters relating to Dr. Ryder are outside my purview."

"Well, within your purview, how do you respond to Dr. Ryder's statements about a so-called resonance event at HARC?"

"Every independent scientific authority involved in HARC's oversight has declared the project to be safe, secure, and reliable."

"State troopers discovered liquor at the spot where the teens, in the company of Dr. Ryder's son, killed themselves. Do you think alcohol abuse was behind the suicides?"

"I cannot comment on the fatalities, beyond stating that they are unrelated to the HARC project. What I can say is that, as project director, I have a responsibility to insure public safety, and that extends, naturally, to the welfare of the scientists and technicians working on this important research undertaking. I feared that Dr. Ryder, in his present unpredictable state of mind, might pose a danger to himself and to others."

Mike's heart was pounding. *Lies!* And the blithe assurances that HARC was safe . . . the malicious innuendo about Lucas . . . those hot-button words: "illegitimate," "Native," "suicide," "alcohol abuse." It was as though the questions and Burdett's answers were all part of a propaganda script.

Jesus, that's it. *That's* who the interviewer is— Miguel, Carol's assistant. It hit Mike so hard, it knocked him back in his chair. *She's put her office to work. It's her script. To smear me.*

The program cut to an interview with a white-haired doctor in a lab coat, and under his dour face the caption: Dr. Robert Mosbacher, Chief Coroner, Fairbanks. "Autopsies of the two teens show a high level of alcohol in the blood of both. The cause of death for the female was drowning, perhaps related to incapacitation from alcohol. For the male, death by rifle wound, self-inflicted."

Miguel's off-camera voice asked, "No indication of mental breakdown due to electromagnetic interference?"

The coroner made a face of disdain. "I don't know how that would manifest itself, and I doubt such a thing could even occur. Certainly, I saw no evidence of any chemical neurological imbalance. Of course, alcohol can produce severe depression."

Mike was livid. The whole slant was, *A couple of Indians got drunk and killed themselves; what's new?* He clicked to the competing local station, Channel 8, and was startled to see Jacob Porteous talking. "The University of Alaska's Geophysical Institute has enjoyed a harmonious and productive collaboration with HARC which has brought the U of A international acclaim. I earnestly hope that the psychological problems of one man will not jeopardize the advances which our top research team at the Institute—"

Christ, Jacob, you wouldn't even *have* a team if it

weren't for me. He clicked again. ". . . and here at the Chamber of Commerce we're concerned it would severely impact the local economy. The HARC project provides needed income to so many of our residents. If HARC closes, it'll throw an awful lot of good people out of work. That's—"

Click. Governor Dainard in the capital, Juneau: ". . . absolutely safe. More than safe—HARC represents future security for Alaska. It is my hope, and my belief, that success with this fine research venture will lead to more joint projects with the federal Department of Defense and the Department of Energy, bringing even more top-level jobs and high-tech industry to our great state. As you know, I have long envisioned—"

"Shit, Mike, this is bad," Wayne said quietly, watching. "They've really got their act together."

Mike's mouth was dry as canvas. "It's Carol. She lined them up." This was her specialty, supplying PR videos to TV stations. They invariably ran them since it was free fodder, and easier than doing coverage themselves. Now, just as the local stations were scrambling to cover the HARC story, she'd supplied these interviews. The perfect smear campaign.

Wayne gave a low whistle of dismay. "Did I say she was busting your balls? Looks like she means to cut 'em *off.* And I'd say she just bagged one."

Mike felt a rage he'd never known before. *How could she do this to me?*

Then he felt fear . . . as though the earth had lost its solidity beneath his feet. Everything he'd risked by going public had been for nothing. *Ben will go ahead.*

"What's this mean for HARC?" Wayne asked nervously. "Mike? What now?"

Got to tell the truth. The whole truth. Tell them *Ben's agenda.* "Hit back," he said.

But how? Sunday night, who could he call? He didn't know any reporters. Crazily, he envied Carol's rapport with these people. She so conscientiously curried their favor, whether in Boston, Washington, or Fairbanks—remembered their spouses' names, congratulated them on promotions, took them out for drinks. Mike didn't know anybody.

Reid D'Alton, he thought—he has media contacts. He grabbed his cell phone and called D'Alton's office. No answer. Was he with Dana? Mike hated calling her house. But rage and fear were telling him: *Get the truth out tonight. Stop Ben.*

Dana answered his phone call. "Mike? My God, are you watching?"

▲

"Are these books of Aunt Carla's going?"

No answer. Lucas, on his knees, looked up from the piles of stuff he was sorting in his uncle's messy cabin, but Thomas, sitting on the edge of the bed, went on staring in silence at old photographs in his lap. Lucas sat back on his heels, exasperated. The village airlift was tomorrow, and he'd been trying all afternoon to organize his uncle. But Thomas hadn't packed or made any preparations for leaving, and the effort of doing it for him had left Lucas worn out. Not that he wasn't glad to be finally up and around. On Friday his mom had got him out of the hospital past that swarm of reporters, and dropped him off here before she flew back to Fairbanks, and after two days of resting in Takona he felt a lot better. Everything was awkward with his left arm in the cast, though, and his bruised face sure wasn't going to win any beauty contests. But his uncle needed his help. Anyway, he *had* to get Thomas organized, because he was going with him. Lucas had decided that last night. Though he hadn't told Thomas yet. Or his mom.

He tried again. "Uncle Thomas? These books. Going, or garbage?"

"Leave 'em. Leave everything."

"Come on, you'll need *some* stuff. Clothes, tools—"

"Don't want nothin'." Thomas grabbed his rifle propped at the foot of the bed, picked up a rag, and began to clean the barrel. "Got all I need right here."

Lucas groaned inside, and moved on to the cardboard boxes of clothes. "Well, I'm putting these shirts and jeans in the 'going' pile."

"Leave it *all*, I said." Thomas got to his feet to grab a can of gun oil, and the photos spilled from his lap to the floor. Lucas glimpsed one, of Thomas and Aunt Carla readying their dog team in the snow. Must have been taken years ago, because Ron was a baby on his mother's back, just a blanket bundle topped by a little face with cold-reddened cheeks. Looking at his uncle, Lucas felt such a hard sadness. Thomas had lost Aunt Carla in the spring, now Ron. He was all alone.

But he didn't look beaten, and that made Lucas kind of proud. He'd always looked up to his uncle. Thomas was a great shot, a skilled hunter, and as upset as he was about Ron, he still looked strong, looked together. Lucas remembered his mom once saying that she and Aunt Carla both had a crush on Thomas when they were teens, and it was easy to see why. The powerful body, rugged face, thick black brush cut—it's where Ron had got his movie-star good looks. Lucas admired the way Thomas had provided for his family by hunting and trapping and fishing, just taking the odd job downriver in Hanley for a little cash, like on the road construction this summer. It seemed now to Lucas the best way a man could live—at home in the place where he belonged.

That's why he'd made his decision. He would drop out of his senior year in Fairbanks and live with his uncle in the new village. What could school teach him anymore? He'd learned all he needed this week: Don't trust the white man, and stick with your own. You could get too educated for your own good. Like Mike. To hell with school.

It was going to be hard to tell his mother. She wanted him to help her people but live in the white world too, like she did. But who was she to criticize? Who was *she* helping? She'd all of a sudden dropped her fight against the village relocation, just like that. She was becoming more white all the time. And she was going to marry that lawyer, D'Alton. It gave Lucas the creeps.

He lay awake these days wondering what it would have been like to marry Sophy and live here. He would have taken care of her, the way Thomas had taken care of his family. Would have made Sophy's life easier. A man had to make a choice, Lucas knew that now—had to live in one world or the other. His mother wasn't going to understand, but she didn't know how he'd felt about Sophy. Lucas had such nightmares about her, reliving those terrible moments on the bluff. In his dreams he tried over and over to smother the fire he'd felt for her. Tried again and again to stop her from jumping. From plunging into that cold river. With her mind messed up, she'd suffered and drowned . . . *been* drowned, by HARC.

Lucas hated HARC. Wished he could wipe it off the face of the earth. It made him sick to think that he'd actually worked there, helped it kill Sophy. Helped Mike. He'd caught a radio report of him going public about what HARC had done and saying it should be closed. *A little late, Mike.* It didn't stop the nightmares about Sophy. Or stop his uncle brooding about Ron. Quite a pair, the two of us, Lucas thought. The only good thing about the horror of it all was that it had brought him back to Takona. Wherever his people went, Lucas was going with them.

"Better feed the dogs," he said. Thomas's sled team was supposed to get a meal now, then nothing until the tranquilizers for the flight in the morning, blue pills the vet had left.

Thomas didn't answer, so Lucas went outside alone. The rain had stopped. In the evening sunshine a rainbow arched above the forest behind the village, and the smell of soaked earth was fresh and pungent. The dogs, lying in the wet grass, chained to their stakes, eyed Lucas with hopeful curiosity as he came among them.

"Where's Thomas?" a gruff voice asked.

Lucas turned. It was Archie Paul, Sophy's dad. A little unsteady on his feet, he stood too close, as drunks will, a tic twitching his cheek, the sweet stink of bourbon on his breath. Takona had been dry ever since Lucas's mom had persuaded the council to vote for prohibition, but everybody knew that Archie went downriver to Hanley to drink. Tonight though, he had a bottle in his hand, and Lucas was startled by the open defiance. Still, he could only feel pity. Archie had lost both daughters in one week. First little Francie, then Sophy. Like Thomas, he had no one left.

"Where's he got to?" Archie asked. "I got business with him."

"Inside."

"Right here." Thomas appeared at the cabin doorway.

"All set," Archie told him, as if making a report. "Enough shells for us both. I'll be there. Okay?"

Thomas said nothing, but the two men exchanged a conspiratorial nod that sent a dart of suspicion into Lucas. Shells? What were they up to?

Archie shuffled away, drinking from his bottle. It seemed to Lucas that there was something on edge about the whole village tonight, like electricity, as though everyone's nervousness about tomorrow's move had burned the air. It was after ten, getting close to dusk, but everybody seemed frantically busy. A couple in the cabin behind Thomas's were arguing loudly about whether to pack some old cooking pot. An old man sat muttering on his cabin stoop as his children and grandchildren hustled past him carrying out bulging boxes and plastic bags, then went back in, bumping him. Even the kids' voices at the pinball machines over at the store sounded too excited, hyper. The usual peace in Takona seemed to be disintegrating, as though people knew their old life had already disappeared. It made Lucas mad at his mother again. Why had she let this happen?

Thomas came and joined him, and the dogs leaped up at his approach. He opened his fist, and Lucas saw he'd brought a handful of the blue tranquilizers. "I'm supposed to shut down their brains with these." Thomas looked at the lead bitch. "I trained her to *use* her brain. Hell, why don't they just give us *all* tranquilizers." He threw the pills, scattering them far in the tall grass. "Leave these dogs be," he told Lucas. "They're not goin' nowhere."

Lucas stared at him. "You're not leaving. That's it, isn't it? You're staying!" He was shocked . . . but also impressed. Thomas was going to defy the relocation. And Archie was with him. It suddenly seemed stupendous to Lucas, a grand gesture. Thomas was taking a stand.

Then it hit him that the empty village would be burned once everyone had been flown out. That had been made clear: it was to prevent squatters. State troopers would enforce the evacuation, and fire marshals would come a few days later to direct the razing. So even if Thomas and Archie successfully hid out, how long could the two of them survive, with nothing left here?

"Tomorrow, when Dana comes for you," Thomas said, watching the dogs, "you get out of here with her. Leave us be, me and Archie. Everybody, just leave us be."

"But what'll you do if they come with guns?"

"Do what we have to. We got guns too."

Lucas was stunned. Surely the two of them didn't think they could *hold off* the troopers.

Thomas turned to him. "I'm asking you, Lucas, man to man, don't tell your mother. She wouldn't understand. But I think maybe you do. After what happened to Ron. To Sophy." He was looking Lucas straight in the eye. "This is the place my ancestors chose. This is where Carla's buried, and my son. This is home. Damn right I'm going to stay."

As Lucas watched him go back into the cabin, the strength drained from his legs. He did understand: Thomas and Archie didn't *care* how long they survived. He felt a terrible struggle inside. He'd meant to live with his uncle to *help* him, but not this way. Thomas was trusting him to keep his secret . . . but what he was planning was suicide.

Lucas dropped to his knees and looked into the lead husky's eyes. What should he do?

▲

Dana looked aghast. "Why didn't you tell us this before?"

"A weapon that violates the Anti-Ballistic Missile Treaty?" D'Alton said, "and you kept the information to yourself?"

"*That's* why Crewe wanted Takona moved," Dana went on, anger in her face as the truth dawned. "Get rid of the Indians, cordon off the whole area, so the moment

HARC becomes a classified military operation, nobody gets near it. That was the idea, wasn't it, Mike? That was it *all along*."

Her words hit him like blows. They stood in D'Alton's office—the lawyer had been at Dana's house when Mike had called, and they'd agreed to meet here, and Mike had started telling them about the secret weapon plan while D'Alton was still switching on lights. Now, they both stared at him in shock. "I'm sorry, Dana," he said. "I only found out myself five days ago."

"Sorry? The airlift is *tomorrow*. Lucas is out there right now, helping people pack, for God's sake. To leave their homes *forever*."

"I know." There was nothing he could do about that. He still hadn't told them about the money and Carol's part in it, either. Her father was the enemy he had to stop. "Call your media contacts, D'Alton. Get them over here. I'll tell them everything."

"Oh, *now* you'll tell them everything."

"Damn it, Reid, let's get started," Dana said, reaching for the address book on his desk. "This changes everything. Everyone will see now that Crewe has to be stopped."

"Don't be so sure."

"Who do we call first, D'Alton?" Mike asked. "You have a handle on this."

"Neither of you get it, do you?" D'Alton plowed a nervous hand through his hair. "Look, I'm just a lawyer. These people are public relations *pros*. Led by your wife, Ryder, the PR queen. They've attacked your credibility with everything they've got, painted you as disturbed, unstable, even dangerous—and, most important, *wrong*. We're stuck with having to defend and protest. I don't know who'll listen to us now."

"Well, we can't just roll over," Dana said, punching numbers on the desk phone. "Anyway, how can the press not want to hear the awful truth about Crewe's real agenda? It's not just news, it's a scandal. I'm getting them over here, now."

"And I'll set the lies straight," Mike said.

D'Alton gave him a scornful look. "Have you ever watched a jury? Guilty until proven innocent, that's what's in their hearts and minds. 'The police wouldn't have picked him up if he hadn't done something wrong.' 'Where there's smoke there's fire.' People don't think rationally about these things, there's a vacuum in their minds and it gets filled by whatever information's injected first. Oh, I know you blew the whistle first, but that was such a screwup, you keeping in the background, and when you finally did speak out you gave such a low-key statement you looked downright suspicious. Now, Crewe and your wife have blasted back with both barrels, got their message out that you're nuts, that the dead kids were losers, and that HARC is safe. It'll be almost impossible to reverse the squalid images they've created—an unbalanced man, his bastard half-breed son, alcohol-induced suicides. Now you want to tell people, 'Oh, by the way, the general, my father-in-law, has cooked up a paranoid military plot'? Ryder, if you'd come forward with the whole truth at the beginning they couldn't have ambushed us like this. But now . . ." He shook his head.

Mike was fed up with D'Alton's attitude. And his lectures. He looked at Dana, talking on the phone to some reporter, her back turned. She may hate my guts, he thought, but at least she's with me. "People will listen," he told D'Alton, "because, damn it, I'm the authority on this."

"Oh? Did you watch Channel 5's news special to the end?" D'Alton pulled a video cassette from his briefcase and stuck it in the VCR. "I taped it at Dana's." After some rewind jockeying, he hit the play button, and Mike was startled to see Karl Yuill, dean of MIT's physics department.

"Yes, Dr. Ryder was brought before a disciplinary committee hearing on a charge of publishing with fraudulent data. This was, oh, five years ago, when he was an associate professor here, but I vividly recall the circumstances, because he was a brilliant researcher and we'd expected great things from him. But academic fraud is a grave offense . . ." The picture cut to the news anchor who started talking about "scientists who lose their way."

Livid, Mike turned to D'Alton. "I collaborated on that paper with a partner, Meredith Crosbie. The fraudulent data was hers."

"Ah, yes, the great physicist herself." D'Alton fast-forwarded, again hit play, and Mike saw Meredith in the HARC control room, calm and confident as people on his team quietly worked around her. Superimposed below, her name was followed by: "Lead Scientist, High-frequency Auroral Research Center." She turned to the camera and said, "I'm very proud of our world-class ionospheric research facility, and I have hopes that it will one day enhance global communications for both civilian and defense systems. But please remember that our sole function is research—we merely study the properties and behavior of the ionosphere. As for the high-frequency energy we transmit during our studies, much of the signal passes right through the ionosphere and travels into space where it disperses. Even before that, the intensity of the signal is tens of thousands of times less than the sun's natural electromagnetic radiation reaching the earth. Actually, it's hard to see what danger HARC *could* pose. A resonance event? Deadly low-frequency radiation?" She shook her head. "It saddens me, because Mike Ryder is a distinguished colleague and I hate to comment negatively—especially when he's suffering psychological distress. But I must categorically state that his theories are scientifically impossible."

Mike was staggered. Meredith was the responsible researcher . . . he was the crackpot! The smear was complete. Carol had covered every base.

"It's worse than we thought," Dana said as she hung up. "The CBS stringer and both radio stations say they're not interested, they've got all they need on Mike. Don Ichimura at the *Anchorage Daily News* just gave me a hint why. He's a friend, did a story last year on me and Aurora Aviation. He said his editor warned him to back off Mike's message because they're afraid of a defamation suit from HARC. They're nervous that people might claim to be victims of the accident and demand damages, and cite the paper's reports as evidence."

D'Alton groaned. "They're right."

"No," Mike said, "they're being strong-armed by Ben Crewe."

"Same thing."

Mike was furious. D'Alton was caving in. "*I'll* talk to them," he said, grabbing the address book and the phone.

He tried three numbers. The reporters' initial cool reserve changed when he told them about Ben's antiballistic weapon plan, but it was far from the change he wanted. Two were openly scornful, the third dismissive, his tone clearly saying, Don't waste my time. Mike realized they didn't believe a word.

"My turn," D'Alton said, reluctantly taking the phone.

Dana turned to Mike. "What about testimonials? Getting people with credentials to back you up. Scientists."

It was a good idea. The people on his team had not only worked with him for years; he'd gotten most of them grants and promotions. Carol might have the media in her pocket, but he had the solidarity of his colleagues, which would count for a lot. On his cell phone he reached his two senior scientists at home. Bjorn Halveg was flustered, said he couldn't talk about it, "had to run." Roger Donelly was openly critical: "Can't possibly support you, Mike, when I believe you've made an enormous error."

He didn't waste time arguing. He tried Gina DalBello. Not home. He reached her at HARC, working late. She was hesitant, sounded torn—said she wished she could help, and did have a nagging doubt about that negative impedance spike. "But Dr. Crosbie's got us all under review, and hell, Mike, I can't afford to lose this job."

Gina bailing—that threw him. He'd been her mentor.

"Finally, good news," D'Alton said, holding up the phone. "I've got Rosemary O'Neil on hold. She does Channel 5's *Alaska in the Morning,* and she says she'll come right over. Wants the 'human angle,' whatever that means. Her show is fluff, but she says she'll air the story on tomorrow's program."

"Yes!" Dana said, triumphant.

Mike found himself grinning in relief. "Fluff or not, I'll do it. It'll break the full story, that's what matters."

"Not you," D'Alton said. "That's O'Neil's only condition—she's asking for Dana. Personally, I think it's a good idea. You're damaged goods, Ryder. I'm not even sure we have a chance as it is, but we certainly won't with you. Dana's got great credibility—hometown girl, entrepreneur, respected physician. Beautiful, too, which doesn't hurt. I vote yes."

At the "respected physician," Mike caught Dana's glance at him. He kept his face neutral, and she quickly looked back at D'Alton and said, "I'm willing."

Mike hated the idea of hiding in the background again, sending Dana to do battle for him. It was just a variation of their first, botched whistle-blowing, and he wasn't going to repeat that mistake. "If Dana does it she'll be stuck in the same trap as before. 'Who's your source?' this woman will ask. I may as well demand to be heard right at the start."

"And say what?" D'Alton challenged. "That your apocalyptic scenario, which nobody believes, wasn't quite weird enough, so now you want to rat on your own father-in-law, a revered Marine general, and accuse him of treaty-violating subversion? Raving scientist turns malicious? We want a *sympathetic* reaction, Ryder, not hate calls."

Rosemary O'Neil was a skinny redhead in a purple power suit. Young, early twenties, Mike figured, which was maybe why she was hungrier for the story than her colleagues. But her smile seemed genuine, and when she graciously thanked Dana for agreeing to the interview, Mike began to hope. O'Neil marshaled her video crew of three as they set up lights, positioned the camera, and clipped a microphone on Dana's shirt, while Mike stood in the shadows with D'Alton.

O'Neil began the interview. "Dr. James, you made an extraordinary announcement two days ago about HARC, and I understand you want to make another."

"Yes, I've just learned some very alarming information. General Benson Crewe of the Office of Naval Research, which funds HARC, plans to make HARC an antiballistic weapons system. This is in direct violation of our country's international arms agreements. General Crewe has been planning it in secret for years, and that's why he intends to push ahead with HARC, despite Dr. Michael Ryder's explanation of the terrible danger of another resonance event."

"Then you believe Dr. Ryder's warnings?"

"Certainly."

"You appear to be alone."

Mike bristled, but kept quiet. Dana was getting out the facts, that's what mattered.

"But even if the danger didn't exist," Dana went on, "I'm outraged, as a citizen, by what General Crewe is planning. It's illegal, and it's immoral."

"Where did you get this information?"

"A reliable source close to General Crewe."

"Mike Ryder?"

"A reliable source."

O'Neil changed tack. "Aren't you nervous about making unsubstantiated allegations about a respected general?" She added with a sympathetic smile, "I hope you've consulted a lawyer."

"The facts will bear me out. General Crewe has a private agenda that must be stopped."

"You're brave to say so." O'Neil went on in her friendly manner, "Actually, it's your bravery that fascinates me. I'm interested in you, your personal story. For example, your relationship with Mike Ryder. How did that come about, and how did it end?"

Red flags went up in Mike's mind. *What the hell does this have to do with anything?*

Dana looked uncomfortable. "I'd rather leave my private life private."

"I understand. But your private life with Mike Ryder has a bearing on the claims you're making, don't you think? After all, he's the father of your sixteen-year-old son, the boy Ryder claims was mentally affected by HARC's so-called resonance event. You must agree that people have a right to know what's going on."

Dana hesitated. "Nothing's . . . 'going on.' Look, I want to talk about General Crewe, about HARC."

"Of course, but HARC was Mike Ryder's project, and you have been a well-known opponent of that project, and understandably of Ryder too—not only as HARC's creator, but as the man who abandoned you when you were pregnant sixteen years ago, leaving you to bring up your son alone. Now, he's turned against his friends at HARC, including General Crewe, and suddenly, out of the blue, you're supporting him. Dr. James, do you defend his accusations because you hate HARC so much, or is it because you're still in love with Mike Ryder?"

Dana stilled like a doe caught in headlights.

Mike was about to barge forward to speak, when Dana suddenly said, "You're wrong about Mike. He's a caring father . . . and a principled scientist. I have total trust in his judgment." She hurried on, "And it's incredibly important that his message be heard. Please, I'm urging everyone in Alaska—demand an inquiry into General Crewe's secret goal for HARC, and demand that HARC be closed before he causes a disaster."

O'Neil said, "His secret goal. Okay, let's talk about that."

For the next few minutes they did. Dana presented the facts calmly and carefully, and O'Neil asked no more egregious personal questions. O'Neil wrapped up the interview, and as her crew began packing, she came over to Mike. "Dr. Ryder, you seem to be a decent guy. Sorry about that personal stuff."

"Guess it's your job. Doesn't matter, as long as the facts get out."

"My job. Well, yes." She was studying him, her head cocked to one side, as if wondering whether to go on. "You really don't know what's happening, do you? Oh, boy. Look, let me give you a heads-up. My boss sent me to get Dana James's reaction on tape about your personal relationship, especially about your son. *Only* that. I didn't get much—she's a tough nut to crack. Anyway, the rest, all that conspiracy stuff about General Crewe?" She made a gesture of dismissal. "I seriously doubt whether a word of that will make it out of the editing room."

In a flash, Mike saw the truth. *"You're a fool,"* Carol had said . . . and he suddenly saw how much of a fool. This was how war was waged in the public trenches, and this was how it felt to go down. Cut off at the knees, he couldn't strike a single blow, or even make himself be heard. And Dana was going to twist in the wind for his misjudgment, his errors.

"Forget it." He started for the door. He would stop Ben himself. And he knew how he had to do it.

▲

Reaching the boat, he went below to Wayne. "Can you get me inside the site?"

Wayne looked up from the bench where he was torquing down screws on a generator plate. His eyes widened in astonishment. "You mean now?"

"Has to be now. It's Sunday, so there's just the security staff and a few people working late. And tomorrow you have to hand in your keys. Tonight's my only chance."

Now that he'd decided, he felt excited. After days of passivity, sitting and waiting for the next punch, it felt good to be readying an attack. He'd thought it through. Since Carol and Ben had joined forces he couldn't win this war, not as they were waging it. They had the troops and all the heavy guns. He'd have to become a revolutionary. And his target was HARC itself. That brought a pang. He'd never intended his creation to hurt anyone, only to do good—he'd had such dreams for HARC. But Ben and Meredith had subverted it, turned it into a monster. Now, he would have to kill the monster.

Wayne's expression had become wary. "What did you have in mind?"

Energized though he was, Mike was also more afraid than he'd ever been. If he failed, if Ben cut him down this time, there would be no way to prevent a catastrophe. No escape, he thought, for any of us. *So, I can't fail.*

"Sabotage," he said. "Through the computer system. HARC's own brain is going to program suicide."

Sunday, 11 P.M.

CAROL COULDN'T BEAR it another moment. Reaching past her father as he stood grimly watching the video, she punched the stop button. It froze a close-up frame of Dana James's face, which for Carol was almost worse. Dana James condemning Dad . . . defending Mike. The producer of *Alaska in the Morning,* a friend, had couriered the whole uncut video to Carol as a favor, with a note telling her that the interview, taped just hours before, would air tomorrow, Monday. Carol had brought it to her father in the Fairbanks observation center he was preparing for the VIPs; the interior wasn't finished yet, and electricians and carpenters and technicians were working around them in a din of drilling and hammering. Carol felt cold and miserable. Her shoes were soaked from puddles as she'd run in from her car. Paint fumes inflamed the headache she'd had for two days, ever since Mike had left the house—she didn't even know where he was. And now this frozen video image of Dana James.

She felt the edges of her professionalism fraying. She wasn't sure how much more she could take.

She longed for her father's guidance, his strength. His expression was determined, as always, but Carol noticed lines of anxiety at the edges of his eyes. That frightened her more than anything. "Dad . . . is Litvak going to get us?"

He turned fierce eyes on her, took her by the elbow and led her into an office, away from the workmen, and shut the door. "Don't *ever* speak of this in front of others."

Carol had never seen him so nervous. It meant he feared the worst. Her legs went weak. This can't be happening, she thought wildly. Not to me, my family. This happens to *other* people . . . bad people, stupid people. She saw the future like an avalanche rolling to smother her. Disgrace, ruin, arrest. Prison . . . strip searches . . . rape. "Oh, God," she cried, "I'll never live through it!"

He gripped her shoulders. "Stop this."

She was shaking. Dad had failed . . . and her heart was crying out, *What went wrong?* All she'd ever wanted was to create *success*—for Mike, for Dad, for everyone. The weapon was Dad's dream, and HARC was supposed to make Mike happy, make a secure future for him, for her, for Lindsay. How could that be *wrong* of her? Yet somehow she'd lost Mike . . . and she and Dad were under attack. "I've lost everything . . . lost Mike . . . and if—"

"Mike *betrayed* you. Isn't that obvious? This woman has some hold over him, and he's told her everything. He's informed on us, *knowing* it will destroy us. Carol, he sold you out!"

It was true. But the voice inside her wailed, *Why?* What had pushed Mike to lose touch with reality, to lash out against his family, to desert her? She snatched at her father's words. *"This woman has some hold over him."* That's it. Mike made this terrible choice because of Dana James. She'd manipulated him, changed him. Moments ago Carol had looked into that Indian face, eyes wide at the question, "Are you still in love with Mike Ryder?" No reply, just a stunned pause, but Carol knew the answer. *She loves him. She means to have him.*

"Carol, stick with me in this fight. I can't do it without you." Her father's hands went to either side of her head, and he held her face close to his own, his eyes locked on hers. His grip was unyielding, and the very strength of it, the security, began to steady Carol.

"We're alone in this, you and me," he said. "We're the only ones who understand the stakes, not just for ourselves, but for the defense of this country. We alone had the courage, the nerve, to do what had to be done. It's up to us. We've got to stick together, and if we do, if we fight back—with your expertise—we can still win."

A ferocious new energy surged through her. I *will* fight back. *I won't lose Mike.* "You're right," she said. "I can wipe out Dana James."

"Yes." He hugged her.

Carol pulled free, her mind already on the task. The small office they'd come into was so new that the desk chair was still wrapped in plastic, but there was a working phone. She called the suite in the Princess Hotel, her war room, where her assistants were working. "Miguel, dig up all you can on Dr. Dana James. She's too good to be true, and that usually means something's a lie. Drop everything else. I need dirt ASAP." Hanging up, she almost smiled. She'd hated engineering the smear campaign against Mike, but *this* one would be sheer pleasure.

"The interview," her father said. "Do you need me to call my lawyers to get it pulled?"

She shook her head. "I know the producer—he'll edit out the references to you. He'll know he's on thin legal ice if he plays such defamatory accusations." She was almost sure that what the producer had gone after was a titillating slant on Mike's personal past: getting an Indian girl pregnant and abandoning her and his son. It made Carol squirm, but it was toothless content. "I'd better get to work."

As she started back through the main room, her father came after her. "Carol, wait." He spoke quietly, though the din of the workmen around them made it impossible for anyone to overhear. "I have no doubt you'll manage this expertly, but there's still a danger that this thing could escalate. I won't take any chances, not now when we're so close to the end. I'm moving up the demonstration."

She was surprised. The demonstration was scheduled for Thursday, four days away. "To when?"

"Tuesday."

She glanced at the workmen. This observation room was a scaled-down replica of the Pentagon's National Military Command Center, optimal surroundings to impress the men from Washington, and no expense was being spared. The giant screen would display real-time depiction of HARC's actual satellite "kill": a Hollywood computer animation outfit, consulting with a Navy satellite expert, was preparing the special effects. Yet, if all went well, this room would be dismantled the moment the demonstration achieved its goal, and then all operations would be confined to the HARC site eighty miles away, hidden behind Marine-patrolled razor wire. "Can everything be ready in time?" she asked.

"Crosbie's already ahead of schedule. I know Graham Sloan will rearrange his schedule. Can you manage the change in our other guests' agendas? On Tuesday we must be good to go."

Carol felt a shiver of excitement. Nothing was going to stop Dad. "Kaplan's on holiday in Oregon, but he's very keen—I think I can get him. Secretary Montcrief's agenda may be harder to interrupt, but I'll do my best." Sloan and Kaplan—the chairman of the Joint Chiefs and the national security adviser—were key. Montcrief, the secretary of defense, could be briefed after the fact.

"Good." He called for his car, and they stepped outside together. It was eleven but not quite dark, the dusk of near-midnight in Alaskan summer. Carol couldn't wait to get back to the East Coast world she knew, with days that ended properly in dark nights. Back to civilization. As her father walked her to her car, he said, "There's something that might help you with Dr. James. The deal we made was that she would agree to the village move if HARC endowed a clinic in the new location. I gave her a substantial sum. Could you somehow use that against her?"

"Gave it directly to her? Not to the village council?"

"To her. I wanted to avoid publicity about it until the move was completed, so I asked her not to speak of it until then. That's my point. Because she agreed to keep silent, I doubt she deposited the check into an account that other council members had access to. Too many questions. I imagine you'll find it went into a business or personal account of her own."

Carol quickly saw how to make it work. "She's a leader on her village council, yet this money, meant for the welfare of her people, ended up in her account? Yes, I can use that." She opened her car door, then looked at him. "How much?"

"Three million."

For the first time in days Carol's headache began to subside. "Enough to hang her."

▲

"I'll need another piece of photo ID, sir," the guard at the HARC gate told Wayne.

Listening, Mike lay inside the coffin-sized toolbox in the back of Wayne's Chevy pickup. Coffin-sized for somebody shorter, maybe—he was crammed up in it. Ralph, the former night watchman, would have waved Wayne through, no questions, but Ben had brought in a new private security outfit, preparing for HARC's delivery into military hands, so Mike had climbed into the emptied toolbox a mile back. Now, chin pressed against his chest, he strained to listen through the galvanized steel.

"What, you don't like my smiling mug on my HARC

ID?" Wayne cracked. When the guard didn't answer, Wayne's tone hardened. "You're new, buddy. I'm the maintenance foreman here."

"You're terminated tomorrow, sir. That's what's on my manifest."

"Yeah, well, tomorrow isn't for another half hour, and I've got stuff to clear out of my desk."

"At midnight?"

"Hey, no time's a good time to leave love letters lying around. Jeez, what if somebody sent them to my house. Give me the half hour, you'll be saving my old lady a lot of grief. And saving my sorry ass, too."

Mike thought it was an inspired bit of bullshit, but the guard repeated stonily, "Another piece of ID, sir."

Mike prayed Wayne could rustle up the proof. He had to get into the control room. The computer disk in his shirt pocket held all his hopes. Using Wayne's laptop, he'd written a subroutine to upload onto the HARC program, changes so subtle that Meredith wouldn't notice. When she and Ben launched their demonstration, the system would crash: Ben's mighty new weapon would prove a dud. But to achieve that, Mike had to access his terminal in the control room: it had an administrator access level, allowing the user to write code to HARC's systems programs. Five minutes to upload the subroutine, that's all I need, he thought as he lay still, hardly daring to breathe. That is, if the systems manager hasn't changed the passwords, and if I can get in without being stopped. *If . . . if.* The odds seemed more impossible the longer he waited, praying this by-the-book sentry wouldn't open the box, call out the dogs, call Ben . . .

"Twenty minutes, sir," the guard said grudgingly. "After that, you must hand in your keys and depart the installation."

"Thanks, buddy." Wayne gunned the truck, and Mike bounced and banged inside the box `as they raced up the gravel road. When Wayne swung a hard left, Mike's head and knee whacked the side. The truck stopped. Mike pushed up the lid a crack and looked out. They'd come to the back of the ops center where there was a single back door. No one around. He climbed out. Wayne got out too, pulling off his worn blue rain jacket. He handed it over, along with his yellow hard hat, and Mike put them on. He only had to create a general impression, to look like Wayne from a distance. He wasn't sure what he'd do if anyone got close, but with any luck he'd be in and out before that could happen. Luck . . . how he hated relying on something so uncontrollable.

"I got a look up at the control room as we drove past," Wayne said. "The window was dark. Looks good." He used his keys to open the back door, then glanced at his watch. "Seventeen minutes, Mike. I'll be here."

Mike hurried up the back stairs, then took one corridor after another, heading for the control room. He didn't see anyone, even in the offices he passed. Then, just outside the control room, he spotted a security guard sitting at the far end of the corridor, flipping through a magazine. Beefy guy, pencil mustache, holstered sidearm. Mike ducked into the control room. It was dark, like Wayne said—which meant empty, thank God. In the gloom, he switched on his terminal. The monitor cast its blue light on him, making him feel exposed. He slipped

the disk out of his pocket . . . waited for the system to
boot. His eye fell on the crayon drawing of Lindsay's
that he'd taped to the ionosonde monitor. A kid's vision
of HARC's bright future: sun beaming through a rainbow over a lush irrigated field . . . *"Daddy's Dream."* A
longing to hang on to that dream made him snatch the
drawing, stuff it in his jeans pocket.

"Mike? Is that you?"

He twisted around. Gina lay on the couch by the window, propped up on one elbow, squinting as though she
were waking up, her hair mussed. "It *is* you." She looked
bewildered. "What are you doing here?"

He was still holding the disk. Could he insert it and
input the command before she saw? He glanced back at
the screen. The machine was still booting. "Catch you
napping, Gina?" he asked, forcing casualness, feeling
the seconds take forever. "They're working you too
hard."

She got up off the couch and started toward him.
"Seems you're working late too." Suspicion in her voice.

She reached his side. Her nose stud glinted in the
monitor light. "Make them let you rest, Gina," Mike
said. "You know you need it." She had a history of
epilepsy. Medication kept her condition under control,
plus a strict regimen of rest.

Her mouth curved in a smile. "I will, Mom."

The computer had booted. Mike logged on. No access
changes—he was in. He felt light-headed with relief.
"Just want to verify our data about that test, Gina. Maybe
I was hasty. I've got to know if I'm right or wrong." He
hoped that would satisfy her. But she was staring at the

disk in his hand. Whatever . . . he was committed now. He reached across to slip the disk into the computer, but before he could insert it, the guard said at the doorway, "Problem here?"

Mike froze, cursing under his breath.

"Sir, I don't recall you signing in with me." It was a clear accusation as the guard walked in. Mike lowered the disk to hide it.

"Stop right there," the guard said, hand on his sidearm. "Could I see some ID, please?"

"Sure, no problem. It's over there in my coat." Mike indicated a couple of orphan jackets on a rack by the door. Getting up, he slipped the disk back in his shirt pocket and threw a look at Gina, a silent entreaty not to give him away. Her wide-eyed expression told him nothing. He could only hope their friendship still meant something. He started for the door.

"You wore a coat over *that*?" the guard said, frowning at the bulky rain jacket Mike had on.

Mike was already at the door. He stepped out into the corridor. Then ran.

"Stop!" the guard called.

Mike ran on, heart pounding, expecting a bullet any second to rip into his back. He heard the guard running heavily after him. "Stop!" Then the thudding footsteps stopped. Mike didn't waste time looking back. He veered into the hallway and almost collided with Wayne.

"Crewe just drove up, Mike. Let's get the hell out."

They reached the back stairs and bolted down. Bursting outside, Wayne got into the truck cab and Mike jumped onto the flatbed. Wayne gunned it and they roared down the gravel drive. Mike hung on as he opened the toolbox, about to climb in again, then looked back. No one was following. But somebody might if Wayne kept driving like a maniac. He slid open the cab window between them. "Slow down, no one's coming."

"Because they'll alert the gate. That's procedure," Wayne called back, eyes ahead, foot to the floor. "We gotta get past our buddy before he gets the call. Hide."

That's why the guard stopped chasing, Mike realized—to call. He looked at the road ahead. The gatehouse was just visible in the gloom beyond Wayne's headlights. The guard *had* to have called by now. The guy at the gate would search the truck. They'd never get past . . . not together. Alone, Wayne might have a chance.

"Stop!" Mike said. As Wayne braked, Mike hopped out. "As far as this guy at the gate knows, you arrived solo and you're leaving solo. Give him your song and dance and tell him you didn't see anything. Meet me on the access road up by the three boulders." He turned to go.

"Mike! Did you do the upload?"

"No."

"Shit." The truck roared off.

Mike started toward the forest wall that rimmed the site. He didn't know if Ben's new razor-wire perimeter had been completed, and it was dark enough that, in that bush, he'd wish he had a flashlight. But he knew the general topography—he'd built this place. Getting through and reaching the road was his only way out: there was wilderness all around. As the red glow of Wayne's tail-lights disappeared, he ran toward the dark trees.

▲

"He had on a blue jacket and yellow hard hat. I believe he's still somewhere on-site, General. None of the vehicles is missing, and the gate reports that no one's gone out but a Wayne Hingerman, the former maintenance manager, came by to clean out his desk and drop off his keys. The perp can't get far. We'll find him, sir."

"He's gone, Lieutenant. With Hingerman." Ben was seething as he stood looking out the control room's wall of windows, trying to detect any motion at the boundary line. Lieutenant—he'd used this ex-cop's former title with the Anchorage PD, but he wanted to call the man an idiot. He ran the new security outfit and had let Mike slip away. *Just thirty-six hours to go*, Ben told himself, gritting his teeth. Then he could turn the site over to professional soldiers, men not afraid to shoot. If he saw Mike now, he swore he'd pull the trigger himself.

He felt a jab of remorse. Pull the trigger? This was *Mike* . . . once, as close to him as a son. Now, enemies. His hands balled into fists at his sides. Mike had become a menace. It was getting harder to fend off his attacks. Things were falling apart . . . *Can we hold out for thirty-six hours?*

He heard Crosbie, behind him, typing at the terminal where the guard had discovered Mike. She'd been down-stairs in her office working late when Ben arrived to brief her about the schedule change, but the alarm had sounded and they'd rushed up here. They'd found only the young post-doc, DalBello, Mike's protégée.

"Inform the state troopers, Lieutenant," Ben ordered, turning from the window. "Tell them to issue an APB for Hingerman's vehicle. Ryder will be with him." Until they reach Fairbanks, he thought as he watched the idiot leave. After that, if Mike and Hingerman split, it would be much harder to find him. I'll call the trooper commissioner myself, he decided.

"Well, he didn't get any further than logging on," Crosbie said, sitting back from the keyboard.

"Can you tell what he was trying to do?" Ben asked.

She shrugged. "Who knows?"

DalBello suggested hesitantly, "I think . . . he had second thoughts about his theory, his accusations, and wanted to check the data. At least, that's what he said. And I've never known Dr. Ryder to lie."

Ignoring her, Crosbie came to Ben and said quietly, "My guess? He was planning to upload some subroutine to sabotage the demonstration." She added with a thin smile, "It's what I'd do."

Ben was horrified. "You mean . . . it can be done?"

"Sure. But don't worry, he didn't get in."

Ben held up his hand, a silent command to say no more in front of the young scientist. Turning, he said, "Dr. DalBello, thank you for identifying Dr. Ryder. I understand he interrupted you trying to get a little hard-earned rest. We won't keep you from it." He gestured for Crosbie to follow him out.

Downstairs in Crosbie's office, he asked her, "I don't

understand. If Mike had been successful, wouldn't you have spotted this new subroutine?"

"Probably not. It's not something I'd look for. Besides, there's miles of code. It's how I got that fix for the EM shadow past *him*, remember?"

This was appalling. "Could he still do it via a link off-site?"

She shook her head. "He needs a terminal that has administration level access to write code to the program. That's why he took the chance of coming here. Besides, if he does attempt it off-site—if he's crazy enough to try hacking—the new security feature we installed will trace his modem."

Ben was glad he'd taken her advice days ago and brought in a Department of Defense computer security expert. Though Mike didn't know it, the new feature ensured that if the system detected a hacker, it automatically turned from passive to aggressive: after three failed passwords, it went after the hacker. But Ben could hardly rely on Mike falling into that trap. No, I'll have to track him the old-fashioned way, with men and guns. *Nothing will be secure until he's arrested.*

Where would Mike go? To Dana James? That would be bad—she'd never turn him in. To Carol? The thought struck a deep vein of worry. Could he rely on Carol's loyalty? Just hours ago he'd seen her almost fall apart. She had rallied, but that glimpse of hysteria made him wonder, could she stay the course? She loved Mike and seemed caught up in a fantasy that they could be reunited. *If it comes down to a choice between Mike and me, who will Carol betray?*

"So, General, you came to discuss some business?"

"Yes . . . urgent business," he said, collecting himself. "We need to advance the demonstration to Tuesday. My daughter is rearranging our guests' itinerary. Can you be ready?"

"Tuesday? That's the day after tomorrow."

"I can count. Can you do it?"

"If you get your Navy people to reschedule the satellite's engine burn."

"Done." He'd already called his office in Arlington and left a detailed message. Given the time difference, his ONR staff would soon be arriving at work. "The satellite thrusters will be fired by oh-nine-hundred on Tuesday."

"Then Tuesday it is."

"Good. You understand, no one must be told the new date except personnel with a need to know."

"No problem." She gave him the first genuine smile Ben had ever seen from her, as though she realized how near they were to success. "Well, General, looks like it's almost showtime."

Ben felt they were far nearer disaster. If Carol couldn't take out Dana James, as near as tomorrow's news.

And a small fear was gnawing at the far reaches of his mind. Mike was so desperate to stop HARC. Could there be a possibility . . . that he was right?

A memory flashed. *Man-eating tiger.* That had been Granger's terror, the youngest of Ben's platoon survivors, all captives. The five of them, including Ben, spent three years in bamboo tiger cages under the Vietnamese sun, one to a cage. Three years of hanging on to sanity. But Granger had lost his. Then came the day Ben overwhelmed his torturer, killed the guards, got all of his four guys free. They were about to head into the hills, other guards sure to come within moments, when Granger froze, refused to leave. *Man-eating tiger in those hills,* he said, teeth chattering. *Don't go.* Ben knocked him out, dragged him into the jungle. Granger's terror had almost got them all killed . . . for a phantom menace.

HARC had become Mike's man-eating tiger. A phantom fear. Ben would drag him out if necessary. He wouldn't stop now.

▲

Mike sat in the parked cab, watching his house. It was almost 5:00 A.M. and Carol's silver Lincoln was in the driveway. He imagined her sleeping. How could she? After what she'd done to him, how could she even lie in their bed?

Forget that. His mission was to get inside, get to the computer in the den. He knew how Carol worked. She would've brought in her assistants, set up a war room in some rented office or a hotel. She'd go there soon, to carry on her campaign against him. He would wait.

He paid the cabdriver and got out. Standing on the deserted street, he looked down at his muddy sneakers, ripped jeans, scratched hands. At the site, stumbling in the dark through the dense pines, he'd reached the new perimeter barrier—ten-foot fence topped with razor wire. Impossible to climb. He followed it about a half mile, through muskeg that left his sneakers caked with mud, until he reached the spot where the workmen, replacing the old chain-link fencing, had stopped for the day, and there he'd grappled his way over, tearing the knee of his jeans. He reached the road and met Wayne in the truck, and they raced away, but twenty minutes later, as they turned onto the highway, they spotted two trooper cruisers waiting ahead on the shoulder. Had Ben called them out to intercept him? Wayne cut onto a logging road, then onto a skidoo trail that eventually led to an old back road that paralleled the highway into Fairbanks. The rough detour had added a tense two hours to the trip, and it was a sunny 4:00 A.M. when they reached the city outskirts. On the way, Mike had called Gina on his cell phone.

"You want *what*?"

"Your ID and password. Gina, I've got to get into the system." She had global administration access, because she often networked off-site, and with her password Mike could still upload the program changes, could still sabotage the demonstration. He hadn't turned to her before—after all, she'd refused to help him with even a testimonial—but something in her eyes when the guard had stopped him in the control room made him hope the bond of friendship still held. "Gina, I'm right about the resonance, and right about the danger. Lives are at risk. *You're* at risk. You've got to help me."

When she spoke again she sounded torn. "I told General Crewe that I've never known you to lie . . . but, Mike, what you're asking me to do is criminal."

"No, just give me your password, that's all. I'll do the rest."

"Oh, Mike . . . I wish I could help, but . . . I just don't know."

He sensed her wavering, as though trapped on a fence. He had to tip her his way. "Gina, think about it, can you take the risk of—"

"Someone's coming . . . Dr. Crosbie . . . I've got to go."

"Gina, call me back! Soon as you can! On my cell." She knew his number. Without another word she hung up.

Mike had Wayne drop him at the city limits, then took a cab into town, still unsure, at that point, where to go. If Gina relented and called back with the password, he would need a computer and modem to access her terminal, but he couldn't go to Wayne's—if Ben had the state troopers looking for him, they were probably already staking out the boat. He couldn't risk going to the U, either; Jacob Porteous's people would turn him in.

So here he was, staking out his own home, waiting for Carol to leave. At least there were no troopers. Yet.

No word yet from Gina either. If she didn't call, he grimly decided, he'd have to try hacking.

Meanwhile, he couldn't hang around on the sidewalk. The street was quiet, people still in bed, but not for long. Few Alaskans wasted the precious days of summer sleeping late. Soon people would be up, leaving their houses, starting to work. So would Carol.

He walked to the all-night donut shop on Cushman Street. He went to a rear table by a window and pretended to read the *Fairbanks News-Miner,* watching cars come and go, on the lookout for trooper cruisers, feeling like a wolf being hunted. Still no call from Gina. By six-thirty he'd had three coffees and was getting hostile looks from the woman behind the counter. He walked back to the house. Carol's Lincoln was gone.

He went to the back door and used his key. In the kitchen he stood still for a moment, gauging the silence of the house. What if she'd only gone to buy orange juice and came right back? What if, what if . . . he couldn't make himself crazy with that game. With any luck he'd have a few hours on the computer.

He hurried up to the bedroom and quickly changed out of his muddy ripped jeans into clean ones. The room was a mess. Carol, usually obsessively neat, had left a dress on the floor, a slip on the unmade bed, makeup scattered across the dressing table, some red stuff ground into the ivory carpet. Mike grabbed his hiking boots, about to leave, when he remembered Lindsay's drawing in the dirty jeans pocket. Its purity was something he wanted to keep near him. He fished it out, stuck it in his shirt pocket, and went downstairs with the disk.

In the den he switched on the computer, logged on . . . and waited for Gina. He'd give her an hour, then give up and start hacking. The minutes crawled by. He turned on the TV to watch Channel 8's morning news. He didn't expect they'd play Dana's exposé of Ben, but there was nothing he could do except watch and wait and hope.

"Thank you, General Sloan," Carol said. "Believe me, you'll be glad you made the trip. We'll meet your helicopter in the morning."

She hung up, worn out, the last of her phone calls done. Sloan, chairman of the Joint Chiefs, would be here for the demonstration tomorrow. So would Ronald Kaplan, the national security adviser. The secretary of defense couldn't juggle his agenda on such short notice, but he'd told her he was eager to hear the results. It was the best she could do. She was hungry and tired, her headache a full-blown migraine. She hadn't had even an hour's sleep, driving home at 5:00 A.M. just to pick up some files, then rushing back here as she and Miguel worked feverishly to get their material on Dana James off to the media outlets for the morning newscast. It was done, and Carol was exhausted. All she wanted was to go home.

She turned and saw her father walk into the suite. *What bad news is he bringing now?* "What is it?" she asked as he reached her.

He glanced around. Her assistants were busy with phone calls. "It's okay," she assured him. "What's happened?"

He said quietly, "Mike broke into the site, tried to sabotage the computer program. He failed, but he's escaped. I've got the state troopers out looking for him. Has he tried to contact you?"

She was overwhelmed with sadness. That Mike would even *try* something so crazy . . . he *did* need help. Yet Dad was hunting him down like a criminal. He'd have him arrested, thrown in jail . . .

"Carol, *has he tried to reach you?* Do you have any idea where he's gone?"

She looked into his eyes. "No." And she was no longer sure she'd tell him even if she did know. Not tell Dad? He relied on her. It felt like treason. "I haven't heard from him in three days," she said, her hands at her throbbing temples. "I may never hear from him again. I can hardly think straight anymore. I've done all I can, Dad. I'm going home."

▲

Mike was hacking. No call from Gina, no sight of Dana's exposé on TV. This was his last option. The most obvious passwords—Gina's birth date, the date HARC opened, the fourth of July—had been unsuccessful, but he meant to exhaust the obvious before flailing at random. Seven futile attempts later, he caught the announcer's voice on the TV.

". . . to bring you an update on the HARC controversy."

He looked over at the screen. The news anchor, an earnest blond, said, "There has been a development in the story of Dr. Michael Ryder, the former lead scientist at the High-frequency Auroral Research Center who claimed that radio waves from a HARC test drove two local teens to suicide. His claims have been unsubstantiated, and Dr. Ryder has been placed on mandatory medical leave."

Hardly "breaking news." Mike turned back to the keyboard.

"Now, one of Michael Ryder's most vocal defenders, Dana James, a local resident and the mother of Ryder's son, has come under suspicion."

His eyes snapped to the screen. There was an unflattering still photo of Dana opening her truck door, looking startled, almost furtive.

"Channel 8 has just learned that Dana James, who has practiced medicine in the Fairbanks area for over a decade, has done so without a medical license."

Mike's chest tightened. As they cut to an interview with the president of the Alaska Medical Association, he saw the interviewer was Carol's assistant, Miguel.

"Doctor, is Dana James a danger to the public?"

"I can't comment on that, beyond stating that my office is examining the facts which have come to light."

"What facts are those?"

"Eleven years ago Ms. James was expelled from the University of California's medical school. We don't yet know the circumstances."

"But, since then, she has posed as a physician in the Fairbanks area?"

"That appears to be the case."

"Will charges be laid?"

"I've authorized an investigation, and the results will determine our course of action."

Mike felt sick. That Carol could sink so low . . . to dig this up, leak it, supply the taped interview.

The blond anchor: "Whether Dana James risked the lives of patients remains to be seen, but other allegations against her have surfaced as well, allegations of financial mismanagement in her position on the council of her Indian village."

Now Miguel was interviewing a well-dressed Native man, the caption under him: Leonard Titus, council elder of the village of Takona.

"Mr. Titus, you negotiated a relocation agreement with HARC on behalf of the Gwich'in Indians of Takona?"

"That's right. A good arrangement for our people. Modern new homes, a fair cash settlement, employment opportunities."

"Dana James is also a village council member. What position did she take on the relocation?"

"First she opposed it, then she suddenly changed her mind. I guess I see why now. I just found out she's moved three million dollars meant for the village resettlement fund into her personal business account."

"So you believe that she has abused the trust of her own people?"

"Sure looks like it. But I guess that's for our lawyers to check into."

The anchor: "Both these allegations against Dana James—for embezzlement and for medical fraud—are now under investigation. Charges may be laid. As for—"

A sharp sound at the front door. Troopers? *Got to get out.* Might make it through the kitchen and out the back door. Adrenaline pumping, he started to go, when Carol walked into the room.

"Mike!" Her shock at seeing him turned instantly into a smile. "You came back."

It disgusted him, that smile, as though she'd murdered

Dana and was grinning at getting away with it. Murder would have been kinder than what she'd done. He wanted to wipe the grin off her face.

"I was so afraid," she said. "I thought I'd never see you again. Mike, I honestly don't know how things got so crazy. I'm not sure . . . about anything anymore. Except that you came back. That's all that matters."

"That *is* all that matters to you, isn't it? That your life stays exactly the way you want it. Everything in its place, everybody playing their role."

She seemed distracted, wasn't listening. "Oh, God, Dad's called the troopers about you. We've got to go. Right now. Come on, I'll take you. We'll get you away from them, get far away from here. What you did will all blow over, and later we can go home. *Home*, Mike." She was tugging his arm. "Mike? Please . . . let's go. *Please*."

He stood like a rock. Going anywhere with her was the last thing he'd do. "You've done this . . . this hatchet job . . . and you've trashed me too, all just so your life won't be derailed. Even after I told you I'd go to jail for you, for God's sake. But that wasn't enough. You had to destroy *other* people's lives."

"Mike, I'm trying to save you. Save *us*. I had to stop what you were doing, you were acting so—"

"I'm not talking about me. Christ, why can't you ever look beyond what *you* want?"

She stiffened. "Oh. You mean her."

"That's right. Dana. I just saw. She put herself on the line to help me. She was trying to save lives, Carol. Now, the way you've savaged her, you might as well have left her dying in the bush. Threatened her livelihood, her dignity, the respect of her people. You've cut her off from everything she loves and needs."

Her voice turned hard. "Not everything. There's still you. Apparently, still available."

Mike couldn't believe it. The whole scene was too bizarre: Carol warped in her jealous fantasy, the TV babbling a commercial, the computer monitor frozen at his futile hacking . . . while Ben was off readying HARC. "Has it even occurred to you that you've crushed the last chance to stop a catastrophe?"

"Has it occurred to *you* that you're wrong about HARC? Deluded by this woman and her stories about her son's accident?"

"I'm not wrong! And Lucas is *my* son too."

"Oh, I know, how could anyone forget? The question is, who's your wife, Mike? Me? Or this Indian piece of ass you used to fuck. Maybe you're *still* fucking her."

He let the vicious words fall. It struck him that he felt absolutely nothing for his wife. And that he was seeing her clearly for the first time: creating artificial realities was how she lived. By what she'd done she had made herself such a stranger to him that she had removed herself beyond his anger, even beyond caring. He said, "All you know how to do is build lies."

He saw that she had no idea what he meant. She was adrift. He almost felt pity.

His cell phone rang. *Gina . . . the password.* He grabbed the phone from his belt. "Gina?"

"I'm sorry, Mike," she said dully. "I can't help you."

"Gina, please—"

"No, you don't understand. I was going to, I *wanted* to. But Dr. Crosbie's just changed all the passwords. And fired me." Her voice went thin. "Things are getting so weird, Mike. Ibrahim just quit. At this rate Dr. Crosbie's going to be out here practically by herself."

Mike swallowed. First Wayne thrown out of work, now Gina. No more allies on-site. "I'm sorry."

"Me too. For not listening to you earlier. I don't know what Dr. Crosbie and General Crewe are up to, but it scares the shit out of me if what you say about a resonance event is true. I'm getting out, taking the first flight back to Philly. I'm just . . . sorry I let you down."

He closed his eyes. Said lamely, "Good luck."

"Thanks. And, Mike? Don't even *think* about hacking. Not only have they changed the passwords, but there's also a new computer security feature. If it logs three failed attempts, it'll alert HARC security and trace your modem."

Three? His eyes shot to the computer screen. He'd just tried *ten* times. The troopers must already be on their way. *Got to get out. Now.*

He turned to go. Carol stepped in his way. "You're going . . . without me?"

"They're after me. Coming here. I have to get—"

"Forgive me, Mike . . . what I said. I'm out of my mind with . . . I love you . . . can't live without—"

"Carol, I'm asking you, tell them you haven't seen me. Give me that. Just that chance."

"Yes . . . yes, get away. Escape. And when you're safe, call me. I'll come get you, wherever you are. We'll be together, Mike. You can count on me."

He looked at her. This was insane. "Good-bye, Carol."

"Mike? . . . *Mike?*"

He bolted out the back door and headed for the woods by the river, not sure where he would go after that, where he *could* go, knowing only that he had to run, had to stay free, had to find some way to stop what was coming.

Time froze for Dana. In Takona's crowded general store where people were preparing for the airlift, she stood with a dirty-faced little boy on her hip, a plastic garbage bag of someone's clothes in her free hand, and everyone's eyes on her—everyone silenced by the news report they'd just seen on the store's TV.

"... *expelled from medical school ... practicing medicine without a license ... diverted three million dollars of the resettlement fund to her personal bank account ... charges may be laid ...*"

Dana's heart seemed to have stopped. She'd treated people in shock, and a voice inside was saying: This is what shock feels like. She'd come to help organize the departure and take Lucas home to Fairbanks, and moments ago there had been a noisy chaos of men and women fussing over bags and boxes, lost children crying, old people whining in bewilderment, confused dogs running in and out. The first airlift plane, a Twin Otter, was waiting on the grass airstrip. But now everyone had gone still.

"Dana?" old Mildred Dance asked, her wrinkled face screwed up in confusion. "You're not a doctor?"

The garbage bag slipped from Dana's hand. "No."

"Then . . . the ear medicine you gave me's no good?"

"It's fine, Mildred, don't stop using—" She couldn't go on, mortified by the waver in her voice.

"How about the three million?" an angry man called out. "I'll bet *that's* good too, eh? Buy you a big fancy house in town."

Sarah Elroy pushed through and lifted her little boy off Dana's hip as though to remove him from danger. "Oh, Dana, how *could* you?"

Dana turned, and came face-to-face with the most accusing eyes of all. Lucas. And Thomas beside him. Lucas's face, drained of color, looked as cold as the day she and Mike had found him near death on the bank of the Wahetna.

"That's why you caved in about the move." His voice was raw. "They paid you off. At HARC. You sold us out."

"No, Lucas, it's not like that. The money is *for* the village. For a tuberculosis clinic. I only—"

"News to me," Jim Titus said behind the counter. "Council didn't know anything about this." He scowled at Dana. "But you can bet we'll be looking into it."

"I can explain," she said to Jim, to everyone . . . most of all to Lucas. But, could she? She *had* taken HARC money. In another day she would have announced the project, but right now the evidence was so damning . . .

"So you ain't a doctor?" Archie Paul called out. He stood in the doorway, looking drunk. "That why I lost my little Francie? You gave her some drug, that day she died. What'd you do? Poison her?" He stared toward Dana with sudden ferocity. "If you killed my little—"

Thomas stepped between them and slapped a thick hand on Archie's scrawny chest, stopping him. Archie staggered, but he snarled at Dana, "She fooled us. Ain't no doctor, just a liar and a cheat. All high and mighty about people having a drink, when it's her that's *killing* people." He spat on her face.

Her hand shaking, Dana wiped the spittle from her cheek, reminding herself that Archie had lost both his daughters.

Thomas kept a restraining hand on Archie, but gave Dana a look that made her burn with shame. "Never took you for a thief, Dana." His eyes went cold. "Guess we all do what we have to." He turned his back on her. "Let's go," he told Archie.

"Yeah," Archie growled at her, "do what we *have* to."

"Shut your mouth," Thomas told him. They walked out together.

As she watched Thomas go, Dana heard a raven's rusty call outside, and imagined the spirit of her sister Carla crying out at this rift between her husband and her sister. She turned to Lucas and reached for his arm. "Let's go home."

He shrugged off her hand. His mouth trembled. "I *am* home."

When Lucas, too, turned his back on her and walked out, Dana felt it like an arrow through her heart.

▲

Lucas hurried up the path behind the village, following Thomas and Archie as they headed for the woods, but keeping as far back as possible so they wouldn't spot him. He made himself squelch the hot tears, concentrated on keeping his eyes on the yellow stripe down the leg of Archie's old blue track pants, faint at this distance as Archie and Thomas moved into the trees. He was afraid to think about his mother . . . how she'd lied about being a doctor, stolen money meant for her own people. It was so terrible it scared him. He had to be strong now. Like Thomas.

He walked on, never letting the yellow stripe out of his sight, and reached the edge of the trees. Tracking was something he'd always been good at; Thomas had taught him. Behind him, the village was noisier than he'd ever heard it—all the commotion over at the airstrip in the cottonwoods, people getting ready to leave. But soon the planes would take them away and Takona would be silent, for good. A dead village. Killed by HARC . . . just like Sophy. In a few days, they'd burn it down.

His breathing quickened as he entered the woods and picked up his pace to keep up with the distant yellow stripe. Thomas and Archie were moving fast. Where were they going? Lucas stumbled on a gnarled root and glanced down, and when he looked up again, the yellow flash was gone. He'd lost them. He stopped and slowly scanned the woods to his right, then his left. Nothing. A snap sounded behind him and he twisted around. A ptarmigan had taken off from a stump. He turned back . . . and gasped. Thomas stood in front of him.

"Plane's that way," Thomas said, jutting his chin toward the village. He held his rifle, the barrel resting on his shoulder.

"I'm not leaving," Lucas said steadily. "I'm staying with you."

Thomas raised the rifle. "You're leaving. Now."

"You going to shoot me, Uncle Thomas?"

"You got no life here, and no life where the village is going either. I'd be doing you a favor."

There was a hard gleam in his eye that made Lucas wonder if Thomas was mad enough at the world to do it. But Lucas was mad too. They had that in common.

"Let me stay, Uncle Thomas. Please. Ron and Sophy are dead. And my mother isn't . . . who I thought she was. What else have I got?"

"Well, you got nothing here."

"I have you. You're family."

Thomas blinked, scowling, as though fighting tears. "Get the hell out."

Lucas didn't move. "You're not lying down for those bastards at HARC, and that's what I want to do too. Look, I didn't tell Mom that you're planning to stay, so that proves you can trust me. And I can help you, getting meat. Well, as soon as my arm's better. Until then I can still do lots—fish and get firewood and stuff. As for getting through the winter, you know I'm a better shot than Archie, better at trapping too. And, if I don't make it, well . . . I'm not afraid to die."

"That's a boy talking." Thomas lowered the rifle. His

eyes bored into Lucas's. "You can shoot a moose, but can you shoot a man? Archie and me got a camp. We got guns and traps and even a little dynamite. Anyone comes to interfere, we'll take them out. Can you do *that*?"

Lucas swallowed. "I can do that."

▲

Squinting at the evening sun's glare in her face, Dana brought her Aeronca Chief down over the smooth surface of the Fairbanks float pond. She'd left her sunglasses back in Takona, a slip-up she would never normally make, and she'd flown with her numbed mind on automatic. The pontoons touched down and she taxied toward the dock. But the accusing eyes of Takona seemed to be on her still . . . Thomas's contempt . . . Lucas's hurt and anger. It felt as if her life were spinning out of control. *"Charges may be laid."* Back in the village an inner voice of self-preservation had warned her: You need a lawyer. She was going to see Reid. To get his advice. His help.

She hadn't called ahead. What could she tell him on the phone? *"I'm a fraud . . . may be prosecuted . . . accused of embezzlement too . . . and we haven't stopped HARC."* She couldn't trust herself on the phone to be coherent. Beneath the pain, she felt such fury. Mike's family had done this to destroy her. Only his father-in-law could have told about the three million, and only his wife could have organized the instant media attack. And Mike? He was the only person Dana had ever confided to about her expulsion from medical school. Had he handed that to his wife? She could hardly believe it of him . . . yet his wife had struck so quickly. And where *was* Mike? The last she'd seen or heard of him was last night when he'd stalked out of her interview. Those humiliating questions about their past. After seeing his own reputation savaged, had last night been the breaking point when he'd finally surrendered to Crewe? Something told her Mike would never do that, would never give up—yet everything seemed to be unraveling . . .

She tied up at the dock and headed into her office. Aurora Aviation was ominously quiet, no phones ringing, her other pilot and her mechanic nowhere in sight. When she saw her receptionist's face, Dana knew the news had hit.

"I didn't know what to tell people," Sherry said, distraught. "Everybody's canceling. That geologist's team booked next week for Nome? They were the first. And the New Jersey couple so excited to do a flightseeing over Denali? They just called, changed their minds. Dana . . . what should I tell people?"

She felt such frustrated anger. She'd built this business by gritting her way through fourteen-hour workdays and walking tightropes of debt. How dare Crewe and his daughter jeopardize it. "Tell them we'll be happy to accommodate them anytime they'd like to charter in the future. And say it like you mean it."

"Dana, that's not all. The FAA sent an inspector, and he's grounded the Beaver and the Piper Cub. On silly technicalities."

Had Crewe pulled strings to sick the FAA on her too?

"Dana . . . is it true? What they're saying . . . about you?"

"We'll talk about this later, Sherry. I'm going to get legal advice."

In her truck on the way to Reid's office her mind felt bombarded with worries. The most painful was Lucas. He'd run off, and she had no idea where. But she did have some idea why: Thomas. He hadn't showed up, either. Nor Archie. As the packed planes had carried the people of Takona away, she was searching through the empty cabins. No sign of Lucas or the two men. With the last Twin Otter set to take off, Jim Titus told her they couldn't wait, that she'd have to ferry Lucas and the other two out herself in her Chief. Left alone, Dana desperately eyed the thick woods behind the empty village. Where had they gone? What could Thomas be thinking? She stood in the unnatural silence, feeling so alone in this deserted place, the graveyard of her ancestors—and now of her people's way of life. The enormity of her problems roared in on her. Her exposé hadn't stopped General Crewe . . . the cataclysm at HARC was on the verge of happening. Mike's warning echoed in her head: *"Being next door, Takona would be the hardest hit."* And Lucas was there, somewhere.

▲

Mike emerged from the woods into Dana's backyard. He'd spent a tense afternoon in the marshy woods by the river, constantly on the lookout for troopers as he made his way here, and he was dirty, hungry, and tired. But he had an idea. No computers this time, no high-tech tricks, this plan was unsophisticated, even crude: HARC's state-of-the-art glory crippled by a sprinkling of dust. And Ben himself had given him the idea.

But to make it work, Mike needed Dana.

Her house was a modest bungalow with gray aluminum siding and blue trim, and it covered most of her small lot, screened on either side by young aspens and birches. He quickly crossed the yard, passing the cedar deck with its barbecue, and went around to the front. Her truck wasn't in the driveway. And no one answered his knock on the door. He wasn't surprised—she had said she'd be in Takona today for the village airlift. But she'd also said she'd be bringing Lucas home. Mike would wait.

Couldn't hang around outside, though. Some neighbor might get nervous and call the police. He tried the door. Locked. Going around to the rear again, he found the back locked too. He bent to look under the deck, and saw a basement window. He ducked under the deck and started for it. The sloping ground rose toward the house, forcing him onto his hands and knees in the dirt, and as he crawled up the narrowing space, something gouged his shoulder blade. Wincing in pain, he looked up. A nail protruding from a deck joist had ripped off threads of his shirt. He felt blood trickle into his armpit. Crawling on, he found the window unlocked. He opened it, went in feet first, and lowered himself to the basement floor.

Strange to be in Dana's house. The basement wasn't finished, just unpainted drywall, with old trunks and boxes, discarded kitchen furniture, a bike, all neatly stacked on the clean, concrete slab floor. An open wooden staircase led upstairs.

He climbed the steps, thinking he'd better somehow clean up his bleeding shoulder, and opened the door at the top. Walking down the unfamiliar hall, he glimpsed the lemon-colored kitchen. A smell of apples. He'd been here only once before. Three years ago, arriving to build HARC, he'd called Dana and asked to meet Lucas. The three of them spent a strained half hour at her kitchen table, arranging for Mike to spend some time with the thirteen-year-old. Dana had put no obstacles in his way. It was HARC she fought, later—and his power to lure Lucas away. Mike thought now how badly he'd fouled up both. Protected HARC, hurt Lucas.

He found the bathroom. Pale blue walls and clean white tiles, blue shell designs on the shower curtain. Straightforward, unfussy, like Dana. The curtain was closed. He flashed on her in there, showering. Remembered swimming with her naked in the river sixteen summers ago, making love after in a grove of white spruce, the heat of the day wafting pine resin on the air. He was startled by his face in the mirror. Grass in his hair, mud-streaked cheek, evangelist eyes. *And you expect her to trust you?* He stared back, as if facing down an opponent. *She has to. We can beat Ben. This idea can work.* It was inspired by Ben's own words.

It had been back in Boston, on a wet evening in spring. Ben was having dinner with him and Carol, telling how back in the eighties the Navy had experimented with a bomb to dispense chaff to confuse enemy air defense, and had stumbled on a discovery. During an exercise in southern California, the chaff drifted and landed on power lines, short-circuiting them and blacking out a section of Orange County. The Navy realized it had a new weapons system: carbon filament packed into the warheads of cruise missiles could incapacitate enemy electrical facilities. In the Gulf War, they used filament-spitting missiles in attacks on Baghdad to cut off power and create confusion. Ben had enjoyed telling this parable of low-tech success amid a high-tech war, and Mike had agreed, over coffee that spring evening, that accidental discoveries were often the sweetest. He liked the concept even more now. A carbon filament drop over HARC's open switching station could disable the entire array.

Wayne could get the materials—carbon fiber was available at boat yards—and Dana could do the flyover. Mike would need a place to hide while he prepared the attack, but he'd thought about that too. As of today, Dana's village was a ghost town. It would be razed later, but until then, deserted and remote, it was a place Mike doubted the troopers would look for him. And, so close to HARC, it made a perfect staging spot. Thinking about it as he looked in the mirror, he felt sure it could work. A crude sabotage, but one that might save countless lives.

But he needed Dana for all of it—to get him to Takona, and to do the flyover.

His shoulder stung. Blood was sticking his shirt to his back. Turning on the sink taps, he grabbed a towel.

The sound of a vehicle . . . pulling up in the driveway. He tensed, turned off the water. The engine cut out, and doors slammed shut. Dana and Lucas? Mike moved down the hall, stopping at the living room. Through the picture window he saw a trooper cruiser pulling up on the street, joining the one in the driveway. He ducked back into the hall. Had they come for Dana, to investigate the charges against her? But, two cruisers? *No. It's me Ben wants.*

A knock on the door.

His timing couldn't have been worse.

▲

Dana found Reid packing boxes of files into the trunk of his maroon Volvo sedan as she pulled up outside his office. Leaving her truck, she came toward him, and as he turned and saw her, his sober look told her everything. *He's heard. He knows.*

Before she could speak, he slammed his trunk lid down. "Can't talk now, Dana. Something's happened, maybe the break we need. A friend in Governor Dainard's office tells me the governor has concerns about HARC. He did his public reassurance speech, and he's being advised by Crewe's experts, but he'd be open to hearing our side. I'm on my way to the capital now."

It was like sun breaking through clouds, the first ray of hope. "If we can convince the governor, he could pull the plug on HARC overnight."

"Exactly. I have an appointment tomorrow morning—Dainard will give me fifteen minutes over breakfast. I didn't call you because . . ." He looked away, pulled his key out of the trunk lock. "It's a crucial fifteen minutes, and I think you'll agree I'm the only one now who can credibly present our case."

Her heart twisted. "You've seen the news."

"Yes."

"Reid, let me explain—"

"Later. I'm sure you realize how serious the situation has become. With you discredited, your accusations about Crewe are meaningless. And I haven't heard a word from Ryder—he seems to have vanished—so we can't count on him anymore. I've got to go, Dana. Alone. You see that, don't you?"

She nodded, mortified. "Of course."

"I'm taking the detailed notes Ryder gave us about the resonance event, and other background material. I was just leaving for Anchorage."

Dana looked at the car, incredulous. "You're driving?" It was three hundred miles. Then a five hundred mile hop to Juneau. And it was eight o'clock now.

"No direct flight to Juneau from here tonight. I'm booked on a 6:00 A.M. flight—best I could get." He looked at her. "Unless . . ."

She didn't hesitate. "If I fly you you'll be sure to make the meeting." It meant leaving Lucas. A kid with a broken arm and a broken heart, and an uncle embittered enough with grief to endanger his life. But this might be the last chance to stop Crewe—and no one would be safe if she failed to do that, including Lucas. "I just need to pick up some things from home. Let's go."

They took his car. As he pulled out into the sparse traffic on Fourth Avenue, heading for her house, he asked, looking straight ahead, "When were you planning to tell me?"

He sounded emotionless as a judge. Dana struggled to keep a lid on the tumult inside her. "You're hanging me without a trial? What happened to due process?"

His smile was fleeting. "Okay, let's do the Q&A. *Were* you expelled from medical school?"

She explained, as she had to Mike: alone in L.A. with a pre-schooler, falling behind, and so desperate to come home with her degree that she'd cheated on a test. "No excuse, I know," she said, "but I've been a good physician, Reid, M.D. or not."

He glanced at her. The light ahead was yellow, and he accelerated through the intersection. "Next, *did* you accept three million dollars from HARC?"

"To build a TB clinic. Crewe himself gave it to me—to drop the injunction. The resettlement seemed inevitable, so I saw this as a way to get something good for the village. He asked me to keep the deal private until after the move."

"I see. You didn't feel you could trust me with either of these secrets?"

"It wasn't about trust, Reid. I just . . ." She didn't finish. How could she even begin? Her abiding need to help her people fight the diseases of poverty that drained them, a need so deep it transcended the rules of white medical societies and had even led her to make a clandestine deal with her enemy—all of that was something Reid would have understood, so why hadn't she told him? It struck her that it all came down to one reason: *I didn't feel close enough to you.* She had told Mike. Had confided to him both her secrets. But the bond with Reid wasn't strong enough. How long had she felt this way? Always, it seemed. It was a secret she'd hidden even from herself . . . until this moment. She offered Reid all she could think of to say. "I'm so sorry."

He let out a troubled sigh. "I love you, Dana. But I wonder if I really know you."

She looked at the rusted blue pickup ahead, where a malamute sled dog sat on the open flatbed, staring back at her. She felt Reid's eyes on her as well.

He asked quietly, "Isn't this where you say: I love you too and we can work things out?"

"Oh, Reid, so much has gone wrong . . . and so much is at stake with HARC, I don't see how we can think about us right now."

"I see." In the silence, he made a small needless adjustment to the rearview mirror. "Which brings me to my last question. About your capitulation to the resettlement. Did Ryder play any role in your sudden change of heart?"

This was crazy. How could she think about such things when she was facing so many problems? Maybe the governor could stop HARC now, but could she ever repair the shambles of her life? *"Charges may be laid."* The Alaska Medical Association. The FAA. The village council. Lucas. "Reid, I need your help . . ."

It was a raw plea, and she saw that it startled him. His expression softened. "I know." He said in his old, businesslike manner, "I'm sure you had good reasons for everything you've done. Tell me in detail, later, and we'll prepare a case."

She nodded, grateful.

He glanced at her. "Something else?"

"It's Lucas. He's run off. At Takona. I'm afraid he's done something stupid—gone into the bush with a couple of holdouts."

They had reached her street, and Reid turned onto it. "He'll likely show up. But if you want, I'll put in a call to the troopers' post at Coldfoot."

"No, one of the holdouts is my brother-in-law, and I don't want to draw the law down on him. But when we get back, would you come and help me look for Lucas?"

His face clouded with worries of his own. "Let's take this one step at a time, Dana. First, the governor."

▲

Mike was sitting on the floor by Lucas's bed, trapped. It was the only spot in the bedroom where he couldn't be seen through the two windows, and outside one trooper at least was stationed in Dana's backyard. He knew they couldn't have a search warrant or they'd be inside by now, but the windows overlooked the yard, one by the desk and the other straight ahead, and with the curtains wide open he didn't dare get up.

He'd never seen his son's room before today, but in the last forty minutes he'd memorized it. The flea-market wooden desk, its computer surrounded by candy wrappers and video games and science fiction paperbacks. Above the rumpled bed, the framed first-prize certificate from the Fairbanks District High School science fair. The schedule for last term's exams tacked on the cork board, photos tacked around it. One was a dramatic aerial view of HARC from the official publicity package. He realized that Lucas hadn't been home since the tragic night nine days ago—hadn't had a chance to rip the picture down. Beside it was a snapshot of Lucas grinning in his yellow kayak, paddle flashing. Beside that, one of a tall, pretty Native girl in a red parka in the snow, nuzzling a husky pup. Was this Sophy? And then, the photo he kept coming back to—Dana in shorts and T-shirt picking salmonberries with Lucas, maybe five years old, in baggy little dungarees, both of them grinning at the camera. It hurt Mike to look at it. What a great job she'd done bringing up the kid . . . and how much of his son's life he'd missed.

He forced his mind off that, off the pain in his shoulder too, and focused his thoughts. How long before she came home? Everything depended on Dana.

▲

As Reid drove down Dana's street she saw the parked cruisers outside her house.

She threw him a look. "Why are they here?"

"I don't know. But I doubt they'd come in such force to arrest an individual for medical fraud, or even for the alleged embezzlement. Let me handle this."

He pulled into her driveway. "What's the problem, officer?" he asked the lanky trooper who reached them as they got out of the car. The man was middle-aged and gaunt, with the sunken eyes of chronic low-level ill health, it seemed to Dana, but his steely expression under the wide-brimmed hat conveyed authority, and so did his holstered gun. She made her face impassive, but she was gripping her house keys so tightly they were digging into her palm.

"Dana James?" When she nodded, he said, "I'm Sergeant Howe. We're looking for Michael Ryder. When did you last see him?"

Why were they after Mike? She was about to answer "last night," when Reid cut in. "Ms. James doesn't have to answer that, Sergeant. I'm Reid D'Alton, Ms. James's attorney. Do you have official business here?"

"We have reason to believe that Ryder may attempt to come here. I'd like to have a look inside."

"You have a warrant?"

"I can get one."

"I suggest you do that."

The men locked eyes, and Dana's alarm grew. If she was uncooperative, Howe might delay her, and she couldn't afford that if she was going to get Reid to the governor on time. "Sergeant Howe," she said, "I'm just leaving for a business appointment. I'll be back tomorrow, and I'd be glad to show you around then."

"Where's your appointment?"

Reid gave her a sharp look of warning, but it seemed to Dana there was no sense hiding it—she'd be filing a flight plan. Anyway, the police hadn't told her not to leave town. Not yet. "Juneau," she answered. "I've just come to get some things. Will you excuse me?"

Howe turned back to Reid. "I'll get the warrant, Mr. D'Alton, but meanwhile I'm leaving my men posted outside."

Going inside with Reid, Dana closed the door on the troopers, but uneasiness about Mike gnawed. This manhunt had to be at General Crewe's instigation. "I'll just be a minute," she told Reid. She went to her bedroom, quickly threw a change of clothes and toothbrush into an overnight bag, and went to get her spare Serengeti sunglasses from the dresser. She wouldn't fly into the evening sun again without them. They weren't there. Had Lucas been using them again? She went down the hall and into his room . . . and saw Mike.

Cᴌᴏsᴇ ᴛʜᴇ ᴄᴜʀᴛᴀɪɴs," Mike said.

He saw Dana's surprise, but she went to one window after another and pulled the drapes. With the evening sun shut out, Lucas's bedroom was suddenly cast in gloom. She turned and whispered fiercely, "What are you doing here? Why are they after you?"

Mike got to his feet. "No time to explain. Dana, I need your help."

"I'm this close to *jail,* Mike, I can't afford one false step. If you expect me to keep up the charade with the sergeant out there, tell me right now—what's *happened*?"

"Dana, are you all right?" It was D'Alton, in the hall. Reaching the doorway, he saw Mike and stopped. "Jesus. You."

Mike hadn't counted on D'Alton. Would the lawyer feel duty bound to inform on a fugitive?

"Ryder, you're endangering Dana by being here."

D'Alton's hostility, and Dana's antagonism, made

Mike fear his plan was dead in the water. But he reminded himself that they were on his side. Anyway, his fate was in Dana's hands. "They haven't got a warrant, right?" he asked D'Alton.

"They're working on it. It seems they're here in case you arrive—I don't think they suspect you're actually inside."

Good, they wouldn't be barging in. Not yet. "I broke into HARC last night," he said. He quickly told them about his attempt to sabotage the computer system, his failure, Ben sending the troopers to track him, and his day in the woods by the river. "Dana, you're the only one who can help me. You've got to fly me to Takona."

"Takona? Why?"

He explained the plan to drop carbon filament over the switching station to disable the antenna array, and her role as pilot. "And until we're ready to strike, Takona's one place they might not look for me."

They both stared at him, dumbfounded. D'Alton said flatly, "Impossible."

"No, it can work," Mike said.

"He means I can't take you," Dana said. "We're leaving right away for Juneau. Reid has an appointment with Governor Dainard. He's heard that the governor's ready to listen about HARC. Mike, it's exactly the chance we need."

Mike felt a flash of hope. Dainard could shut down HARC with one phone call! Then reality dragged him back. He'd been burned too often pleading with people to believe his warnings, only to have Ben and Carol twist his words back on him. "That's a dangerous long shot.

Besides, Crewe can pull strings at the governor's. I won't put my trust in others anymore. The only way I can be sure of ending this is to do it myself."

"But you *can't* do it yourself," D'Alton said. "You're asking Dana to be part of it—to risk herself." He turned to her. "Don't listen to this crazy idea. We've got to get going."

Her eyes flicked to the window, out where the troopers were, then back to D'Alton. "What happens to Mike?"

"He took his chances coming here. We have a more important priority. Dana, the governor is our last chance, and if we're going to make it we've got to go now."

She looked at her watch. For Mike, her indecision was torture. "Dana," he said, "you've seen how futile it is trying to get the truth out. Nobody *hears*. Ben's made sure of that. And we have just two days left."

"The governor's ready to listen," D'Alton pressed her. "And he has the power to act. Don't give up the last hope we have, all for this wild idea."

"It's not wild, it's dog simple," Mike said. "That's why it can work."

"Can it?" Dana challenged. "Crewe always seems one step ahead of you, Mike. He and your wife. And they've just about destroyed me."

It knocked him back. Not just the truth of it, but the struggle in her voice—that after everything Ben and Carol had brought down on her, she was still here, still listening to him. "Dana, I saw on the news what they did to you. I can't tell you how sorry I am. But you've got to trust me just one more time. I can't do this without you."

He and D'Alton watched her, waiting. She looked away. But when she finally spoke, her voice was steady. "How can we get you past the troopers?"

He could have kissed her.

D'Alton groaned. "Dana, please think of—"

"Reid, I'm going to do *both*."

"What?"

"The flight north to Takona is just fifty minutes. A detour there and back will add only two hours to our time south to Juneau. It's nine-thirty now, so you'll still make the governor's breakfast meeting. Then after I drop you off I'll come back to help Mike prepare the airdrop. This way we'll have *two* chances."

D'Alton looked far from convinced, but he nodded with a sigh, as though resigned. Dana gave him a smile.

Mike felt a twinge. She was going to marry this guy. "We need a diversion," he cut in, "for the troopers." As he turned to look for something to use, he heard Dana gasp. "Mike, your shoulder."

He'd almost forgotten the bloodied rip in his shirt, the sticky gash. It was the least of his worries. "If we could draw them around to the front," he said, "then I could get back out through the basement window and make a run for the woods."

"Not a diversion," Dana said. "Cooperation."

"What?"

"I'll just invite them in, tell them I want to get the search over with right now so that it's not hanging over me. While they're coming in, you can get out the basement and sprint to the woods."

Mike had to smile. Simple was always best. "Once

I'm out," he told her, "I'll have to stick to the woods along the river, so pick me up at Bartlett's Landing. That dock by the old dredge."

She nodded.

"Okay, Ryder, I guess there's time," D'Alton conceded. "We'll drop you off in Takona, then we can carry on to Juneau."

"Not we, Reid," Dana said. "An FAA inspector grounded the rest of my fleet. The long arm of General Crewe, I suspect. I have only the Chief, and it's a two-seater."

"Then drop him off, and I'll meet you back at the airport float pond." He took her in his arms. "It's going to be tight. Can you manage it without taking risks?"

"A little late for that," she said wryly. "Don't worry, I should make it back before midnight. Then we'll head south."

Mike wanted the lawyer's hands off her. "Go," he said.

She and D'Alton reached the door. "Dana," Mike whispered, stopping her. "If I don't make it past these guys, head straight to Juneau. Give the governor your best shot."

▲

The Aeronca Chief swooped over the radio tower on a campus rooftop, dipping so alarmingly close that Mike felt he could reach down and touch the antenna. Swallowing the peanuts he was wolfing, he threw a look at Dana. "You okay?"

"I don't even know how to answer that."

But Mike saw calmness in her face as her eyes swept the horizon, and he was satisfied that she was in control. Hell, more than satisfied. Her simple plan had worked. Waiting by her basement window, he'd heard her call in the troopers, then hauled himself out the window and bolted across to the woods. Dana had finessed her own way past the troopers, even sneaking out a gym bag with some of Lucas's clothes for him. She'd got the plane and picked him up, and she was taking him to Takona. She was amazing. She'd also given him the peanuts from her plane's emergency rations, since he hadn't eaten anything but a stale Danish and several coffees at the donut shop this morning, and though the nuts were a lump in his empty stomach, he didn't care—he was on a kind of high. This had been the first victory in days, and it felt sweet.

The weather was something else. He'd seen distant flashes of dry lightning in the west as he and Dana took off from Fairbanks, and now he noticed a band of dark cloud on the horizon. It seemed to be moving in.

"Thunderstorms," she said, following his gaze. "I'll be pushing it to get back and pick up Reid before this hits."

Mike didn't like to think of her flying in a thunderstorm. "Maybe you should abort Juneau. D'Alton could make his pitch to Dainard on the phone." For what it's worth, he thought. He had no faith that the governor would shut down HARC. "Besides, what if you got there but then weather stranded you in the capital. Remember,

I need you back." The double meaning struck him. He quickly clarified, "You're my bomber pilot."

Double meaning . . . mixed signal. A memory flashed of sixteen years ago, that day she'd told him she was pregnant. She'd looked so happy, and he'd felt such a thrill. They were far too young, of course, Mike twenty-one, waiting to hear from graduate schools in the lower forty-eight, though the University of Alaska was wooing him to stay; and Dana just eighteen, a U of A freshman. But Mike knew she was the one. They immediately planned to get married. Then, days later, he got the great news that he'd been awarded a fellowship at MIT, a dream come true. Bursting with pleasure at the thought of surprising Dana, he handed her the letter as he walked her to class.

"Too bad to turn it down," she said, handing it back.

He grinned—she had to be kidding. "Turn down MIT for Alaska? Why would I do that?"

"To be U of A's star physicist, and live with your wife and child."

"What do you mean? You're coming with me." He'd never imagined anything else.

"To Massachusetts?" She'd looked shocked. "Never. This is my people's home."

Visions as opposite as night and day . . .

"Getting stranded is a definite possibility," Dana said, tuning the VHF for a weather report, "maybe sooner than later. And I didn't file a flight plan." She shook her head, muttering, "For the first time in my life."

Right. She could hardly file a plan when she was helping a fugitive escape to a restricted area to plan criminal sabotage. Not behavior to endear a pilot to the aviation authorities. Mike realized he'd better reach Wayne right away if he was going to get his hands on enough carbon fiber. He unclipped his phone and called Wayne's boat. When he got a recording, he didn't leave a message—no telling who could be listening in. Try again later.

Dana shot him a sardonic smile. "Never a dull moment with you, is there?"

After all the grief he'd brought her, she could manage a smile. It moved him. He grinned back. "You ain't seen nothin' yet."

The logistics, though, were daunting. This was Monday night and Ben's demonstration was set for Thursday. That left just two days for Wayne to get the materials to Takona, then for Mike to shred the carbon fiber into enough filament. And everything was contingent on good weather conditions for Dana the day of the strike: no gusting winds, no heavy rain. Still, he believed it was doable.

"There's something I haven't told you," Dana said. "There wasn't time. It's about Lucas. At Takona today everybody left on the airlift except my brother-in-law and his friend, and afterward I couldn't find Lucas either. I'm sure he's gone off into the woods with them. Mike, I'm afraid. Those two men are bitter with grief. They're the ones who lost their kids to HARC. Thomas lost Ron, Archie lost Sophy. I'm afraid Lucas has joined them in some desperate last stand."

Sophy and Ron. *The kids I helped kill.* And Lucas

loved the girl—Mike knew Lucas was as bitter as the two fathers. "You searched?" he asked.

She nodded. "But I was alone. Thomas knows the bush for miles around Takona, knows it like his own cabin, and Lucas has spent days on end with him out there, hunting. Together they can disappear." She looked at him. "You grew up in the bush. You have the skills Thomas has."

"You want me to find them."

"Yes. Mike, I want him out of there before Thursday. I want all three of them out, before it's too late."

He met her gaze. Takona . . . next door to HARC. The thought of Lucas there, if the worst happened, turned his blood cold. "I'll do my best," he said.

Dana looked out her window. "Here we are."

Mike saw a hodgepodge of ramshackle cabins spread out along the riverbank and backed by forest. Not a soul in sight. As Dana banked over the water, the wind was rippling the surface into tight wavelets. The pontoons bit into the low chop, and Dana skimmed toward the village wharf. Mike hopped out onto the dock and wrapped a line from the pontoon around a cleat, leaving it loose, expecting Dana to wait only while he grabbed his bag, and then take off again. Instead, she cut the engine. "I'll gas up here," she said. "Better safe than sorry. And you need a dressing on that shoulder before I go." She grabbed her first aid kit.

Mike looked at the gas tank on the dock, just a big covered barrel, a gravity feed arrangement. "I'll do the gas," he said. First he unloaded the gym bag, and as he tossed it on the dock, something inside it clunked.

"Lucas's fishing rod," Dana said as she climbed out. "I thought you'd need it. The village has been cleaned out."

"Thanks." He carried over the gas hose and unscrewed the cap on the plane's wing tank.

"I don't know what else you'll do for food."

"Fishing looks good. I'll get by," he said, running gas into the tank. "Those salmonberries look ripe, too."

Dana followed his gaze to the berry bushes near the water's edge, and Mike caught her wistful look. "My sister and I used to pick pails of them for my grandmother. We brought her fireweed too, and she made jelly from it, sweet as pie." She looked out at the river. "Those summers, Carla and I would spend all day out in the boat with my uncles. Fishing, fixing nets, chattering, goofing off. Good days."

Mike could almost hear the two little girls' laughter. Maybe it was a trick of the eerie quiet of the deserted village, the wind sighing through the trees. He looked upstream. HARC lay about three miles beyond the bend. HARC had forced this silence on the village, and etched the sadness on Dana's face. He remembered how mindlessly he'd gone along with Ben's resettlement plan. It had meant nothing more to Mike than a simple logistics solution to enable his project's smooth operation—not uncles and grandmothers and laughing little girls, their world uprooted. Now, he wished the ground upstream would shudder with a new earthquake and swallow the whole godforsaken site.

The tank was full. He replaced the cap and hung up the hose.

"Take off your shirt and turn around." Dana held up a dressing and a swab.

Her fingers touching his bare back brought a jolt of arousal. He forced his mind on carbon filament, willing the urgency to subside, and when the swab made contact, he welcomed the bite of antiseptic. As she placed the dressing over his wound, her hands were gentle, her movements assured. If skill and compassion made a physician, Mike thought, she was a good one, whatever papers she lacked. Doctoring was in her blood, and he was ashamed at how brutally Ben and Carol had cut this artery of her life.

With his wound dressed and the plane gassed up, Dana was ready to go. They stood together on the dock, Mike buttoning his shirt. He hated to see her leave. And he could tell, from the way she kept glancing toward the woods behind the cabins, that it was all she could do to drag herself away when Lucas was out there somewhere.

"I'll find him, Dana. I promise."

She looked up at him, and the lines of worry on her forehead melted. "I know." She looked as trusting, as beautiful, as the day he'd fallen in love with her all those years ago.

"Mike, I'll be back—"

A loud crack split the silence. Something splashed the water beside them. Mike thought: *rifle shot*. He yanked Dana behind him, shielding her from the shore. The shot had to have come from that direction.

"Hold it right there!" a voice called. A scrawny man in grimy track pants and T-shirt stepped out from among the cabins. He was carrying a rifle, raised toward them. He stopped on the dirt path that led to the dock.

Dana gasped. "Archie."

Mike's mind raced. Archie . . . Sophy's father.

"I seen you on TV," Archie yelled, his voice high-pitched, aggressive. "You're the big brain from HARC. You're a murdering son of a *bitch!*" He dropped to his knee in the dirt. His balance looked unsteady, but he braced himself, taking aim at them.

Mike pushed Dana to the edge of the dock. "Dive!"

She plunged into the water. Mike was about to dive after her when he saw someone run out from among the cabins. Lucas.

"Archie, no!" Lucas yelled. "Don't shoot!"

But Mike knew that hunter's focus—Archie was intent on a kill. Mike turned again to dive, but stopped as he saw Lucas lunge for the rifle. Archie swung the butt, smashing it against the boy's jaw. Lucas staggered, and dropped at Archie's feet.

"Lucas!" Mike didn't think of the lack of cover, the odds. He bolted toward his son.

Archie took aim at Mike. Barreling down the dock, every nerve straining, Mike could almost see it coming as Archie squeezed the trigger.

Swig?" ARCHIE STOOD holding a plastic pint of Johnnie Walker, goading Mike, who sat on the ground. In his other hand, Archie held a .30-06 Winchester. Mike had had plenty of time to get to know the rifle. The shot on the dock had missed him, thanks to Archie's shaky aim, but this would be point-blank range.

"No." His fists were clenched, wrists raw against the rope binding them behind his back. He'd been straining at the rope all through the twilight hour, trying to loosen it as he'd watched half the whiskey go down Archie's throat.

"Sure?" Archie tilted the open bottle over Mike's head. "I'll pour." He snorted at the joke.

Fuck off. "I said no."

"Suit yourself." Archie shuffled back to his log, skirting the campfire, and sat, the rifle across his knees.

Mike took a break from straining at the rope and leaned against the cold metal at his back. The camp where he and Dana were captives in the woods lay in the split-open belly of a crashed World War Two bomber, and he was sitting against a twisted wing. The olive-drab fuselage, partially sunk into a moraine, was long overgrown with spruce and alders and cottonwoods, and the only edges still visible were shrouded with rotted camouflage netting. The hulk looming around him in the twilight shadows seemed a ghostly embodiment of failure, literally a wreckage of technological dreams.

"How 'bout you?" Archie asked Dana, raising the bottle. She was sitting cross-legged beside Lucas, who lay on a sleeping bag, a bruise purpling the side of his jaw. Sorting the contents of her first aid kit, Dana ignored Archie's offer.

"Go on, do you good after the scare. What d'they say? 'Medicinal purposes.' After all, we got no *doctors* out here." He gave her a sour grin.

Dana was examining the label on some painkillers. "Drop it, Archie."

Mike admired her cool. The two of them were this drunken idiot's prisoners, and Lucas was hurt, but there had to be some way out. At least the drunkenness had saved his life back on the dock: Archie's wild shot had hit the plane's propeller. Charging, Mike had hoped to tackle him before he could shoot again, and Lucas, too, was getting to his feet. Then, Archie swung the rifle around to aim at Dana as she swam to shore. Mike yelled, "No!" and Lucas lurched to block the shot, crying, "Thomas doesn't want this!" and Archie finally snapped out of his hunter's trance.

He'd searched Mike, taken his cell phone, and, with the rifle trained on Dana as she reached shore, ordered

Lucas to tie Mike's hands behind him. Mike groaned as he'd watched Archie heave the phone into the river. Archie pocketed Dana's ignition keys, gave her two minutes to change aboard into a dry shirt and jeans—she'd insisted on another minute to stuff her first aid kit into a backpack—and then he marched her and Mike out of the village, with Lucas leading the way. Mike could see that Lucas was trudging on in a fog of pain and doubt, but when he tried to speak to him Archie jabbed Mike's gashed shoulder with the rifle, forbidding all talk. They went deep into the woods, across a creek, up a rocky moraine of scrub pine, walking gradually uphill for about an hour, it seemed to Mike, though with his hands tied behind him he couldn't check his watch; he was judging by the deepening orange of the setting sun. Reaching the camp, he glimpsed sled dogs chained in the woods, a few barking at their arrival. Since then, he and Dana and Archie and Lucas had been sitting in uneasy silence around the fire, waiting for Thomas Fraser to arrive. Thomas, Archie said, would decide what to do with them.

Archie had immediately begun rummaging for liquor in his stores aboard the wreckage, and Dana told Mike about the plane. "It's a B-24," she said, helping Lucas sit, and kneeling to tend to his cut lip. "A middle range bomber out of Eielson." The Air Force Base in Fairbanks. She said everyone in Tokana knew about the half-century-old hulk. It was embedded in her people's lore, a fluke of history that had become part of their landscape. "Wish I'd remembered it before," she said.

"Shut up," Archie told her, opening a bottle.

The collective memory of Dana's people wouldn't help anyone find them now, Mike thought: they were in their new settlement over a hundred miles away. And even if D'Alton alerted anyone of Dana's failure to return, outsiders searching would almost certainly not know of the wreck, while the dense leaf canopy would make it all but invisible from the air. Not that Mike wanted to be found—that could only lead to his arrest. But he did want Dana and Lucas out of danger. And he needed to get free. He had to find a way.

"I'll have some of that," Lucas said. With a sullen scowl he turned away from Dana and got to his feet, awkward with the cast on his arm.

"Atta boy!" Archie said, handing him the whiskey. "Bottom's up."

Mike caught the pain in Dana's eyes as she watched Lucas drink . . . and the bitterness in Lucas's. The kid's so angry at the world, he thought. So mad at me. He looked up at the pale stars flickering in the darkness, a darkness deepened by storm clouds moving in. It had to be midnight. Sunup in another hour. Tuesday.

Two days left to stop Ben.

The carbon filament plan was dead. He had no way to reach Wayne without the phone. No Wayne, no materials. There was the radio on Dana's plane, if they could get to it, but that could only connect him to some authority looking to arrest him, or to a stranger, unlikely to help a fugitive. Dana's hope of getting D'Alton to the governor was also dead: too late now to make the meeting. Anyway, Archie's erratic shot had clipped a wide shard off one propeller blade, so Dana couldn't fly until the prop was repaired. And Mike sensed that she wouldn't even try to leave without Lucas: thinking that the HARC disaster was all but inevitable, she'd be wanting to get him away to safety in the time left. So did Mike—though he could see that the last thing Lucas wanted was to run away with his mother. *Great timing, kid. What a day to decide to be a man.*

He forced his thoughts on HARC. Its immense power. If he *could* get free, how could he kill that power? He stared into the campfire flames, thinking: How do you kill a fire? Drown it, smother it. But of course you can't really kill power, only transform the energy. From heat and light, back into the latent energy of the combustible material. Wood from a tree that began as the energy of the sun. It's all the same power. It's all the sun . . .

"Let them go, Archie," Lucas said, handing back the bottle.

"Shut up."

"We can't keep them prisoners forever. And Uncle Thomas never meant for this to happen."

"I said shut your mouth!" He threatened Lucas with the rifle butt. Mike tensed, wrists straining at the rope, ready to scramble to his feet and charge Archie.

Dana came to Lucas's side. "If you hit him again, Archie," she warned, "you'll turn him against you. That would make it three to one."

Mike was thinking the same thing. If Lucas would side with them, they could overpower Archie.

"I can fix that," Archie growled at her. "If I blast the kid it makes one less of you. So shut up and sit down, or I'll do it." His bleary gaze took in Mike. "Think I wouldn't?" He swung the rifle barrel between Mike and Dana. "Why not? Between the two of you, you killed both *my* kids!"

Mike didn't dare budge. One false move, and Archie could cut down Lucas or Dana.

Archie suddenly looked morose. "Aw, shit, siddown, kid." When Lucas didn't move, he barked, "Siddown, both of you! And split up!" Lucas and Dana moved apart and sat, and Archie seemed satisfied. Pleased, in fact, at being lord of the situation, three captives subdued under his weapon. "Yeah, we're doing things *our* way now. Nobody tells us what to do no more." He grinned at Dana. "You're just lucky you landed on the river, 'cause me and Thomas, we got charges laid out on the airstrip and we're gonna blast a goddamm hole in it big as this wreck. That'll keep the troopers off. And if they come back in a chopper or a boat, we got enough firepower stocked here to take 'em out. Nobody's gonna burn that village. Yes, sir, we're doing things *our* way now. So you—"

"What the hell is this?" a deep voice demanded from the shadows.

Mike looked over his shoulder. A powerfully built man carrying a rifle walked into the camp. Camouflage shirt, green headband, black brush cut. Mike glanced at the others. Archie looked nervous, Dana looked relieved, and Lucas got to his feet as if in respect for a leader. Even the dogs in the trees were whimpering, excited. This had to be Thomas Fraser.

"Christ, Archie, what have you done?" Thomas said.

He stood in the center of them all, scowling at Mike, then Dana.

"Nobody interferes with us, that's what you said," Archie protested.

"You'll get interfered with plenty if these two don't show up home."

"But this is the bastard that runs HARC. He as good as killed our kids!"

Thomas turned to Mike. His scowl grew more ominous. "You're Ryder?" He glanced at Dana, then back to Mike. "You're Lucas's father?"

"Yes. Let him and Dana go. No one's responsible for your son's death but me."

"I know. He lost his mind. *You* did that."

Dana cut in, "Thomas, he doesn't run HARC anymore. He's been trying to shut it down."

Thomas said darkly, as though passing judgment, "A little late." He moved suddenly toward Mike and pulled a long hunting knife from his belt. He bent, and with one clean jerk, cut the rope binding Mike's hands. "Get the hell out. And take her with you."

"But . . . you can't just let them go!" Archie sputtered as Mike got to his feet. "They'll tell. They'll bring the law!"

"Law's coming anyway. Hostages would just make it bloodier."

Archie slumped down on the log and grabbed his whiskey, his moment of glory past.

Mike wanted Dana and Lucas out. Going to Archie he held out his hand. "Keys." Archie dug in his pocket and handed them over. Mike tossed them to Dana, then turned back to Thomas. This was the man his son was following, and Mike sensed that any appeal to Lucas to leave would depend on Thomas's response. "You're right, they'll come," he said, "but they won't back off and leave you, if that's what you're hoping. You've got a bigger enemy than you know in General Crewe. He means to secure his five-mile empty perimeter around HARC. He'll remove you, dead or alive, count on it. Best you get out, now."

Dana said, "Thomas, you've got to come, all of you. A terrible thing is going to happen, a disaster at HARC. The same thing that hurt Ron and Sophy is going to hit again, but on a massive scale. You've all got to leave."

"With you? No thanks."

"*Listen* to me. Mike says that everyone for hundreds of thousands of miles will be at risk—sent out of their minds. Brain damage, Thomas. It's going to happen in two days. There's still time to get away. We can fix my prop and I can ferry you out, one at a time."

Mike said nothing. Escape beyond the hemisphere? No, there was only time to kill HARC. But, how? He had no fresh ideas. He had nothing.

Thomas turned from Dana and set down his rifle, propping it against the battered fuselage. "We'll take our chances."

"That's *crazy*," she said.

"It's our decision, and it's final," Lucas said.

Dana ignored him. "Thomas, throw away your life if you want to. But Lucas is just a boy. And he's hurt. He's useless to you. Let him leave."

"I'm not just a boy. And I'm not useless."

Mike was struck by his forcefulness. Lucas was taking a stand. A foolish and futile one, but Mike couldn't help being impressed.

Dana didn't seem to have heard. "Thomas, don't endanger him like this. Please, let me take him with us."

"I'm not *going!*" Lucas shouted.

This, Dana heard. She turned to Mike, desperation in her eyes. "Mike, make him see."

But Mike knew that his son had made up his mind to stay no matter what . . . just as he'd made up his to fight Ben to the end. He and Lucas seemed to be moving on parallel paths of futility. It made his heart heavy, but he understood.

Lucas threw a sullen look at Dana. "This is where my ancestors chose to live and die. I will too."

"They didn't choose, Lucas!" she cried. "They wound up on a riverbank and never left. You have your whole life ahead of you. You *can* choose!"

"Got to die sometime, somewhere," Thomas said flatly. "Might as well be this way."

So much useless energy, Mike thought, watching them. Thomas's fatalism, Lucas's bitterness, Dana's desperation, Archie's hate . . . so much goddamn wasted energy. Then it hit him. *You can't kill power . . . it's just energy transformed.* Could the useless energy of this ragtag band be transformed? Focused? Archie's words echoed: *"We're gonna blast a goddamm hole as big as this wreck."*

That's it.

"Thomas," he said, "you have explosives. How much?"

"What?"

"Archie said you're going to blow a crater in the airstrip to prevent anyone landing. How much explosive material do you have?"

"All I need." Thomas's look was wary. "Why?"

"Enough to take out a small power distribution station?"

They all stared at him.

When Thomas said nothing, Mike pressed, "Where did you get it?"

"Hanley," Lucas cut in. Mike knew of the town—ten miles downstream from HARC, it was beyond Ben's cleared perimeter. "He's been working on a road crew there," Lucas added. "They do blasting."

Mike saw Lucas's excitement: Lucas understood.

Thomas said, "I brought home a couple sticks to clear away a rock after the quake last week. It was damming up the village creek. Didn't get to it, though, before all this happened."

"Can you get your hands on more?" Mike asked. "A lot more?"

"If I wanted to steal."

Everyone was watching Mike.

"You're going to blow up HARC!" Lucas said, eyes alight. "I want to help."

Mike felt an ache in his chest, part pride and part dread: the kid had courage. He'd had this split feeling once before, watching his daughter on her horse as she jumped her first fence: *Go for it! Stop!* Looking at his son, he forced himself to let go of the dread, hold on to the pride. "Good, Lucas. I can't do it alone."

"Good?" Dana's face had gone pale. She turned on Mike. *"Good?"*

His words had the opposite effect on the others, though. Thomas had caught the spark already afire in Lucas, and even Archie jumped up, eager.

"That'd be justice," Thomas said with satisfaction. "And not hard to get the dynamite. At that Hanley outfit they just lock up the shed with a chain, no guard or nothing."

"But how do we get there?" Lucas asked. "All the village boats are sold and gone."

Thomas's smile was sly. "Not mine. I hid her up the creek. That's what I went for, just now, brought her back."

"Hell, yes!" Archie said, dancing a crazy little jig. "Blow that motherfucking HARC to kingdom come!"

"No," Mike said. "There are people working there. We'll carry out a minimal strike, well planned, disciplined. And, believe me, we'll need to plan very carefully, because a tough security outfit's guarding the site. And don't fool yourselves about the risks. We'll only get one chance, and there'll be no glory. If we fail, it means disaster—if we succeed, we'll likely face jail. Either way, there's a chance of getting shot. Anybody wants to change his mind, it makes sense. Just say so now."

He tried not to look at Lucas. But Lucas remained silent. So did the other two men. Dana let out a small sound of despair, and walked away.

She thinks I'm going to get him killed. Mike blocked that out. "The planning starts right now," he said. "Thomas, give me all the specifications you know about the explosives. I'll do the math and work out what we need. Lucas, you know the HARC site, draw a map for him, explain the layout." He turned to Archie. "And you—you'll follow my instructions to the letter or you're out. Understood?"

"Sure, sure." Archie raised his hands defensively. "I just wanna see the damn place go up. Hey, you're the boss."

Mike turned back to Thomas. "How big's your boat? You sure it can take the four of us, plus all the explosive equipment?"

Thomas frowned. "Guess not. It's just a skiff."

"Then we'll get another in Hanley," Mike said. "Buy it, or steal it. How about the river between here and HARC? Is it clear? No rapids?"

"Clean as a whistle. Come on, I'll show you." He led Mike around to a homemade ladder of saplings and rope propped against the hulk. "See for yourself."

Alone, Mike climbed the sapling rungs and walked across the fuselage roof. The bomber wreckage was on a high moraine, and from this vantage point he could see all the way down, beyond the wilderness of trees, to the river flowing in the distance—a highway of molten silver in the dusk of the new day. At the bend upstream, he could just make out HARC's shadowy forest of towers on the opposite shore, their rigid symmetry in stark contrast to the rolling forest itself. His heart beat faster as he spotted pinpricks of light at the power building and the operations center. Ben and Meredith were working late. *Not for long.*

Lightning flashed, a jagged bolt so vivid, it filled

Mike with all his boyhood awe at the power of the electric universe, its magnificent dynamic balance. Then darkness rushed back, and a roar of thunder vibrated the metal under his feet, and he felt the first fat drops of rain. He shivered. If he failed, HARC would connect with all this raw power. It would violate the balance, and millions could suffer.

He shut his eyes. *Can't fail.*

"What do you see?" Dana said.

His eyes sprang open. She stood beside him, gazing down at the river. Raindrops pinged the hulk around them, and hissed in the campfire below. The others were dragging sleeping bags and rifles and camp gear into the shelter of the wreck. Mike looked out at the river too, searching for an answer that would convey his hope. "Clean as a whistle, just like Thomas said."

She nodded. "Nothing to stop you."

It seemed she wasn't going to try. Mike was relieved. He looked at her. Rain speckled her denim shirt. The campfire glow burnished her blue-black hair, and flickered in the hollow of her throat.

"Mike, I came to ask one thing."

Don't take Lucas . . . was that it? Yet something about her steadiness told him she hadn't come to fight. Raindrops hit her face, upturned to his, but she didn't flinch. She accepts the rain, he thought; she's a part of this balanced energy. It struck him how driven he'd been in the last sixteen years. Had to have it all. Academic glory, hot career, stunning wife, state-of-the-art breakthrough project. He'd got it all . . . and lost his balance.

"Hold off for one day," Dana said. "Give me today to try to reach the governor."

It surprised him. "Still? That schedule's shot, Dana. D'Alton expected you back hours ago. He'll be worried sick, waiting."

She shook her head. "No, he'll be trying to get to Juneau on his own. He believed the governor was our only hope. He'll likely have alerted my office that I'm late, but he wouldn't wait for me."

A raindrop hit the hollow of her throat and slid down to where her top buttons were open. Mike forced his eyes up. "He'd wait."

She said quietly, "I've let him down in more ways than this. I don't expect him to wait for me anymore." She went on, "The point is, though there's a chance he might get to Juneau on his own, I can't be sure. But I *can* get there. I can repair the prop and be in the capital this afternoon. And then, try to somehow get Governor Dainard to see me." She managed a wry smile. "Maybe land on his mansion grounds."

Mike was listening, but barely concentrating. *D'Alton's out of her life?* Bizarre to feel such a rush at a time like this . . . and he had no right to hope. But that voice inside wouldn't shut up: *She's free.*

"Say you'll hold off until I've had a chance at seeing the governor," she urged. "Just this one day. Promise me that much, before you commit to dynamite and guns."

Her plan seemed futile to Mike, but at least it would get her six hundred miles away from HARC. Anyway, he'd need all day to get another boat, get the dynamite, and organize the mission, and the chances of infiltrating

HARC would be best during the two hours of midnight. "I can hold off until evening, wait to hear if you've had any luck. But how can you reach me?"

"Could you get a handheld VHF radio in Hanley?"

"Good idea." Better yet, two, so he could talk to Thomas in the other boat, and when they got to HARC. "Let's make the cutoff point eight tonight. Can you live with that?"

She said somberly, "I'm hoping *you* can live with it."

She feared for his life. It moved him. Looking at her, he realized how steadily it was raining now, how oblivious they'd both been to it. Water was trickling down his cheeks, and her hair was gleaming wet, and their clothes were almost soaked. But Mike didn't want to be anywhere but here. "Dana, I think we can pull this off. They won't be expecting us at HARC, and I couldn't have three more motivated guerrilla soldiers. I feel good about it." It was true. After so many days of powerlessness, this felt like liberation. "There are risks, sure, but I won't let Lucas get hurt, I promise. And this is something I've got to do. You understand, don't you?"

"I understand more and more these days. I think that even if you knew the governor was about to pick up a phone and end this, you'd still want to destroy HARC."

Mike looked toward the far-off site. She was right. "Weird, huh? After I built it. Trying to remake the world."

"Is that what you wanted? To remake the world?"

He saw that she was sincerely curious. "In a way." How could he explain the dream that had fueled him? He suddenly remembered Lindsay's drawing and dug into his shirt pocket for it. As he unfolded the damp paper, they huddled over it, shielding it from the rain. He hoped she could make it out in the dim light—the crayoned field of green crops, the rainbow, the horse, all bathed in a golden beam. "My daughter did this."

Dana read aloud, "Daddy's Dream." She smiled up at him. "How old is she?"

"Nine." He had no intention of ever living with Carol again, but he'd fight to keep Lindsay. "I'd mentioned irrigation systems to her, told her I hoped HARC would one day tap into auroral power and convey inexpensive energy globally—give a boost to even the poorest, most remote areas. Make a better world? I hoped so, yeah." He thought, with a pang: *That dream's dead.* The drawing was getting damp. He folded it and stuffed it in his pants pocket. "Well, that was the idea."

"I never knew. Guess I . . . never wanted to know." She added, like a confession, "That's something else I'm beginning to understand." She raised both hands and smoothed her wet hair back from her face—an unconscious gesture, but it stirred Mike. Raindrops clung to her lips. Her shirt clung to her breasts.

"I was wrong about Lucas, too," she said, meeting his gaze. "Lucas . . . and you. The village would have drained the life out of him. Going to university close to you, that would open up his world. You were right."

"Was I?" He could almost feel her body heat reach him through the space between them. All he could think of was kissing her wet mouth.

"I even understand that Lucas has to go with you now, if you do this thing. It's what he wants."

"He knows he needs to, Dana. For so many reasons. To avenge the girl he loved. To see justice done for the deaths he couldn't prevent. I know how he feels, because I need this too, to set right all the harm I've caused with HARC. Just like I wish I could set right . . . choices I've made in my life. Like leaving, sixteen years ago."

He realized he was gripping her shoulders.

She didn't resist. "Mike, if you'd stayed it would have drained the life out of you too. You had to go. I knew that. You had to go . . . to be *you*. And I had to stay."

"To be you."

"Only, what I gave up . . . I didn't know it would be so hard. All these years without you."

A spark shot through him. No matter what lay ahead, no matter what dangers, nothing could smother this spark, this certainty of her love.

He pulled her to him. Her mouth opened under his.

"Ryder?" It was Thomas, calling up. Mike felt Dana slip out of his arms.

Thomas had come out of the wreckage, and he shouted up through the din of the rain, "We gonna plan this or not?"

Mike and Dana stood staring at each other, both breathing hard. He subdued the ache for her. "Yeah. On my way."

▲

"Liftoff in five minutes, sir. Buckle up," the pilot advised.

Reid D'Alton fastened his seat belt in the rear of the

troopers' search-and-rescue helicopter. He was hoping he hadn't waited too long to call them; he'd waited as long as he dared. Dana had said she would return before midnight, but she hadn't reckoned on a thunderstorm. It was 4:00 A.M. now, the sun strong, and the three-man SAR team were climbing into the seats around him. In a few minutes they'd begin following Dana's assumed route to Takona. They knew Ryder had gone with her— Reid had told them. The only thing he hadn't told about was Ryder's carbon-filament sabotage idea. He still wasn't sure he'd made the right decision in calling them at all.

He hadn't decided lightly. Alone in the Aurora Aviation office at midnight as the thunderstorm peaked, he'd tried for almost two hours to raise Dana's plane on the VHF. No reply. He'd called every fifteen minutes, wondering whether to alert the troopers. The meeting with the governor was impossible now. That was no longer Reid's objective. The situation with HARC had become grotesque, insurmountable—the peril that loomed had spiraled out of his control. All he hoped for now was to find Dana . . . and find her alive. As for Ryder, if he, too, was still alive and the troopers arrested him, that wasn't Reid's concern. He had one goal: to get out of Alaska with Dana before the disaster hit in two days.

If she was dead, he'd get the hell out alone.

The helicopter lifted off and they left Fairbanks behind, and soon the vastness of tundra and taiga stretched out below them like a universe. The pilot reached the Gatana River and followed it north, and soon Reid saw the village. "There's her plane! There, by the dock!"

The pilot landed on the dirt path to the dock, muddy from the night's rain, and Reid climbed out with the team. They found Dana's plane empty. No sign of her or Ryder.

The village, too, appeared deserted.

Reid remembered Dana's anxiety about Lucas: *"I'm afraid he's done something stupid."* He turned to the team leader. "Captain, they may have gone on foot to search for her son." He explained what Dana had told him about two village holdouts taking off into the bush. He felt bad about being an informer—Dana hadn't wanted to bring down the law on her brother-in-law—but how could he expect these men to find her if he withheld information?

It was 6:00 A.M. when they lifted off to fly a search pattern over the surrounding terrain.

▲

Mike emerged from the woods behind Takona, Thomas beside him, the three others following. Mike and Thomas were laden with gear they'd carried down from the camp: rifles, ammunition, tools, coils of rope, several backpacks for the dynamite. Despite the load, Mike felt energized, braced by the morning's clean smell of ozone after the lightning, and refreshed by the few hours rest. Hard keeping away from Dana's corner of the wreck, but a welcome rest nonetheless.

They headed along the muddy path to the river, then down the dock, slippery from the rain, and reached Thomas's boat. A dented aluminum skiff with a twenty-horsepower Mercury outboard, it was tied up beside Dana's Aeronca Chief. Mike and Thomas tossed the gear into the boat and set down the rifles, and Dana went to the plane. As Thomas unhooked the hose to gas up his tank, Mike checked his watch. Six-twenty. Should make it downstream to Hanley before eight. If he and Thomas could get another boat, and then steal the dynamite as easily as Thomas predicted, they should make it back here around noon. Mike picked up the Winchester he was taking, Archie's rifle, to check it one last time. He didn't want to use it, but he would if he had to.

He caught Dana's anxious glance at the weapon, then she quickly turned back to her own task. "I have a hacksaw aboard," she told Archie as she climbed into the plane. "We'll cut a piece off the opposing blade to balance the prop, then file both edges smooth." She added over her shoulder, "Should only take a couple of hours."

"Will it fly, though?" Archie asked her as she stepped back out with a tool kit.

"She'll lose a little power, but she'll fly."

Lucas said eagerly, "Mike, I should come with you and Thomas. If there's trouble in Hanley I could handle the boat for you. You know, getting away?"

Mike shook his head. They'd already been through this. "You help repair Dana's prop, you and Archie. Plenty for you to do once we get to HARC." He knew Dana was cherishing these last hours with Lucas, unsure when she'd see him again. The kid seemed oblivious to her fears. Mike wanted to cuff him.

Dana suddenly left her tools and walked to the other side of the dock. Mike had caught her troubled look, as though she was fighting tears. He put down the rifle and went to her. They stood looking out at the calm river. So much he wanted to tell her . . .

A flock of trumpeter swans had settled near the far shore, lazing in the sunshine. "Peaceful here," he said, hating the lame platitude.

"My ancestors called it a sacred place."

Mike remembered his friend Ravi's words. He quoted: "The hiding places of the gods."

She looked at him. "Pardon?"

"Takona's on a fault line. Electromagnetic discharges from tectonic strain can produce anomalies in EM fields, which could be what gives this place a special feel. A friend of mine studies the effects of geomagnetic forces on perception, and he's found that certain anomalous fields can produce a heightened sense of well-being." *Shut up,* he told himself. *She doesn't want a dissertation.*

A smile curved her lips. "Everything's science to you, isn't it?"

Lord, no. He took her face in his hands. "Some things are pure magic."

She said quietly, "The river spirit lives here, Mike. I'll ask him to watch over you."

She softly kissed him, then stepped back with an embarrassed glance at the others. Mike caught Lucas watching, wide-eyed. *Time you knew, kid.* He took Dana in his arms and kissed her hard.

She whispered, "Bring him home."

"I will."

Minutes later he and Thomas were roaring off in the boat, breaking up the flock of honking swans. Mike smiled in the fresh breeze. He thought: They won't stop us in Hanley, and they won't stop us at HARC. I'll be back. Now that there's so much to come back for.

▲

Ben strode under the slowing blades of General Graham Sloan's helicopter as America's top soldier climbed out onto the tarmac at Fort Wainwright in Fairbanks. The chairman of the Joint Chiefs had a stocky, unimposing physique that, like his bland face and sparse gray hair, led some to underestimate his dynamism. Ben knew the smart ones did that only once. A Marine colonel climbed out after Sloan, carrying his boss's briefcase.

"No bag, Graham?" Ben asked, shaking his friend's hand. Thirty-two years ago, escaping, they'd helped each other survive the jungle hills north of Dien Bien Phu. Now, they would help each other again. "Didn't Carol tell you she booked you a suite?"

"Getting right back in the air for California after your show this morning, Ben. Speech to give at Camp Pendleton tonight."

My show. Ben felt a thrill. For five years he'd been preparing for this moment. He'd done everything he could to simultaneously advance and shield his project so that he could present it to the country's military leaders as a fully operational weapons system, ready to deploy, with no political fallout for them. They alone had the power to embrace it, and then to shut the public window on it. Forever. Ben's moment had come.

"The observation center's just ten minutes away," he

said. "Mr. Kaplan's already there." Ronald Kaplan, the national security adviser, had interrupted his vacation in Oregon to attend. A political hawk who'd savaged his share of opponents, Kaplan had shown keen interest at Ben's hints of an antiballistic breakthrough. "The demonstration will begin on schedule at oh-nine-hundred, Graham. After, if you have time, I'll give you both a tour of the site, a ninety-minute drive away. I believe you're going to be very, very pleased with what I have to show you."

As they walked toward Ben's car, where his driver stood with the rear door open, Sloan said, "My office has been tracking your little media storm up here, Ben. I understand your lead scientist went rogue. What's the score?"

"Small problem, just overwork. It's been taken care of."

Sloan frowned. "Small? Isn't this fellow your daughter's husband?" He stopped before they reached the car, out of earshot of the driver. "Ben, that's got to hurt."

It did. But he wouldn't let the top man see that, friends or not. "The important thing is HARC, Graham. Dr. Crosbie, who's running the program now, is exceptional. We're in great shape." Crosbie was ready, had been ready since yesterday. It seemed to Ben she was almost as eager as he was.

He checked his watch as they slid into the backseat. Oh-seven-three-five. His thoughts jumped to Mike. Where was he? The last update from the state troopers had been at oh-four-hundred—a SAR mission to find a plane in which Dana James had been carrying Mike to

Takona. Why Takona? It made no sense: the place was deserted. All Mike's actions lately seemed frantic: recklessly breaking into the site Sunday night, terrifying Carol back at the house, then disappearing with the James woman. Yet Ben felt a certainty that Mike was still a player, an adversary to be reckoned with. Takona was only three miles from HARC.

As the car pulled out of Fort Wainwright and onto the Richardson Highway, heading for the observation center, Ben told himself to relax. Mike believed the demonstration was set for Thursday, two days away. He couldn't know that in less than an hour and a half, HARC was going to prove itself in all its power and glory.

Tuesday, 8:50 A.M.

How's the prop repair? Over." Mike spoke into the handheld VHF radio as he steered the outboard motor with his free hand.

"Got airborne thirty minutes ago, no problems," Dana's voice crackled back. "Hell of a head wind, though. Next stop Juneau. Your status? Over."

"On my way too." A chevron of snow geese flying above the river mirrored the V wake from Mike's boat as he headed back toward Takona. The battered, fourteen-foot aluminum skiff stank of fish guts, and its cranky outboard needed a tune-up, but he'd been glad to get it. Boat, motor, and radio had been part of a quick and dirty deal he'd done with a retired fisherman in Hanley, a grungy little river port of fishermen and loggers and a temporary road construction crew. Thomas had gone ahead in his own boat with the dynamite, and now, as Mike watched the geese overtake him above, he was glad of the moment of solitude. He was alone on the broad river, but as he talked to Dana he felt connected to everything that mattered.

She'd soon be out of radio range, though. He scanned the sky, hoping to see the distant speck of her plane. Instead, he spotted a helicopter. Far off to his right, it was heading west. Mike was going north. He watched it for a few moments until he was satisfied it was maintaining its course away from him. Wherever it was going, it didn't seem concerned about him.

"The job went off without a hitch," he told Dana, turning his attention back to the river. Dimpled water ahead to the right indicated a barely submerged rock, and he could discern more past it. He steered left. "We got all we need. We're in good shape." Anyone could be listening on this channel, so he wasn't giving details about stealing the dynamite. It still surprised him how simple it had been for him and Thomas to cut the chain on the explosives shed at the edge of town, fill their backpacks, and carry them back to the wharf. "Thomas left loaded up a half hour ago. I got delayed a bit getting gas, but I'm on my way now. Wish us luck. Over."

"Thought you scientists didn't believe in luck. Over."

"I do after last night." The excitement of her kiss, her body against his, still lingered. "Dana, when—" He broke off, the din of the ailing outboard suddenly loud. No, not the motor, he realized, looking up over his shoulder. The helicopter. It was banking about a quarter mile behind him, following the river. Following him?

Its colors—and that dot of insignia. Troopers.

"Sorry, Dana. Gotta go."

He tossed the radio to the floor and twisted the throttle, gunning the motor. *Where to? Can't outrun a heli-copter.* He spotted cottonwoods crowding the shore in the distance ahead, branches overhanging the water. He glanced back. The chopper was still so far away it looked like a toy. There was a chance it hadn't spotted him yet. If so, he might hide under the cottonwoods canopy. Spewing a foamy wake as he jerked the boat to the right, he sped toward the shore.

"Mike? Do you copy?" Dana's voice crackled. When he'd tossed down the radio, it had skidded and landed under the bow seat, and he could barely hear her over the roar of the outboard. "Mike . . . come in . . ."

Racing on, he couldn't reach for the radio and steer as well. Couldn't answer.

▲

"Five minutes to initiation, sir."

"Thank you, Lieutenant."

Optics. Visuals. That's what mattered now. Ben stood in command in the HARC observation center in Fair-banks, flanked by his two guests, while his ONR assis-tant, Lieutenant Gopnik, a lanky Texan, sat quietly managing the communications interface with the HARC site and with U.S. Space Command. Ben glanced over his shoulder at Carol, the only other observer. She was in an elevated area in the rear, behind a glass partition, and she stood watching, arms folded as though hugging her-self against a cold world. No wonder, he thought; what a price she'd paid, with Mike. But he was proud of her: she'd remained loyal. Now, HARC's moment had come, and she knew as well as he did how much depended on the visuals.

Ben had designed the room to be a mini replica of the Pentagon's National Military Command Center to make his guests feel at home, and he was pleased with the success of the effect. The subdued lighting, the soundproofed hush, and, of course, the centerpiece: the big board, a high-definition display screen fifteen feet wide and ten feet tall. On it, a Pentagon world situation map was surrounded by video windows showing silent feeds from the six networks, CNN, and MSNBC, while a larger central window overlaying the map depicted computer animation of the target satellite—today's "kill"—above the South China Sea. Crowning the big board, a digital clock's large red numerals indicated four minutes and fifty-five seconds until initiation.

Ben was satisfied by all this, and even more by the looks of anticipation on the faces of the men for whom he had created it. His friend Graham Sloan sat to his right, arms folded over his chest—a chest that the public usually saw uniformed and bright with campaign ribbons, but today was dull with a beige shirt and tan sports jacket. To Ben's left was Ronald Kaplan, the national security adviser, a dark-haired, wiry Manhattanite wearing a green polo shirt and gray chinos. Neither man looked imposing, but their power was. The opposite of this room, Ben thought. The real power was out at HARC eighty miles away, but the nondescript scientific instruments there wouldn't have impressed these men. In this fabricated room, with its high-tech luster, they were comfortable. This felt big. And soon the displays would show them something very big indeed: success. As a professional soldier, Ben knew how vital such visuals were, from the hard lessons of Vietnam, when horrific casualty images every night on America's living-room screens had derailed the war effort, to the application of those lessons in the Gulf War, when the Pentagon's management of every inch of news videotape had kept the public happily focused. Even Sloan and Kaplan, sophisticated in Washington spin-doctoring, would not be immune to the impact of the images they were about to see. If all went well, this would win Ben his goal.

If. He stifled his anxiety as he glanced at the clock. Time to set the stage.

"Gentlemen," he said, "as you know, our satellites can detect a missile launching anywhere on the globe, but we've never had the means to shoot down an ICBM in flight. Until today. In four minutes, you're going to see how. Let me give you a preview."

He nodded to Lieutenant Gopnik at the controls, and instantly the computer animation in the center of the big board enlarged and split into two windows. One was a virtual view from outer space of the target, a defunct Navy satellite, 1986 model, metallic-gray, pockmarked from minute asteroids. It was orbiting in serene obsolescence above the sapphire South China Sea. The second window was a landscape view of Earth's horizon with HARC pinpointed near the north pole and the satellite hovering half the globe away. And, in a preview depiction of the kill, a golden beam from HARC streamed up on a diagonal, struck the ionosphere, and was reflected down to bombard the satellite. These were all virtual images. However, the satellite itself was real: USNS1287, an obsolete piece of orbiting hardware. The kill would also be real.

"Gentlemen, the defunct satellite 1287 is our stand-in today for an enemy missile. It has been recalled to duty for the purposes of this demonstration. A signal has been sent to reactivate its engines. In a few moments HARC will change that."

"General Crewe," Lieutenant Gopnik said, "Dr. Crosbie on the line."

"Excuse me," Ben said to his guests as he picked up the phone. He thought of Crosbie out there at HARC with the remains of Mike's team. After the rash of firings and resignations, they'd been reduced to a minimum— just five manning the array from the ops center, and a handful of technicians overseeing the reactor. Tenacious as a bulldog, Crosbie had assured Ben it was sufficient.

"We're ready here, General," she reported. "Are you?"

"Affirmative, Dr. Crosbie. You may proceed. I'd like to add that you have done fine work under trying circumstances in your wilderness post, you and your team. Godspeed." He hung up, aware that Sloan and Kaplan had overheard, as he'd intended. His aim was to convey a sense of scientific-military occasion, something approaching the excitement of the first atomic bomb test a half century ago in the New Mexico desert. Extraordinary new weapon—extraordinary new power.

If it works. He'd been forced to push ahead so fast— had it been too fast? Did Crosbie really know what she was doing? *If only Mike were there instead . . . I could trust Mike's judgment.* The thought shook him. No, he reminded himself, Mike had been the one person he *couldn't* trust. But it was too late for Mike to stop him now.

"Sir, I have Colonel Mason of U.S. Space Command."

"Open it up, Lieutenant."

Gopnik hit the button to open the channel so that when Ben spoke to Cheyenne Mountain everyone in the room could hear. U.S. Space Command tracked some of the myriad pieces of space debris orbiting Earth, ranging from rocket fragments to abandoned satellites. At latest count, the total number was over a hundred thousand; Space Command tracked about eight thousand. Earlier, Ben had relayed his request to Colonel Mason. "Colonel," he asked now, "have you established observation on 1287?"

"Yes, we're on it, General. Engine reactivation is confirmed."

"Good. I'm going to hand you over now to General Sloan." Turning to his old friend, he made a gesture that said, Go ahead. Ben had planned this moment carefully: he wanted Graham to feel in command.

"Colonel, this is General Sloan."

"Yes, sir, General." Ben heard the controlled awe in the colonel's voice at speaking to the chairman of the Joint Chiefs.

"I want you to watch the target satellite carefully," Sloan said, his eyes on the big board clock. "In one minute thirty-five seconds we're going to take it out."

"Take it out, sir? I . . . don't follow."

"Just maintain observation and stand by."

"Standing by, sir."

Ben nodded to Lieutenant Gopnik, who adjusted his controls, and the room dimmed. On the big board, the windows with the network feeds went to black, and the overlay of the world map dimmed. Then the two central windows with the simulation enlarged: the target satellite in close-up, and Earth with HARC and the satellite highlighted. The five people present silently watched the bright color images as a taped countdown began, a male voice intoning the ten-second units:

"Sixty seconds to initiation . . . fifty seconds . . ."

▲

Motor screaming, the skiff was planing, the aluminum hull skimming the river's surface. Gripping the open throttle, Mike squinted into the wind. He knew he wouldn't make it.

The helicopter was almost on top of him, rotors roaring, the water mounding in circular ripples. Looking up as he raced on, he was shocked to see Reid D'Alton's face peering down at him. D'Alton had brought these troopers! Or they'd brought *him*. Whatever, they were here, and Mike had no time to think about how or why. Every nerve in him was straining to escape.

"Dr. Ryder, this is the Alaska State Troopers," a loudspeaker boomed. "Please, stop your boat!"

Fuck you. Mike crouched lower to reduce drag, and sped on. The race was hopeless . . . but he couldn't bring himself to give up.

"Ryder, it's me, D'Alton! You've got to stop!"

▲

"Ten seconds to initiation . . . nine . . . eight . . . seven . . ."

All eyes were on the big board: the virtual satellite and the virtual HARC. Ben's heart was banging so hard, he thought the others must hear it. *Let this work . . .*

"Three . . . two . . . one . . ."

HARC's beam on the big board glowed a dazzling gold, a depiction of the invisible waves that were actually beaming up from the site eighty miles away. In the simulation, the patch of ionosphere struck by the beam blazed red-hot for an instant, then cooled to a shimmer, like molten silver: a gigantic space mirror. HARC's precise beam reflected down from the mirror and bombarded the satellite image. The satellite exploded.

Silence in the room.

Ben held his breath.

Sloan asked over the open channel, "Colonel Mason, can you give me confirmation on the target? Do you show a direct hit?"

"That's affirmative, sir. We've lost telemetry with 1287. It's now off our screens. It appears that you . . . took it out."

Ben finally breathed. *It works.*

Sloan and Kaplan were both studying the vacant point in space above the South China Sea. In unison they nodded, impressed.

Ben fought to suppress his jubilation. *Make the pitch.*

"Gentlemen, you've just seen HARC knock out the

target's electronics systems, sending its engines out of control and causing its solid fuel propellant to explode. In this way, it can destroy any incoming ICBM. HARC's focusable energy beam, and its ability to incapacitate electronics—including missile guidance and detonation systems—gives us a unique new antiballistic defense. In effect, HARC renders enemy electronics brain-dead, and the units destroy themselves. And, it also can extend HARC's supremacy far *beyond* missile defense. Let me show you."

He nodded to Lieutenant Gopnik, who tapped at the controls. On the big board, the Pentagon's world situation map intensified, and three windows sprang to the margin showing actual, real-time visuals from three U.S. surveillance satellites: a North Korean military airfield, a sprawling Baghdad factory, and a Chinese battleship plying the Straits of Taiwan.

Gopnik hit another button, and special effects were superimposed on the surveillance images: a computer-animated jet lifted off from the Korean airfield, a truck drove away from the Baghdad factory, a missile was launched from the Chinese battleship. Then, the central window depicted a simulated series of HARC activations, its reflected beam directed at one target after another, destroying them. The Iraqi truck burst into flames, the Korean jet exploded in air, the Chinese missile's flight became erratic, spiraling in free fall.

Ben said, "Gentlemen, in HARC America has a weapon that can reach around the globe to take out enemy targets without having to fire a shot. It can strike with the speed of light. Surgical, over-the-horizon kill capability. Zero risk to our military personnel. No cost increase, whether it's one kill or a thousand. HARC introduces a new concept of warfare. It is fully operational, ready to deploy. And it is now at your disposal."

He was done. His palms were sweating, his heart still thumping, and all he could focus on was the frown on Kaplan's face.

"It's in contravention of the ABM treaty," Kaplan said, mulling.

Ben drew hope from his tone: Kaplan *wanted* HARC, was annoyed he couldn't have it, and was looking for a way around the problem. The very response Ben had hoped for. Now he needed to strike the right note: coach them, but with deference. "Mr. Kaplan, my authority allowed me to build HARC only as something insignificant, a research project. As such, I have hidden the weapon in plain sight, temporarily impotent. You and General Sloan have the authority to make it potent. But to do so, you must hide it permanently."

"Yes, I see," Sloan said, seeming to realize the solution. "A national security obligation." He and Kaplan looked at one another. Suddenly, they were both grinning.

Kaplan got up and shook Ben's hand. "Congratulations, General Crewe. I believe you've just delivered this country an astonishing new advantage."

Sloan stood too. "Outstanding, Ben. Just outstanding. I want to arrange in-depth briefings with you and your lead scientist, but first I'm going to black-box the whole operation immediately." He gestured to a phone. "May I?"

Ben was elated. Years of secrecy and strain, weeks of setbacks . . . now, instant success. "Please do." From this moment on HARC would be top secret. His troubles were over: Litvak's investigation could not touch him. He was vindicated, his country strengthened, his mark on history made. He had won.

He turned to Carol, watching behind the glass, and gave her a brisk victory nod. Relief swept her face, followed by a tenuous smile. Then she slumped into a chair and covered her mouth with her hand, as though to hold back tears.

The tension, Ben thought. His own joy, however, could not be deflated. Jubilant, he thought of Crosbie, and decided to congratulate her. He asked Gopnik to get her on the line.

A moment later Gopnik said, puzzlement in his voice, "No answer at the site, sir."

"No answer?" He watched as Gopnik tried again.

"None, sir. The line's gone dead."

Ben didn't have time to speak before the visuals on the big board vanished, and all the lights went out. A vibration like a fluttering wind swept the pitch-black room.

▲

She'd turned back after Mike's last transmission. *"Sorry Dana. Gotta go."* No response to all her attempts to raise him. And he was alone on the water. She'd headed back to look for him, and now she was almost at the river as she tried again. "Mike, come in, this is—"

A vibration startled her—an odd fluttering against her body. Then static in her headphones, painful in her ears. She swiped off the 'phones. She noticed her electronics in surprise: her instruments had died. She tapped the GPS, then the fuel gauge. Dead as the radio. The altitude indicator was out too, and the VOR. A short in the system?

The engine died. A chill of adrenaline shot through her. Magneto failure—no power. *Got to glide.* Manipulating the ailerons and elevator and rudder, she headed for a treeless stretch of tundra. Could she make it?

A jolt inside her head—like a shock. Then dark emptiness in her mind—a void. Her hands dropped from the controls. Her body's energy drained. She slumped back in her seat. Heard the stall warning sounder: a whistle of wind. Saw the left wing drop . . .

She forced a thought: *Stop the spin—full right rudder.* But she couldn't move. The earth rushed closer, pines and rocks funneling toward her. Fear engulfed her.

A huge raven swept out of a cloud, so dazzling that Dana's breath caught. Black body iridescent in the sun, eyes agleam, it swept into the cockpit, hovered before her eyes. Its light-jeweled wings spread out like a totem, filling her with wonder. Iridescence trembled the cockpit air.

"Why're you flying so low, Dana-rayna? Follow me, *this* way."

Carla's voice! Raven-rusty, laughing!

Dana watched wide-eyed as her raven-sister swept back out of the cockpit and hovered, waiting. The feathered wings, undulating, pulsed such emotion through her . . . love, homesickness, girlhood delight. She longed to follow Carla . . .

But, Carla's dead. What's happening? *It's not real.*

The raven vision vanished and the sky dimmed, cold and lonely. Dana looked down. Real world. *Crashing* . . .

Carla again soared out of the clouds. "Race you to the river!"

Dana groped for the controls, eager to follow her wondrous iridescent sister. *Carla, take me with you!*

▲

Mike jerked the throttle, spinning the boat a hundred eighty degrees in a wild, splashed wall of foam, and sped south. It was a desperate maneuver, and futile. He couldn't escape the helicopter hovering behind him like a massive bird of prey. Glancing back, he saw it bank, unable to spin as fast as he had, but soon it would swoop to follow him and . . .

A vibration shuddered the air . . . pulsed through Mike's bones . . .

The huge machine above seemed to hit some invisible wire and stagger. It skidded across the sky as if dragged along above the trees. It stalled, immobile for a breathless moment. Then dropped like a boulder. Stunned, Mike saw the forest swallow it, heard the muffled explosion. Birds burst up like scattershot, screaming. Orange flames boiled, and black oily smoke, and . . .

A wild disorientation nailed him. It wrenched his hand from the throttle, knocked him off the seat, slammed him against the side of the skiff. Incapacitated, he sat sprawled on the floor of the speeding boat, his shoulder blades pinned to the stern seat.

The world blurred past him, incomprehensible. A fish leaped, thrashing. A bird plunged to the water like lead. His mind groped for meaning in the nightmare panorama. Pointed pines on shore seemed like rumbling rockets . . . the cloud-clumped blue above was an ocean of icebergs . . . the wind on his face, a smothering plastic film. Why was everything so wrong? Chaotic, senseless. *Where am I?*

He groped for the throttle in a desperate need to take control. But his hand was shaking, his mind and body beyond his will. He saw the dimpled water ahead, too late to swerve.

The aluminum hull crunched over the submerged rocks. The boat felt airborne, a missile, twisting Mike into the air. His lungs sucked air . . . sucked water. His mind plunged into darkness.

Tuesday, 9:07 A.M.

GASPING, MIKE FORCED his face above the surface. His eyes sprang open. He was lying on the riverbank, face lolling in the shallows . . .

Coughing water, he struggled up onto his hands and knees. Pain shot through his left hand. He lurched backward out of the water, flopped onto his back, and lifted his throbbing hand. His index finger was broken.

Wincing, he lay on the muddy grass, catching his breath, blinking in the sun. A welter of aches through his body . . . a residue of fear in his mind. He tasted blood, and sat up, spitting blood. He touched his mouth. His lower lip was split.

What happened? How had he got here? He'd been in a boat . . .

He looked at the river. The skiff was drifting in a tangle of reeds a stone's throw from where he sat, its bow nudging the shore. He thought: Grab it before it drifts off. He started to his feet, but at the sudden wallop of dizziness he thudded down again. The boat wasn't going anywhere, and neither was he until he could get himself together.

What happened?

A noise startled him, a flapping sound. A chum salmon the size of his arm was thrashing on the grass. He looked around. Along the thin beach, a scatter of fish were flopping in their death throes or lying dead. Just past his boot was a dead trumpeter swan, washed to shore. He saw a few more floating dead birds, smaller ones, snagged among the water grass. Drowned? He thought of Sophy's floating corpse snagged by boulders. His skin prickled. He scrambled to his feet.

What in God's name happened?

He stood at the river's edge, dripping water, his legs shaky, and saw, across the river, oily black smoke snaking up from deep within the trees. The troopers . . . with Reid D'Alton. The horror rushed back: the helicopter skidding across the sky and crashing. *No way they could have survived.* He remembered his boat speeding on unmanned, his mind disintegrating in bizarre petrifying visions: *drowning with Sophy . . . blasted apart with Ron.* He slammed shut that terrifying memory.

Focus on now, on reality. He wished he could check for survivors, but there was no way he could bushwhack over to the helicopter. Better to retrieve the skiff and report the crash on the VHF emergency channel. What time was it?

His watch had stopped.

The fact, so trivial, made him freeze. Like the neutral line under a column of figures that leads to a total, his static watch led him to an answer. It staggered him. The watch was powered by a computer chip—it had failed. The helicopter relied on electronics—failed. His *mind*—failed. *All at the same moment.* And before that, the vibration . . .

His heart banged in his chest. He knew. He had no scientific proof, but he knew. ELF radiation. HARC.

Words Ben had once said came rushing back. *"A good commander doesn't wait for the enemy to come to him."* To Ben, I'm the enemy, so he's produced the demonstration *early.* He's powered up HARC. The resonance event . . .

It's happened.

He struggled to take it in. The world seemed unchanged. Water lapped placidly at his soaked boots. A breeze rustled the aspen trees behind him, chilling the back of his wet neck. Everything seemed peaceful. But around him was the evidence. Suffocating fish, drowned birds, smoking helicopter, drifting boat.

The implications crashed in on him. Were jetliners falling from the sky? Was there carnage on the roads? Violence in the cities? Were people all over Alaska affected? Alaska and beyond? The whole hemisphere? *How far? How many people? How terrible?*

He felt sheer, runaway panic. He forced a brake on it, forced himself to think. How long had he been lying unconscious? Minutes or hours? Can't be hours, or I would've drowned. And the helicopter's still smoking. And the sun hasn't moved. Minutes, then . . . it's gone on for just minutes.

Only, why can I think clearly *now*?

He looked up. A hawk drifted overhead, rising in a

thermal, recovered, unconcerned. *It's over,* Mike thought. The stab of relief was so sharp it hurt. If it's over . . . I must have been wrong. About HARC going out of control, the resonance escalating, unstoppable. If that had happened my mind would be jelly.

He'd never been so glad to find he'd screwed up. Grinning, he felt his split lip sting. *Thank God, I was wrong.*

He thought it through. Meredith must have managed to shut down HARC before the resonance escalated. He'd been in the same position himself ten days ago, during the test, when he'd lost those seven seconds. That was the first tiny resonance pulse, and the moment he recovered he'd shut everything down before the next pulse could build. Meredith must have taken the same quick action. She'd caught it in time.

It's over *now*, he thought with a pang, but what's it done? It's over like a bomb: one deadly blast. How many has it killed? Planes falling from the sky . . .

Dana.

He looked up at the blue expanse, empty but for the hawk. He felt a wild thumping in his chest. Maybe she'd made it beyond the area of the ELF strike. Maybe she was fine, still flying, as unconcerned as the hawk wheeling above him. *Please, let it be.*

Call her. The VHF.

He splashed through the knee-deep water and grabbed the skiff and clambered in. The aluminum hull was badly dented from hitting the rocks, but not ruptured. But the radio was gone, lost overboard. No way to reach her. He thudded down on the stern seat, his chest hurting from dread about her.

His thoughts were skidding. The ELF-affected area . . . it would almost certainly have included Takona. Lucas. Thomas and Archie.

Got to get there.

He yanked the pull-cord to start the engine. Dead.

Oars. They were still clamped under the seats. He fitted them into the oarlocks and was about to start rowing when a new thought hit him like a punch. His theory—his *whole* theory—had been that if a runaway resonance event occurred, the ELF radiation would strike randomly and intermittently. *Intermittently.* He remembered his own words to Dana: *"It'll be like random sniper fire that never quits."*

Is this just a lull . . . between strikes?

Fear clenched his gut. Think! Competing theories. A: Meredith has shut down HARC after one ELF strike. B: She's incapacitated, and everyone else on-site is too, unable to stop a runaway disaster, and the strikes will keep coming. Which one's true?

He looked downstream toward Hanley. Could he get information there? Less than a mile, and he'd have the current with him. He looked upstream toward Takona. It meant leaving Lucas, which wrenched him. But he had to find out what was happening. If they were in the middle of an ongoing disaster, he was the only person who even understood the *problem.* He knew it was likely that all communications equipment in Hanley was wiped out, but he had to take the chance. Unless he could find out what was happening there was no hope for Lucas, Dana, or anyone.

He pushed off from the reeds and started rowing, leaving the dying creatures on the beach.

▲

Approaching the Hanley wharf, Mike saw that a runaway trawler had plowed up onto a dock. A half-dozen men were working at securing the craft and hauling debris, but others were shouting, a sense of panic in the air. Rowing in through splintered dock flotsam, Mike reached the wharf and hopped out, his clothes clammy, his broken finger aching fiercely. A woman in a dirty rubber fish apron bumped into him, dazed, and walked on. Dying fish lay twitching on the wharf.

"Somethin' happened. Don't know exactly what." It was the old-timer who'd sold Mike the skiff. He was sitting on a pylon, slumped in shock. Somewhere beyond the wharf, a car horn was blaring, stuck.

Mike felt a wave of pity. The ELF blast had devastated these people.

"Is there a phone in the office I can use?" he asked. "Or a VHF radio, or CB?"

"Don't work. Nothin' works."

Mike had half expected it. The ELF blast had probably disabled every unprotected phone wire, computer chip, electronic engine ignition, and power cable. The only question was, how far afield? As far as Fairbanks? Farther? Was the damage here just the tip of the iceberg? Worse—far worse—was the thought that this might be just the beginning. On the other hand, it might be over. It all depended on what was happening at HARC. He couldn't go there. If his worst fear were true, anyone entering the site would be incapacitated.

But there might be a way to find out. The realization came over him like nausea. Ben was the one person who might be able to tell him where they stood. Ben wouldn't be at the site with Meredith. He'd built an observation center in town for the demonstration he'd just unleashed; that's where he'd be. Mike had to get to Fairbanks. To meet his enemy.

It meant abandoning Lucas. What if he'd been injured during the strike? What if he lay in pain, fighting for his life, and the danger from HARC had ended? Mike's heart insisted he go back to Takona. But his mind told him there was no time. If this was just the beginning, he had to get to Ben. The decision was excruciating. But horribly clear.

He needed a vehicle. Two cars and a pickup truck were parked at the wharf, but their ignitions would be shot after the ELF blast. He looked up the main street. It went up a low hill that backed the town. On the far side of the hill the road construction outfit had its trailers and explosives shed. Mike had been there with Thomas just hours ago, getting the dynamite. They'd have diesel trucks. No ignition.

He ran. Near the top of the hill, between the scattered houses, he could see the road crew halted in its work down the other side, trucks stopped helter-skelter. He heard dogs begin to howl. The sound lifted hairs on the back of his neck: dogs heard frequencies humans couldn't. Fear crawled over him. A part of his mind cowered in a corner. *Not again . . .*

The fluttering vibration buffeted his ears . . .

Among the road crew a fuel truck barreled down the grade, out of control. It plunged off the grade, flipped, and burst into flames. Mike found he was shaking.

Not again . . . please . . . no! . . .

▲

General Sloan was dead. On the lawn outside the observation center Ben stood over the body of his friend, ashamed that his bowels were churning, his hands trembling. The street in front of him was like a war zone. People running, shouting, crying, crawling. There were wounded. Crippled vehicles lay slewed on the road. A car had hit a concrete post and sat crumpled and smoking. Traffic lights were out. Flames licked from the window of a carpet store in the strip mall across the street. Thick black smoke.

Are we under attack? Ben wondered, dazed.

"No breath, no pulse," Gopnik said in a thin voice, kneeling on the grass by the body. "Maybe heart failure." Face pale, he looked up at Ben. Moments before, they'd all groped their way out of the observation center after the lights went out—after the terror of feeling caged had swept Ben, sent him crashing out of the place . . . *escape*. Behind him, Graham Sloan had come out gasping, clutching his chest, and the others followed. Then Sloan collapsed. Now, Ben was struggling to comprehend what had happened.

He latched on to Gopnik's statement: heart attack. Could happen to anyone. Poor Graham. The very banality of it brought some relief that Graham hadn't died of fear . . . as Ben had felt, back inside, might happen to *him*. His whole body still prickled, as if from a massive electric shock. The terror he'd felt in that black, windowless room. The panic of being held captive . . . the Viet Cong's cage.

"What in the name of God . . . ?" It was Kaplan. He stood in the doorway eyeing the people in the street, bracing himself against the door as if to reassure himself of the stronghold at his back. "Keep them away . . ." His tone was belligerent.

"He was right . . . oh, God, he was right . . ." It was Carol, crying. Ben was startled to find her sitting on the grass at his feet. One of her mauve high-heeled shoes was gone, and she was huddled by his leg like a child afraid to be left alone. He felt inexpressibly sad to see her so out of control, and he patted her disheveled hair to comfort her. If he could only grasp what had happened . . . what the danger was.

"Just like Mike said," Carol sobbed, looking up at him. "It's HARC . . . he was right . . ."

HARC? Ben turned his head away. He'd worn his dress uniform for the demonstration, and the silver stars reflected pinpricks of sunlight that needled his eyes. He looked up at the sky. *HARC?*

The chaos of shouting around him seemed to reach a crescendo. For one long, tortured moment he fought the truth . . . fought it with all the strength of his will. But the truth was stronger. It slammed into him.

Crosbie was wrong. Mike was right. The disaster he predicted . . . it's happened.

He struggled to recall the full scenario Mike had warned of. It came back in one terrible rush. Mind-altering ELF radiation . . . the whole upper hemisphere affected . . . personnel at the site incapacitated, unable to shut it down . . .

"Oh, God," Carol wailed, "what are we going to do?"

Do. The word flipped a switch in Ben's brain. From panic to containment. *It's happened—now, stop it.* The taste of fear was still in his mouth, bitter as bile, but forty years of training and experience kicked in. He was the commanding officer of HARC.

Communications were out. Gopnik had established that, moments before it happened. No phones, no computer links. A massive power failure. No way to contact the site.

Mobilize. Fort Wainwright's down the road. Eielson Air Force Base is just twenty miles away. Get to the commanding officers. Impose martial law and secure the HARC site. Did Kaplan, as national security adviser, have that authority? Ben's breath snagged in his throat. What did such authority matter now? *I've got to get troops to the site to shut this down.*

"Lieutenant Gopnik, get my car. Carol, we're going to Wainwright." He helped her to her feet. "Mr. Kaplan, you're with me. We'll take the general's body with us."

The only way to proceed was as though they were at war.

▲

Mike clung to a gnarled pine, pressing his forehead against the trunk to force the tortured visions from his head . . .

. . . *chained to Sophy, face-to-face, drowning with her, crabs gnawing her eyes . . . blasted by the shell splitting Ron's head, both of them exploding in blood and brains and bone . . . pulling Lucas over the bluff, plunging together through the frigid abyss . . .*

The visions suddenly fractured . . .

Mike staggered a step back from the tree. His forehead throbbed where he'd been grinding it against the bark. The hallucinations had vanished, but they left him shivering, chilled all over with sweat. He swayed on his feet, sucking breaths, his throat parched. *It's over, it's over,* he told himself.

He turned, leaned back against the tree, and struggled to get his bearings. Underfoot was a carpet of dead orange pine needles. Above, visible through the pine boughs, a faint rainbow. Somewhere, there'd been a shower. It settled him a little to imagine a soothing rain.

It's over?

He suddenly felt a dread so deep, his blood seemed to stop moving. The hallucinations had been a *second* ELF hit. It could mean only one thing. The resonance event was continuing.

His legs went weak. *It's still happening. Intermittent random strikes, exactly as I predicted.* Meredith hasn't shut it down because she can't. She's been hit too hard. And everyone else on-site. Too debilitated to function. Or dead.

The resonance will continue, amplifying in power, expanding its range, the saturation ELF zone at the site slowly widening . . .

Then the full terror hit him. *The rainbow . . .*

He looked up through the branches at the bands of color shimmering in the blue, and knew it wasn't a rainbow. It was the aurora. In the sunlit sky. An impossibility. The soft hues rippled like something alive. Beautiful, mesmerizing. But Mike knew what it meant. Unprecedented electromagnetic energy had already amplified the ionosphere's solar electron activity to a threshold level, and broached that threshold. The resonance had escalated to a magnitude greater even than he'd theorized.

Tears stung his eyes, blurred the colors. "What have I done?" he whispered to the sky. To Dana . . . to Lucas . . . to the world. *"What have I done?"*

▲

He pulled himself together. *Can't give up.* He had no idea yet how to focus his mind on the problem, but his mind was all he had. Maybe not for much longer . . . but that wasn't up to him. For now, he could think. He had to find some way to stop HARC.

He pushed away from the support of the tree trunk. Pain shot up from his broken finger. He blocked it out. Blocked out, too, the faint sounds of shouting and screaming down both sides of the hill—on the Hanley wharf and among the construction crew. He wouldn't think about those poor people. He had only one goal, one focus. Get to Ben.

He spotted a green gravel truck halfway down the grade among the road crew. Diesel exhaust pipe.

He ran down the hill. More like staggered, his legs were so rubbery. He reached the crew, twenty or so men. One wandered past him as though sleepwalking. Another was on all fours, vomiting. Several stood slack-jawed around the flipped fuel truck that was engulfed in flames. A man in a yellow hard hat was trying to move them back to safety, and whether he was the foreman or just a guy taking charge, he seemed to Mike the one to talk to.

"I need that truck," Mike told him, pointing up the grade. "I'm with the HARC project. There's been a power surge that's blacked out the area, knocked out electronics." Impossible to explain what was *really* happening—might as well tell a tale of abduction by a UFO. All he wanted was the vehicle, however he could get it. "I'll take that truck to Fairbanks and alert the authorities, have them send help. But I'll need some of your men to get me rolling." The computer chip in the starter system would be fried, but once the rig was rolling, Mike could start the diesel engine. "Can you round up a half-dozen guys to push?"

The man seemed too stunned for questions, and relieved by Mike's take-charge attitude. They pulled together a gang of five. Mike hopped in the truck cab, and the men pushed. The truck crept down the grade, then began to roll, and by the time it reached the bottom Mike had the engine running. He couldn't shut it off between here and Fairbanks or he'd never get it going again.

Eighty miles. Whatever lay in his path, he wouldn't shut if off.

Shifting gears, he barreled along the rough dirt road that would take him to the highway, the serrated skyline of pines sliding past him on either side. It would take over an hour to get to Fairbanks, and he had no idea how quickly the locus of lethal ELF saturation would spread beyond the site. How soon would it engulf this area . . . engulf Fairbanks? And what about the sniper blasts of ELF radiation that were almost sure to keep coming? Would the next one hit him at the wheel, incapacitate him before he could reach the city?

In his side mirror, he caught the ribbon of aurora lights shimmering behind him in the blue sky. The intensifying beauty hit him with an illogical but crushing image: that Dana was dead, and the aurora was gathering brilliance from her rising soul. He blotted out the awful thought, but he couldn't blot out the aurora itself, and it warned him of a terrible new deadline. A solar deadline. Because there was a phenomenon he hadn't calculated into even his worst-case scenario: the added energy of solar excitement. It was around noon now, so the energy increase would be negligible until the end of the day as HARC's location on the globe moved away from the sun. But after midnight, that trend would be reversed. As HARC moved back into the area of solar energy the resonance would be amplified by several orders of magnitude. What was only sniper fire now would become an endless machine-gun barrage. He had only until the small hours of tomorrow morning to do something to stop it. Once the sun rose again, it would be too late.

CAROL WAS LOST.

"Go south, ma'am," the out-of-breath young corporal told her. A troop of soldiers hurried past in the street, disorganized, out of formation. "Bassett's right past the airfield. Things are pretty crazy there, lots of hurt folks, but maybe they can fix you up. Go south." He pointed, then ran on toward Fort Wainwright's headquarters.

Carol gazed after him helplessly. She was trying to get to Bassett Hospital on the base, hoping to find a doctor. Soldiers were passing singly and in groups, some looking confused, some afraid. Somewhere a car horn was blaring, and men were shouting. Carol felt drained by fear and exhaustion, and still disoriented. Which way's south? The only other time she'd been on the base, at a dinner for the new commanding officer, she'd been chauffeured. Now she was walking, all alone, one shoe lost and the other abandoned, and sharp tiny flints of asphalt had shredded the soles of her stockings. She felt dazed by the terrifying last hours, by the fear that they were all going to die. Dizzy at the thought, she drifted into the road.

A car horn blasted and she stumbled out of the way. The car passed, a rust-pocked old Chevy, at the wheel a disheveled officer. The roads were littered with new-model vehicles that would not run, the base airfield with planes that would not fly. When they'd found her father's car useless outside the observation center, Lieutenant Gopnik had stolen an old Camaro and hot-wired it to get them here to Wainwright. They'd had to leave General Sloan's body on the grass.

She shuffled along, not sure where she was going, wincing at the rough asphalt abrading her soles, her right leg still sluggish. At least she could walk again; her right arm was still partially numb. When the second attack had hit, just after they'd arrived at the base commander's office, her body had seized up, her right side paralyzed. And a vision had engulfed her, a terrifying sense of herself alone in a silent world . . . *Don't everybody leave me!* As the disorientation lifted, she'd found that the thing had affected everyone, each person surfacing from some private hell. Her father had smashed a window with a chair as though to make an escape. Kaplan had curled up whimpering on the floor. Colonel Braden, the base commander, had cocked his sidearm at a female lieutenant and was yelling obscenities at her. Even after feeling and mobility gradually returned to Carol's side, she'd still felt panicked, and was sobbing for her father's help. But by then he was busy in the war room—no time for her, for her pain.

Another horn blasted on the road behind her, then a

cacophony of horns. Carol turned. A mud-spattered gravel truck belching diesel smoke had roared through the Richardson Gate and was barreling up the road, soldiers dashing out of its path. Two Jeeps were chasing it, horns blaring. One raced around to cut it off. The truck swerved to avoid the Jeep, fishtailed in front of the base Burger King, and screeched to a stop. Carol couldn't believe her eyes . . . Mike at the wheel!

She watched as MPs piled out of both Jeeps, weapons raised, and pounded toward the truck. With rifles pointed at him, Mike climbed out, his face bruised, his clothes filthy. Soldiers surrounded him.

His hands shot up to show he had no weapon. "Let me through! I've got to see General Crewe!"

"You'll see the command sergeant major, sir," an MP said. Two of them took his elbows and started to lead him away.

"Mike!" Carol cried.

His head snapped around. "Carol!" He dug in his heels against the MPs. "Carol, tell them! I've got to see Ben!"

Her thoughts were spinning. Mike knows *everything* about HARC . . . *can he make it stop?* "Wait!" she cried. "Let him go!"

▲

Mike took the stairs two at a time, with four MPs and Carol behind him. They'd brought him here to the Arctic Battle Simulation Center—Ben's war room. In reception there were about twenty uniformed people working in what looked like barely controlled confusion. Two more MPs guarded the closed door to the war room. As Mike pushed through the crowd, he was astonished to see Wayne and Gina sitting in a corner.

"It's Mike!" Gina gasped, jumping up.

"Hey, buddy!" Wayne said, pushing through to Mike, Gina behind him. "Where you been?"

"Long story," Mike said, thinking theirs must be too as he took in Wayne's nose crusted with blood and Gina's pale face. She said in a rush, "I was at the airport waiting for a flight out. Saw a prop plane crash. Then the ELF hit us all." She gave him a contrite look. "Just like you warned, Mike." She said she'd come here to offer what help she could, and had found Wayne waiting too.

Mike thought she looked very rocky. "How've you managed the hits?"

"Not too good, they trigger my epilepsy. Just brief seizures, though. I'm keeping medicated. I can handle it."

Mike felt the tug of a smile: Gina was always game. He turned to Wayne. "How about you?"

"Found myself pummeling some poor jerk on the dock. When it was over, he was a mess." Wayne shook his head, looking ashamed. "Hate to say it, Mike—I was crazy for a drink."

Mike felt a lump in his throat. "Yeah, this thing finds our weak spots." It had hit while he was driving. Only the fact that he'd been on a flat stretch of tundra had saved him. When it lifted, he'd found himself with his face in his hands, weeping, overwhelmed by visions of the people he'd killed with HARC, and the truck was plowing into the hard-packed earth. He'd wrenched back the wheel, his heart banging, and turned again onto the highway.

"Dad!" Carol was calling at the closed door. "Dad, it's Mike!"

The door opened, and Ben stood before them. Seeing Mike, he froze.

So did Mike. Part of him wanted to go for Ben's throat. But there was no time for personal fury. If there was to be any hope, he had to work with Ben. He found his voice. "Tell me what's happening."

Ben, too, had quickly got his surprise under control. "I'm hoping you can tell *us*. Come in."

Mike said he wanted Gina and Wayne in too, for their specialized knowledge. Ben gestured for them all to come. As Mike started forward he felt Carol grip his arm. "Mike . . ." It was a whimper that said: *Don't leave me.* He wondered: How much more can she take? Or any of us? She stuck close behind him as he followed Ben into the war room, followed by Gina and Wayne.

Inside were banks of high-tech equipment, unmanned and silent, a conference table littered with maps, and four men—three in uniform, one civilian.

"Gentlemen," Ben said, "this is Dr. Michael Ryder, the principal creator of HARC. He's come to help us." As they all looked at him, Mike felt the weight of their expectations. Ben briskly introduced them. "Mr. Kaplan, the national security adviser." Mike recognized Kaplan, though he looked unkempt, nervous, completely unlike his media appearances. Mike thought: He came for Ben's demonstration and now he's stuck here. "Lieu-

tenant Colonel Lou Braden, the base commander."
Braden—grizzled, jowled, wearing fatigues—was busy
conferring with an exhausted-looking soldier at a phone.
"And Major Figgis from the 354th Fighter Wing at Eielson Air Force Base." Ben indicated an officer writing
notes at the table. "His CO sent him here for information. He came on a bike." Mike exchanged nods with the
major, a clean-cut guy in Air Force blue, though his uniform was grimy and sweat-stained.

Mike knew how wild he must look himself. Gashed
lip, filthy clothes, hair matted with muck from the riverbank. He couldn't help staring at Ben. Dress uniform
spotless. Martial bearing, ramrod straight. And the old
aura of authority and control. But his face looked gray,
and Mike saw how he kept balling his hands into fists at
his sides, fists so tight his knuckles went white.

Mike asked him, "Do you have any idea what the situation is at HARC?"

Ben shook his head. "Lost all communication with
them. However, assuming incapacitation of on-site personnel we've dispatched commando units to secure the
facility and shut it down. Five six-man teams, for redundancy."

Mike stopped himself from saying how pointless
sending anyone was. "What information *do* you have?"

"Very little." Ben explained that all local telecommu-
nications links were out, computers down, most vehicles
malfunctioning. They'd managed to patch into an old
mechanical phone switching system and were trying to
get through to the Pentagon—he indicated the soldier
manning the phone beside Colonel Braden—but there

was only one line, and it was operating sporadically. He said that on the base there was disarray, hundreds of personnel injured, several fatalities. Over ten thousand people lived at Fort Wainwright, and the base hospital was overwhelmed, unable to cope with all the accident victims, the medical staff suffering the same effects as their patients.

Ben's expression turned grim as he went on. "We know of three major airline accidents in this state alone—two jetliners collided above Anchorage International, an Airbus crashed in the Brooks Range, and a 747 went down in the Gulf of Alaska. We've had patchy reports of highway accidents throughout the state and into the Canadian Yukon and British Columbia, and of widespread outbreaks of violence. Hospital ERs are overloaded, in chaos. We've also had erratic reports of power blackouts in locations across the upper Northern Hemisphere. Thule, Greenland. Severodvinsk in Russia. Baie-Comeau, Quebec. Even as far south as Saint Cloud, Minnesota. All this as a result of three strikes so far of the—" He stopped, seeming to struggle for the words.

"ELF radiation," Mike said, his mouth dry.

Ben met his gaze. "Yes. I have some concern about maintaining a command structure here, as each of us has experienced the debilitating effects of the ELF strikes. The effects vary widely—according to Wainwright's chief physician, it triggers a spectrum of neurological disorders, affecting every individual differently. On the base alone we've seen behavior similar to that of Alzheimer's victims and stroke victims, also manic confusion, hallucinatory states, suicidal despair, outright dementia. Though we in this room have recovered each time, I've noticed that each attack lasts longer, and is more debilitating. So I've had Major Figgis taking notes. Since there's no knowing when the next strike will come, I want written information available to pass along in the event of our . . . incapacitation."

Mike looked around. Everyone seemed to be stoically dealing with the situation. Carol alone was in bad shape, huddled in an armchair across the room, sniffling quietly.

There was a commotion outside in reception, raised voices. Colonel Braden went to the door and opened it, and the voices got louder. "Bring him in," Braden said. He turned to Ben and the others. "It's a sergeant reporting from one of the commando teams."

A sturdy black soldier in dirty SWAT gear came in. His arm was bound in a bloody cloth, soot smeared his fatigues, and he looked shaken. "We didn't make it, sir," he said to Braden. He explained that his six-man unit had left the base in a hot-wired Humvee, but it broke down about seventeen miles south of HARC. On foot, they'd reached a gas station fifteen miles from the site.

"Lieutenant Bowden and I fell back to help people at the filling station, sir. A vehicle had rammed a propane tank and there was a fire, casualties, people very agitated, some of them armed, so the captain ordered the lieutenant and me to help the people while he led the team up the road. One of the civilians shot me"—he indicated his blood-soaked arm—"and then . . . well, it happened so fast, sir. I saw the thing hit our guys, like machine-gun fire, only invisible. It didn't hit me and the lieutenant where we were with the civilians, but the guys ahead on the road, they just . . . crumpled. Fell apart. I mean, the thing didn't let up like the hits we'd had before, sir. Those were bad, but this . . . I saw the captain trying to cut off his own foot with his knife like he didn't feel a thing, just sat there in his own blood till he fell over. Saw Corporal Yates crawl into the swamp by the road . . . saw him go right under the water. The other two looked comatose. I don't know if they were dead or alive, sir, I was trying to cope with my wound and the civilians, but Lieutenant Bowden ran up the road to help our guys and I saw him crumple too. I was the only one left, sir, and it seemed so . . ." He stopped, looking lost. He pulled himself together: "Sir, I judged you'd need this information."

"Thank you, Sergeant," Braden said. "Get your wound seen to." The sergeant left.

Ben addressed them all, "Remember, that's just one team. There are four more on their way. One's bound to get through."

Mike shook his head, sick at the commando's story. "Ben, *no one* can make it into HARC." He turned to take in everyone. "ELF waves are bombarding the site nonstop. HARC's mainframe is protected in a steel room, but any *person* who tries to get near will be cut down, just like those men. That's why this thing is out of control, because Dr. Crosbie and the others out there aren't . . . functioning. It's not a case of temporary hits and then recovery, like we've been experiencing. They're in a zone of continuous saturation ELF bombardment. We're talking permanent brain damage—"

His voice broke. Lucas was in that zone. He gripped a chair back, cleared his throat, and plowed on. "And I believe that zone is slowly expanding. The filling station the sergeant spoke of is fifteen miles south of HARC, so the saturation zone has expanded at least that far. And the resonance will keep increasing and intensifying as long as any power is being transmitted from the site. Since HARC is powered by a nuclear reactor, that could be virtually forever."

There was a long moment of silence. Even the soldier at the phone sat motionless. Then Ben addressed everyone, his voice steely, "We now know the extent of the problem. Let's hear solutions."

They all moved to the conference table. But no one sat. Mike noted that the three officers and Kaplan were at one end, he and Wayne and Gina at the other. Carol stayed curled in her chair, her eyes big with fear.

Colonel Braden said, "I'd bomb the place, but the electronics on all our aircraft are fried. Figgis says it's the same over at the Eielson base. However, if we can reach the Pentagon, they can send bombers."

Mike shook his head. "Their electronics would fail in HARC's airspace, and so would the pilots."

"I'm talking about hardened aircraft," Braden said.

"Hardened?" Gina asked.

Kaplan explained, "Planes with specialized metal shields. It's to protect them from the electromagnetic pulse from a nuclear detonation."

"But Mike's right," Ben said. "The *pilots* would still be incapacitated. Even in gliders or balloons. Unable to position and fire."

"How about tunneling, sir?" Major Figgis asked. "Send sappers with demolition charges."

"Through miles of permafrost?" Ben pointed out. "Anyway, the EM waves penetrate underground. They'd disable the equipment and the operators."

Colonel Braden said, "A battleship could shell the site from the Bering Strait or from the Gulf of Alaska."

"There's no ship close enough," Figgis said, indicating the table maps. "The nearest one would take three days to steam into firing range."

"In any case, shelling HARC's nuclear reactor would release deadly radiation," Kaplan said. "Can we risk that?"

"Can we risk doing anything less?" Ben asked.

"Three days to get into range?" Kaplan said, plowing a hand through his hair. "Jesus, a good part of the population of the Northern Hemisphere could be vegetables by then, including us."

Three days—way too late, Mike thought, thinking of the aurora deadline. He watched Kaplan and the officers continue their debate down the table, and sensed Wayne and Gina beside him anxiously following the discussion. He glanced at Carol. She sat quietly sobbing and . . .

Quietly? He stared at her, an idea dawning. She was crying, but the sound wasn't reaching him because of the officers' talk. *Sound waves canceling sound waves . . .*

That could do it! The Eureka prototype.

"Ben," he cut in, "no bombs or shells. There may be a way to get someone out to HARC to shut it down."

Braden said, "You just told us anyone getting near would be too debilitated to function."

"Not if we could create a skip zone."

"A what?"

"An area of interference."

"Yes," Gina whispered, her eyes on him, alight. She turned to the officers. "It's like when you're driving and suddenly lose the radio signal, then you leave the area and get the signal back. That area is a skip zone."

"Look," Mike said, pointing to the corporal at the phone. "If he's talking there while I'm talking here with Wayne and Gina, then you officers, where you're standing, would have a hard time making out the corporal's words. Our sound waves are disrupting his. It's not because of volume, but interference. A coherent wave—his voice—is disturbed, and becomes mere noise."

"Okay, I get the principle," Ben said, "but how does that apply to HARC? How can we do it?"

"Radio waves," Mike said. "We massively propagate radio frequencies."

Ben tried to grasp it. "Like, from a broadcasting facility?"

"Far too small. And no way to focus it. But Eureka could do it."

Colonel Braden said, "I don't follow. Eureka?"

Ben answered for Mike, a new excitement in his voice, "The HARC prototype. We called it that because it's near the town of Eureka, fifteen miles north of here. It's three hundred high-frequency transmitting antennas that—"

"Christ, yes," Wayne jumped in. "Sixty acres of them."

"And focusable," Gina said. "We can fight HARC II with HARC I."

Carol got to her feet. "I knew Mike could save us!"

Mike saw the hysterical hope in her eyes. Looking at the others, he saw their hope, too, more controlled but just as strong. It caught him up short. "Hold on," he said, "Eureka's been mothballed for over two years. I don't know if we can get it operating."

"I can," Wayne said. "The antenna array's intact, and all ten diesel generators too. I had them pickled, so they'll need some adjustments, but that's doable. The challenge will be fuel, but if we can get our hands on enough, I'll get those gennys running."

"Mike?" Ben asked. "Is this feasible?"

Mike's heartbeat was doing a dance. "Yes. We tune Eureka to disturb HARC's wave pattern. It's a matter of setting up a frequency that's out of phase with HARC's harmonics, so the peaks of HARC's waves meet the troughs of Eureka's waves, neutralizing them. We carve a corridor through the ELF zone."

He looked at the rapt faces. Time for a reality check. "Eureka, however, can't produce anywhere near the power or control of HARC, so that means the corridor will be narrow, and probably shifting. And even inside it, the ELF radiation won't be completely canceled, just reduced in strength. But if we can reduce it enough, someone might make it through, reach the site, and—"

"And flip the fucking switch," Kaplan said.

Mike nodded. "That's the idea."

He took in Kaplan's smile, heard Braden heave a sigh of relief, saw the gleam in Ben's eyes. They all thought they had some time. He hadn't explained about the aurora.

"I haven't yet told you the worst," he said. "The disaster is of a magnitude even exceeding what I predicted. It's because of the added energy of solar excitement. On my way here I saw the aurora borealis—a virtual impossibility in the daytime sky. It indicates how incredibly powerful the resonance event has already grown. It's as if there's a rogue wave building. Maybe a solar storm has kicked in—I could check the data if we had the access, but it doesn't matter, it's happened. The point is, it forces us to a deadline. It's just after noon now, and solar augmentation will decrease gradually for the next eleven hours as our location on the globe moves away from the sun, so although the resonance will continue to grow, it will be somewhat tempered by this distance from the setting sun. However, after midnight, the trend will be reversed. Once the sun comes up, the added solar excitement will increase the resonance by several orders of magnitude. In other words, the rogue wave will hit. Even the Eureka corridor would collapse. We have until sunrise tomorrow. In Alaska in July, that's 1:00 A.M. If we can't shut down HARC by then, it'll be too late."

Everyone was silent, taking it in. There was only Figgis's pen scratching notes.

Ben said, "I'll send runners to notify the Navy to prepare shelling. But we all know now that it's really up to us. Mike's given us a possible way out. We have twelve hours—let's not waste another moment. Mike, what do you need?"

"Manpower."

"That I can give you." Braden said.

"Not me, Colonel, it's Wayne who'll be getting Eureka running. He'll need mechanics, and a small army to ferry enough diesel fuel to the site—truck it, hell, roll it in barrels if they have to. Anything he needs, men or materials, see he gets it. Meanwhile, I'll work out the frequency equations, Gina and I. If there's anyone on your staff with a background in physics, I can use them too." He looked at Gina. "You okay for medication?"

"I could use a refill."

"We'll need the base pharmacy to fill a prescription," Mike went on to Braden. "Then, I need a ride over to Eureka." He looked at his aching left hand. "And a splint for this damn finger."

Carol said, "I can get that."

Everyone went into action. Braden was at the door calling in aides, Figgis was organizing notes and maps, Carol left to get a first aid kit, Wayne and Gina went to tell the aides coming in what they needed.

Ben reached Mike. Amid all the activity, they were alone. "Mike, as I understand this, whoever goes into the corridor can't be sure whether your counterwave will work or not. They might get inside and be knocked out by the ELF effects after all. They'd suffer brain damage and . . . never get anywhere."

Mike faced him—the man who'd refused to believe all his warnings. "It's true, there's no guarantee it'll work. It's a hypothesis. But a reasonable one."

"Still, it's a mission so dangerous we'll have to inform any volunteers among Braden's men."

"His men won't be going. It'll take a little more specialized knowledge at the site than just flipping a switch. Anyway, I won't ask others to risk their lives to end a disaster you and I created." He caught the flicker of surprise in Ben's eyes. "Yes, both of us, Ben. You didn't do this alone. I built HARC." He tried to block out his fear of the visions, those twisted, agonized faces of the people he'd killed. Instead, he hung on to the hope of this last chance. "*I'll* be going through the corridor. I'm going to kill our monster."

▲

The soft sound of lapping water was the first thing Dana was aware of.

She sat up, her neck stiff. She'd been slumped against the cockpit door, and was startled to see a smear of blood on the window. What had happened? She looked out. She was on a river, forest on both sides, and her plane sat perpendicular to the slight current. Didn't make sense. She twisted in her seat, and saw that she was actually on a gravel bar midstream—at least, her starboard pontoon nudged the gravel, so she was partly afloat and partly beached. The gravel bar was familiar because of a distinctive landmark on it, a quartz-rippled boulder the size of a young bear. Dana let out a breath of relief. She couldn't remember what went wrong or how she'd got here, but she knew exactly where she was: on the Gatana between Takona and Hanley.

From what she could see of the plane there was no obvious structural damage. Both floats were sound, and the prop was intact, though blunted; she remembered mak-

ing the repair this morning. She did a quick check of herself for injuries. A goose egg on her forehead with a little tacky blood, but no wounds, no broken bones. Her
hip felt bruised where the seat belt had bitten into her,
nothing more serious.

As she reached down to untangle the radio headset
with its cord caught around her feet, recollections surfaced that chilled her. Something had voided her mind,
blotting out thought. Then terror as the aircraft had
begun a spin. Then a vision of iridescent light and . . . a
raven? Carla! Dana remembered her sister sweeping out
of the clouds, remembered following her. She blinked in
wonder. *I followed a vision . . . to safety?* Could it be
true? Not literally—she knew that. Probably her own
skill at managing a controlled crash landing on the water
had kicked in unconsciously. Yet she also knew, with a
certainty she trusted beyond facts, that the vision of
Carla had guided her to this safe spot.

She had no idea what all that had been about, but she
was grateful. Alive and afloat, on the river she'd loved
all her life.

The warm feeling fled. What about Mike? She'd been
searching for him, fearing he was in some kind of trouble.

She tried the ignition. Dead. What had disabled her
engine?

How long had she been here? She saw that her watch
had stopped. The sun seemed near its noon zenith, so she
calculated she'd been out of it for maybe an hour or two.
She looked upstream. Takona was less than two miles
away. Could Mike have made it back? Logical first place

for her to check, she decided. If he wasn't there, she'd do a search downstream from that point. She had an emergency inflatable raft aboard with oars. She felt strong. She could row to Takona. Besides, a shadowy concern made her want to check that Lucas was all right.

She grabbed a coil of line for securing the plane and slung it over her shoulder, then leaned across to open the starboard door, intending to climb out onto the beached pontoon and hop down onto the gravel. But the door was jammed, maybe from the impact of landing. She opened her port door instead; getting out here she'd have to swim around. She climbed out onto the pontoon and jumped into the water. Cold. If she'd needed her head cleared, that did it. She felt an unexpected exhilaration as she did a breast stroke around the plane. Weird; the goose egg should have given her a splitting headache, but instead she felt fine, felt a mild euphoria. Psychosomatic response, she told herself: the acute relief at finding herself alive after a brush with death. She smiled. *Thanks, Carla.*

She scrambled up on the gravel, then stood a moment, dripping wet, and looked up. In the cloudless eastern sky bands of color shimmered in the blue, just like the aurora. Strange in broad daylight, she thought. An alarm she could put no name to clutched her, then let go. She got busy. She tied the line to the float cleat, stretched it to the boulder, and wrapped it, securing the plane. Hopping up onto the starboard pontoon, she wrenched the door open, climbed aboard, and tossed out what she needed onto the gravel: the folded raft, foot pump, oars, and a life jacket. She inflated the raft, and was soon on the water, rowing for Takona.

▲

As Dana climbed out on the village dock there was no one in sight. But Thomas's skiff was tied up, its bow crammed with bulging backpacks. She checked inside one of them. Dynamite. No other boats, though. Thomas had got back, it seemed, but not Mike.

She walked up from the dock, her clothes almost dry from rowing in the sun. She scanned the cabin yards for Lucas or Thomas or Archie as she went, hoping to spot Mike too in spite of the evidence. She hated the silence. Where were they? They wouldn't have gone all the way back to the camp. Maybe at Thomas's cabin; it overlooked the river. As she approached it, a low moan came from inside.

She stepped in. Thomas lay on his back on the bed under a gray blanket, eyes closed, face pale. She went to him. "Thomas?"

No answer. His breathing was shallow and ragged. She checked his pulse. High and thready—alarmingly low blood pressure. Dried blood flecked his chin.

"Mom? Why're you back?"

She turned. Lucas stood in the doorway. She was thrilled to see he was all right. She quickly told him she'd had to make a controlled crash landing on the river, then asked, "What happened to Thomas?"

Lucas lowered his voice as he came in. "He's in bad shape. Lost control of his skiff—hit a log and went overboard, broke a rib it looks like, almost drowned. It happened just downstream. Archie and I saw it from the dock, saw him go under and the skiff go up on the sand. We fished him out, carried him in here, and got the skiff back. I figured he shouldn't stay in his wet clothes, so we cut them off him."

She nodded. "You've kept him warm, you did fine." She sat on the edge of the bed, and rolled the blanket down to Thomas's waist, exposing his bare chest. There was extensive bruising.

Lucas said, "Something happened on the river that made him dizzy, he says. Says he saw some kind of ghost, saw his dad, and lost control. He's talking a little weird, maybe from the pain. He's hurt pretty bad, I think."

Very bad, she thought. From the slight concavity in the chest wall, plus the bruising and the labored breathing, she could see the injury was critical—a "flail chest," bones broken at the sternum. When he was thrown from the boat, his chest must have hit the log. She gently placed her palm on his sternum. With his every breath, she felt a grinding of bone.

Thomas's eyes opened. "Dana." He didn't seem surprised to see her. He gazed at her as if her walking in and placing her healing hands on him was what he'd expected. He coughed, and bloody saliva frothed at the corners of his mouth. Hemothorax? Dana wondered in alarm. If a broken rib had pierced his lung, blood seeping in would have caused the lung to collapse.

Lucas whispered, "He's been coughing blood like that since we got him here."

Dana felt a pang. Thomas was slowly drowning in his blood. A hospital trauma center could save him—open his chest to stop the bleeding and reinflate his lung. But, stranded here, there was nothing she could do for him.

As she pulled the blanket back up to cover his chest, he said, "I saw Carla."

It startled her. *So did I.* "Where?"

"Outside. Picking fireweed." His words were spaced with frayed breaths. "She gave me . . . that wicked smile . . . told me to get up . . . off my backside, stop faking it. Saw my old man, too. When I was . . . under the river. He was fishing for grayling. Casting that old net . . . the one Carla mended with Juju's embroidery threads . . . remember? Looked like a rainbow in the sun?"

"I remember."

"My old man . . . said he could use a hand fishing."

They looked at each other. Thomas's father had been dead for years. His eyes seemed to say to Dana, *You know.* Far away, dogs were barking. Thomas winced in pain, and shut his eyes.

"Mom," Lucas said, his voice hushed, "he's not the only one who's seen things. Me and Archie both have. Well, I didn't *see* anything, more like felt it. Kind of a nice buzz. A couple times. Colors inside my head, and a sound like a guitar, and bits of memories." He shrugged. "Guess it's all just getting to us, huh?" He looked puzzled, but far from apprehensive.

But Dana was. A suspicion was needling at her nerves, its threads weaving a web she didn't want to look at. So *many* threads . . . She needed to think.

"Thomas, we're going out for a bit," she said, getting up. "Try to get some sleep."

"Don't want sleep. I'm finished, Dana. Going . . . to the river. Soon's I rest up and . . . get my breath back." His gaze held her. "Hear my dogs? Back at the camp? They know . . . and so do you."

She felt a cold finger run up her backbone. Because she did know. *"I'm finished, Dana."* Her throat tightened with the threat of tears, but she reminded herself of Juju's wisdom: the circle of life. Maybe it's just a beginning.

He reached for her hand. "I'll need your help . . . getting to the river. Then, after, I want you to . . . set them dogs free."

She squeezed his hand. "Rest first, Thomas. You'll need the strength."

She nodded for Lucas to follow her outside.

In the yard, she found Archie sitting on the weathered wooden table that Thomas used to clean his fish on. He was rolling a cigarette. "You back?" He didn't seem fazed. He licked the cigarette paper, sealed it, and dug in his pocket for a match.

Dana sat down on the cabin stoop in the sunshine. Something was different about Archie. Cigarette lit and dangling from his mouth, he was picking idly at a scab on his finger, and she realized what the change was: *He's relaxed.* The alcoholic tremor in his hands had disappeared. So had his facial tic.

Lucas stood under the aspen by the cabin door and looked out at the river, poking a finger under his cast to scratch. "Mike's awful late."

"Lucas, I talked to him on the VHF. He was on his way, then we suddenly lost contact."

"Think he got into some kind of trouble?"

"I don't know."

He seemed to consider this for a moment. "He'll make it."

But Dana had to face the awful suspicion that was growing in her mind.

Lucas sat down beside her on the stoop. They both watched a yellow moth land on his sneaker. "What did Uncle Thomas mean, he's going to the river? The shape he's in, he couldn't even make it to the shore."

"We'll carry him."

"But why? Won't it make him worse?"

"No, it'll take away the pain." She watched the moth flutter off, then looked into her son's eyes. "He's going to walk into the river, Lucas. He's going home."

She saw his shock. He stared at her for a moment, taking it in, then looked out at the water again.

Dana caught the scent of fireweed blossoms. The purple stalks were crowded close to the yard, and the scent enveloped her in memories. She wanted to take refuge in those memories . . . wanted not to examine the tangled threads in her mind. But she had to. She began to follow them, groping toward their common source. One by one, they led her on.

One. After Mike's abrupt last transmission, she couldn't raise him.

Two. Her electronics had failed. Then her engine. Even her watch.

Three. Thomas had lost control of his boat.

Four. *"I saw Carla,"* Thomas said. And so had she. Visions. Hallucinations. Just what Lucas had gone through, in his own way, that tragic night on the bluff.

Five. The aurora. She looked up at the eastern sky above the forested far shore, where bands of lurid green and violet were shimmering against the blue.

She thought: The whole string of events is too bizarre—unless you look at what could be common to them all. An extreme electromagnetic disturbance. In that light, all the threads could lead back to the same source. HARC.

Pins and needles ran down her arms. Crewe must have gone early! The demonstration. The resonance event. It's happened. *It's happening.*

She remembered Mike's terrible prediction: ELF waves bombarding the HARC site in a brain-damaging barrage, and making random temporary strikes far beyond. Were people all around her suffering, dying?

An arrow of pain pierced her. *Mike.* Had the ELF waves blasted him in the boat? Did he capsize? Drown? She clamped her hand over her mouth to bottle up a cry.

Lucas and Archie didn't seem to notice. The lazy atmosphere unnerved Dana. A breeze rustled the aspens' leaves, bees hummed in the fireweed. So peaceful . . . it suddenly struck her how impossible that was. *If the resonance event is going on, why aren't we debilitated by the ELF radiation? How has Takona escaped it?*

Like the final piece of a puzzle, a thought snapped into place. "Kind of a nice buzz," Lucas had said, and Dana had felt it too, ever since awakening on the river— a sense of well-being, so out of keeping with their grave situation. She could see it in Lucas and Archie, both so calm. Even Thomas was quietly bearing internal injuries that would leave anyone else whimpering at the pain. *"So peaceful here,"* Mike had said as they were saying good-bye on the dock, and Dana remembered his next comment. *"Takona's on a fault line. Electromagnetic discharges from tectonic strain can produce anomalies in EM fields, and that could be what gives this place a special feel . . ."*

She felt a tingling. Mike had believed, naturally, that anyone here, being so close to HARC, would be the most severely affected. But what if it was the exact opposite? What if Takona's distinctive electromagnetic field, amplified by the ELF radiation, *enhanced* its benign effect on the brain? Boosted that special feeling to a pervading sense of contentment? Could it be that the stronger the ELF waves grew, the more euphoric she and the others here would feel?

It's protecting us, she thought in awe. This little village is safe.

A sacred place.

She felt a surge of hope. Maybe it's protecting Mike, too. Maybe he's nearby, recovering on the riverbank, or drifting in his boat. No, she thought, that fantasy dissolving. Last night she'd seen his zeal to lead this small group. If there was any way on earth he could get back here, he would have made it by now. Nothing could keep him from his mission to stop HARC . . . except HARC itself.

Her heart banged against her ribs. She thought: The horror's happening right now. Can it be stopped? The authorities must be trying, frantic. But they're miles away. How could they even get near, through the ELF waves?

A thought lit up her mind like lightning. The dynamite. If Mike can't do it . . . somebody has to. Not Thomas; a different mission was claiming him. Lucas and Archie? A sad old drunk and a sixteen-year-old boy? They were willing, but leaderless. Mike should be leading them . . . but Mike hadn't made it. Grief swelled in her, but she pushed past it.

"Lucas," she said. "I saw the dynamite in Thomas's boat. Did he explain how to use it?"

He nodded. "Last night he gave me and Archie a crash course."

"Good. You can teach me everything."

His eyebrows lifted. "You're coming?"

She wished she could do it by herself, but that was impossible. She needed Lucas and Archie. "Something's happened," she said. She looked at Archie to include him, and saw that he was already listening. "The resonance event at HARC . . . it's going on right now." She told them everything: her certainty that Crewe had run the demonstration early, the accidents, the visions, the aurora. They both looked up at the colors in the sky, then back at her in quiet astonishment. She told them her belief that Takona was protected, and why. As they stared at her, Lucas seemed to be thinking it through. Archie finally just shrugged. Dana saw that, in their separate ways, they accepted it—they'd lived through too much to doubt it. She explained that it was up to the three of them to carry out the mission against HARC, and put an end to the disaster going on around them.

They sat for a moment in silence, looking out at the water.

When Lucas's calm gaze met Dana's, it touched a nerve of love, and threw her. How could she think of leading her son into such danger? If she was right about Takona's protection, then the moment they left the village, like leaving Shangri-la, the devastating ELF radiation would hit them. No end to it . . . no help. A voice inside her cried: *Stay in the village. Here, he's safe!*

"Mom, I know what you're thinking. But I *want* to go. And . . . Mike would want it too."

Never before had she seen so much of his father in him. Pride caught in her throat like pain. She saw a boy ready to become a man.

"Listen to me, both of you," she said. "It may be that this protected area—this safe zone— extends quite close to HARC. If Takona's special quality can protect us right up to the site, then it might take just one determined sprint through the ELF zone to get us inside. We'll lay the charges the way Mike said, detonate them, and end this."

One sprint. Yet the ELF barrage would be terrible. Could they handle it?

She remembered her vision of Carla, how she'd let herself be guided by her raven-sister. Could she help Lucas and Archie in the same way? Be their guide in facing the hallucinations? Visions held no terror for her. When she was a child, her grandmother's dream-visions had been a parallel reality woven through Dana's everyday experience, and her uncles had induced visions in their sweat lodges. Dreams and the spirits of dead loved ones were enmeshed in her culture; ghosts didn't frighten her people. But Lucas had lived mostly outside that culture. As for Archie, he'd never had strength of character, though he did have nerve. She needed to prepare them.

"You're going to see things that aren't real," she began. "But remember—" A sound inside the cabin stopped her.

"Dana," Thomas called, his voice faint.

She took a breath and stood. To help Thomas she needed focus, and courage. She saw Lucas watching her, his eyes wide. "It's time," she said. She explained that the three of them had to carry Thomas down to the riverbank. Archie nodded gravely. Lucas swallowed, then got to his feet.

Inside, Dana found a cloth and gently wiped away the sweat on Thomas's face, and the blood trickling from his mouth. "So hot . . ." he said.

"The water will cool you," she told him. It was hard to hold back the tears.

"Ready," he said, his voice thin as a reed.

They carried him naked on a blanket down the dirt path. It was tough going, just the three of them, but it wasn't far. At the water's edge, they set him down, and Thomas struggled to his feet. Dana knew how excruciating it had to be for him just to stand. But his willpower was stronger.

He tried to focus on her face. "Carla?"

Tears blurred her vision. "She's waiting, Thomas. Wonders what's been keeping you."

Lucas and Archie touched Thomas's shoulder, a last

connection. Their faces were stony at the solemn moment. No one spoke. Thomas nodded, then turned to the water, bending in pain. He took his first step.

It ripped something inside Dana to see his powerful body stooped, see blood dripping from his mouth into the water, see him courageously go on, one halting step after another. But she made herself move back on the sand with Lucas and Archie, leaving Thomas alone, allowing him the dignity of the end he had chosen.

Once he started, he didn't stop. An uninterrupted passage from land into water. For the last few steps, he straightened, and his motion became as smooth, as in harmony with his world, as when his sled dogs had carried him gliding over the endless snow. Finally, he spread his arms and gave himself to the river.

Dana heard Lucas's breath catch. On the water, she watched the ripples radiate, the circles moving wider and wider, extending into nothingness. A sandhill crane skimmed the treetops across the river and landed serenely on the far bank. Archie began to hum an ancient chant, his voice surprisingly melodious. Thomas's dogs far behind in the trees howled.

Dana looked up. The aurora's livid colors shimmered. The river had taken Thomas before his time, felled by HARC, and in her heart she feared the river had also taken Mike. HARC was voracious.

Here, we're safe . . . but no one else is.

She gathered her courage, as Thomas had, for the steps that lay ahead. But there was time for one last duty.

"Thomas is on a new journey," she said as the ripples subsided. "Let's go and set his dogs free."

Tuesday, 3:00 P.M.

"HAVE YOU GOT POWER?" Wayne called from the doorway. His chest was heaving from the run, his broad face glistened with sweat, diesel blackened his hands and smeared his hairline, but Mike saw hope in his eyes.

"Hold on," Mike called back as he plugged in the imaging riometer. He was on his knees on the floor behind the console in the crowded Eureka operations room, Gina watching him and waiting. "Operations" was stretching it—half the equipment had been moved out over two years ago. He'd built the Eureka prototype with no thought of permanence, and the ops room was only a prefab trailer with linoleum flooring, fluorescent panels in the low ceiling, a film of dust on every working surface, and since the air-conditioning was out, a ripe body odor from the milling soldiers and scientific assistants, and himself. Still, Mike had found enough equipment here to work with, and because it had been unplugged—unlike the base's computers that operated twenty-four hours a day—it hadn't been damaged by the ELF strikes.

Outside, among the three hundred high-frequency antennas, they'd found that a few towers in the northwest quadrangle had suffered wind damage—snapped guy wires and twisted dipoles—and platoons of soldiers were working to repair them. Once they did, the array would be ready to transmit. A bigger problem was the huge generators. Wayne had been faced with dirty fuel tanks, gummed pistons, and no diesel supply on-site. Nevertheless, he'd now got one of the generators running, and as Mike reached around to flip the ionosonde switch, a sweet electronic hum met his ears. "Yes!"

"Fantastic!" Gina said with a grin. A nervous grin, Mike knew, but he also knew he could rely on her. He'd have to. Once he set out into the corridor, Gina would be fine-tuning Eureka's controls, his life in her hands.

And in Wayne's, whose job would be to keep the power flowing.

"Great, buddy, you've got us going," Mike said, hopping to his feet. "Now, get back out there."

Wayne dragged his arm across his face to mop the sweat. "Yeah, one down, nine to go." He turned and hurried out.

Mike wiped his own sweaty forehead, wondering if they could do it. Nine more generators to bring on-line, each one as big as Wayne's boat, and the first had taken over an hour. Meanwhile, they needed thousands of gallons of diesel fuel. With the power blackout, and so many vehicles either out of order or breaking down, procurement was a nightmare. Fuel was being trucked in piecemeal, in barrels commandeered from service stations, even jerry cans from stores; Colonel Braden's sergeants were running the operation like a combat mission. They were doing a great job, and Wayne was busting his ass, but could he finish in time? Jammed against the midnight deadline, Mike had only nine more hours, and he needed every single watt Wayne could squeeze out if he was going to make Eureka's transmissions effective. Meanwhile, everything depended on his calculating the correct wave pattern, a complex web of shifting mathematical parameters, and the only computer he had was a dated laptop. Switched off when the ELF radiation had hit, it was functioning, but Mike didn't know what the next ELF strike would do to it, or to any of this equipment. Still, the laptop was a big step up; on the ride here, before they'd scrounged it for him, he'd been scribbling equations on scraps of paper.

"Where do you want this stuff, sir?" a private asked him, holding up a shoe box, while behind him, three young soldiers, electronics specialists, hustled past with armloads of manuals. Colonel Braden had assigned the three to Mike, and they were about to sit down with two physicists from the university's Geophysical Institute. Mike felt lucky that Braden's men had been able to find the pair of scientists, since a lab explosion on campus had left untold casualties and chaos. He'd asked them to help Gina, and set the three soldiers to bone up on Eureka's apparatus to assist them, but now he shook his head as he watched the young soldiers go past, thinking he must be crazy to expect this to work.

Don't think, he told himself. Just do it.

"I'll take that," he told the private. Inside the box were the few items he'd requested, including a plastic slide rule Braden had got from one of the base pilots. Taking it and the laptop, Mike headed for a small desk in the corner, the only spot where people weren't working. It was cluttered with spare parts and greasy rags, and he shoved the mess aside. Outside the trailer's thin walls, trucks were rumbling in and out over the gravel road, delivering the precious cans of diesel, Wayne shouting for more soldiers to give him a hand. A group of them pounded past on the double. Mike glanced at Gina as she tuned the VHF riometer and the Raleigh LIDAR, explaining the rudiments to the soldiers. On all their faces, Mike read tension. Everyone was awaiting the next ELF strike, holding at bay their own private terror. So was he. Like waiting for the next jolt from a torturer.

He sat down amid the noise. Everything rested on his calculations—with a plastic slide rule, an old laptop, a pad of paper and a pencil.

Don't think. Just do it.

▲

"Hold it there!" The corporal stiff-armed the air to hold back the yellow Volkswagen van, and motioned a truck to go ahead. Conducting traffic in and out of the Eureka site, he looked frazzled.

Obeying the signal, Ben hit the van's brakes. Carol, sitting beside him, lurched at the sudden stop. The traffic-cop corporal did a shocked double take, seeing a general at the wheel. Shame heated Ben's face under the corporal's gaze. He wore the uniform of a general but he felt like an imposter. Felt like this soldier's enemy.

"Sorry, sir . . . sorry, General . . . go right on through."

Ben shifted gears and drove across the gravel toward the ops trailer. The VW van, a seventies vintage he'd commandeered from a Baptist church, was in good condition, its interior immaculate, if slightly threadbare and smelling of sweet patchouli car deodorant. Ben was just relieved that it ran. All afternoon, at Wainwright, he and Braden had been organizing the part-military, part-civilian brigade to locate working vehicles and transport diesel fuel. With intermittent communications, disorder on the base, and panic throughout Fairbanks, he'd felt lucky to get the van. It would get him to HARC. He hadn't yet told Mike that. Nor Carol. On the backseat lay a .22 Winchester and ammunition. His sidearm was a Glock nine-millimeter. He was as ready as he could be.

"Wish I had a lipstick," Carol murmured. She had lowered the visor for its mirror, and was examining her reflection, listlessly touching her pale lips. On her feet were borrowed sneakers, incongruous with her chic dress. She flicked at her messed hair. "I look like hell." Ben saw that her hand was trembling. "It fits," she added bleakly, "since we're sending Mike into hell."

Ben felt an overwhelming sense of failure. That's why he was going to HARC. He couldn't let Mike face this alone.

Carol stared at her reflection in defeat. "Couldn't have been more wrong, could we?"

"Me. My fault."

She looked at him. "Oh, Dad." She sounded exhausted, but her voice was tender. "You didn't mean this to happen."

But it was happening. On the base, they'd got some computers working, and by E-mail had reached the Pentagon and received more information, and Ben was staggered by the reports. Intermittent power blackouts were hitting communities all across the northern states and Canada. Sporadic ELF radiation was striking down men, women, and children in random spots. Portland, Oregon; Billings, Montana; Grand Rapids, Michigan; Thunder Bay, Ontario. The death toll in Grand Rapids alone was in the hundreds. Aviation, transportation, and commerce were crippled in those localities. Chaos on the roads. Even livestock herds were affected. Yet Ben had had to warn the Pentagon not to scramble any jets toward HARC, because once in Alaskan airspace, neither aircraft nor pilots would make it.

He pulled up outside the ops trailer. With vehicles grinding past, soldiers running, sergeants shouting, it was like a battle staging area. A battle against the terrible thing he'd unleashed. He sat staring at his hands on the wheel, not wanting Carol to look into his face. "I meant to protect my country," he said, a sharp tightness in his throat. "Instead . . . I'm killing people."

He took a breath. He had to go on, had to tell her. "I'm trusting Mike's plan will work." He knew the guy would get to the site and kill HARC, even if his brain was mush and he had to crawl. "But the moment this crisis ends, my world ends too. You see that, don't you? I'll be stripped of command. Court-martialed. For me, it's over." Disgrace. Dishonor. The worst thing he could imagine. Worse than death. "I'm only glad your mother isn't alive to—" He stopped, swallowed. "But you and William and Maureen . . ." The thought of bequeathing such shame to his children felt crushing. He turned to her.

Carol, who'd always looked up to him as a master, was watching him with pity. It only intensified Ben's decision. He had no intention of returning to dishonor and disgrace. He needed her to understand that, because this was the last time he would see her.

"I've failed in command, Carol, but—" He searched for words to express the one thing he knew to be true. "I am still a soldier."

▲

"It's working," Mike said, looking over Gina's shoulder at the imaging riometer screen. The oscillating wave patterns were textbook perfect: HARC's red crests and troughs, in precise opposition to Eureka's green crests and troughs, together formed an undulating chain across the screen, depicting neutralization. "God damn, the skip zone is going to work."

"You think?" The hours of tension showed in her anxious eyes. "I'd believe it better if I saw you juggling."

He smiled. Looking around, he asked, "Where's Wayne?" He'd called together the core Eureka team—Gina and Wayne, the three soldier specialists and their lieutenant, and the two Institute scientists—and in the stuffy trailer, they were all watching him.

"Here." Wayne stood by the door, wolfing a chocolate

bar, his face streaked with diesel. "And all I want to see you juggling is pieces of the HARC grid."

Mike laughed, and so did the others—a spontaneous release of tension.

"I don't know how you did it," Mike told Wayne. "All ten gennys on line in less than five hours. Incredible." He applauded him, and the others joined in, clapping enthusiastically. Someone even whistled. Wayne nodded, grinning.

Mike looked at the eager faces. "You've *all* done a fantastic job. We're ready. I'm going to drive through the safe corridor up to HARC, nice and easy, and I'm going to shut that sucker down. And it'll all be thanks to you." He gave them a double-fisted thumbs-up, and everyone grinned and clapped again, for him, for themselves, a room full of hope. Mike started for the door.

"Give 'em hell, sir," the lieutenant supervising the soldiers said.

Mike nodded. "Follow Dr. DalBello's orders. Do whatever the lady says, got it?"

"Yes, sir." The lieutenant turned to his men. "Now, listen up." They crowded round him for instructions.

Gina caught up to Mike. "Take this," she said, lifting over her head a thin gold necklace with a crucifix. She handed it to him.

"Thanks." He slipped it into his pocket.

"I just wish I could talk to you as you go, on a phone or a radio. I know, I know, everything's dead, but if I could only *somehow* hear how you're doing . . . I mean, if you felt some ELF disturbance, I could tune things here faster." She bit her lip. "Mike, what if I screw up?"

"Then you'd have to hand back that Penn State fellowship."

She gave him a feeble smile.

"You won't screw up, Gina. Just keep a careful eye on the frequency modulations, trust yourself, and you'll be fine." He squeezed her shoulder. "And so will I."

She quickly hugged him, then hurried back to work.

Mike reached Wayne at the door, and together they stepped outside. "Fuel supply's good, Mike. Enough for four, maybe five hours. Plenty to get you to the site. Hell, you could stop for a picnic on the way."

They shook hands. Mike said, "I meant it, buddy. Outstanding."

Wayne smiled. "Just don't do it again." He slapped Mike on the arm. "Now, go be a hero." He strode off.

The moment Mike was alone, his legs felt so rubbery he had to lean against the trailer. *It's not going to work.* Soldiers hustled past, and vehicles were grinding over the gravel, and somebody was shouting commands, but all Mike could think was: It's pointless. He'd lied to Gina, to Wayne, to the soldiers, to everyone here who was expecting him to save them. For the last five hours he'd buried himself in calculations, equations, estimates . . . *guesses.* For five hours people had been tiptoeing around his desk as though he were some genius at work, not to be disturbed. But he wasn't a genius, or a hero. Just a scientist with bleary eyes, a cramped hand, an aching back, and terror in his heart. *It's not going to work.*

"Mike." Carol's voice, behind him. Her hand on his shoulder.

He turned, drawing away from her hand that felt like a weight. Ben was with her. Anger twisted through Mike. Do I have to pretend even to him?

"I had to come, Mike," Carol said. "Had to say—"

"Good-bye?" He was tired of faces staring at him for reassurance.

"No," she said quickly, "good luck."

Luck. He thought of prayers against a plague. Thought of Gina's crucifix. Pointless. He nodded, hiding it all. "Thanks."

Ben asked, "Ready?"

"All set." Everyone hungered to hear the lie, and what was the alternative? Blind panic. "On my way." He was looking for a car. At least, for Major Figgis, who'd said he was bringing a car. No sign of him.

"Mike," Carol blurted, "forgive me."

He nodded, still looking for Figgis. "Sure."

She stepped closer and timidly kissed his cheek. "And come back to us. If not for me . . . for Lindsay."

It was a blow Mike hadn't expected. She'd meant no harm, he knew; meant the invocation of their daughter to inspire him. But for hours he'd cleared his mind of everything except frequency equations and wave patterns, allowing no thoughts of the people he loved, people who were suffering right now, or dying, or dead. Dana. Lucas. Now this extra torture, that he might never see Lindsay again.

He saw the yellow VW van behind Ben. "Did you come in that? I'll take it, I need it." He started forward.

"Hold it," Ben said. "I'm coming with you."

Mike stopped. Ben's face was grave. Jesus, he was serious. "No. Nobody goes but me."

Ben went on as if he hadn't heard. "I've brought weapons. No way of knowing what we'll find out there. People are out of their minds, and a lot of them are armed. I'm coming to protect you, Mike. The fact is, you're too valuable to lose. I'm dispensable."

Something like affection swelled in Mike's throat, surprising him. "Don't need protection. I'm going alone."

Ben opened his hand to reveal the keys. "I'm still the commanding officer of HARC. It's my decision." His fingers closed over the keys.

"And I'm telling you, you're not coming. There's no reason for you to die with me." They both stared at him, but he couldn't keep up the lie any longer. "Christ, Ben, do I have to spell it out? This neutralizing buffer is a fantasy!"

Carol gave a small gasp. "But . . . you said—"

"I know." He was sorry he'd started this in front of her, but maybe she should hear it after all. It might help Ben see the truth. "I really hoped I could generate enough of a neutralizing wave. I've even got the damn thing working—Gina's in there right now tuning it. It seems we've done it, created a safe zone between here and HARC. But the problem is we're dealing with the ionosphere, a wildly dynamic system, and the variables are overwhelming. The resonance disturbance is in flux, constantly shifting, constantly creating subtle frequency changes. Gina will have to continuously adjust and focus Eureka's frequencies, trying to match the changes in the resonance wave pattern. But the moment she loses it, anyone inside the corridor will be hit by full-blast ELF radiation. It's like a surfer trying to move with the changing wave—lose it, and he wipes out. Only here, Gina will have to keep me riding the wave by remote control. She'll be trying to follow the shifts, match the moves, but she's got nothing to go on but my calculations." He plowed his hand through his hair, sick at the odds. "Even if she could keep on top of it, the skip zone *itself* will be shifting. Patches of it are going to fade, other patches might attenuate to nothing. And meanwhile the whole corridor will probably be moving, a quarter mile this way, a half mile that way . . ." He pictured it like a giant snake pinned at both ends but still wriggling. No one could predict its action. "Damn it, Ben, it's almost impossible for this to work."

"I know. That's why I'm coming."

Mike looked at him. It struck him that, once again, Ben was one step ahead, just as he had been through the whole life of HARC. Life, and death. Strangely, it lit a faint glow of relief, to know he wasn't alone with the truth. "You know?"

"I've watched you work for years, Mike. I've admired your vision, but I've also seen the shadow in your eyes when you're not positive about a course of action, and that's what I saw when you told us in the war room about the corridor."

If only you'd listened days ago, Mike thought, but he bit back the words. Ben was the only person besides himself who was looking the truth in the face, and regardless of the betrayals that had brought them to this

point, it somehow forged a bond. Part of him craved
Ben's clearheaded presence beside him. But his coming
would be senseless. "This is a one-man job." He reached
out, open-handed. "Let's have the keys."

Carol moaned. "Mike, if it's *not* a safe corridor . . .
you can't go."

"Got to try. It's almost ten. I've only got till midnight." He forced a smile. "Let's just hope Gina's good
at surfing."

Ben said, "You don't understand, Mike. This is a
command decision. It concerns not only your protection,
it's also a procedure of redundancy. The corridor might
work, or it might not, but it's all we've got, and if we go
together we can help each other . . . through the effects.
One of us might make it." His gaze was unwavering. "In
case that one is me, you'd better tell me, on the way,
what needs to be done to shut the thing down." He indicated the van. "Ready?"

"No!" Carol clutched Ben's arm. "Dad, don't. Please
don't! I can't lose you *both*."

Her face was white, her body rigid. Mike didn't think
he'd ever seen anyone so frightened. Carol would rather
die than be alone.

"Ben," he said, "Carol needs you, and so do all the
people here. You might be able to save some of them,
manage an evacuation . . . I don't know, get them to just
start walking. Better than staying and waiting for the
end, isn't it? If so, these people will need a leader. That's
you."

"No go, Mike. If we don't stop HARC, no one here
has a chance. And that goes for millions of others. I've

already told Braden to send volunteers after we set out. They'll come in pairs, every hour—for as long as they can." A ghost of a smile tugged his mouth. "I've always believed in redundancy."

He opened the driver's door. "We're the first pair. Let's get started."

▲

They had been half an hour on the river in Thomas's dented skiff, heading for HARC: Lucas in the stern, steering; Dana in the bow; Archie between them, surrounded by the dynamite-filled backpacks. It seemed that the extended protection of Takona's peculiar EM field—its "magic circle"—had kept them safe this far. Safe, and oddly serene, considering their mission, Dana thought. The river was placid, the motor hummed a soothing drone, the gold-red glow of the setting sun burnished the water to a sheen, and the breeze on her face felt clean and elemental as she watched the primeval forest glide by. It was as though the evening were as uneventful as any other in the eons since the glaciers melted to form the Gatana. Only this evening wasn't like any other—Dana knew that. In the reddish sky, the patch above her pulsed with the garish purple and green of the aurora, like a proclamation of the devastation happening beyond this peaceful stretch of river. And she and Lucas and Archie were on their way to blow up HARC.

Beneath her surface serenity, Dana felt fear. Takona's magic would soon run out. Could they endure the ELF zone?

Then, as though her thought of peril had created it, she saw the grizzly. A huge male on all fours at the river's edge just ahead, the bear was heaving its head back and forth like a massive pendulum—a motion of sheer derangement. It lumbered up onto its rear legs, and the red sunset glow lit its eyes like blood-wet stones. Throwing its shaggy arms wide, it let out a bellow of agony.

A claw scraped Dana's heart. This was the border of Takona's protection. The bear was suffering . . . within moments, so would they.

She turned to Lucas and Archie, and found them both watching the grizzly too. "We're coming into the ELF zone," she told them. "Hang on."

An intense vibration suddenly quivered the air. *This is it . . .*

Her mind seemed to empty . . . then to fill up with the river. The whole world turned blue, misty, liquid. It was all river, all water, all peace. She longed to float in it. With Thomas. Just plunge in, drown herself in the everlasting blue . . .

No . . . it's not real. Don't give in!

Amazed, she found she could do it, with great effort. Could divide the real from the unreal. No, not divide, incorporate . . . realize that she was *already* in the world, in the water, part of its energy.

But she saw that Lucas had frozen. And Archie was suddenly on his feet, his eyes locked on the grizzly. "He's a beaut!" Archie cried. "I'm gonna bag him!" His scrawny body was trembling all over, his teeth were chattering, but he was grinning like a death's head. Dana thought: It's the alcohol in his system. The ELF effects were boosting it into a chemical-electrical fire in his brain, a false sense of potency. She reached out to calm him, but he took a step closer to the gunnel, oblivious, dipping the side of the skiff.

"He's mine!" he yelled. There was a wild gleam in his eyes—the hunter in ecstasy. He unsheathed the knife at his belt and dove overboard.

Dana watched in horror as he swam like a demon toward the bear. "Archie, come back!" she called. But he reached the shore and scrambled out of the water. Before her stunned eyes, he raised his knife and, with a battle cry, charged the grizzly. The animal's maddened red eyes glinted. Its roar shook the air. Its massive arm slashed, claws ripping flesh. Archie screamed, and bright arterial blood sprayed. Horror-struck, Dana saw the massive jaws clamp Archie's middle, and the grizzly lifted him and shook him like a huge salmon. The violence of it had to break his backbone, and he went suddenly limp. Sickened, Dana couldn't watch. She knew Archie was dead. She turned, and saw Lucas. He sat still as a totem, his gaze ahead unfocused, apparently oblivious to the horror on shore. The boat, with no one steering, was swerving toward the opposite shore.

Dana staggered to the stern and sat beside him, and with one hand took control of the throttle and steered. Her other arm went around Lucas's shoulders. His body was rigid and cold. Archie was gone, but Lucas needed her. She held him close to her, trembling herself, and rocked him, willing her warmth into him as the boat sped on. "I'm here," she said. "I'm here."

But she couldn't stop shaking. Clinging to Lucas, she could still see Archie's broken body, and she cringed, shutting her eyes. She felt her will, her self, draining away. *Can't do this . . . can't go on . . .*

"Hey, Dana-rayna, sure you can."

Her eyes sprang open. A raven winged past and alighted on the gunnel. Black feathers iridescent, eyes aglitter. Carla!

"Rested up? Good, let's go." Carla cocked her head at her. "Come on, you can do it."

Dana stared in wonder. "Can I?"

"You and me," Carla winked. "They never could catch us."

"No . . . they couldn't." Dana felt determination surge back. Oh, thank you, Carla. *Thank you.*

She felt a breath shudder through Lucas. "I can't . . . stop her falling," he mumbled. "Can't ever . . . stop her falling . . ."

"Shhh. It's not you, Lucas. It's something in your head. A trap that's closed on your mind. Open it. Sophy's not falling, she's flying. She's free. Make *yourself* free."

Gradually, she felt his terror thaw. She rubbed his shoulders, his chest, his good arm. He blinked at her, blinked away tears. Dana had to hold back her own fear and confusion. She knew the ELF effects were still happening. Every few seconds a fish would leap from the water, thrashing. She saw a squirrel in a treetop, screeching. It was still happening and she had to keep it from overwhelming her. For a moment, she thought she saw faces in the water—Archie, Thomas, others she hadn't been able to help. Disoriented again, she asked her sister with her eyes, What's real?

"It's all real," the raven said. "Take what you need."

That's it, she realized. Layers of reality. I can choose the one I need. To accept the altered state of mind, not resist—that's the way to survive the ELF zone. And to help Lucas through it.

The raven, impatient, danced from one foot to the other. "Lots to do. Let's go." The glimmering black wings flapped and Carla lifted off. "Race you up the river!" Away she flew.

Dana was ready to follow. She looked upstream. HARC lay just around the next bend. "Stay with me, Lucas. It's not far." She opened the throttle.

She asked him questions to keep him focused, questions about kayaking, school, his hurt arm—anything to keep them both on track, rooted in reality. He stuttered answers, sometimes just a word, sometime a babble that barely made sense, and Dana's heart swelled, knowing he was struggling to stay on the surface, not sink. She pushed him on, pushed herself on, glancing now and then at the raven guiding her from far ahead, a glittering shape between the river and the sky.

Suddenly, there it was. HARC. The west riverbank rose abruptly to a rocky bluff, and beyond its crest she saw the tops of antennas, a forest of towers etched against the livid sky. She knew they filled a square mile, an immense machine pulsing electromagnetic destruction. But she didn't have to blow up all of it, just the open distribution station; Mike had explained that last night. It was half a football field in size, he'd said. Blow a hole in the machine.

"There's a wharf past the spit, around there on the north," Lucas said, looking ahead. "We sometimes got shipments by boat. I helped build that new dock."

She stared at him, astonished that he was talking lucidly. *And I'm thinking clearly.* And Carla had vanished. "Lucas, how do you feel?"

Their eyes met. Though he looked bewildered, Dana sensed that he was calm and rational. "Okay," he answered. "You?"

"I feel . . . all right." She looked around. On the near riverbank a beaver was dragging a sapling in its mouth, unconcerned, busy at its task. Three Canada geese flapped blithely overhead, honking. What's happened? she wondered. Had the ELF radiation subsided? Why?

"Is it over?" Lucas asked, surprised, hopeful. "The resonance?"

A prickly uncertainty settled over Dana. "Mike said it wouldn't end."

"Maybe we've adjusted. You know, got used to the effects?"

Dana could see the wharf now, and steel stairs going up the bluff. Everything seemed normal, and she *felt* normal. They were far past Takona's protection, but Lucas was right—*something* had made the ELF effects ease up. It was as though they had entered a corridor of calm. Something clutched inside her. Not fear, ice-cold anger. This out-of-control machine had killed Archie, killed Thomas, and probably killed Mike. She had come to destroy it, and whatever was causing this lull, she didn't care. She was beyond analyzing. She would finish what she'd come to do.

"What about fences?" she asked Lucas as she eyed the crest of the bluff.

"Just low chain link, a strand of barbed wire along the top. We can climb it and cut the barbed wire." She turned to him as he, too, scanned the bluff. His face looked so young, but his resolve was rock-solid. In one day, he'd grown up.

The skiff nudged the dock. She grabbed hold and Lucas hopped out and tied up. "Let's unload," she said.

▲

"I'm pulling you out!" Ben cried. "We'll run for the hills!"

Mike was suffocating under bodies. "Can't move . . . can't breathe!"

He felt himself being dragged . . . his back banged over metal, then his heels carving channels through dirt. Ben was dragging him . . .

He found his feet, fought for balance, stood rockily. Gulping breaths, he stared at Ben's wild-eyed sweating face before him. They stood grappling each other for support, Mike's hands gripping Ben's shoulders, Ben's gripping his. They were both breathing hard, disoriented. Mike finally realized they were surfacing from hallucinations. He felt the terror of it still: entombed with all the people HARC had killed . . . *he* had killed. He'd felt their thrashing limbs . . . heard their screams . . . Sophy, Ron, Reid D'Alton, hundreds more, writhing around him. He'd felt a tortured hope: *Maybe they're not dead yet . . . maybe I can save them!* Only he couldn't move! All around him, thousands were drowning, falling, bleeding, burning . . . Dana . . . Lucas . . .

He shook his head hard, willing the horror to subside.

Ben's own horror, he saw, had been just as unrelenting. Mike asked, his voice hoarse, "Was it . . . Vietnam?"

Ben nodded, sucking breaths. "Escaping. We were . . . on the run."

When they found the strength to stand alone, Mike looked behind him. Down the road, their yellow VW van lay overturned in the ditch, its left tires looking afloat on the tall grass. It had been a particularly intense ELF strike. Ben had driven off the road.

Before that, the skip zone had been working . . . to Mike's amazement. For a good hour they'd sailed along the highway toward HARC. When they'd set out the odds had appeared so hopeless to him that for a half hour he'd sat grimly waiting to hit the invisible ELF wall that would annihilate them. But for mile after mile there had been no ELF onslaught, not a single strike. It was working. At first, leaving Fairbanks, they'd had to maneuver around vehicles abandoned on the roads, and injured people wandering in shock. A house on fire. A lost child crying. And Mike bleakly aware that they couldn't stop to help. But once on the open highway, nothing had slowed them. Scattered people in roadside hamlets groggily watched the van go by. Soon, the few isolated victims they passed seemed literally stunned: a couple were slumped in a Cadillac stopped on the opposite lane; an Indian kid sat propped against the gas pump at the burned-out filling station. Mike couldn't tell if they were dead or alive, but it seemed clear that they'd suffered ELF saturation bombardment—and permanent damage—before the skip zone had kicked in. Soon after, he and Ben passed the corpses of the first three commandos. It was pitiful and chilling, but it was also proof, as they sailed along, that the corridor was working. They'd turned off the highway onto the dirt road that led to HARC—just twelve miles to go!—and Mike had allowed himself the first words of hope. "Shit, Ben, we're going to get there."

Then it had hit. Either they'd driven into an ineffective patch of the skip zone, or maybe they'd been at its edge and it had shifted off them. Whatever, they had skidded into the ditch, the van was thrown on its side, and they had both veered into madness. If they'd stayed there, the ELF radiation would be bombarding them still. But Ben had clambered out, apparently spurred by his hallucination of the Viet Cong coming after him and his men. He'd pulled Mike out and dragged him down the road . . . and now it seemed they were safely back inside the skip zone. Maybe this patch had suddenly resumed the neutralized state, or maybe the whole corridor had shifted back to reengulf them. Mike didn't know. He was sure only that Ben had saved them both.

Saved his weapons too, Mike noticed. Ben had slung the rifle by its strap over his shoulder, and tucked his sidearm into his belt. Uniform grimy, nose bleeding, he looked as though he *had* escaped through a jungle. He was looking up the road toward HARC. "Twelve miles," he said, wiping sweat off his face with his sleeve.

"Can't do it on foot," Mike said, still catching his breath. "No time."

"Have to. No vehicles in sight."

"Except that one." Mike was looking past the brushy woods that edged the road to a small farm. There was a dilapidated metal barn, and beside it was a red tractor. "Let's get it."

▲

It was the most malignant dusk Mike had ever seen. A twilight sky eerily awash with garish aurora colors. A nightmare sky. As he looked up at it from the rattling tractor seat, with Ben sitting shotgun behind him, his heartbeat was racing. The solar deadline was less than an hour away. Yet he couldn't get any more speed from this tractor. Lumbering over the gravel road, it belched diesel smoke above the engine's rumble and grind. Twelve miles back, the farmer had been nowhere in sight, and they hadn't wasted time looking for him. The starter worked, there was fuel in the tank, and it was faster than walking.

Mike drove past the three boulders, the landmark where Wayne had picked him up that night he'd escaped Ben's security detail. In five minutes they would reach the gates of HARC. Ten minutes, they'd be inside. Excitement and relief coursed through him.

The guard's corpse changed that. He lay on the side of the road just beyond the gate, a dark patch of blood-soaked earth beneath his head. A revolver lay on the ground by his hand. Suicide. Driving past, Mike didn't need to turn to know that Ben was looking at the dead man too.

"We knew it would be bad," Ben said.

"Yeah."

As Mike drove the tractor up the site road, he heard a wailing alarm coming from the buildings ahead. The ops center came into view. In the dusk, it was just a massive block, no windows on this side, no indication of what was going on inside. He hadn't known the dead guard, but he did know every scientist on Meredith's reduced team. What state would he find his friends in? Or Meredith? Was anyone even alive?

The road was clear. About fifteen vehicles were in the parking lot, no one in sight. As Mike pulled up in front of the ops center, he realized that the wailing from the stuck alarm was coming from the power building next door. He looked out at the shadowy vista of antennas that stretched into the dusk. He knew the array was still transmitting, still in the throes of the resonance event. The skip zone neutralized only the space up to it. Eureka couldn't dent the power of HARC.

Something on the ground in the distance caught his eye. A dull flash out there at the beginning of the array, near the distribution station. A moving shape. A woman?

Ben said, "Mike, look."

He turned and followed Ben's gaze toward the power building. It sat on a slight rise across a lawn that separated it from the ops center, and outside the front doors three or four men in technicians' navy coveralls were moving slowly in the gloom, indistinguishable as ghosts. They were moving in different directions, as though aimless, the alarm wailing behind them, and their shuffling gait made Mike profoundly uneasy. These were people not in their right minds. But there was no time to help them. There was only time to end this.

Get into the control room, he told himself. Switch off the HF beam, and end the nightmare.

▲

Wayne heard it before he saw it. A soft sizzle, behind him. He was walking through the Eureka power shed between the No. 3 and No. 4 generators, each one the size of a truck. An instinct told him to back off, even as he turned to look. A leak in the fuel line?

The line burst. Pressurized fuel sprayed out, an explosion of scalding vaporized diesel: Wayne dove to the floor. Only the fact that the No. 3 genny stood between him and the ruptured copper line saved him.

"Fuel leak!" he yelled.

Soldiers came running.

"Let's get this repaired, Corporal," Wayne called out above the hiss of the spray as they all stood back.

"Yes, sir," the young soldier called back, "but we'll have to shut off the generators to do it."

"No. Can't shut off the power till Ryder and Crewe are done. I'll repair it on the fly. I'll need three of your guys to help. First, we get suited up. On the *double*, kid!"

He was running out with the three designated soldiers when he heard someone back near the spraying fuel yell, "Fire!"

In the ops trailer, Gina was bleary-eyed from constantly fine-tuning the Eureka transmissions. The first hour had gone okay, and she'd felt confident the skip zone was working, and that she could hold it. On her screen, the oscillating pairs of wave crests and troughs had looked like perfect hourglasses, HARC's red line and Eureka's green line undulating in harmonious opposition. But she hadn't dared let her concentration waver for a moment, and now exhaustion was beginning to drain her. The two scientists from the university Institute were doing their best to help, and so were the soldiers, but no one was capable of spelling her off. Worse, the frequency modulations at HARC were getting more unpredictable, because the resonance was growing. On her screen now, the oscillations were sometimes ragged, Eureka's lagging behind HARC's. Gina had to be quick to keep up, to compensate.

She heard soldiers shouting outside. Something about the generators.

She blocked it out. *Keep focused.* But her hands on the keyboard were sweaty, and she had to keep wiping her palms on her skirt. On screen, the ragged oscillations looked like a stormy seascape. She was afraid . . . if she lost the skip zone, saturation ELF bombardment would engulf Mike and General Crewe. Tuning quickly, she got the wave pattern under control again.

"Ma'am? Take this."

The lieutenant beside her was pouring a glass of

water. Eyes fixed to the screen, Gina took the glass and gulped a few mouthfuls. Better. She sat up straighter, shook her head hard to clear her vision, took a deep breath, and settled back to work. She could not let the harmony on her screen slide into chaos.

MIKE THOUGHT HE HAD prepared himself for whatever he and Ben might find as they walked into the ops center lobby, but when he saw Roger Donelly hanging from the open staircase, a fist of sickness shot up his throat. Roger had tied a rope to a crossbeam and hanged himself.

"Jesus!" He bolted forward and grabbed Roger's legs, lifting to ease the pressure on his neck.

"Leave him," Ben said.

"He could still be alive." Mike grunted as he held up the dead weight.

Ben grabbed his shoulder. "He's gone. We have to get to the control room."

Mike let go, sickened as the body slumped. He'd known Roger since grad school. *No time for this,* he told himself. At any moment the skip zone could fade or move off them again. He turned to Ben and nodded.

They didn't see anyone as they went down the second-floor corridor, and as they walked into the control room, it looked deserted. Along the console island, computers hummed and screens displayed wave patterns and bar graphs, but no one was at the workstations. Had they all wandered off, like Roger?

Then Mike saw Bjorn Halveg. On his knees in the corner, writing on the wall with a black marker, he'd covered the wall with senseless equations. The scribblings of a madman.

"Bjorn—"

Halveg turned to Mike, the look in his eyes catatonic. Then he went back to writing.

Mike went to the console and initiated the "shutdown" sequence. Nothing happened. Computers went on humming. Screens still displayed HARC's changing data.

Ben came beside him. "What's wrong?"

Mike reentered the command. Nothing. "It's frozen."

"What now?"

"This room's just an interface." Mike was already on his way around the corner, pulling his magnetic key card out of his wallet. "I'll do the shutdown at the mainframe." It was in a steel-lined, climate-controlled room, protected behind a steel door.

As he turned the corner he saw Meredith, and his breath caught. She lay sprawled on her side in front of the mainframe door. Her cheek on the carpet, she was staring up at him, making a strangled sound. But she didn't move. *Paralyzed*, Mike realized. A string of saliva drooled from her mouth.

"Meredith—"

"I'll see to her," Ben said. "Go shut it down."

Mike wrenched his eyes off Meredith's stricken face. He reached the door and slid his card into the slot to activate the electronic lock.

Nothing happened.

"... ouer ... ah ..." Meredith moaned.

Mike twisted around to her. A new code? He went down on his knee in front of her. "Meredith, did you change the key code?"

She stared at him, making that tortured sound. Was her brain even functioning?

"Maybe the new key's on her," Ben said, rolling her on her back and checking her pockets.

"No. Here." Mike lifted the thin chain around her neck, drawing out the card from inside her shirt. He felt like a grave robber, but he needed her card. "I'm sorry, Meredith." He tugged the chain gently over her head.

Going back to the door, he slid the card into the slot. Nothing. "The code's not the problem. The lock's jammed."

Ben was unslinging his rifle. "Stand back."

"You can't shoot through two inches of fire door. And the wall's concrete and steel rebar."

"Can we cut the cables from the mainframe to the array?"

Mike shook his head. "Underground."

Meredith moaned again. "... ur ... ouer ... ah ..."

Mike finally knew what she was saying. *Turn the power off.* She was right. "Ben, there's no way to stop this from here. We have to turn off the main switch at the reactor substation."

"Let's go."

Mike told Meredith they'd be back, and they headed for the door. As they passed the wall of windows that overlooked the array, Mike saw that the gloom of midnight had lightened to a murky dawn, sinister with the blue-green fire of the aurora. His eye was caught by a movement near a sodium light atop the distribution station fence. Two figures moving in the shadows.

▲

Lucas was glad of the nearby sodium light. It was hard enough to see in the gloom, and his one good hand was still shaky as he pressed a blasting cap into the dynamite stick he'd wedged between his knees. *All* of him was still shaky. His mom had cut an opening in the wire fence around the distribution station and they were working inside, laying charges among the squat towers. Lucas was trying hard to concentrate, but the alarm wailing at the power building sawed at his nerves, and he couldn't stop thinking of the technicians he'd glimpsed outside the doors there, moving slowly on the grass. Those poor guys had looked crazy. He hoped none of them would stumble over here among the charges.

He'd almost gone crazy himself, back in the boat. The way they'd lost Archie . . . then his own mind had gone, nothing in it except Sophy falling, and wild terror. When it had suddenly lifted, he'd been weak with relief just to be able to think straight. But he had a terrible feeling it wasn't going to last.

He glanced at his mom. She was attaching a fuse line to the last charge he'd set, and it amazed him how together she seemed. He remembered her voice back in the boat, so calm, something he'd been able to hang on to to make the terror go away. Now, her willpower as they worked inspired him: though shaky and scared, he would finish this. The two of them *had* to—there was no one left but them. But he could see how exhausted she was after everything they'd been through, plus hauling the equipment up from the river, and now she was organizing all the fuse lines. He wished he could help her more—he was taller and stronger—but with this damn broken arm there was so much he couldn't do.

Still, he had the detonator switch. To flip it, he'd only need his thumb.

He tucked the dynamite against the foot of the tower, and looked up at the other distribution towers around him. The smooth black ceramic insulator disks capping them looked eerie, reflecting the aurora colors. It made his skin crawl.

What was that, up at the ops center window? Someone moving. More crazy people? He turned back to grab another blasting cap from the pack. *Can't let anybody stop us.* Just another fifteen minutes to finish the job. Can't let *anything* stop us now.

▲

Mike and Ben ran up the sloping lawn toward the power building, the alarm inside screaming louder as they approached. Mike saw evidence of how hard the saturation ELF had hit people. A Jeep had run up onto the grass and smashed into a lamp post and sat crumpled, the driver slumped at the wheel, apparently dead. A technician in blue coveralls was rolling on the concrete walk, as if he felt on fire and was putting out the flames, and another was shuffling along the walkway, back and forth, like an animal in a cage. They'd been too debilitated to think of shutting down the power, Mike knew, and even now, protected by the skip zone, they were too far gone. As he and Ben passed a gray-haired technician sitting dazed on the grass the man called to them, "No . . . don't go in! Containment . . . don't . . . go near!"

They stopped.

"Stay back . . . radioactive steam . . . rads off the chart. The guys inside . . . too late . . ." He lowered his head between his knees and vomited.

Mike turned to Ben, and saw his own horror mirrored in Ben's eyes. He fought it down, got control of the panic. "Somebody's got to go in."

Ben nodded. "A one-man job."

Mike looked at the technician who was watching them, dying as they stood there. *So many dead.* "I'm . . . sorry," he told the man. "I'm going in to end this, right now."

"Forget it, Mike." Ben had pulled out his Glock pistol, and after checking it he stuffed it back in his waistband, then reslung the rifle on his shoulder. "It's suicide."

Mike's eyes were already on the building, steeling himself. "Yeah, well . . . when I left Eureka I was pretty sure that was the deal."

"It was. But my deal, not yours. I'm going in."

Mike glanced up at the blazing aurora. "No time for

this, Ben." More words would not come. He started for the building.

"Stop right there."

He heard the safety catch unlock. He turned. Ben was pointing the pistol at him.

"You're not going to kill me, Ben. You know it, and I know it."

"You're right, but a bullet in the leg would slow you down. There's something you don't know, Mike. I brought weapons for two reasons. To protect you, then to kill myself. I'll do it anyway, after the mission—I won't live with dishonor. So, you see, your death in there would only be a waste."

Mike stared at him, shocked. Saw that he meant it.

Ben gave him a wry smile. "The guy with the gun *always* makes the rules." He took a deep breath. "My life is over, Mike. I will not allow you to sacrifice yours."

Something swelled in Mike's chest, an awe that felt like grief. Ben was always one step ahead.

"Mike, I've been so wrong. Done so much harm. I have a chance—a last chance—to do one right thing." There was a plea in his eyes. "You've been like a son to me. And no man can send his son to his death."

Mike felt torn apart. "I'm going in. I know the layout . . . know what to do."

"So do I." Ben aimed the gun at Mike's leg. "You're not taking one step nearer that building."

The siren wailed.

"Damn it, Mike, you've got kids who need you. I've got kids who need to forget me. I'm going out with this mission accomplished. One shred of honor to leave them. Understand?"

Mike's heart crammed up in his throat.

Ben gave a grim shrug. "Besides, if I don't make it, you'll still be here, in reserve."

"Redundancy."

"Yeah."

Their eyes locked. Mike said, "But you *will* make it. Nobody stops Ben Crewe."

Tears glinted in Ben's eyes. "You have a life ahead. Go live it."

Mike had to hold himself back as he watched Ben stride across the grass toward the doors.

▲

Gina felt it in her left leg first. A spasm. As it crept up her left side, panic crept with it. *A seizure . . . please, no!* Her left foot kicked. Her body shook. "Lieutenant!" she cried. "Medication! My pills—"

The convulsion clamped her teeth together. No words . . . She twisted around to the two Institute scientists, and tried to grab the closest one. *He's got to take over . . .* Her arm went into spasm before she could touch him.

"Ma'am?" the startled lieutenant said. *"Ma'am!"*

Gina fell off the chair.

In spasm on the floor, she heard the two scientists in panic yelling beside her screen, felt the pounding vibration of boots as soldiers ran in, felt the lieutenant wedging a cloth between her teeth. "Medication's on the way, ma'am! Hang on!"

Too late . . . the skip zone . . . Mike!

"Jesus Christ," one of the scientists at the screen said. "The zone . . . it's gone!"

▲

Ben staggered at the vibration that shuddered through his skull.

He dropped to his knee on the grass, whipping the rifle around. Viet Cong, there in the jungle brush! His guys were taking fire all around! One was down—there, down the slope, vomiting. Alive, but in shock, it looked like. Was it Maloney? Can't leave him. Can't let the sons of bitches get him and torture him. Another guy stood near Maloney. Ryder? Good man, Ryder. Ben glanced over at the smashed Jeep. It would give them some cover from the enemy fire.

He ran toward the two men. He grabbed Maloney by the collar, keeping his rifle in his free hand aimed at the jungle. "Cover us, Ryder! I'm taking Maloney to that Jeep. Once I get him there, I'll cover you. Then run like hell!"

He backed away on the double, dragging Maloney. He reached the Jeep, sweating, out of breath, and propped Maloney against the rear wheel. Their left flank was exposed, but it was the bastards in the jungle ahead that he needed to worry about. He turned to look back at Ryder. Still standing. Good kid . . . can't lose Ryder. Can't let them capture him and torture him. "Ryder, run! Now!"

A yell from the jungle. Ben swung his rifle, ready to aim. *Can't see the bastards.* Frantic, he looked again at Ryder. *Come on, kid! I'll hold them off, but you've got to run!*

▲

Mike sank to his knees on the grass, tears streaming down his cheeks. The dead and the dying engulfed him as he plunged through the freezing abyss. The faces of the dead were terrible . . . Roger, Sophy, D'Alton . . . choking, drowning, burning. But the faces of the dying were worse . . . the red-eyed technician, and Bjorn, and Meredith, and thousands more . . . screaming, suffering, pleading for him to stop their pain. Dana and Lucas, in agony, tumbling away among the cold stars, trying to reach back for him . . . He tried to reach for them, to stop them going, but he couldn't move! Corpses crushed him . . . ice encased him . . . the dead were frozen with him, pinning him in ice. And Dana and Lucas were floating away in the darkness . . . *If only I could move, I could catch them, keep them alive!*

▲

Dana had felt the vibration too. She stumbled back amid the squat towers, and looked up, dazed. Bodies lay atop black platforms . . . cache poles at the edge of the village, they held the frozen dead aloft through winter, waiting for spring burial. But it was frightening . . . so *many* dead.

"No, Dana, it's *endji*. Don't get lost in your mind."

Carla's voice! Dazzled, Dana looked higher, up to the shimmering aurora. Carla's voice had come from there . . . to guide her away from *endji*, the work of dark powers.

Don't get lost!

She forced her eyes down, forced herself to think. Not cache poles . . . distribution towers. Gravel underfoot. Dynamite, fuse wires, battery. *Lucas.* She saw him by the fence, under the sodium light, frozen by this ELF blast, the detonator switch in his hand. In horror, she realized that in his unstable state he might flip the switch. He was standing among the dynamite charges. So was she.

She rushed to him and gently lifted the switch from his hand, then took him by the arm and led him away. "Lucas, we're moving back, to a safe place. Slow, steady . . . that's it. Don't get lost inside your mind. Stay with me . . . we've almost finished what we came to do. It's nearly over."

He was shaking, and his eyes were huge with fear, but she knew he was trying to hang on to her voice, so she kept talking, guiding him away from the dynamite. Fifty feet back . . . a hundred feet back. Finally, they were clear.

Do it now, she told herself. *Detonate.* She took a last look around to check that everything was set. Her breath stopped. Mike? Over there on the lawn?

Or . . . just another vision? Could she believe in it? *If he's not real, I can't let a vision stop me.* But when she closed her eyes and opened them again, Mike was still there.

Joy shot through her. He's alive!

But he was dangerously close to the dynamite. She had to move him away. "Lucas, I'll be right back." To be safe, so that Lucas couldn't accidentally trip the switch, she disconnected the lead and shoved the switch in her pocket. "Stay here," she told him.

She ran. Over the gravel, across the asphalt driveway, onto the grass between the buildings. When she reached Mike he was on his knees, weeping, out of control, trapped in some terrifying world his mind had created. It wrenched her heart. She had to lead him out. Lead him to Lucas. Only there could she be sure they'd both be safe from the blast. And only by detonating it could she end the horrors torturing them.

She bent over him. The alarm inside the building was loud and shrill, but she needed to speak gently and not frighten him, so she put her mouth to his ear. "Mike, can you hear me? It's Dana. Lucas and I are here. We've set the dynamite, just like you said. We're ready. I know you're going through something terrible, but in a few minutes it will all be over. Can you hear me? Can you stand and come with me?"

He looked up at her, disorder in his eyes. It tore her apart to see him struggling to make sense of her. "Mike, let go of the fear. That's all that's trapping you. You've got to leave the fear behind and leave this place."

He made a strangled sound. Didn't budge.

She went down on her knees with him, face-to-face, and placed her hands on his wet cheeks and brushed away his tears. "Mike, whatever's inside your mind, you're seeing it for a purpose. You can make it a good purpose. You can let it help you. A vision isn't something that's not there—it's something that's *always* there. Like my love for you. Use the vision, Mike. Make it what you want. Let it guide you to where you need to be."

She took his hand and got to her feet. "Come now, with me and Lucas. We're going to end this."

▲

Her voice reached Mike through his terror like a warm hand in the arctic night. He held on to it—her warmth, her voice, the vision of her face. Dana. He put his mind in her guidance, and let her words thaw the ice that encased him with the dead. His terror melted, and the ghosts fled, releasing him. He gulped breaths, letting himself see only her.

"Can you stand?" she said.

He knew she wasn't real. It didn't matter. She had set him free.

He got to his feet, legs shaky. Her hand helping him up felt as warm and firm as if it were real. He gripped her arm, not wanting to ever let go of this new vision.

"Ryder! Come on! Run!"

Mike turned. It was Ben yelling, across the lawn. He had hunkered down with his weapons behind the Jeep, and was shouting at him to run and join him. Mike fought through the layers of disorientation. *What's a vision . . . what's real?*

Ben was real, he remembered that now. Remembered

what they'd come to do. Stop HARC. He struggled to remember it all. The power building flooded with radioactive steam . . . Ben had started on a suicide mission to go in and shut off the power. But now it was clear that Ben had been stopped by visions of his own. Watching him gesture wildly from behind the Jeep, Mike realized: He's a captive of his fear. Unable to go in.

I can go in. Dana freed me.

It meant certain death. He longed to turn away, to escape with the vision of Dana. But she wasn't real, he knew that. Only her guidance was real. *"A vision isn't something that's not there—it's something that's always there . . . Let it guide you to where you need to be."* He felt a surge of contentment at seeing the truth. Dana and Lucas were alive, somewhere—he *felt* it—and he could keep them alive by going in and ending this. *My life to save theirs.*

He started walking toward the doors.

"Mike, no, this way!" Dana said. "Come with me. *This* way!"

He blocked out her voice. She wasn't real. That's why he could make himself walk away from her—could make himself do what he had to, even as she kept calling.

▲

Lucas faintly heard her voice calling. In the dark desert where he found himself alone, where nothing made sense, it was all he *could* hear. His mother's voice, calling . . .

But why? What's she saying?

He was shaking. His vision was blurry. He tried to focus on the wire at his feet. He remembered what it was . . . the lead to the fuses. The dynamite.

His mother's voice, calling . . . he suddenly realized why. *She must be telling me to detonate.*

But . . . where's the switch? He dropped to his knees, searching. His fingers scrabbled in the gravel. No switch. How could he do it without the switch?

Can't let that stop me. Got to finish. Mom's calling.

He forced his mind through the dark labyrinth. He had the lead, and over there, by that fence, he could see the battery. He could connect the lead to the battery. That would complete the circuit.

He got up. His legs were weak as straw, but he forced himself to move, to take a step, then another, moving toward the battery. Vision blurry . . . something seemed wrong about going to that fence . . . but he couldn't let stray thoughts break his concentration. Couldn't let anything stop him from this one task he had to do: complete the circuit. Detonate. *Then, we'll all be okay.*

He stumbled forward.

▲

Ben was astounded to see a woman running after Ryder. He hadn't noticed her dash out of the jungle. Black hair, slanted eyes . . . Viet Cong! *Pick her off now, before she gets to Rider!*

He lifted his rifle and took aim.

It struck him that she had no weapon . . . confused him.

Makes no difference. So many enemy, they'll kill us or capture us. I know how they torture prisoners . . . I remember.

Can't let her torture Ryder. Got to save him.

He aimed at the woman. He fired.

▲

Mike heard the rifle shot and whipped around as Dana fell. His heart thudded. She lay sprawled on the ground. "Dana!"

No, don't go back to her, she's not real!

But the blood soaking her shirt, and her eyes glazing over, and her finger twitching . . .

Uncertainty tore at his guts. Every instinct pulled him to go back to save her. But the voice of intellect said: *She's not real, go inside, finish what you have to do.*

▲

Ben watched in shock. The shot he'd fired had galvanized him . . . a psychic catalyst. Everything came back like a bullet. Reality.

Not Vietnam—HARC. Not a soldier beside that body—Mike. Not the enemy who'd been cut down—Dana James.

He slumped against the Jeep and his rifle clattered to the ground. Sickness roiled in his stomach. Comprehen-

sion roiled in his mind. A staggering certainty of all the
harm he had done.

He forced himself to think. The reactor. Go in. Finish
the mission.

He walked across the lawn toward the door. He
passed men on the grass dying from radiation poisoning,
their faces beginning to bloat. He opened the door,
walked into the lobby, and felt stunned by confusion.
Bodies, alarms screaming, acrid smoke in the air . . .

As though clawing his way through a jungle, he
clawed back toward reason. *Find the control room.*

He walked on, turned a corner. He took the steps to
the control room, stepping over bodies on the stairs.

▲

On his knees Mike cradled Dana in his arms. *If she's not
real, nothing is.* He knew that now . . . she was truly
here. Was he too late? Looking at her unconscious face,
her blood-wet shirt, feeling the warmth drain from her
body, he thought his heart would crack.

But he had to go inside, had to shut down the power.
Had to leave her. He shook his head to clear the tears,
gently laid her down, got to his feet. Then saw another
ghost. Lucas. Dana's words rushed back: *"Lucas and I
are here. We've set the dynamite, just like you said."* Not
a ghost . . . Lucas is here!

Can't save Dana . . . or myself . . . but I can save our
son . . . *if I go in now.*

Only, something was wrong about Lucas. Mike could
clearly see him moving under the light atop the distribu-

tion station fence. *"We've set the dynamite..."* That meant the charges were set among the distribution towers. Lucas was there.

Mike saw the battery. Saw that Lucas was walking straight toward it, the lead fuse line in his hand. Saw the fierce concentration on his face. *The poor kid's out of his mind. He's going to detonate the dynamite.*

Mike burst into action. Lifting Dana, he ran with her across the lawn to the ops center wall and set her down in a safe corner. Had her breath stopped? He couldn't check. Had to get back before Lucas could connect the circuit. He took off on the run.

▲

Ben reached the control room. It was a chaos of flashing panel lights veiled in smoke, shrilling sirens, the hiss of ceiling sprinklers spewing spray, water already inches deep on the floor. A moaning man was crawling through the water. Ben stalked by him, splashing toward the control panel. He fought past the disorder in his mind... past the knowledge that he was already dead. *Not yet... finish the mission.*

Steps from the panel, he groped the back of a high-backed desk chair that was in his way. The chair swiveled and a man sitting in it staggered to his feet, blocking Ben. A security guard, young and muscled. "Stop there!" the man shouted in a slur. His face was puffed, red, his bloodshot eyes were wild. He backed up to the panel, arms wide, clumsily shielding the controls.

He's defending the installation, Ben realized. Doing his duty.

Me too. Ben pulled out his pistol. But his motion was as clumsy as the guard's, his mind struggling to make his limbs operate. His gun arm felt like a club.

An explosion of sparks above their heads startled Ben, broke his concentration. The guard raised his leg in a sloppy but powerful kick, knocking the gun from Ben's hand. It splashed in the water.

The guard grinned, demented. Ben's fist hammered the man's face. The guard sprawled into the water. Ben lunged for the controls. He forced his whole mind onto remembering the shutdown sequence. With thick, insensible fingers he flipped switches one by one. It seemed so slow. Smoke was stinging his eyes, his throat.

A heavy weight walloped his shoulders. The guard, apelike, had leaped onto his back. Ben staggered like a wrestler, trying to shed the burden. He lumbered a few steps beside the panel console, twisted around, and smashed the man's back against the console. The guard groaned in pain, let go, and slid down heavily, out of Ben's vision fixated on the panel. Ben reached again for the switches, but from the floor the guard grabbed his leg and clamped teeth into his calf—a searing pain. Ben hauled the man up by his shirtfront. They groped each other like bears. The smoke made them both choke, but Ben saw in the red eyes the guard's crazed will to stop him. *We're both dead men, soldier. No time left.* Ben's hands savagely clamped the thick throat. The guard gouged and thrashed and wheezed. Ben crushed with all his strength, foggily obsessed with stilling the flailing limbs. The wheezing stopped. The bulging red eyes turned dull. Ben let the dead man drop.

Again he reached for the panel. One by one, he flipped the switches. He input the power line shutdown command . . .

Instant mental clarity. It was such a shock, it made him gasp.

Was it over? So fast? Like pulling an electrical plug!

He stood still for a moment, weak-kneed, catching his breath, unsure. The frantic commotion of sirens and sprinklers continued. But his mind was clear and calm. That was the evidence: It was over.

He picked up a phone and tried Fort Wainwright. It rang. The duty officer answered. Ben closed his eyes, overcome with relief. *It's over.*

"This is General Crewe. HARC is now out of commission." He told them to send nuclear containment specialists, and medevac personnel for the victims still alive. He hung up.

He was shaking. The guard's corpse lay by his foot. *Just doing his duty.* Ben took rocky steps through the water and smoke and found his gun. He righted an overturned desk chair. Its beige upholstery was sodden. He sat down. How long would it take? He knew the sequence of nuclear radiation sickness. Nausea. Bloating beyond recognition. Disintegrating internal organs. Dementia.

He wasn't afraid. But he didn't want to wait for death. He lifted his pistol. *I did my duty. I killed HARC.*

He shoved the barrel in his mouth. He fired.

▲

"Lucas!"

Running, calling to Lucas, Mike had almost reached him when suddenly the whole world shifted. Mike staggered on the spot, unbalanced by the sudden freedom, the clarity, as though the dungeon darkening his mind had been flung open. He could think, could understand.

And what he understood in a flash of horror was that he'd been right. Lucas, on his knees, held the lead in his hand just inches from the battery terminal. He was going to detonate the charges.

"Lucas, come away from there!"

Lucas looked vaguely his way, as though in bewilderment. "Mike?"

The dungeon's open for him too, Mike thought, but he's stunned by the freedom. "Come to me, Lucas. I need you here!"

"Sure, Mike." Fixated on his task, Lucas lifted the battery and started to walk toward Mike, still holding the lead as well, unconsciously stretching both of the long slack wires as he came. Mike held his breath. When the battery wire became taut, Lucas stopped. "There. That's it."

Lucas reached with the lead to make the connection.

"No!" Mike ran for him.

The explosion shook the ground. In the split second Mike could still think, he thought: Like an earthquake. Then he was deafened, was hurled across the gravel, felt searing pain. Then he felt nothing . . . and the world went black.

Fourteen Months Later

OVER ALASKA'S WILDERNESS, a chill of autumn was in the air.

Last of the great camping weather, Mike thought. He flipped the arctic grayling fillets sizzling in butter with mushrooms, set the skillet down again on the glowing coals, and checked the tin pot where the sourdough bread was baking. The yeasty aroma and satiny brown crust told him it was ready. So was he. Hungry enough to eat a . . . well, there was nothing he'd rather have than this very meal. He smiled to himself, remembering how Lindsay had asked on the flight if there would be a deli out here. Better that that, he'd told her. He had caught the plump grayling just a half hour ago, he and Lindsay had picked the chanterelle mushrooms, they'd have wild blueberries for dessert, and—best of all in Mike's opinion—Lindsay had baked the bread herself, Indian style. With a little help from her stepmother. Not bad for a ten-year-old.

He glanced at the woods. Where were they with those blueberries?

A bottle of verdicchio was cooling in the lake beside the plane. He went over to where the yellow Beaver aircraft was tied to two stout spruce trees, the bows of its floats nudging the grassy bank, and he lifted out the wine. A loon plunged into the glassy water, fishing for its dinner. Across the small bay, a moose was nibbling willows. Mike stood watching, the bottle dripping water beside his boots as he took in the dappled beauty all around. The woods beside him were a mosaic of yellow aspen leaves, magenta cranberry bushes, white birch trunks, and swaths of green ferns. The sunset-tinted lake mirrored spikes of black spruce and bunches of rose-colored clouds. Mike drank it in. People said this was a bittersweet moment in the changing seasons, with summer slipping away and winter closing in, but he didn't feel the bitter part. Not this September. The HARC disaster fourteen months ago was far behind him. All he felt was the ripe goodness of life gathering him in, the way a campfire gathers you to its warmth.

The air held the spice of resin and woodsmoke—air so still, Mike thought he could hear the moose across the bay munching. He lengthened his focus over the forest. Looming in the distance was the white immensity of Denali—officially Mount McKinley, the highest peak in North America, but the Indians here for millennia had called it Denali, the Great One. Mike felt a small thrill at seeing its peak this evening; so often it was shrouded in cloud. Denali was a mountain so high and so cold, it created its own weather—roiling clouds that formed in a minute, sudden storms, gale-driven blizzards. Big always means unpredictable, he thought. Unpredictable consequences, like with HARC. He'd tried so hard to tell Ben.

In the end, Ben had killed HARC . . . and HARC had killed Ben. Technically, the bullet he'd fired into his own brain had done it, and later, everyone said they understood his desire for a quick end instead of the slow agony of lethal radiation poisoning, but Mike knew it was HARC itself that had taken Ben's life. It had messed with his mind long before the crisis, in the guise of that age-old devil, pride. Not for himself, for his country. Still, Mike imagined that by the time Ben had lifted that pistol to his head, he'd done so with sober satisfaction, knowing he had slain the monster he'd let loose. Later, the president had awarded Ben a posthumous medal for sacrificing his life to save others. A perverse irony, it seemed to Mike, yet he couldn't find it in himself to feel cynical, then or now. He was just glad to be here.

The dynamite explosion had hurled him across the gravel, broken his leg, dislocated his shoulder, and knocked him unconscious. But the commando teams Ben had ordered out earlier from Fort Wainwright had soon arrived and evacuated the survivors, and specialized crews came to contain the radiation leak. The moment Mike woke up in Fairbanks Memorial Hospital, doped up on painkillers, his first question was about Lucas and Dana. "Rifle wound . . . dynamite," were about the only words he could remember getting out after their names. When the nurse gave him the news that they'd both survived, he had felt such a shock of happi-

ness it had actually hurt, and he'd slid back into a
drugged oblivion.

The Pentagon had immediately stepped in. They'd
sealed off the HARC site and evacuated residents within
a fifty-mile radius, a sparsely populated area in any case.
Communications and transportation were quickly re-
stored, and Fairbanks, eighty miles away, had recovered,
mourned its hundreds of dead, and returned to normal.
With the situation under control, the Pentagon had
turned to spin control. Their statement to the country and
to the world was that an industrial accident had occurred
at a Navy funded high-frequency research facility in
Alaska, but was now completely contained. Though the
loss of life at the facility due to a nuclear radiation leak
was tragic, they said, and though any technological dis-
ruption further afield that HARC's high-frequency irregularities might have temporarily engendered was
regrettable, their position regarding the phenomenon of
mental incapacitation was unequivocal: the alleged
causal link to HARC, they said, remained unproven, and
the event would require a comprehensive internal investigation, a process that could go on for years. The Office
of Naval Research had immediately terminated the research project, classified the files top secret, and dismantled the site. Mike had been astounded at how
quickly they had thereby cauterized any incipient
protest: a preemptive strike, with surgical precision. No
acknowledgment that the thousands of deaths in Alaska
and the Canadian Yukon and the north of Russia and
Scandinavia—a total of over thirty thousand fatalities,
by one intrepid Swedish journalist's account, plus ten

times that number of injuries—were anything but accidents, completely unrelated to HARC. Never had Mike been so chillingly aware of the ancillary scope of his country's military power: a mighty wall of silence. With scant hope of denting that wall, he had nevertheless continued to give media interviews for several weeks, finding he was a top story whether he wanted to be or not, though he answered no personal questions, just scientific ones. Until suddenly a "hotter" story broke: one of Hollywood's most popular female stars declared she was actually a man. A new media frenzy was on. Mike, and HARC, were history.

But he hadn't had time for outrage. He'd needed a job. He was pleased when, before he'd even got out of the hospital, Jack Schiller at NASA called with an offer to head up the wave plasma group with their Geotail project. Since it focused on high-latitude polar regions, it meant staying in Alaska. Mike had accepted on the spot. Gina had joined his team. Part of the International Solar-Terrestrial Physics Program, Geotail's mission was to examine global energy flow in the magnetotail, and for the last eleven months, from his new lab in Anchorage, Mike had directed his group on determining auroral plasma acceleration outflow. Through NASA, the aurora had again become his scientific turf.

He walked back to the campfire with the wine. Going to be a chilly night, he thought. He had on a fleece pullover, but it was through his jeans, in his knee, that he felt the cold—twinges of stiffness leftover from the fracture. Tonight, they would be glad they'd brought the thick sleeping bags.

Or maybe it wasn't the autumn coolness chilling him, he thought. Maybe it was that surprise visit from Kaplan.

Three days ago, the national security adviser had walked into Mike's lab in Anchorage. He had come to Alaska for a meeting with the governor, he'd explained, and stopped by to say hello. "After all"—Kaplan grinned—"you and I were comrades in arms that day in the war room. Like sharing a foxhole under fire."

Not exactly how Mike remembered it. As he recalled, Kaplan had been scared shitless. *Just like all of us.* But he let it pass. He offered him coffee.

"So, Dr. Ryder," Kaplan asked as they stood sipping from foam cups, "how's NASA treating you?"

"Good." In fact, Mike was happy. The work was fascinating, his colleagues were solid people he'd been conferring with for years from MIT, and he found it inspiring to know that his contribution to an increased understanding of magnetospheric processes would directly impact all future space exploration. But he didn't think Kaplan had come to discuss electrostatic cyclotron harmonics.

"Let me know if there are any bureaucrat's cages you need rattled," Kaplan offered. "To fast-track matters."

Mike looked at him. Fast-tracking—it made him think of Ben's obsessive push for HARC. "Thanks, sir, but I'll just keep plodding."

"You're no plodder. You saved all our asses, Ryder, creating that skip zone with Eureka. You were the only one with the brains to do it, and the balls. The president publicly cited General Crewe's courage, and of course we needed to get that message out—that there were heroes in this story, not just disasters—but for my money, you're the real hero."

Mike's coffee tasted sour. Or maybe it was the conversation. He couldn't forget all the misery HARC had inflicted. Strangely, the tale that had humbled him most was Dana telling him about Thomas Fraser's chosen end, walking into the river to die. "Was there a reason for your visit, Mr. Kaplan?"

"We'd like you back, Ryder."

Mike didn't follow. "Sorry?"

"There's a new high-frequency project in the works. Right now, it's headed up by Dr. Crosbie, and her commitment is one hundred percent. Unfortunately, though, her stamina falls short. Naturally."

Naturally. Mike had seen her on TV in her wheelchair, praising Ben. She had suffered neurological damage, but the saturation ELF radiation had affected individuals differently; in her case the damage was not to her mental abilities, which seemed as sharp as ever, but to her central nervous system: Meredith was a paraplegic, likely for the rest of her life. Her televised eulogy of Ben had sounded like a put-up job to Mike, and now he thought he was beginning to see why. Had she struck a deal with the Pentagon? For delivering their PR knockout by lauding Ben's heroism, had she been handed a plum directorship? "What's the project?" he asked.

"It's top secret, you understand."

Mike had an uneasy feeling that he *did* understand.

"Success often comes out of failure, Ryder. Of course you, as a scientist, know that better than anyone. The experimental process. Ben Crewe demonstrated HARC's potential to deliver a remarkable antiballistic defense strategy, and that's something we're keen to explore. But the accident also gave us a glimpse of something even more remarkable: the power to mentally incapacitate an enemy. Properly managed, the resonance factor could give this nation an extraordinary new defense capability."

"Properly managed?" Mike controlled his dismay. HARC had killed Ben, but it seemed his fixation on an ultimate weapon hadn't died with him—had only been transferred to others. "Mr. Kaplan, what we went through with HARC taught us that power like that *can't* be managed."

"You're too modest, Ryder. You *did* manage it, using Eureka. It's what I've always said—take this country's best talent, give them cutting-edge technology and the resources they require, and they'll find a way. There's *always* a way."

Mike was about to object, but Kaplan held up his hands to forestall protest. "We're well aware that it's an embryonic technology. It will require a great deal of refining. That's exactly why we want you." He gave Mike a shrewd look. "If working with Dr. Crosbie is a problem, I'm sure we can interest her in a position elsewhere. As for remuneration, I can promise you that no scientific facility anywhere, public or private, will match the offer we're prepared to make you."

Mike looked him in the eye. "Mr. Kaplan, a day doesn't go by that I don't think of the people HARC killed, and I expect it'll take me the rest of my working life to balance, in some small way, the harm I couldn't stop Ben Crewe from doing. Nothing in this world could induce me to help you kill more people than we already have."

Kaplan looked startled. But only for a moment. "I take it that's a no."

"It is. And I advise you, with the strongest possible urgency, to give up this new program."

Kaplan set down his coffee. When he looked again at Mike, his smile was sardonic. "Dr. Ryder, I advise the president. Giving up is never among my recommendations."

Laughter in the woods. Mike turned from the fire. Dana and Lindsay, each hugging a berry pail, were coming through the trees to camp, eating blueberries as they chattered. Mike felt a tug at his heart at the way his daughter's fair hair bobbed alongside Dana's shoulder. Lindsay's outfit, as usual, was schizophrenic—half Alaska, half Boston: a fawn-colored old wool sweater, too big, that she'd borrowed from Dana, over trendy lime pants stamped with a fashion corporation's logo. Mike noted with satisfaction the grass-stained knees and the blueberry streaks where she'd wiped her hands. Alaska was winning.

"Dad!" Lindsay ran the last few yards to him, excited. "I'm going to look into a deer's eyes! Dana says!"

Mike was lifting the skillet off the coals. "Come again?"

Dana said, "It was something my grandfather had me do." As she reached Mike, she held out her pail for him to sample the berries. She had on jeans, a yellow flannel shirt, a blue down-filled vest, and her hair was in a ponytail. Mike scooped a handful of berries, thinking how beautiful she was. "They left me alone in the woods," she said, "and my task was to look into the eyes of a deer. So I had to wait for one. I waited a day and a half, but I saw my deer, a young buck. It was beautiful."

"Great idea, Lins," Mike said, munching berries. He looked at Dana and deadpanned, "And I'll be nearby with a .30-06 in case a bear decides to look into her eyes."

Lindsay groaned, "Oh, Dad."

Dad, Mike thought. Not Daddy anymore. How suddenly she'd decided to grow up. Dana had been a big part of it. For the first few months, Lindsay, missing her mother, had been shy with her, but Mike had noticed her big eyes following Dana's every move with fascination. Dana hadn't made a fuss over her, hadn't treated her like a hothouse blossom trembling from the upheaval of divorce, and she hadn't changed herself, either. Instead, she gave Lindsay flying lessons. Gave her an orphan husky pup to care for. Gave her all the time Lindsay needed to talk about her new school in Anchorage and her new friends, but also expected her to help out at the village of New Takona when they visited there. Lindsay was thriving on it. Dana had become her ideal. The rapport between the two of them pleased Mike enormously.

"She doesn't just want to be *like* you," he'd said to Dana one night in bed, "she wants to *be* you."

Dana had laughed. "You know why, don't you? Because I'm the girl who got *you*."

The divorce had come through late last fall; the wedding had been at Thanksgiving. But Lindsay had come to live with Mike in Fairbanks right after the HARC disaster, while Dana was on a visit of condolence to Reid D'Alton's parents. Mike had been prepared to work out a joint-custody arrangement with Carol, but that wasn't how the judge had seen things. At Ben's death, Carol had suffered a breakdown. She'd spent some time in McLean Hospital in Boston, and had developed a phobia about going outside. She'd been living with her sister ever since. Mike had felt terrible when he'd first gone back with Lindsay to visit Carol and saw what a fragile state she was in. It was going to be a long time before she would fully recover, if ever. Her sad situation certainly wasn't what Mike had wished for, yet he couldn't regret that it had led the judge to award him full custody of Lindsay.

He had shaken his head at the final irony. Senator Litvak had decided to throw his hat into the presidential ring, and dropped his investigation into military research spending. Ben and Carol had rushed HARC into catastrophe . . . for nothing.

Last year had been a watershed for Dana, too, only a far more positive one. She had faced the charge of practicing medicine without a license, but so many former patients came to testify in her defense, and other physicians, too, vouching for her fine work in a remote area, and pointing out that she'd never taken money for her services, that the judge gave her not only a total acquittal, but a commendation. It had inspired her—with a nudge from Mike—to finally go for that M.D. She was enrolled in the University of Alaska's brand-new school of medicine at its Anchorage campus. It had meant selling her charter business, but when Mike saw the light in her eyes the day she was accepted, he knew it was right. Dana was going to be a doctor, just as she'd always wanted.

"Ladies," he said, pulling the wine cork, "dinner is served."

It was so good, they all ate too much. What was it about food outdoors? Nothing inside ever tasted so great. Polishing off the fresh bread, they talked about the schedule for tomorrow to pick up Lucas in New Takona. He'd spent the weekend helping paint the clinic, built with the three million Ben had given Dana, but he had to be back in Anchorage for Monday classes at U of A where he was an engineering freshman. Another irony, Mike thought: his son was getting a scientific education in the same city as Mike's lab, exactly the way he'd once visualized it happening in Boston . . . only it had come about in Alaska.

He and Lindsay took a quick dip in the dusk-purpled lake. As Lindsay scrambled out, happily shivering, Dana rubbed her with a towel to warm her up. "You're like a salmon," Dana said with a smile. "Returning to your source."

"How come?"

Dana looked out at Mike, who was doing a lazy breaststroke toward them. "Because your source is your father," she said. "And he was born here."

Mike grinned. "Yeah. It's been a long swim back."

Lindsay broke up laughing.

They talked around the campfire for a while, Mike and Dana sitting together on a log, Lindsay on the ground between Mike's legs, wrapped in a blanket and watching sparks fly upward on the still air. Night closed in quickly. Lindsay fell asleep. Mike picked her up—that wonderful dead-to-the-world weight of a sleeping kid—and carried her inside the nylon dome tent, and settled her into her sleeping bag.

Outside, he reached Dana as she stood spreading the blanket on the ground. His arms went around her. Her face was cool, her body warm.

She looked at him. "Mike, I love having a little girl. No, that's not quite right. I love having *that* little girl."

They sat on the blanket, their backs against the log, the wine bottle at their feet, and looked at the stars. With summer over, the nights were finally dark enough to see stars. They talked for a while, about the kids, about an upcoming NASA conference, about planning a visit to Wayne, who'd become a manager on the pipeline in Valdez, about the leaky basement at home. Mike reached for the wine to top up Dana's glass.

"Mike. Look."

It was the aurora. Green and gold and violet streamers were softly rippling across the western sky. As he watched the dazzling show, Mike felt the old thrill. And something more. Ben's wasn't the only mind HARC had been messing with for years. Once, Mike had dreamed of taming the aurora, controlling it. Now he knew better. To spend a lifetime exploring its mystery, that would be challenge enough.

"Ionized particles," Dana mused, watching too. "Seems a pretty inadequate description for something so wonderful."

"It is. I like yours better. Dancing spirits of children not yet born."

Their eyes met. He poured the last of the wine.

Dana grinned. "Not exactly roughing it, are we?"

"We're not out here to rough it, my love, we're here to smooth it." He kissed her. "The rough part's over."